VAULTS OF TERRA

THE HOLLOW MOUNTAIN

More tales of the Inquisition from Black Library

VAULTS OF TERRA

THE HOLLOW MOUNTAIN

CHRIS WRAIGHT

BLACK LIBRARY

A BLACK LIBRARY PUBLICATION

First published in 2019.
This edition published in Great Britain in 2020 by
Black Library,
Games Workshop Ltd.,
Willow Road,
Nottingham, NG7 2WS, UK.

10 9 8 7 6 5 4 3 2 1

Produced by Games Workshop in Nottingham.
Cover illustration by Igor Sid.

A CIP record for this book is available from the British Library.

ISBN 13: 978 1 78999 030 0

See Black Library on the internet at

blacklibrary.com

Find out more about Games Workshop
and the world of Warhammer 40,000 at

games-workshop.com

Printed and bound by CPI Group (UK) Ltd, Croydon, CR0 4YY

To Hannah, with love.

It is the 41st millennium. For more than a hundred centuries the Emperor has sat immobile on the Golden Throne of Earth. He is the Master of Mankind by the will of the gods, and master of a million worlds by the might of His inexhaustible armies. He is a rotting carcass writhing invisibly with power from the Dark Age of Technology. He is the Carrion Lord of the Imperium for whom a thousand souls are sacrificed every day, so that He may never truly die.

Yet even in His deathless state, the Emperor continues His eternal vigilance. Mighty battlefleets cross the daemon-infested miasma of the warp, the only route between distant stars, their way lit by the Astronomican, the psychic manifestation of the Emperor's will. Vast armies give battle in His name on uncounted worlds. Greatest amongst His soldiers are the Adeptus Astartes, the Space Marines, bioengineered super-warriors. Their comrades in arms are legion: the Astra Militarum and countless planetary defence forces, the ever-vigilant Inquisition and the tech-priests of the Adeptus Mechanicus to name only a few. But for all their multitudes, they are barely enough to hold off the ever-present threat from aliens, heretics, mutants – and worse.

To be a man in such times is to be one amongst untold billions. It is to live in the cruellest and most bloody regime imaginable. These are the tales of those times. Forget the power of technology and science, for so much has been forgotten, never to be re-learned. Forget the promise of progress and understanding, for in the grim dark future there is only war. There is no peace amongst the stars, only an eternity of carnage and slaughter, and the laughter of thirsting gods.

CHAPTER ONE

Niir Khazad was alive.

It had been borderline, for a while. Erunion, Courvain's chirurgeon-philosophical, had worked patient hours over her, adjusting the vials and the sutures, snagging and twisting the flesh, until she was finally stabilised and her heart was beating and her lungs were pulling in air. When she awoke at last, it was his skinny face that she saw first, peering over half-moon spectacles as if scrutinising a disappointing lab specimen.

'You're tough,' he admitted.

She knew that. Being born and raised on a death world had given her no alternative. During her long career, she'd suffered frequent and significant physical trauma and had always pulled through. On the mag-anchor platforms in low orbit over Dramde XI she'd taken a bolt-round through her shoulder that had pulled a fist-sized chunk of flesh with it. That should have killed her, as should the poison-laced spike in her stomach under the hive-slums of Hydra Demetrius. Back then, though, she had been able to draw on the services of Inquisitor Hovash Phaelias. Her old master had been a thorough man, with a well-supplied armoury and well-maintained apothecarion, and so her medical care, when needed, had been exemplary. Now, through a fog of pain suppressors, she barely knew where she was, let alone how reliable her treatment had been. Looking at Erunion, with his ghost-pale skin and flickering gaze, it was hard to be confident.

'Yes,' was all she croaked, proudly.

She gained strength after that. The chirurgeon shuffled away, coming back every few hours with more tinctures and needles. Servitors clunked and drooled around her cot, attending to the antiquated machines with their dumb, clumsy movements.

Her sense of self, of place, of memory, began to return. She remembered the long hunt, when it seemed like the world itself had turned against them all and her master's retinue was picked off, one by one. During that time she had never tried to persuade him to leave, to flee off-world from a Terra that had become their enemy. An inquisitor did not flee, not when there was quarry to hunt. Right until the end, she had assumed that he would discover who their hidden enemies were and then find a way to counter them, but in that she had miscalculated. Phaelias was dead now, as were all the others. Only she remained, a fugitive plucked from the shadows of the great hive-spires and absorbed into another coterie of killers and misfits. Even then, death had still come for her in the deep catacombs under the Palace itself, where xenos and myth-pulled gods had fought amid the swirling shadows.

But she had cheated it again, one more time. Now she breathed, painfully. She blinked, painfully. She swallowed, and felt the rawness of her throat where the tubes had been.

By the time she came fully back to her senses, the lumens in the chamber were dialled low. In the hazy murk, it took her some time to realise she was not alone.

'Welcome back, assassin,' said Erasmus Crowl.

She had never spoken to him before. She had only ever heard the name 'Crowl' when Spinoza had mentioned it, and such references had been fleeting and in haste. By the time the two of them had ended up in the same chamber at last, the las-bolts were already flying and the greatest of Rassilo's hunters was coming for her with murder in their eyes.

Still, it was hard to mistake him. He wore black robes trimmed with silver. His hair was slicked back to his skull, pulled away from a gaunt face of scars and sickness. He sat calmly, hands on his lap, still as the shadows around him. Only his voice, which had a soft, dry surface timbre, gave away a little more humanity.

She tried to lift her head from the pallet, and failed. 'Inquisitor,' she croaked.

Crowl got up, tipped away the metal can of water by her cot and replaced it with a fresh one. She took a cautious sip.

'I wished to give you longer to recover,' Crowl said. 'They're serious wounds. Spinoza thought you might die from them.'

Spinoza. Luce Spinoza. The woman – Crowl's interrogator – who had tracked her down and in all likelihood saved her life. She was cut from exceptional cloth, that one – rougher, harder, more ebulliently physical. Khazad and she were similar in many ways – warriors schooled in the Imperium's imaginative arts of combat – but the man before her was a breed apart. Frailer in body, it seemed, but with an evident mental strength that even now, even here, was capable of chilling with a word.

'Does she live?' Khazad asked. It was hard to remember

precisely how things had ended, down there in the deeps under those immense walls.

'She lives, Emperor be praised. I think it would be very hard to end her, and I am grateful for that.'

Khazad swallowed again. It was slowly getting easier. 'Then, can I–'

'Peace,' said Crowl, quietly. 'You are not under edict of interrogation. Questions will have to come when you are stronger. For the time being, I wish you to know you are safe.'

Khazad smiled weakly. 'Nowhere safe.'

'Ha. Maybe not. But there are degrees of danger. Do you know where you are?'

Khazad nodded.

'Most who come here never leave,' Crowl said. 'You, of course, may leave whenever you wish. I know a little of the Shoba doctrine. You will need to locate those who wronged you.'

'Yes,' she said vehemently. 'I know names. If any still live–'

'Indeed, and I approve of the sentiment.' He leaned forward, into the pool of murky light, and Khazad saw the deep rings of black under his eyes. 'You must take whatever path seems right to you,' he said. 'Either alone, or, if you choose, with us. Spinoza might have told you I habitually worked alone. That was partially true, for a long time, but things are becoming perilous here. An assassin of the Shoba school would be of use to me. It wouldn't be the safest option, given how things are, but think on it, when you're recovered.'

Khazad looked at him directly. 'No time needed. I stay here.'

Crowl raised an eyebrow. 'Really? You don't wish to consider it?'

'Spinoza trust me. I trust her. Have no other master – you will do.'

Crowl chuckled. 'I see.' He got up, and Khazad saw for the first time how lean he was out of the armour she'd witnessed him wearing before. In his long robes he looked like a coiled whip, frayed and flaking from overzealous use. 'Get better then,' he said, seriously. 'Get stronger.'

Khazad began to feel her awareness slipping away again. Erunion must have piped something down the tubes that still ran into her arteries, something that would knock her out and accelerate the healing that still needed to be done.

'Will be ready,' she said fiercely, keeping her eyes open as long as she could.

'Good,' said Crowl. 'They'll come for you again, now. They'll come for me, too.'

'Yes.'

'Just so you know. It isn't over.'

Sleep rose up to smother her again, hot and cloying.

'Never is,' she murmured, thinking back over all those injuries. 'Always start again.'

Maldo Revus, too, was recovering.

His body, too, was a thing of consummate toughness, honed and shriven over decades until every muscle was like boiled leather, held together by its scars and bearing the marks of its armour pieces. He had limped out of the catacombs with Spinoza, his carapace plate riddled with dents and his helm visor blurred with his own blood. That was the way such things usually ended, of course, so he had no complaints about it.

Perhaps, though, as he aged, the recovery times were lengthening a little. It had been eight years now, with Crowl. Before that he had served as a sergeant with another Inquisitorial detachment, and before that he had been a private soldier in a storm trooper division on permanent void duty. His memories beyond that were blurred, perhaps due to the strain of near-constant combat, perhaps due to the after-effects of the mind-wipes he had undergone multiple times during preliminary training. There was no true beginning for him, no commencement, just a growing set of impressions, steadily becoming firmer, solidifying into his current state as Crowl's loyal killer.

At times, he would dream of another time and another world – empty skies of pale green, a dusty plain stretching away towards gauzy horizons, a child running in terror from the iron ships hanging in the grit-blown air. Even now, after a routine action, while recuperating in Courvain's medical bays, he might remember the nights he had endured in the schola, stinging from the welts left by the instructors' electro-whips, his lips bloody from constant recitation of battle-doctrine. He could revisit himself as an adolescent sometimes, crying angrily into the thin sheets of his cot, fists balled against the bolsters, exhausted, broken. All that psycho-training had left its mark, bludgeoning out the weaker elements, leaving only what was necessary for his vocation. Like so many others in the service of the Throne, he had been forged, hard-tempered, then re-made.

Courvain, for one of Revus' experience, might have been considered a less than optimal posting. Another man in his position might have agitated hard for promotion, for transfer to a personal detachment in a more prestigious location, or even command of an active-duty regiment in some branch of the mainstream Militarum. Revus, though, knew what Crowl offered. Some inquisitors were sadists, treating their troops as expendable resources. Others were flamboyant mavericks, swaggering around the Imperium's possessions like temporal lords and holding sway over fiefs in the name of none but themselves. Crowl was simpler to understand. He cared little for the outward ostentation of his office, but maintained an orderly, active programme of investigation. He had high expectations of those in his service, but was solicitous over their wellbeing. That engendered loyalty in excess of that guaranteed by standard indoctrination alone. For those who served long enough, it inculcated something close to devotion.

And yet, it was still possible to have one's faith shaken; to be exposed, even briefly, to a wider world. For a very short time, down in those lightless pits, Revus had fought alongside Custodians. They had barely noticed him, in all likelihood, and his own contribution to the encounter under the walls had been little better than nominal, and yet, still, he had served alongside them. A man might live for a hundred years and never see such a sight. He might tell stories of it with every detail perfectly represented, and none would believe him.

Now, in the shadows of the citadel's interior, Revus stood on the edge of the training square, his linen jerkin soaked with sweat. He tried to recall how they had moved, how they had handled those crackling staves. Perhaps there was something to learn from it, however imperfectly or clumsily. There was always room for improvement, to become a better servant of the Throne, and it was hard to imagine more exalted role models.

But in truth, there was no emulating such paragons, not even by degree. They were as far above him as he was above the wretched and disease-blighted masses of the underhives. Already the experience had begun to seem like a dream, a too-vivid vision provoked by fever. Back in Courvain, all was dark again, all was stained and old. They had been like shards of gold in an imagined sunrise, fleeting, seen from a distance, a reminder of another possible world of myth and forgetfulness.

He pushed himself from the wall, flexing his aching arms. The baton was greasy in his grip. In the centre of the training square was a padded column two metres high, a static opponent of limited use for honing his skills. It would make him stronger though.

The overhead lumens flickered as he padded on to the mat, rehearsing the litanies of manual combat, the same ones he had been taught in the schola and had used ever since. The sodium tubes above him shook as he thudded the baton home, swinging heavily, panting and throwing sweat from his forehead. As he worked, as he pummelled and struck, he had the golden giants in his mind's eye the whole time, those titans of combat whose movements had been so fast as to be nearly impossible to follow.

There was so much to do still. So far to go before he reached the limit of his potential and the absolute satisfaction of what the Throne could demand. Once they had been seen, they could never be forgotten, and could only remain there, visions, goading him towards greater accomplishment.

There would never be fighting like it again. If he had never lived to see another day, it would still have all been worth it, just for that.

'Again, now,' he murmured to himself, getting ready for another bout. 'Faster this time. More accurate.'

The lumens pulsed, as if in readiness. Sweat ran in thin trails down his flushed skin.

He hefted the baton, and started again.

* * *

Now Terra was her home.

Spinoza's time on the Throneworld had been so short. She had seen many planets in her time and each had left their mark, though none had claimed her so completely as this one. She had ingested its poisons and breathed its soot-heavy atmosphere. She had observed the blush fade from her skin, to be replaced by the grey pallor that all wore here. She had already been swallowed up, enveloped and weighted down, until there was nothing left but this place, this endless city, this press of thousands upon thousands of souls, all of them clamouring for something, anything.

Now she stared at herself in her small mirror above her personal hygiene station, lit on all sides by unforgiving lumen strips. She saw the harder edge to her jaw, the deeper lines around her eyes. Her hair, which had always been a pale blonde, was now bleached almost entirely white. Terra's mark had been made, and the process could only continue.

She had a choice now. She could either do what Rassilo had done and indulge in augmetics and rejuvenat to hide the damage, or adopt her master's policy of letting the world do its worst. The latter was the more honest course and appealed to her innate sense of conventional piety, but the temptation to fight against the grime was still strong. There were things she could do, techniques she could adopt, all of which required coin, which she had enough of, and time, which she didn't. It was most likely, then, that she would let it slide and gradually become one with this place, just another grey-skinned, dark-eyed cadaver stalking the labyrinths.

She splashed cold water over her face, rubbed the skin dry, and turned away from the mirror.

Her private chambers were set on the northern wall of

the citadel, near the summit and only overhung by the top-most gun emplacements. Her sole view of the city outside was through a single set of narrow, reinforced windows. She could see towers crowding the night beyond, rank upon rank of them, each one surmounted by glowing marker lights and glittering from their thousands of tiny viewports. Palls of smoke from the incinerators and cathedral-furnaces rolled lazily across the darkness, snagging on the gothic turrets and spilling back down into the narrow canyons between.

The Palace itself was far to the north, a long way out of sight. Its grandeur might have been a world away from the crumbling mazes before her, and yet it never left her mind. She had come closer to it than she had ever dared to hope, albeit via buried ways that gave her little sight of the immense structures above. Since returning to Courvain, she had pon-dered little else – the ranks of statues forgotten in the deep dark, the foundations buried under centuries of accumula-tion, the smell of ancient dust in her nostrils, deposited in another age and only stirred again by their brief intrusion.

Crowl had gone further in, she knew. He had said nothing of what he'd seen, and she had learned better than to ask, but something had changed in him. He'd been brought out uncon-scious. When he'd finally stirred again, his first expression had been almost rapturous, as if he were still in the presence of something phenomenal, before he'd blinked, winced, and real-ised that it had gone. After that, there had been a change, some faint mark left on him. She could never quite put her finger on what it was – he remained dry, soft-spoken, occasionally sardonic – but an alteration had taken place.

Perhaps that was inevitable. You did not come so close to such powers without being changed by them. Even as Terra was moulding her, so the Palace, or what had taken place within it, had changed Crowl, and only time would tell where those changes would lead.

And then there was the heresy of it – the xenos, the monster, dredged up from the profane reaches of the void and delivered into the very precincts of holiness. The thought of it disgusted her beyond endurance, just as the memory of its many depravities still polluted her mind. She had seen foulness before, but never so close to the heart of what she had been charged to protect. It should never have got so far in. Now, whenever she closed her eyes to begin her devotions, she would see its hollowed-out face. Crowl said it was dead now, killed by the Custodian Navradaran, its body destroyed. She had to believe that. And yet, in the dark hours of the night, when she awoke, she would still catch it staring at her through the window, or back at her in the mirror, or from behind her altar, licking its dark tongue around its bone-pale lips.

Just visions. It was weakness to entertain them at all. To combat them, she read the catechisms aloud. She returned to the Pradjia rhythms again, clutching to their solidity and simplicity, trusting that, in time, faith would dispel such phantoms from her unconscious mind.

She donned her robes, pinning the rosette to her breast and adjusting the heavy fabric of her cassock. In the far corner of the chamber, hoisted on a metal rack and surrounded by ritual candles, was Argent, the modified crozius arcanum gifted her by the Space Marine Chaplain Erastus. Simply laying eyes on it made her fingers itch to grasp it, to take it out into the darkness and use it to tear the shadows apart. Physical violence was easy – it was pure, and it was sanctioned. Other forms of service, particularly those practised here, were harder.

A chime sounded, and a corresponding lumen-bead spread a soft blush of red across her wax-stamped purity seals.

'Interrogator,' came a thin voice over her private comm – Aneela's, by the sound of it.

'I am aware of the hour,' Spinoza replied, pulling a cloak over her shoulders. 'I shall be there presently.'

The link cut out. The candle flames fluttered in the hot air, sending their warm light flickering over Argent's sacred outlines.

It had never been over. The short time for respite – a mere breath, a single heartbeat – had passed. Now it would all start again.

CHAPTER TWO

Crowl moved through one of the many snaking capillaries that twisted and interlocked within his home's old and deteriorating heart. Drifting suspensors cast weak light over the dark metal walls. Every panel he passed was inscribed with worn-smooth homilies or excerpts from Inquisitorial manuals. The air smelled both antiseptic and musty, as if the grime of ages were perpetually warring against endless efforts to erase it. Strange noises welled up intermittently from the levels below, muffled by distance and distorted by the citadel's many interior crannies.

As he made his way higher, climbing up narrow spiral stairways, a servo-skull swooped in close. It bobbed at his shoulder, its lone eye a dull, thoughtful orange.

'Where have you been, Gorgias?' Crowl asked.

'*Armorias*,' the skull replied. 'Requiring *repleneo*. Not enough.'

Crowl nodded, still climbing. 'It's being looked into. Revus is working all the hours he can.'

The skull dipped and swerved around a floating suspensor caddy, making its lumen-bulbs wobble. '*Furioso*,' he blurted.

'Yes, they will be.' Crowl paused. 'And what do you think of that, then? Who has the right to be angry at whom?'

Gorgias spun around on his vertical axis. For a moment, the skull seemed genuinely nonplussed. Then he darted off again, leading the way up the spiral. '*Periculo*,' he murmured aimlessly. '*Periculoso*.'

Given its prestige and age, Courvain was not a particularly well-appointed citadel. It was by turns too cold and too hot, its air gritty from the overworked processors, its foundations slowly sinking into the silts below, but the upper apartments had at least a semblance of civility to them. Candles burned in deep alcoves, breaking the monotony of the sodium-yellow lumens. Fine statuary on devotional themes stood in recesses between the carved doorways. Much of the accumulation in such places was due to Crowl's forebears, but now and then there was a piece that he had collected himself – a jewelled copy of the *Reflections of Saint Adsel*, or a chalice from one of the ruined chapels in the Renata purge-zone. All such items were cared for rigorously, their plinths free of dust, their protective ward-shields glistening faintly like spiders' webs.

Spinoza was waiting for him in front of the doors to Crowl's council chamber. She, too, was out of armour, but somehow the reduction in bulk didn't seem to diminish her essential solidity. She stood unconsciously in a military stance – spine straight, shoulders back – as if she were still somehow serving alongside the Adeptus Astartes rather than occupying a shadier role within the Ordo Hereticus.

Spinoza might have made a fine Space Marine, Crowl thought, had she been a man. And if she had been a product of a different schola she might instead have ended up in the Adepta Sororitas, something that he suspected she would have preferred if the choice had been presented to her. As it was, fate had dragged her into the bosom of the Inquisition, where she was now condemned to spend the rest of her mortal existence.

There were so few real choices in the lives they all led, he reflected. Only different varieties of duty.

'My lord,' she said, bowing her head a fraction.

Still she persisted in that. Trying to get her to use *names* was, it seemed, a doomed endeavour.

'Khazad will live,' Crowl informed her, signalling for the doors to open. 'Just like you, Spinoza – hard to put away.'

The interrogator followed him inside. As they entered the chamber, a glow of lighting bled up from recessed panels, gilding the moribund space with a scatter of soft amber. 'I am glad of it,' she said. 'What did she make of the offer?'

'She accepted,' said Crowl, reaching for a goblet of wine. Experience taught him that Spinoza wouldn't drink, so he poured just the one glass, adding the powdered narcotic-mix from a dispenser at his wrist. It was a movement so practised and familiar that he could have done it in his sleep. 'Which does her credit – we are hardly a choice employer at this time.'

'Nonetheless, I believed she would.'

Spinoza stood beside her usual place at the long council table, making no move to pull the chair out. That, too, was a minor irritant. Crowl had at times wondered just how long she'd stand there if he never invited her to sit. All night, probably. There had been times when he'd been tempted to test the hypothesis.

'Sit, *please*,' he said, lowering himself into the iron-inlaid throne at the head of the table. As he did so, a chime sounded from the other side of the room, where a second set of slide-doors were half-lost in shadow. Spinoza raised an eyebrow.

'I wanted Revus here for this too,' Crowl said, unlocking them with a gesture. 'This is about survival.'

Gorgias adopted his favoured position hovering between Crowl and Spinoza. Revus entered, acknowledged both of them, then took his place at the far end. The captain of the storm troopers looked battered, as if caught out in bad weather for too long.

There was a faint crackle as the chamber's sensor-baffle field activated. Crowl took a long sip of his wine – a trifle foxed by age, but not bad – then flexed his gloved fingers.

'One thing is certain – we cannot remain static,' he said. 'We must move again, despite what remains unknown.'

Spinoza and Revus listened. They had both been with him under the Palace. No doubt they had also spent time contemplating what had to come next. The dust had settled in the old tombs, the great mass of pilgrims had reeled away from the final Sanguinala rituals, drunk on religious fervour, but Terra never rested. It was always a crucible, always in a churn of movement.

'So, this is what we know,' Crowl went on. 'A xenos creature was brought to Terra. Its presence, it seems, was required for some purpose connected to the Throne itself. Whatever the intention, the creature carved its own path under the Palace and was ended there. It is possible that those behind its deliverance will let matters drop now. It is possible they will have learned their lesson and repented of consorting with such monsters.' He took another sip, then let slip a wry smile. 'But it is also possible that their folly knows no limit, and that having come this far, they will attempt to finish what they have started. We must understand what they wish for. We must understand who they are.'

'You mentioned Lords of the Council,' said Spinoza warily.

'Three of them,' said Crowl. 'That is what Khazad's master Phaelias believed, and that is what the xenos told me.

No evidence, no names, just accusations from unreliable mouths.'

Gorgias began to agitate. '*Traitoris!*' he blurted. '*Castigatio!*'

'Yes, very possibly,' said Crowl.

'But...' Spinoza began, then trailed off.

Crowl looked at her tolerantly. 'Go on,' he said.

'All of us were hunting it,' she said. 'All of us rejoice that it is dead. Perhaps, beyond that... The truth of these charges. Perhaps that is less clear.'

'I know you wish to think that,' said Crowl. 'I understand why. But I spoke to Rassilo at the end. There is division within the Council. The Three – if it is Three – have kept their task secret from the others, and a virtuous policy is not kept secret. They can't stop now. They will carry on, maybe attempt the same thing again, maybe try some other scheme, but they can't stop. And if our involvement in this becomes known, they will come for us, too.'

'Surely too late for that,' said Revus.

'Maybe not,' said Crowl. 'Consider this – Rassilo was killed. All those she took with her into the catacombs were killed, or taken away by the Custodians. They will not be coming back, at least not with the same minds they entered with. The same can be said for those led by the heretic Lermentov, whose life was ended here by my own hand. So, who is left to witness our presence? Who among those who commissioned this can truly know what happened in the vaults? I do not know. It may be they have gleaned nothing at all, and are left to guess what took place, or it may be they know everything. We cannot presume, one way or the other.'

'The Custodian, though?' asked Revus.

Crowl sighed. 'Ah, yes, Navradaran. I would very much like to speak to him again, but my attempts have failed. I should not be surprised – either he chooses to remain silent, or he has been assigned to some other mission and cannot hear me. They are not servants to be held at one's beck and call.' He drank again. The narcotic blend was taking its time to work, and he felt pain throb in his glands. 'We are on our own, with limited information. Our first task must be to change that. We must uncover the complete picture.' He leaned forward, placing his elbows on the table. 'Phaelias believed that the Speaker of the Chartist Captains was involved. That would seem likely, given information I received from Navradaran. There was a contact in the Speaker's service, a woman named Glucher, who was in correspondence with those responsible for bringing the xenos out of the deep void. Phaelias discovered that she had been dead for five years before this started, and so the name itself is a cipher, but there was clearly some involvement there. Remember also that bringing such cargo to Terra undetected is hard – I find it difficult to imagine any such scheme being enacted without the Speaker being somehow entangled.'

'That's one, then,' said Revus. 'Another two to find.'

'The second must be the Fabricator-General,' said Crowl. 'The cargo was first landed at Skhallax, and the final ship used in the transit was a Mechanicus vessel. Again, I cannot imagine that happening without his knowledge. Phaelias was also of this view.'

'The third, then?' asked Spinoza.

'There, we reach the end of certainty,' said Crowl. 'If there was indeed a third party, we have ten more names to consider. We may be inclined to reject the Provost Marshal, whom Phaelias had persuaded to conduct the orbital cordon, but that still leaves nine. Too many. We can hardly knock on their doors to ask.'

'Nor can we go to Mars,' said Revus flatly. 'Not in secret.'

'True enough,' said Crowl. 'So we have the Speaker, the Provost Marshal, and not much else. That is where we start, though we must pursue this without leaving a trace – the moment our involvement is revealed is the moment we lose the power to investigate.'

'Then you already have a procedure in mind,' said Spinoza.

'At present, Spinoza, that is all I have,' said Crowl. 'We must access the archives in the Halls of Judgement. We need to establish what the Arbites know, or knew, and whether they are still pursuing an investigation. Even if they are not, there may be material there that can aid us. In addition, we must check for the remnants of Rassilo's forces. It seems likely to me that Gloch, her oversized henchman, never left the Palace, but we must be sure. His network stretched into Salvator – we must find out if he lives, and whether he is capable of directing harm towards us.'

Spinoza still sat stiffly, her hands clasped before her on the tabletop.

'And the Speaker?' she asked, carefully.

'She shall be my quarry,' said Crowl. 'I see no way of discovering what we need without getting close to the centre of her web. We need a name, just one, plus knowledge of what was intended.'

'And when all this is done,' said Spinoza, 'and we gather a case – what then? Are we to set ourselves against the Council?'

'A part of it.'

'I… see.'

Crowl sighed. The pain suppressors didn't seem to be working – the dull ache that accompanied his every move was morphing into something sharper. 'What would you have us do, Spinoza? Turn away?'

'No. No, of course not.' She looked pained. 'But there is the Lex.'

Revus smiled privately to himself.

'Yes, there is the Lex,' said Crowl, patiently. 'But at present there is no one we could go to, not with these rumours and half-heard whispers. We would be laughed out of the Council, even supposing we were somehow granted an audience, which is doubtful.' He placed his fingertips to his temples and began to massage the flesh slowly. 'We discover the truth, we can discuss what is to be done with it. But the first step, as always, is to discover the truth.'

Slowly, grudgingly, Spinoza bowed. Gorgias rose up over the centre of the table, swinging wildly.

'*Tempus* short-supply!' the skull crowed, turning to face each one of them in turn. 'Now hurry-hurry.'

'Quite,' said Crowl wearily. 'So, unless there are additional points, I see no further purpose in discussion here.'

Revus looked at Spinoza. Spinoza looked at Revus. Neither spoke.

'Very good,' said Crowl. 'Then we take up the hunt again.' He rose. 'A new beginning. May the Emperor be with us all.'

After that, he sent them away. All of them, even Gorgias, who clattered back to wherever Gorgias went when dismissed, grumbling bitterly all the way.

Crowl climbed the narrow staircase leading up from the council chamber, limping more than usual. He was already at the limit of the narcotics he could ingest, but glanded a sliver of something mildly sedative to take the edge off.

Was it getting worse? It was likely. He had known for a long time that there was no ultimate escape from this slow decline – the only question was how long it would take.

The poisons lodged in his bones and his organs were too deep-seated to expunge without killing him, and now Erunion's palliative cocktails were the only thing holding him together, like rusty bars clamped around a sagging wall.

But there was more to it than simple bodily decline. He had breathed the same air as that thing, just for a few moments. Recalling the foulness of its breath still made him want to gag. This was a world full of decay, and yet nothing, *nothing*, could compare with the rank debauchery that had been present in those few coughed-up breaths. Everything about that monster had been uniquely despicable, a nauseating mixture of cruelty, horror and sheer *other*ness that went far beyond that possessed by any human heretic or sadist. He had looked into its eyes, down in those deep pits. They had been blacker than the void itself, twin points of nothingness that sucked all life and hope out of the air. Across his many decades of service, he had never witnessed anything so completely, irredeemably corrupted.

Still, he should have been able to shake the memory off. He had seen many bad things and absorbed them all. An inquisitor was expected to be able to cope, to process such poison and transmute it into something useful. A lifetime of labour, of constant training, of psycho-conditioning and ritual observance, should have given him the tools to rise above anything.

He reached his private rooms. His fingers danced twice, and the lumens reduced to a cold blue glow. From somewhere, a vox-emitter began to play music. As so often, it was Bacque. Crowl's old master, Levi Palv, had been fond of saying that Bacque was the only truly incontrovertible proof that humanity was worthy of continued survival, and in the years since, his pupil had come to agree with him on that, if on little else.

So he sat, heavily, in a real-leather armchair and reached for the ever-present lead crystal decanter.

It might have been the xenos. Proximity to such debased specimens was proscribed for a reason. Or perhaps it was the things Navradaran had shown him before that fateful meeting. Down there, in the hallowed halls leading to the Eternity Gate itself, Crowl had felt the colossal tug of the one immortal presence that guided them all. He had not slept since, not truly. Erunion's concoctions could knock him out for a while, but only far enough to provoke dreams of black gums under white lips, laughing in the shadows. What was he seeing there? The xenos wretch? Or something closer to home, buried hard and fast and deep under that continent-sized Palace?

Spinoza had already noticed. He had seen similar signs with her, though not as acute. In addition, she was younger, stronger, more apt to bounce back. He found himself envying her. The iron certainties were still intact in Spinoza, so much so that it was hard to know how best to tutor her further. Inquisitors of her ilk generally had two courses ahead of them – to double-down on their puritanism and become fanatics for the Throne, or have it steadily worn away until they became like he was.

From the outset, for ignoble reasons, he had sought to turn Spinoza away from her inclinations and show her the folly of cleaving too close to the literal core of Ministorum doctrine. Now he had no idea where to lead her, or even if he were capable of leading her anywhere at all. It was almost certainly too late now. Preoccupied with survival, with seeing this thing through to the end, there would be little space left for instructing his interrogator as she ought to be instructed.

Still, she was no one's fool. As new to Terra's labyrinthine politics as she was, she understood that maintaining an investigation into this scheme was taking them into treacherous territory. In principle, an inquisitor was beholden to no one but the Emperor Himself, able to take his or her enquiries where the evidence led without fear of hindrance or obstruction. In practice, some members of the ordo were more powerful than others, and even the very greatest would hesitate before following a thread into the Senatorum Imperialis itself. It was not fear, though, that made her hesitate. It was that she still had faith in the institutions, resisting the notion that such exalted servants could possibly behave less than perfectly. That was what stayed her hand – the belief, cultivated and maintained through her diligent recitals of the catechisms, that the High Lords could do no wrong.

Crowl smiled briefly in the dark, a flicker across his scarred face. Perhaps, once, he too would have thought the same.

'Summarise,' he said.

A translucent hololith spiralled into life ahead of him, hanging in the gloom in a gauze of flickering green. Runes scrolled across it, followed by raster-barred images.

'Speaker of the Chartist Captains, Kania Teledh Dhanda,' came a disembodied voice – a vox-recording linked to the cogitator's spool-record. *'Female. Estimated age: ninety-seven standard years. Terra-born. Held Speakership for forty-one years. Held seat on the High Council for thirty-one years. Known Inquisitorial investigations: none. Known suspect tendencies: none. Political affiliations, list follows.'*

'Halt,' Crowl ordered, thinking. He studied the gently rotating three-dimensional image of Dhanda's head. She looked incredibly young, even for one with access to the very best rejuve treatments. Her hair was pulled back into a tight bun, and she carried two small tattoos on her right cheek – charter-marks, no doubt, from her ascent through the hierarchy. Her expression on the hololith was blank, with a tight mouth held firm and flat. She looked unaugmented, unlike the grotesquely altered Fabricator-General. Normal, almost.

And yet no High Lord was normal. They held truly massive amounts of power in their hands, accumulated collectively over thousands of years. Each one was an emperor in their own right, a potentate capable of drawing on near-untrammelled volumes of patronage and resource. Some were flashier than others: the Grand Master of Assassins, say, or his own ultimate mistress, the Inquisitorial Representative – they tended to attract the most fear. Dhanda, though, was as quietly influential as any of them. It had been estimated that nine out of ten ships in the Imperium fell under her purview. If the merchant fleets stopped plying their trade across the yawning void then the Imperium would swiftly fall apart. Whether it was hauling ores from mining asteroids to forge worlds, or munitions from those forges to the Militarum regiments, or foodstuffs from agri worlds to the teeming hive spires, the merchant charters were the mortar that held the tottering structures of the Imperium together. A word from Dhanda, and billions could prosper or decline, live in ease or starve.

Crowl had often wondered what such power did to a person. The High Lords were not genetically enhanced constructs like Navradaran, as limited by design as they were powerful – they were men and women like him, capable of doubt, capable of weakness. Even, as seemed possible now, capable of treachery.

He took a long swig, emptying his glass, and the hololith flickered out. It had been a long time since sleep had been restful. He had doubts that this night would be any different.

There was so much he didn't understand, and so little time to discover the necessary truths.

'Aneela,' he said out loud into the darkness, activating his comm-line.

'Lord,' came the crackling reply, crisp and ready. Aneela was so perfectly reliable.

'I require a meeting with a colleague,' Crowl said. 'Slek Nor Jarrod. His details are in Huk's records. Speak to his people. Impress upon them the need for haste.'

'By your will.'

'Secure channels.'

'Of course.'

Then the link cut out, the hololith span away, and Crowl was alone again, in the dark, thinking hard.

CHAPTER THREE

At dawn, following her regular devotions, Spinoza resumed her research. Her cell had been piled with books for some days, and more were scheduled to arrive soon. They formed mouldering stacks on the metal floor, all dusty, flaking spines and – in the case of the most proscribed – coils of rusting chains. The light from the window was as grey and weak as ever, and so candles burned, casting a wavering yellow blush over the vellum.

Spinoza had always been a diligent student, and knew more of the technicalities of the Lex Imperialis than most of her peers, but Terra, needless to say, had its peculiarities. The Lex, already complex beyond mortal calculation, was further complicated here by ancient treaties and pacts, some pre-dating the Imperium itself, all relating to the institutions that only existed here. The task of a judge was hard enough in any context; on the Throneworld, where billions of illiterates lived desperate lives crammed up against one another in the dark, occupying chambers and roles that had been old even before the myth-age of the Great Heresy, it was nigh-impossible.

Lermentov, the heretic, had told her exactly how it was.

The people here have precisely three fears – the monsters, each other, and you.

She snapped closed the tome in front of her. She admonished herself. Lermentov was dead now, and his execution had been just. She should not be recalling anything he had told her, not even in scraps of unbidden memory.

Spinoza pushed herself back from her desk and rubbed her eyes. She got up and paced around her cell. Argent was under wraps, a dormant presence in the shadows, something to be pushed away too, lest it prove another distraction.

She needed to begin her investigations soon, following Crowl's direction, and she was not making good progress with her preparations. The cause, she knew, lay within. Too many doubts refused to be quashed through the usual methods. If she were to return to full operational effectiveness, there was little point hammering away at the same worn-out seams – she needed a change.

She pulled her cloak across her shoulders and activated the door release. The candles fluttered as she swept out into the corridor beyond. After that, she trod a practised route through Courvain's convoluted inner pathways. Menials, more of them than usual it seemed, bowed and scurried around her. Many were carrying bundles of sensitive parchments, and some were escorted by storm troopers from the house detachment. Revus was working hard, further ramping up security in a citadel where it had already been ratchet-tight. The work created an atmosphere of more-than-usual tension, one that made the thrall-classes nervy.

She descended rapidly, finding her way, as she had done before, to Yulia Huk's little realm. The place was just as she remembered it from the last time – a circular well, lined with parchment and synth-leather book spines, its symmetry broken by the scampering servitor-creatures in their retrieval baskets. More of them were working this time, hauling on the chains with their metal-clamped fingertips and throwing books jerkily into their shoulder-strapped hoppers. She wondered where Huk kept them when they were not on duty.

The archivist herself was facing away from her as she entered, observing the clattering progress of her creatures, and only turned as Spinoza came up close. For a moment, her crabbed face looked panicked, then it relaxed into a lopsided grin.

'Ah, you,' Huk said, making the heavy cables running from her hunched back wobble as she turned. 'The schola girl. What are you down here for?'

Spinoza was not, by any rational measure, a girl. Before coming to Courvain she might have made something of the insult, but Huk was just one of the eccentrics Crowl seemed happy to cultivate, and who had become such a wretch in his service that it seemed pointless to add to her misery.

'I require information on the Arbites sector command,' she said. 'I thought that–'

'–I might be able to help?' Huk snorted a dry laugh. 'No. Not at all. See this? This is what he makes me do for him now.' She gestured with ironwork fingers to her vaulting gangs of servitors. 'He wants every scrap of every little thing. Xenos? Yes! The Senatorum? Yes! Old Rassilo? We don't have much on her, but yes, yes, yes.' She winked at Spinoza with her one good eye. 'I don't like to refuse him. But you? No capacity. Come back later.'

Spinoza stared at her. The keeper of records seemed more shambolic than ever, as if the augmetics that held her together were slowly coming apart. The pulses running down her extensive cabling were travelling faster than they had done before, a flickering dance of rapid synapse-conveyance.

'It will have to wait for some time, then,' Spinoza said curtly. 'I will be on mission again before this day closes. My thanks, though, for your help.'

Huk sidled up to her. 'Don't be like that.' Her voice could switch to a wheedle instantaneously. 'We're all working hard. What did you find out there? You can tell me.'

'You know I can't.'

'I'll put it together, sooner or later.' She grinned. 'I can work it out from what you file, or don't, given time.' The smile flickered out again. 'But you didn't come down here for papers. You have plenty of those.'

That was true.

'You wanted to talk to me, before,' Spinoza said.

'About Crowl? Of course. But you know all about him now, don't you?'

'Tell me about yourself, then.'

Huk recoiled. She smiled again, though weakly. 'Not sure why you'd want to know. And we're busy.'

'I do not believe you commenced your service in these archives.'

'No, no. Of course not.' Huk's eyepiece whirred, and she pulled at her robes absently. 'Savant. He didn't have a retinue. You hear that all the time! But he didn't, except he needed a savant, and I was training then, and I liked him, and he liked me. I was good. Very good.' She winced. 'But, it is hard. Your mind. It changes. Some do not cope. They do not remember. I began to… forget. A savant never forgets. I made a mistake. A bad one.' Huk began to look anguished again. 'Then they were coming for me. It would have been a poor death. I couldn't have argued with it. It would have been easier for him to stand aside, and let them take me.' She shook her head. 'He didn't. He buried me down here instead. I can still be of service, see?' The grin returned. 'I paid him back, I think, over the years. I got good at this. My mind – never the same. But I'm still good. Very good.'

'It is a dangerous thing,' said Spinoza, 'to interfere with just sanction.'

'And who says it was just?' Huk chuckled. 'Maybe it was. But maybe it wasn't. You'll learn the difference soon enough.'

'I already know it.'

'Of course you do.' Huk limped around her, her tattered skirts dragging on the stone floor. 'You think he's dangerous. You think he's a whisper away from going rogue. Don't deny it!'

Spinoza smiled to herself. 'We have our disagreements,' she said. 'I admire the way he allows me to express them.'

'Then don't be a fool.' Huk sidled up closer, and unpleasant aromas wafted up from under the cloak. 'There's no more loyal servant to the Throne.'

'Though he conceals it well.'

'You know his... condition. It makes him care less about what he says.'

'Words matter.'

'Do they? Not really. Not most of the time.'

They looked at one another for a little while. Spinoza saw the ruin on Huk's features, the slide into half-maintained dereliction. Everything here was falling into ruin, and no one ever queried it. She wondered if Huk saw the same in her.

She pulled away. 'I will return, when I can,' she said. 'Then I will require my information.'

Huk shuffled off, looking uncertain, as if she couldn't remember what she'd just said, or why she had said it. 'Of course,' she mumbled.

'But this place is disordered,' Spinoza added, turning on her heel. 'You were a savant. You should fix it.'

Huk watched her go. 'Some things can't be fixed,' she mumbled.

'Everything can be remade,' Spinoza said, reaching the doors. 'That is the lesson He teaches us every day.'

The locks cycled.

'Not here,' said Huk, as Spinoza crossed the threshold. She turned back to her servitors and her chrono-racks. 'This is Terra.'

It was the first time Crowl had left Courvain since sustaining his injuries. He took a groundcar, with Aneela in the cab, feeling somehow that staying close to the earth might help him adjust, and in any case the distance to travel was small. They pulled out of the vehicle depot in a cough of smoke, then growled up to the main transitway. Crowl sat back, letting the lights from the city filter through the armour-grille viewport, and watched.

For most of human history, orientation on this world had been virtually two-dimensional. There was the ground and the sky, and the entirety of the living occupied a narrow strip between them. By the 41st millennium, that distinction had all but disappeared, to the extent that it was very uncertain where the 'ground' on Terra actually was. The foundations of the great hive spires delved far below the nominal surface crust. Hidden catacombs and pits plunged down further still, honeycombing the world's upper mantle in a deepening procession of worm-eaten galleries. In the filmy air above it all, the jutting hive spires merged and branched in dizzying, almost organic thickets, joined and trussed by spans and viaducts and gothic arches, such that no structure ever really stood independently of any other, and all was lost in a grime-stained haze of fumes and vented condensation.

Transitways perched high up and jutted down low, sweeping round the boles of the spires before toppling back into the lamplit depths, then branching, then re-joining, then coalescing into the vast, echoing transportation nexuses before more routes sprouted and divided away again. Old ordinances governed their use, rigorously categorising the cracked rockcrete avenues by purpose and status. The majority, the Via Exclusiva, were reserved for security personnel, leaving the greater bulk of the population to travel on the wider but more heavily congested Via Ordinaria, jostling and clawing past one another to get to wherever they needed to be. A select subset, the Via Prohibida, was kept clear for the very highest echelons of the Imperial hierarchy – the governing classes, senior enforcers of the Adeptus Arbites, agents of the Inquisition. These narrow conduits shot precariously above the rest, tracing efficient routes between the major administrative centres, though it was rarely possible to complete an entire journey without having to duck down onto less exalted transitways.

For the time being, though, the groundcar travelled at one remove from the great press of humanity, a little higher up, a little further away. Crowl watched as the dim walls of the great spires passed by, flickering through the narrow slats of the grille, a steady march of grey-black terraces and buttresses.

The fervour of Sanguinala was a distant memory now, lost in the resumption of work details and shift patterns. Everywhere he looked, he saw labour-gang transports grinding their way to their silos, or Ecclesiarchy floats pushing their way through the crowds blaring out echoing hymn-loops, or supply haulers lumbering smokily towards the distribution centres. The percentage of Terra's inhabitants who ever left the interior of their home spire was small, but even so every sliver of available space was still taken up, wreathed in a boil of engine exhausts that curled up through the tangle of support columns and flying buttresses.

Aneela did not hurry, keeping the groundcar's ride smooth through the sparser traffic of the exclusive zones.

'Any trouble contacting him?' Crowl asked, tiring of the monotonous view.

'Not at all. I got the impression the appointment was welcome.'

'Hmn.'

They started to climb, following a snaking route that twisted through the very heart of a tower-cluster. Swarms of atmospheric craft hovered around them, both above and below, gliding like dirty fish through the sedimentary layers of Terra's choked airways. A big dirigible – all flabby air-sacs and lazily spinning turbines – wallowed under the archway below, trailing long metallic sensor-fronds. Its swaying skirts bore the imagery of a sector-level Ministorum convent, but Crowl guessed it was probably a surveillance unit from one of the hundreds of scrutiny details that prowled every inch of the world-city's airways. You got to recognise the signs, after a while.

Soon another spire was looming – a horn-shaped mass of dark iron crowned with battered stone angels. Its flanks were speckled with flecks of neon yellow, and its entire northern shoulder seemed to be somewhat slumped, as if dozens of hab-levels had subsided before reaching a kind of equilibrium, a frozen landslide of permacrete and twisted steel.

The groundcar slipped from the privileged zone and on to one of several dozen access routes. The space around them filled with bulkier vehicles, though the other drivers soon recognised the matt-black profile of an Inquisition transport and did their best to get out of the way. Vehicles shunted into one another or dragged themselves along the perimeter barriers just to clear a path, through which Aneela coolly guided them. In time, they reached a yawning entrance chamber, its arched ceiling lost in shadows, its walls studded with smog-caked angelic figures. Ignoring the security teams vetting incoming traffic, they peeled off up a steep ramp, plunging into the spire's innards, then switchbacked through steeply climbing roadways. The space around them shrunk until they were almost grazing the edges of the tunnels, and the murky roof got within a metre of the groundcar's comms aerials.

Eventually Aneela pulled up before pair of bronze gates and got out of the cab. Crowl, still seated, peered out at twin braziers burning in the gloom, and saw armoured guardians at station on either side of a heavy blast-door. He let his eyes run over the slabbed armour-panels above, and spied two needle-gun notches and the glint of a sensor-bead. No doubt there were other devices, better hidden, further in.

'Not very welcoming,' he observed as Aneela got out, opened the doors and stood to attention.

'Not at all,' she agreed.

'Wait here until I return, please.'

'By your will.'

Crowl walked on alone, passing through the gates and limping up chipped stone stairs to the doors beyond. The guardians, who looked much as Revus' soldiers did, saluted as they activated the unlock pistons.

He went inside. The change was instant. The grimy exterior, lost down the dead-end of a hive-spire's buried transit arteries, hid an interior of rare opulence. Crowl's boots sunk into a deep-pile rug. The walls were marble, and high-polished mirrors reflected the warm light of a dozen gold-lined suspensors. Every surface was heaped with artefacts and objects of bewildering variety – a long skull preserved in a glass case, a diamond-tipped sabre, a porcelain vase decorated with strange hiero-glyphs. Music was playing somewhere, though of a type he couldn't place. It was hard to listen to, if you concentrated on it.

He pressed on, walking down a long hall hung with paint-ings, and eventually reached a circular reception chamber. The clutter grew ever more pronounced and strange. Much of the furniture was very fine indeed, but every tabletop and chair seat was stuffed with ephemera. Smells, most of them foreign and difficult to identify, tumbled out of the perfo-rated lips of censers. It began to feel a little confined, a little oppressive.

The circular chamber had three doors leading from it, only one of which stood open. Crowl passed through and found himself in a high-ceilinged room of domestic proportions. The walls were lined with books, most very old and all kept locked behind crystal security screens. More esoterica lay in heaps – antique weapons, precious stones sitting on velvet pads, slow-cycling holo-images imprisoned behind ornate glasswork frames.

'Good morning to you, Erasmus,' came a soft voice from an armchair on the far side of the chamber.

The speaker was an old man, slim, with fine-wrinkled skin and a balding pate. He wore thick burgundy robes that hung heavily over slender wrists, and thick spectacles with silver frames. He looked frail and neat and faintly incongruous, like a tall bird wrapped in a carpet.

Crowl picked his way through the clutter until he reached a second armchair. He removed a few items from the seat, placing them on the nearest teetering pile, and sat down.

'Slek,' Crowl said. 'You've had a clear-out since I was last here.'

The light filtering through the windows behind his host was clear and warm. It appeared as if the space beyond was open to the sky, and the silhouettes of hothouse plants trembled behind the glass. Of course, it wasn't the real sky. They were buried too deep for that, and in any case Terra's sky was never clear and warm.

'You do not look well, my friend,' Slek Nor Jarrod said. 'Will you have a cordial?'

Jarrod's cordials were interesting things. As a long-serving member of the Ordo Xenos, he had things in his caches that were almost certainly illegal, not that anyone would have dared to rummage through them.

'Something restorative,' Crowl said.

A moment later, a slender figure weaved their way through the tottering heaps of taxidermy and real-bronze figurines. He might have been a boy, she might have been a girl, it was impossible to tell. They were slim, almost impossibly so, and dressed in a clinging shift of gauzy silver. Something about their movements was hard to get used to – the poise, perhaps, or the silent way they trod through the mess. They carried a silver tray with two goblets, each containing a turquoise liquid that smelled of rose petals. As soon as they had delivered them, they slipped away again.

'This is very expensive,' Jarrod said, raising his goblet.

'Everything you own is very expensive,' said Crowl, taking a sip. It was good, too, though the impressions it gave were as elusive as everything else in this place.

Alien.

They talked companionably enough. Jarrod asked after Revus. Crowl asked after Ohanna Vroon, Jarrod's captain of storm troopers. They discussed the politics of the Inquisition on Terra, the performance of Kleopatra Arx in the High Council, the prospect of another interminable reorganisation. Crowl admired Jarrod's latest items; Jarrod admired, for the umpteenth time, Crowl's Luna-forged sidearm.

'But you did not come here for cordial and conversation,' Jarrod said eventually.

'I should have done,' said Crowl. 'Both are excellent.'

'You have a question.'

'I have a story.'

'Very good. I like stories.'

Jarrod settled back in his chair, letting his hands cross on his lap. His Inquisitorial rosette – an insectoid of some kind locked in amber – nestled within the folds of his robe.

'I became aware of a foolish plan,' said Crowl. 'It was to bring a xenos creature, alive, to a hive world.'

'Very foolish. What kind of xenos creature?'

'A pain-bringer. I can describe it – you will be able to give me the precise term.' He listed the way the creature had looked – its skeletal frame, its shifting robes, its bone-white skin stretched tight over prominent bones, the metalwork pinned through its flesh, its eyes, its black, black eyes.

'You are describing a haemonculus. Throne. Who told you of this plan?'

'A friend.'

'And for what purpose was one of them brought to... a hive world?'

'I was never sure. But it matters not – the point is this. Once imported, it did not do as intended. It pursued its own course. One that, to my mind, was almost mad. Suicidal. And so it proved – my friend tells me the creature is dead now.'

'Throne be praised.'

'So, I am left with a puzzle,' said Crowl. 'The expense and effort required to bring it to that world were huge. They must have had expectations that it could do something for them, and yet it did not. Why? I do not know. I wondered if you might.'

Jarrod frowned. 'It is dangerous to look for reason in what such creatures do. Very dangerous.' Then he smiled, brightly. 'But also intriguing. What do you understand of the dark eldar?'

'Very little.'

'Keep it that way. They are beyond abhorrent.' Jarrod shook his head. 'Even I do not know enough. No one in the ordo knows everything, for they are almost impossible to capture. I have never met one in the flesh. Few people have, so your friend was fortunate, or perhaps unfortunate, to have done so. But let me tell you what is known.' He reached up to his rosette, and began to toy with it absently. 'They are called pain-bringers for a reason. They live for it. It is not an affectation for them, it is life itself. We do not know precisely why, but there are accounts of them being imprisoned and kept away from any possible prey, and after a time spent thus, even when given solid food and water and kept in comfort, they wither. They begin to rave, then to decay. Given long enough, they will expire. I have seen the footage of this, and it is unpleasant. They are terrified, at the end, clawing the metal bars, pleading. And so it has been postulated that the infliction of agony is in some way essential to their survival. If they are given subjects to... desecrate, then they can survive under such conditions indefinitely.'

'How was that supposition tested?'

'Do not ask.' Jarrod let his rosette fall, and reached for his goblet. 'Let us return to your friend. Suppose someone were foolish enough to bring a haemonculus to a hive world. It would be the very opposite of the confinement I have described. The creature would be surrounded by billions of souls, all of them vulnerable, all of them alluring. You must understand that these creatures experience sensation far more acutely than we do. Their appetites dominate them, if allowed to. For this precise sect of the species, appetite is all that remains. It was placed in an environment of overwhelming, intoxicating abundance. I suspect that your judgement was right, Erasmus. I suspect it went mad. If it had some purpose in the beginning, then that must have been quickly forgotten.'

Crowl rested his chin on his interlocked fingers. 'Then it would be folly for those who arranged this to try the same thing again.'

'It was folly the first time.'

'And what would it do to those who came into contact with it?'

Jerrod shrugged. 'They would die. Painfully.'

'But if they survived.'

He looked at Crowl carefully. 'What do you mean?'

'If a human were exposed to such a creature, even for a short time, and somehow survived.' Crowl held Jarrod's gaze. 'What effects might that have?'

For a moment, Jarrod did not reply. 'It would depend on the context,' he said eventually. 'Any xenos is to be avoided – their vices are legion. In this case, I have been told their speech is treacherous. I have been told their aroma is uniquely repulsive, no doubt partly due to their vile practices. But you will know all this.' He reached for his drink. 'I did speak to the master of the prisons where the experiments I mentioned were carried out. He had trouble sleeping.

Perhaps not surprising. He also told me there were some things he could never get out of his head. He told me that he felt sometimes as if the creature had taken up residence there, even after its documented and witnessed death, and was making him think strange things. He feared that his judgement was becoming tainted.'

'How did you respond to that?'

'How anyone would have done – I reported him to his superiors. His replacement was given more strenuous psycho-conditioning.'

'I see.'

'Is that the answer you were hoping for?'

'It is all useful. I am still trying to make sense of the story.'

'A true story, is it? I struggle to believe it.'

Crowl ran his gaze across the objects around him. Many were of human origin, many were not. One long tusk had been mounted over the mantelpiece, its notched length studded with bulletholes. Polished gems set in rune-carved lozenges hung on either side, glimmering faintly as if animated by an internal light.

'Does it not make you sick at heart, to be surrounded by such grotesque things?' Crowl asked.

'No more so than the witches and fools you treat with, I expect. Your hatred for the alien, given all other possible targets for righteous anger, has always intrigued me.'

'They are the ordained foe of humanity.'

Jarrod laughed. 'So the Cult teaches. I thought you only paid attention to the parts of that you liked.'

Crowl sighed. 'A heretic was a man once, or a woman once, or a child. They were gifted something precious, but chose to cast it aside. That is a tragedy, but an understandable one, for weakness is the condition of the masses. These...

47

things, though. They are predators. They are beasts. There is no morality in them, no judgement or law.'

'They say much the same about us.'

'A dangerous equivalence. If I were cut from a different cloth–'

'Did you discover what you wished to?'

Crowl smiled faintly, and looked down at his clasped hands. 'It was helpful. My thanks.'

'The story was intriguing, though. I may have to investigate it further.'

'I would not recommend that. These things happened far away.'

'Oh.'

Crowl stood. 'Thanks for the drink.'

'Any time. It looks like you could use another one.'

'I could. What was in it?'

'Grotesque things.'

Crowl picked a path through Jarrod's collections as he made his way out. 'Goodbye, Slek. Take care of yourself.'

'You too, Crowl.'

CHAPTER FOUR

Revus marched down past the Nighthawk hangars, followed by half a dozen staff – three storm trooper sergeants, two of Courvain's bound adepts and a lexmechanic. They had been working their way through the citadel's standing defences and supplies for several hours, and more work lay ahead. The internal layout had never been logical, with power generators inserted next to mess chambers, dormitories next to armouries. Simply keeping a handle on what lay where and had links with what was a fiendish and unending task.

'Two gunships are still out of service, are they not?' Revus asked the lexmechanic, studying a data-slate as he went.

'That is correct, captain,' came the reply, sounding more contrite than a Mechanicus lackey was wont to. 'The required parts are on order from the feeder depot at Skhallax, but for some reason–'

'Get it done, Namon. The Lord Crowl was most insistent on that point – we must have them all airworthy within forty-eight hours.'

Ahead of them, menials were working hard. An arc welder

was being deployed over a main portal blast-defence screen, and teams of labourers huddled around it, their faces hidden behind iron masks. The sound of turbo-hammers booming came up from the deeps below, from the larger chambers that housed the big Spiderwidow orbital craft.

'I had reports of a fault in the third external door mechanism,' Revus went on, still striding, causing a servitor hauling a heavy power-wrench to lurch out of the way. 'That is unacceptable also.' He looked up, directly past the main overhead lumen banks to where a thin tube snaked along the peeling plaster, terminating in a cluster of capped-off nozzles. 'And make sure that one's been checked out, too.'

'Understood, captain–' the lexmechanic Namon began, then stopped in his tracks.

Ahead of them, ahead of the scurrying labourers and blundering servitors, stood a woman. She looked unstable on her feet, though was dressed in combat gear of the finest quality. The plates fitted tight to her body, each armoured piece beautifully interlocked, matt-black and sheer. That armour had once used cameleo scatter fields, seemingly, but the nodes appeared to be burned out.

'Reporting, sir, as ordered,' said Niir Khazad, making the aquila to Revus.

Revus stared at her, lost for words. The assassin's face was grey, which was unusual, as her natural colouration was copper-brown.

'I did not ask you to report to me,' he said. 'You do not report to me. You report to the Lord Crowl.'

'I get bored,' said Khazad, then grinned. 'Very bored.'

One of the sergeants grinned too, before catching the look from his superior and extinguishing it. Revus went up to Khazad, extending a steadying hand.

'You are not well, assassin,' he said. 'How did you escape Erunion's care?'

Khazad looked at him conspiratorially. 'You know what I do for living?' Then she got closer. 'You are good at this, too, yes?'

She was not focusing. Clearly the sedatives she'd been given were still having an effect.

Revus beckoned one of the sergeants over, and he took her by the arm. 'Get her back to the apothecarion,' he told him, turning back to his work. 'And find out what that flesh-meddler thinks he's doing, letting her out.'

The sergeant, a young man named Greive, dragged Khazad off. A second later there was a crash, and he was on his back amid a tumbling batch of fuel canisters. Revus looked around to see Khazad standing next to him, perfectly relaxed and smiling blearily. The two remaining troopers drew their weapons.

'Don't be stupid,' Revus growled, waving at them to stand down.

He took a closer look at Khazad. Even half-crazed on meds, she was capable of swatting aside a trained storm trooper as if he wasn't there. That should not have come as a surprise. Both of them, Revus and Khazad, had been there in those final moments in the vaults under the Palace. He had seen the way she fought, albeit in confused snatches amid the flashes of las-fire, and it had been formidable. She was, in her own way, far more deadly than he was. Perhaps she was even more deadly than Interrogator Spinoza, who had proved her worth to the citadel in such a very short time.

'I'll take her,' Revus said, almost without intending to. He turned back to Greive, who was getting up awkwardly. 'Complete the survey, sergeant, then run the next two levels down. Report on my desk within two hours.'

'Aye, captain,' Greive said, looking chastened.

Revus took Khazad by the arm and walked her away, heading back to the elevators that led back up to the medicae levels. This time, she didn't resist.

'What you people doing down here?' Khazad asked, looking around her, wide-eyed.

'These are dangerous times,' Revus said, keeping her moving. 'Lord Crowl ordered a review of the defences, just in case.'

Khazad nodded sagely. 'Yes, yes. They came for us, too.'

'I am aware of that.'

Then she seized him by the wrist, a sudden movement that was so quick, so unconsciously fluid yet steel-trap strong, that he instantly found himself wondering how she'd done it. She seemed on the surface to move without thought or consideration – acting purely on instinct – and yet her aim, even under such conditions, was near-perfect.

'I can help you,' she said, seriously. 'They will come again. I evaded them, a long time. I know how they work.'

Revus wondered if he could shake off her grasp without breaking his wrist. 'Yes, that is why Crowl wanted you,' he said.

'I am very good.'

'I can see that. You do not need to grip quite so hard.'

Khazad laughed, and let him go. Then she looked groggy again, and took a half-step backwards to keep on her feet.

'That thing you did back there, with my trooper,' said Revus, carefully. 'Can that be taught?'

'Everything can be taught,' Khazad said, 'to the right student.'

She staggered, and he grabbed her swiftly, keeping her upright, guiding her to the waiting elevator cage. She appeared to be losing consciousness, and her face went another shade paler.

'Throne knows how you even made it down here,' Revus muttered, bundling her in and hitting the lock controls. The doors ground closed on rust-blotched rails before the cage started to clang its way up.

'I am very curious,' she mumbled, slumping against him with half-closed eyes, a thin line of drool running from the corner of her mouth.

'This is a Hereticus citadel,' said Revus stiffly, holding her up and watching the floors slide by. 'Best you work on that.'

Spinoza remembered Rassilo.

The candles in her chamber were burning low, though due to her imminent departure she would not have them trimmed. She shifted in her uncomfortable fatigues, all greasy synth-leather and plasfibre, and tried to concentrate.

From the outset, Rassilo had been the one she had trusted. Spinoza remembered her calm aura of command, the gentle air of authority. Rassilo had worn the badge of her office with such unostentatious assurance that it had engendered trust from the outset. That had been the skill, of course – the ability to inspire confidence. Crowl did not have it, at least with her, and that was no doubt why Rassilo had been an inquisitor lord with access to the interior of the Palace, and Crowl was stuck in Salvator hunting down gangers and witch-cults.

They had known one another, those two, in some fashion that she still didn't understand. Probably a professional liaison, but you never knew. Even a dried-up old lizard like Crowl must have had romantic attachments once or twice over his long life, though it was admittedly hard to see what the attraction could have been in her case.

Now Rassilo was gone, though, cutting off the last thread of security to another world, one in which the chains of command were simple and well understood. Spinoza did not know what was more unsettling about the situation – that she had been so wholly duped, or that she was now on the other side of the mirror, still working with those whom her original mentor had opposed. There was no one left on the outside, now – Spinoza's entire hinterland had become this citadel, its damaged denizens and its decaying walls.

Well, that was not quite true. Oaths had been made. But she could think of no likely circumstances, even mortal ones, under which she could take advantage of the very last contingency available to her.

Sighing, she reviewed the information a final time. The printed parchment documents would not be taken with her, and so everything had to be committed to memory.

Revre, Haldus, forty-five-standard, access level azure-nine, specialism/modus incom–

She looked up as her door chime sounded.

'Come,' she said, placing the parchment back on the desk and turning in her chair.

It was Crowl. As he entered, ducking under the metal frame of the doorway, she thought he looked worse than he'd ever done, his flesh more sallow, his cheeks hollower. He'd been outside, that was clear enough – the promethium stink of the Terran atmosphere still clung to his armour and robes.

'Glad I caught you, Spinoza,' he said, a little breathlessly. 'I wished to bid you good fortune before you left. And that is fine attire.'

Despite herself, she let a half-smile flicker. She was not wearing her habitual blood-red armour, but had donned civilian clothing of a particular down-at-heel kind. It had been altered and fitted to her, but still felt strange – too light, too flimsy.

'Thank you,' she said.

'You would prefer to pursue this openly, I know,' Crowl went on. 'Creeping around in borrowed clothes and with assumed identities is hardly dignified, and Gorgias is still angry with me about it. Trust, though, that it is necessary.'

'I do not doubt it, lord,' she said.

'We have no defence once we are exposed.'

'Yes, I understand that.'

'So you have the leads you require?'

'I believe so. I intend to take Sergeant Hegain with me – he performed well before.'

'Good.' He shot her one of his crooked smiles, the kind that exposed his yellowing teeth. 'Then, unless there is anything else?'

She hesitated. At times, she thought her master had an almost preternatural ability to catch her at her most vulnerable, displaying forensic insight into her hidden thoughts and intentions. At others, he seemed unbearably clumsy, a clever man who nevertheless misread signals and treated all around him as tools rather than subjects. In all likelihood both presentations were correct, albeit deliberately cultivated and managed.

She looked up at him directly. 'A confession, lord,' she said, firmly.

Crowl raised an eyebrow. 'Go on.'

'I was… in communication with Inquisitor Lord Rassilo before she was exposed,' she said. 'In secret. She gave me the means to get in touch privately, in case…' She searched for the words.

'In case I was too difficult to work with,' Crowl finished for her. 'Or you required advice on how to handle me. Or I was, as many no doubt suspect, a heretic myself.' He brushed the idea aside with his hand. 'Come, Spinoza. I'd have been disappointed if you hadn't been speaking to her.'

'It was a betrayal of trust.'

'You had to be careful. She was powerful.'

'It was not for that reason.'

'For whatever reason.' Crowl blinked hard. Something swam briefly across his vision, a kind of cloudiness in his rheumy eyes. 'If you wish me to be disappointed in you, or find some reason to impose discipline, then you are wasting your time. This work is too important.'

She found herself wanting to press him further then. She found herself wanting to ask when he had last slept. She found herself wanting to ask how effective his medication was proving, and whether he was confident that his desire to press on with this investigation, alone, with such haste, was wise. She found herself wanting to ask whether he still saw the creature's teeth in his nightmares.

'Then take it as a lesson learned,' she said, 'that any question of loyalty is now resolved. It will not happen again.'

Crowl nodded. 'Understood.' He limped over to the desk's edge and leaned against it. 'Though you still think this is all misjudged. Go on – speak. Healthier to get it out into the open.'

Spinoza looked up at him. 'No, lord, I do not know what to think,' she said, truthfully enough. 'I have no certainties left. Only one thing troubles me, though – the reason she did all this. If Rassilo were right, and the Golden Throne were indeed failing, then would not anything be warranted in the search for a cure?'

'Do you think she was telling the truth?'

'Why would she lie?'

'Because she had been in contact with that… *thing*.' Crowl

looked briefly pained, and sighed deeply. 'A creature like that twists everything. You cannot ally with them, control them or reason with them. The only safe course is to destroy them. Rassilo thought she knew better, and died for her arrogance. If there are High Lords truly involved in this too, then they have made the same error, and will share the same fate.'

'But if there is even a risk of it, then should we not at least–'

'I was in hailing distance of it,' said Crowl. 'The Throne itself. I *felt* it. Truly, I never wish to be in the presence of anything so powerful ever again. Having been there, I cannot believe that anything could endanger it. That may be why Navradaran took me inside. At any rate, he was not worried, and do you not think he, of all people, might have said something, if such worries had any foundation?'

'Navradaran's life has always been in there,' Spinoza said. 'I have observed before that when a person is surrounded by something for too long, he stops seeing it truly, and cannot conceive of a time when it might not be as it always has been.'

Crowl raised an eyebrow. He thought on that for a moment. 'That may be so,' he said. 'That may be a blindness we are all capable of suffering from.' Then he roused himself and pushed back towards the door. 'But it is still speculation, and only one fact is truly certain, for we witnessed it with our own eyes – a monster was loosed within the Palace and came within a hair's breadth of reaching the Emperor Himself. Whatever was intended, whatever was believed for whatever reasons, that crime must be punished. I have killed countless souls for lesser transgressions – you have done, too. This is our sacred task now.'

'Then do you still see it?' Spinoza asked.

Crowl halted. 'What do you mean?'

'The xenos. Do you still see it? I do. I hear it, sometimes.'

'You must purge such thoughts from your mind.'

'I have been attempting to. I will try harder.'

'Do so,' he said, sharply. Then he appeared to regret his tone, and offered a final, dry smile. 'The truth is I need you, Spinoza. No greater duty will ever come before us, not if we serve in this Inquisition for another thousand years. We must not fail in this. We must not doubt.'

For some reason, Spinoza immediately thought of Erastus then. That was just the kind of thing he would have said. 'Of course, you are correct, lord,' she said, standing to face him. Already she could see the signals flashing from Hegain, informing her the transport was prepared. 'Once more, I have been remiss. I will do better.'

'Just... do what you do so well,' Crowl said, half-tolerantly, half-wearily, standing aside to let her pass. 'And know that, in so doing, and in all else, my trust is absolute.'

Despite herself, that was good to hear.

'Thank you,' she said. 'I shall endeavour to deserve it.'

CHAPTER FIVE

His review complete and standing orders issued, Revus took a Shade out of the hangar and headed west into the heart of Salvator. It was two hours before dusk, and the sky overhead was turning a deep, dark grey. All across the crowded cityscape, lamps were being lit, searchlights were going on, banks of neon were flickering into life. Diurnal watch-craft were returning to their claw-berths, replaced by nocturnal duty shifts. Auto-bells pealed in the many campaniles, just audible over the grind of the city's furnaces, its engines, its sirens.

He didn't opt for the privileged air-lanes, but mingled with the rest of the sluggish traffic. Just as always, they got out of his way smartly enough. Over on his right-hand side, a glut of crumbling hab-units blocked out the lowering sky. They had once, seemingly, been daubed with bright colours, but Terra's driving grit-squalls had scoured most of that from the bare rockcrete, making them look like pocked and eroded cliff-edges.

On his left-hand side was the glowing shell of a refinery, its heart a throbbing red, barred by cooling towers that rose as high as the crowded pinnacles around them. Sparks from the open furnaces drifted across the columns of air-traffic, swept up by the eddies of the roiling wind and thrown into spirals and plumes of twinkling illumination. Revus watched them dance for a while, letting the Shade's machine-spirit guide him. The points of light were ephemeral, glowing brightly for a few scant moments before the dry gusts turned them to ash-flakes, ready to coat the levels below in another gauzy net of dust.

Ahead of him rose the archaic cluster of a Ministorum diocesan command-chapel, a twisting, tortured mass of age-blackened iron and adamantium. Gargoyles and devils crowded its steep rooftops. Web-like buttresses flew tightly between ranked spires and turrets, piled atop one another in a maze of overlapping construction. A hundred narrow stained-glass windows glowed weakly from the thousands of candles tended within, while autocannon placements slowly rotated atop the spire pinnacles under the blind gaze of cowled stone saints.

The place was a micro-city in its own right, with its own priests, its own gunships, its own servitors and its own power generators. Pilgrims and supplicants processed in endless shuffling columns through its gaping portals, blared at constantly by hovering devotion-drones. Every so often an Ecclesiarchy official would push his or her way through the masses, guarded by a phalanx of masked cathedral orderlies with electro-staves and crozius-poles.

Revus took back full control and guided his transport towards a narrow landing pad set deep in one of the command-chapel's less ostentatious districts. He ducked it under the shadow of an overhanging prayer-tower and pulled it round, finally dropping onto the platform with a gout of yellowish steam. He disembarked, sealed the Shade remotely, and followed a spiral stairway down inside the sprawling structure.

Once within, he witnessed the usual activities in the naves – the congregation waddling past the high altars, servo-skulls swarming up in the vaults with their sweeping red surveillance-eyes, the wild cries of flagellants and Emperor-touched pilgrims prophesying the Days of Wrath. More worshippers were gathered into the precincts than he'd seen before, outside of the great feasts and festivals. They huddled there, like herd-beasts clustering for warmth and shelter while a storm gathered energy outside.

Soon, though, he was moving down more tight-wound stairways, entering a labyrinth of older routes and danker passages. The air got stuffier, smelling of incense and rotting books. Candles as thick as his waist guttered in alcoves, dribbling tallow over heavy stone blocks. Tombs had been set back into long alcoves, each inscribed in various ancient dialects of Gothic and given over to the memory of men and women who had once been powerful in their own parochial way but were now almost entirely forgotten. Even the servo-skulls didn't come this far down often, and the hum and shriek of the crowds gradually faded away.

Eventually he reached a side-chapel – a tiny chamber carved out of mouldering black walls. More candles glimmered against damp stonework. A modest altar took up one end of the chamber, over which hung the faded banner of an Astra Militarum regiment, one of the thousands that carried the Emperor's vengeance to His enemies. Revus had no idea how old the regiment was, where it was stationed, what deeds it had performed, or even if it still existed. Perhaps no one ever came here any more, or perhaps, one day, the regimental commanders would finally make the pilgrimage home again, replacing this standard with a more glorious one and leaving a granite-carved record of their many and famous victories. Whatever the truth, a long time ago someone had seen fit to hang the standard over the altar, and mark it with the words *Religio Nostra ad Sideres Aeterna*, and leave a single lasgun, now cobwebbed and dusty, before the votive candle formation.

Revus took a seat on the hard, metal pew. As he did so, the chamber's only other occupant shuffled a little further up.

'In His service,' the man said.

'For all ages,' Revus replied.

The two of them regarded the standard for a while. The man's eyes were milky, as if he were suffering from cataracts. His thin hands protruded from pale grey cuffs, and the faint smell of something gangrenous hung about his priestly robes.

'It has been a while, captain,' the man said, eventually.

'Always so much to do, Heinwolf,' said Revus. 'How is your health?'

'I still serve. I wish only for the strength to do His work a little longer.'

'As do we all.'

'You have questions.' Revus nodded. The priest pulled a thumbed sheaf of parchment from his cloak, and handed it over. 'Here are names your master will wish to study, when he can. The usual sources – whispers in confession, the accusations of the desperate. Who knows? Some may even be guilty.'

'And have you noticed a… worsening?'

Heinwolf croaked a laugh. 'You feel it too?' He turned to face Revus, exposing a drawn, ash-white face under his cowl. 'Every night, in this place, we have prophets telling us the End Times are around the corner. I never believed them.'

'And now?'

'They may have a point.'

Revus stowed the parchment. 'Inquisitor Crowl wishes he could come in person,' he said. 'He is detained with matters of great importance, but wished me to convey his thanks for the work you do on our behalf.'

'Crowl is a good man.'

'He has one particular query.'

'Does he, now.'

'You know the name Aido Gloch?'

Heinwolf coughed – a dry, cold ratchet. 'Quantrain's thug. Yes, I know the name.'

'Gloch has information that would be of use to us,' said Revus. 'For some reason, he is proving elusive. Has he been here?'

The priest shook his head. 'Not for a long time.'

'Do you know of anyone who might know his whereabouts?'

'Your job, surely? If you can't keep up with your own kind, not much hope we can.'

'Then, if you wish to help us further, keep an ear open. You know how to contact me if you need to.'

Heinwolf pulled his robes tighter around his skinny frame. It was cold in the chapel, and the candles' smoky flames did little to change that. 'I could ask why, perhaps. I might be concerned, if some feud between your agencies were to find its way down here.'

'Nothing to worry about.'

'See, now I'm truly concerned.'

Revus got up, giving the altar a respectful nod as he did so. He admired the Militarum. 'I wish you strength for your sacred duties, father,' he said.

'There is someone you could try,' said Heinwolf, looking up at him. 'I have a contact, out in the Mordant factories. She's reliable. Remember the organ-gangs you broke up three years ago? That came from her. We used to talk a lot, but she's gone quiet. I'd investigate myself, but they keep me busy here.'

Revus hesitated. 'How is this related to Gloch?'

'She informs for him, too. She didn't want me to know it, but you know how these networks are – one person talks, another one hears, it gets around. Quantrain doesn't have much going on in Salvator, so I think she's useful to him. If you're looking for him, you might want to look for her too.'

'A name?'

'Elija Roodeker. Technician in the parchment-works for the scribe houses. Good with a knife.'

Revus nodded. 'My thanks. I'll look her up.' He walked over to the chapel's doorway.

'You know what they're singing, up there?' Heinwolf called after him. '*Though Night Falls, My Faith Endures*.'

Revus paused at the threshold. 'And does it, father?'

Heinwolf sniffed. 'I don't know. Something's up, captain. Maybe one thing's true, and the other isn't.'

Revus hesitated, wondering if that was a weak attempt at a jest, or something he should be concerned about. It was not unknown for a priest to fall into corruption. And yet, Heinwolf looked destroyed already, hunched over in a forgotten chapel to a forgotten regiment. There were some weaknesses not worth worrying about.

'Careful what you say, priest,' Revus told him, walking back out into the dark. 'Not everyone on Terra is as tolerant as me.'

You had, of course, to forget.

That had been Haldus Revre's motto for a long time, and it had served him fairly well. So much of the business of survival on Terra was bound up with *not knowing*. Knowledge, of any kind, was terribly dangerous. To know that a man was a heretic, or that a woman was a trafficker in prohibited items, or that an official was taking bribes beyond a level tolerated by whoever had control over them, was to become complicit in their crimes and thus a target. Perhaps that heretic or arms-runner or official was not what they seemed, and you were merely becoming entangled into something more extensive, which was even worse. Some nets of confidence spread, like insect super-colonies, deep below and high above. It was better, all things considered, not to know. And if somehow, despite your efforts, you still knew, the next best thing was to forget.

But also impossible, in his profession, and so a middle ground had to be sought.

He pushed his RE-4x Condor gun-shuttle down through the grime, adjusting its descent against the perilous inter-spire thermals. The streets – what he could see of them amid the flying grey dust – were still strewn with the detritus from the long-ended Sanguinala. It would take weeks more before the last of it was gathered up by the gutter scavengers, scrabbling around for the cheap tatters of red ribbon and gauze and devotional pamphlets, none of which had any value except for the truly destitute or insanely religious.

He wiped his forehead with the back of his hand, feeling greasy and tight. The air had been thicker, it seemed like, ever since the end of the festivals. It wasn't just him who had noticed – Enyi in the next scribe-chamber along had complained of it so much she'd been given a sanction by the section commander. The watch officers were grumbling, he'd been told, about unrest boiling over in places where you wouldn't expect it. They didn't like it when it got truly hot – frayed tempers and failing air processors made it harder to keep a lid on things. If Revre had been interested, he might have enquired a bit further about what was going on, but he wasn't, and so he didn't. You had to forget.

The platform below – an octagon of dark metal swimming up from the gloom – beckoned him down with a flurry of blinking lumens. Gaudy signage snapped on and off around it, below it, above it. Most of that was religious in nature, some security-related, and a smattering was commercial. Galaganda was not a rich district, despite being in such close proximity to the Hall of Judgement. The kind of thing Revre was after didn't exist so obviously in rich districts. For all that human society had evolved, some things never changed, no matter the heat, the cold, the age or the season.

The Condor was a standard transport for an official of his station and had capacity for four passengers besides the pilot. Normally there would have been another official with him and two bodyguards drawn from the enforcers' close protection cadres, but not tonight. That was a risk, given the location, but then everything was a risk – Terra was not a safe world, not even in the highest fragranced domes of the highest spires, and you couldn't be overlooked all the time.

He touched down with a flex of landing spurs. The Condor whined down to cold, and the main access hatch cantilevered open. Revre unbuckled his restraints and emerged into the open, adjusting the grit-filters over his mouth and nostrils and pulling his plasfibre robes tighter around him. The dull roar of traffic made the air above him thrum. Menials were already hurrying to secure the gun-shuttle, but he ignored them, striding to the edge of the platform where the elevators stood. In every direction, the mighty spines of the hive-towers reared up, filling the sky, glittering like dark mountains limned with lurid spots of yellow. The usual cacophony punched through the background roar – tinny vox-bursts from state-authorised commerce outlets, cries from the clogged pedestrian piers, the snarl and skid of groundcars hemmed into their swirling transit-spans.

A guard was waiting for him at the elevator entrance – a skinny figure in a battered carapace breastplate carrying an old electro-lance. Revre presented his credentials, then waited for them to be verified on a clunking pattern-reader. After the all-clear, he got into the descent cage and the locks slammed back. A moment later and he was clattering down the shaft, holding on to the main roll-bar to keep his feet. The roar of the exterior disappeared, along with the hot breeze and the stink of engine oils. He saw the flicker-pattern of the hab-levels rolling past – just glimpses into worlds he would never visit. They were all much the same – dirty flares of under-powered lighting and long, filth-packed corridors receding into the dark.

The cage hit its destination level, and he disembarked. This was a long way down, far enough that the reek of engine oils had been replaced by earthier aromas – mould, damp, rust, human sweat. A long corridor ran off ahead, and he walked casually down it. At the end, lit by a painfully strobing neon tube, was a hatch. By the hatch was a locked door with no signage. Inside the hatch was a woman with an ironwork grille riveted over her eyes and long, painted fingernails.

'Ser Klenda,' she said, nodding at him. 'How are you today?'

'Fine,' said Revre, handing over his ident-wafer and placing his finger up to the blood-check needle.

'Busy, are you?' the woman asked idly, running the wafer through an old verifier unit.

'You know, we *are*,' said Revre, leaning against the door frame. 'It's becoming unhinged. Something's in the water.'

'Cholera,' said the woman, humourlessly. She handed the wafer back. 'That's all fine, ser. I wish you much pleasure.'

Revre put the wafer back in his wallet and pushed the door open. As he did so, the familiar smell of the place wafted over him, blotting out the urine-tang of the corridor. He unclipped his nostril filters and breathed it in.

'Thanks.'

Time to forget.

The space inside was as scratchily plush as the space outside was grimy. A crimson carpet, frayed at the edges, ran down a narrow walkway. A few dozen doors, all locked, were set into the walls on either side. Some dog-eared picts had been stapled up – images of paradise worlds, or heroes of the Militarum in dress uniforms. One of them had been scribbled over and defaced, and no one had done anything about it. Black spiderwebs of fungus radiated out from the walls' edges, glistening faintly.

He reached his usual cubicle, and used the ident-wafer to gain entry. The space was very small – three metres square, with a single armchair and table. Revre could see the incense-steam tumbling softly through the air-filters, so pungent it made his eyes water. He took off his facial gear and massaged his jawline. He took off his overcoat and his jacket, then rolled up his left sleeve. On the table was a vial and a needle and a tube. He connected them up, sat down, and took a breath.

He knew this room almost better than his own hab-chamber. He'd stared at these faded pink walls for hours, though much of that time was lost to the blur of memory loss. It was a comforting space. Its size made you feel safely enclosed, locked away, cut off from the limitless sprawl above and beyond. What he had told the woman at the doorway was right – his labours had been getting crazy, and it was making him jumpy. The enforcers were always run ragged, chasing a hundred different insurrections across a dozen urban sectors, but it had felt like it was getting out of control for some time now. Keeping order on Terra was essentially a confidence trick – if the masses ever truly realised what power they had in their vast numbers, and somehow coordinated, they would be virtually unstoppable. You had to keep them afraid. Keep them busy. Keep them looking at their feet and their neighbours rather than up at the smog-banks and gun-drones.

Revre sighed. These were not good thoughts to have. He had to break the cycle, get back to thinking more positively.

He popped the lid on the vial, connected the tube, and slipped the needle into a vein. Then he sat back, and waited for the contents to do their work. Almost immediately, the boundaries of the chamber grew fuzzy. The ceiling appeared to recede, the floor to drop away. The sense of gravity, of confinement and weight, that was always present on Terra lifted. He smiled, and sat back in the armchair. Soon he wouldn't remember anything of the last twelve-hour shift. For just a short time, it would all be gone, washed away by the soft blur of this agreeable poison.

He closed his eyes for just a moment.

When he opened them again, he was no longer alone.

Revre sat up sharply, his free hand scrabbling for his service sidearm. A man, one of the two figures who stood opposite him, reached down to prevent him. The other figure, a woman, remained where she was.

'Haldus Revre,' she said.

He tried to focus. She was wearing nondescript clothing – the kind of thing everyone wore down here. Her companion was the same, but his grip was incredibly strong. How did she know his name? His heart began to pound.

'What do you want?' he slurred.

'Haldus Revre, Scribe Primus in Hall processing silo Twelve C? Confirm quickly. The longer you wait, the worse it will get for you.'

He blinked twice, trying to clear his head. 'N-no,' he mumbled. 'Lef Klenda, machine operati–'

The woman leaned over him. She held a little bottle in her right hand. He couldn't see her face clearly, but she was powerfully built and looked capable of hurting him badly.

'You'll need this soon,' she said. 'It's the only antidote to the filth you've put in your veins. Talk to me, and you can have it. Don't talk, and I'll keep it here.'

Revre frowned. He was feeling groggier than usual. 'What're you talking–'

'You normally take five quints,' she said. 'There are fifty quints in that vial. You know what that means. Unless you wish to spend your last hour vomiting your own stomach up, stop lying and start talking.'

His eyes went wide. He suddenly felt the rush, and knew she was telling the truth. He tried to reach out and grab the bottle, but the man kept him clamped in place. 'Holy Throne!' he blurted. 'Why would you–'

'You are a servant of the Adeptus Terra,' the woman said emotionlessly. 'By polluting your body and mind you have already earned the death that now comes swiftly for you. You have one chance to redeem yourself. Take it. You are Haldus Revre.'

He started to sweat. The cramps would begin soon. A cold terror rose up with his stomach and threatened to close like a vice around his throat.

'Yes,' he said, unable to take his eyes off the bottle. He needed it. He needed it quickly.

'I require the location of all records of investigations pertaining to the orbital quarantine enacted prior to Sanguinala. You understand me? The communication between the Hall of Judgement and the Speaker's representatives.'

Revre stiffened. 'I cannot give you that!' he stammered, wriggling in the other man's heavy grip.

'Then you will die here.'

Revre started to cry. 'They'll *know*...' he started.

'That is a risk. No worse than the one you took coming here.'

The room began to sway. He felt his heart rate start to accelerate. 'I... cannot...'

'You are running out of time, Haldus Revre.'

'Hall twenty-six!' he gasped. 'Level four-five-eight. They're sealed, though.'

'You have an ident wafer, and a blood sample. Will that be sufficient?'

'Yes, yes, if you get that far.' His head was swimming now. It felt like insects were crawling through his innards. He could scarcely feel the man drawing the ampoule of blood, nor the ident wafer being taken from his pocket. 'There are security cordons.'

The woman handed him a data storage slug. 'You know the codes. Input them here.'

He looked up at her. 'All of them?'

'All of them.'

The man released him to work. His own fingers had got fatter, it seemed. His mind was following them, turning to mush and making it hard to think. Somehow, he managed to punch them out, the ones he could still recall. Then he added a final one. He tried to hand the slug back, but the woman folded her arms.

'Outer zone access codes. All the way in. Work faster.'

He went as fast as he could. He could feel his core temperature rising fast, and the nausea beginning, and the numbness that rose from his feet and would climb steadily through his muscles until the real pain started.

His hands shaking badly now, he handed the slug back. The two figures before him had morphed into four, overlapping and spiralling.

'Please...' he said, reaching out for the bottle.

The woman tucked the slug into her jerkin and instructed her accomplice to check the door. Then she turned towards him and handed him the bottle.

'It won't help,' she said, her voice cold with contempt. 'Your sins have found you out, scribe.'

Revre pulled the lid off, and cold water spilled on to his hands. For a moment, he just looked at it, appalled, watching it drip through his shaking figures.

The woman walked calmly away, following her companion through the door.

'But you still have your sidearm,' she told him, pulling the heavy panel closed behind her. 'In what time remains to you, I suggest you locate it.'

Frantically, Haldus Revre started to rummage in his tunic, shivering and sweltering. As he slipped to the floor, still scrabbling, the door closed with an echoing clang, sealing him in. The world began to shrink around him, terrifyingly fast.

Spinoza strode swiftly along the perfume-drenched corridor. Hegain came with her, studying the data slug carefully.

'How does it look?' she asked.

Hegain glanced up at her. 'Yes, very much what is required, I think so,' he reported. For once, he seemed somewhat lost for words.

'Unpleasant work, sergeant,' said Spinoza, reaching the main entrance. 'But necessary – time is short.'

'Absolutely,' Hegain agreed. 'Of course, you have the right of it.'

They passed through the main portal. There was no sign of the woman at the hatch, nor of the guards who had been there earlier.

'Retrieve the Shade,' Spinoza said, her mind already on what came next. 'He'll be missed soon enough – we'll need to strike within the hour.'

From behind them, a dull crack rang out – a revolver discharged in a confined space.

'As you will it, lord,' Hegain said, his expression blank, stowing the data slug and calling up the transport on his helm's tactical readout. 'Of all things, it shall be done.'

CHAPTER SIX

Crowl took an unmarked atmospheric transport east. He pulled it high, out of the greater mass of traffic and up into the zone where the summits of the lesser spires grazed the clouds. From such a vantage, one could see wide areas of the cityscape unfurl – a drear, majestic clutter of competing pinnacles, striving towards the light that never quite broke through the stratospheric cover. Over to the north, a long way distant, was the steadily rising continent-mass of the Imperial Palace. To the south was the wide, open sprawl of the major worker conurbations – kilometre after kilometre of tightly packed habitation units. Ahead of him lay more industrial zones, some derelict, some very much in operation, all adding to the snarls of coal-black grime whispering up through the high, hot airs.

'*Tumultus*,' observed Gorgias gloomily, floating up to the transport's viewport and gazing downward. 'More of it.'

Crowl said nothing, but the skull was right. The period of Sanguinala had been restive and unruly, but that was part-deliberate – a chance for the long-suffering populace to let off a little steam. Now that it was all over, things should have reverted to the long-run type – a dull, suppressed tension, locked down by fear and hard labour. Instead, the Arbites were out in force everywhere, and there were fires burning on the southern horizon.

Or perhaps he was imagining things. He felt slow from lack of sleep, and glanding narcotics could only go so far to remedy that. Perhaps he should have brought Revus with him, or even Spinoza, but then the subterfuge would have been that much harder. It was best, in general, to keep things as simple as possible. A part of him was even looking forward to it – a return to older, more secret ways, unable to rely on the terror-inducing power of his rosette and dependent on older powers of deception and misdirection. He had equipment and resources to aid him, of course, but at its foundation this was a human skill, one that had existed for as long as the species had.

After a few hours of sustained flying, the object of his journey appeared on the eastern horizon. Just as the Imperial Palace itself emerged from the press of lesser buildings like a grand massif rising up from a tangled forest, so the Nexus Axiomatic swelled up into vastness from the urban confusion around it. There was no beauty to this place, even of a dilapidated sort – the Nexus was a pale, grey rockcrete hunk, obese and streaked with old dirt, sunk heavily amid its feeder-slums like some grotesque nursing mother. A brace of massive comms towers soared above it, great skeletons of wind-blasted iron studded with sensor clusters and relays. Its summit was further disfigured by jumbled layers of landing stages, some very ancient, some merely centuries old.

Terra's air-traffic, always congested, thickened around that monolithic structure like flies on a carcass. Big orbital landers processed from the upper landing pads in regulated columns, punching through the clouds above the Nexus and making them curdle and split. Unusually, there were few Arbites craft present in those airways, though there were plenty of other armed vessels prowling the perimeters, most liveried in the midnight-blue of the Speaker's own security forces.

Just as was the case elsewhere on the Throneworld, this was another kingdom in all but name, a fiefdom carved from the eternal city by immortal precedent and timeless statute. Many institutions on this world were older then the Imperium itself, and the Nexus Axiomatic was one of them. Its ancestor-bodies had existed in the time before recorded history, stretching back into the legendary age before the Great Crusade when humanity's soul had rotted amid a heretical age of technological wonder. The very first charters given to merchant fleets were still preserved under stasis fields in there, it was rumoured, each one tens of thousands of years old. Every hereditary charter since had been ultimately issued from the same location, and over the millennia the numbers had exploded exponentially, such that the Nexus now housed billions of individual screeds and documents and testimonies and amendments, all cross-referenced and counter-stamped and stored in vacuum-sealed depositories. Every void-capable civilian ship in the entire Imperium, save for those esoteric leviathans falling under the purview of Mars, had its legal origin here, no matter where its hull had been laid down or where it plied its trade. Every prescribed trade route was fixed here. Every statistic on transportation, tithe-collection and inter-system trade eventually found its way here too, where the data was pored over and scrutinised by teams of adepts a thousand strong, all to ensure that raw materials found their way to forge worlds, foodstuffs found their way to ravenous mouths, commercial goods found their way to rich hive worlds and weaponry found its way to the Imperium's endlessly shifting battle-fronts.

The original Nexus had been built on this site, it was believed, though no trace of that first building remained. Subsequent iterations had been constructed atop scoured walls, rising, like so many of the great edifices on this world, over the bones of their predecessors. During the inferno of the Great Heresy, the Nexus had been almost completely destroyed, though such was the institution's importance that many of its records had been spirited away long before the Arch-Traitor had made planetfall. In the centuries afterwards, in that strange twilight age when so much was at once lost and reborn, its current colossal foundations were laid and the gargantuan chambers slowly erected. The records returned to the inner vaults, where they had remained ever since, and the mind-bending task of renewing and reissuing and revoking charters re-commenced.

The Speaker, who had long since been a powerful figure in the politics of the early Imperium, took up residence within this rapidly expanding palace-garrison-archive, and, conscious of what had almost been lost, created an army of guardians to police their new realm. In an Imperium already swollen with overlapping and competing armed bodies, the Praeses Mercatura emerged to oversee this high cathedral of trade and commerce, taking command of old weapons and old technology and hoarding it all jealously. It was not perhaps the most prestigious of the high offices of state, but, due to its proximity to the enormous system of tithe collection, the Speaker's kingdom was wealthy beyond imagination, and competition to succeed the current incumbent was always fierce and often bloody.

Crowl had known all this for a long time. Over the course of his long career, he had had occasional dealings with charter-holders and their masters – the captain of a big void hauler was a powerful person, and to lose one to corruption was a serious matter. That being the case, he had never had reason to probe the source itself. If he had, even in more normal times, he might have thought twice about how to proceed. A High Lord was a High Lord, and for all Spinoza's protestations of rectitude, none of those occupying a place at the high table in the Senatorum had got there by being shy of deploying lethal force – whatever the rhetoric, that was not how the Imperium had ever operated.

'*Immanis*,' remarked Gorgias, sounding a little cowed, for once.

'Yes, very big,' agreed Crowl, staring out of the forward viewers. 'Some coin's been spent here.'

By then they were heading toward one of the many ingress points. The pale grey walls filled the entirety of the sky before them, blotting out the jagged towerscape beyond. Several artificial canyons had been gouged into the outer perimeter, each overlooked by ranks of anti-vessel gunnery. Incoming transports filtered into those canyons, watched the whole time by tracer drones and Mercatura gunships. Once across the threshold, the natural light cut out, plunging them into an artificial dusk broken only faintly by blinking route beacons.

The transport shuddered faintly, and a scrutiny-lock momentarily took control of the engines. Runes darted across the main console as a watcher-script inveigled its way into the vehicle's machine-spirit cortex. A few moments later, the transport's hololith column atop the flight console blurted into life, and the ghostly head-profile of a Mercatura official spiralled into instantiation.

'Declare,' it commanded.

'Inspector Ferlad Calavine, Sol Sector Command,' said Crowl. 'Inward-bound for scheduled appointment with Signals-adept Majoris Harker Bajan. Request entry at berth gamma-fifty-six as arranged by prior communication.'

There was a pause, a faint click over the comm-line, some evident processing of a cogitator.

'Granted, inspector,' came the eventual response. 'Proceed to nominated berth. Welcome back to Terra.'

The hololith flickered out. Crowl smiled. 'Thanks very much,' he murmured, and guided the transport further in, following a blinking line of guide-nodes that now sprung up across the forward scanner lens.

The last of the grey sunlight fell away, leaving them in near-total darkness. Their allotted berth swam up towards them, just one of hundreds ranked against the walls ahead. The berths held transports inside clawed metal fingers, from which umbilicals led back into a complex lattice of metal and stone beyond. This canyon alone could have held more than a thousand vehicles, and there were many others. Spider-like servitors crawled across the entire surface, their spines sprouting lasguns, probing and testing. Great booms and crashes rang out, echoing up the long cleft, as larger craft docked or were released. And then it was their turn, as metal struts unfolded to greet them, sucking them in towards a circular aperture, enclosing them in prehensile iron fronds crowned by sensor-spikes and hull-drills. The transport shuddered, its engines extinguished, and then it clanged to a halt, locked fast against the canyon's inner wall.

Crowl waited for a moment, letting the remote systems do their work. The transport's machine-spirit was still being interrogated hard, and no doubt the spiders would be paying a visit to the outer hull soon enough. Gorgias darted back and forth across the cabin interior, angling his oculus to try to get a view of the outside.

'Doing damage,' he hissed, watching a hull-drill scrape across the transport's flank. 'Careless. *Ridicolo.'*

Crowl got up, pulling the black jacket of his Inspectorate uniform down and donning the high-peaked cap. His face had been rearranged with surface prosthetics and a gesture-lattice that would fool all but the most determined scrutiny. His garb was nowhere near as protective as his usual armour, but the chainmesh under-layer and stiff outer surface offered at least a modicum of reassurance. He had an Inspectorate-issue laspistol in open display on his belt, and other, certainly not Inspectorate-issue, weapons hidden in sensor-reflective caches within.

He was as prepared as he would ever be, and managed to walk up to the transport's outer doors with only the faintest limp evident. The shielding cracked open and rolled away, to reveal a blue-light-tinged interior and a pronounced smell of antisepsis chems.

A circular umbilical lay ahead, polished and clean, but there was no one in it to welcome him as there should have been. Crowl stood alone for a moment, wondering if something had gone wrong. If he had been discovered so soon, this was the last chance to retreat back into the transport and attempt to break out again.

Eventually, though, a circular portal revolved open at the far end of the umbilical, and five figures emerged into the lumens – four masked soldiers of the Mercatura, and a single official in dark blue robes. The official had a smooth, young face with little sign of augmetics. His forehead bore the tattooed mark of the Speaker's kingdom – the ancient star-and-quill of the old void-charterers. He looked disturbingly similar to his ultimate mistress, Dandha, though right now he was failing to hide a certain degree of agitation, and his skin was flushed at his collar.

'Welcome to the Nexus, inspector,' said the man who Crowl recognised from Calavine's private records as Harker Bajan. 'I apologise for the delay – we are busy, my private secretary has been taken ill, we are still catching up.'

'You don't have a replacement?' Crowl asked, sceptically.

'As of two days ago. She is still learning.' Bajan stepped aside, gesturing for Crowl to join him. 'I trust your journey was satisfactory. Warp-stage from Altera-Commodus, was it, this time?'

'Vorlese,' said Crowl snappily, striding out ahead, knowing more about Calavine's actual and intended movements than anyone living and supremely unconcerned about such cursory attempts to trip him up. 'And it was filthy as ever, so let's get this started – I do not have time to waste.'

Raw commodities were the lifeblood of the Throneworld. It was often said, and widely believed, that Terra made nothing and consumed everything, and though that maxim captured the fundamental balance between humanity's birthplace and the rest of its domains, it was not quite correct. Manufactoria on Terra still produced plenty of specialised items, but given the all-devouring press of the choking conurbations across such limited land-space, they rarely had direct access to the raw materials they needed. There was no agriculture or extractive industry to keep them fuelled – all such primary inputs had to be shipped in by the colossal merchant fleets that forever plied the voidways of the Sol System. Primary amongst these were, of course, the ores and the alloys required for the maintenance of the nigh-infinite urban fabric, as well as the freeze-packed carcasses ready to be rendered down for consumption by the equally infinite tide of workers. A bewildering array of other items were imported daily, the sustained lack of any one of which would have swiftly crippled life on this uniquely thirsty, greedy and insatiable world.

One object of particular importance was scarcely present in the imaginations of that ignorant citizenry. Young charges of the scholae, when asked to guess which was the seventh-most-vital import to Holy Terra by weight, almost never landed on the right answer. And yet, the chances were that the product of that importation was staring them in the face, marked with their own scrawl and stamped with the crest of their particular educational establishment.

Parchment. Vellum. Animal-hide. For millennia, it had been the choice material of record throughout the scriptoria of the Imperium. Far more durable than paper, much cheaper than crystal-plate or dataslab, less ideologically suspect than cogitator-wafer and harder to tamper with than audex screeds, parchment remained the medium trusted by scribes on worlds from Ultramar to Hydraphur. It was inefficient, to be sure, and prone to error in onward copy-transmission, and yet still it persisted, clung to by a savant-class so wedded to its smells, its texture, its permanence and its cheapness that the mere suggestion of another method of record-keeping skirted close to a kind of heresy of its own. After so long in use, the infrastructure of vellum-creation had become mind-bendingly vast, spread out across every industrial world in mankind's sprawling possessions. There were whispers in the Imperium's famed archive-worlds of entire wars fought over its production and distribution. Five hundred years ago, the great Master of the Administratum,

Skito Gavalles, had been asked what would make his onerous job more bearable.

'Pigskin,' he was said to have replied. 'More pigskin.'

Of course, few living humans had ever laid eyes on a por-
cine. Unless they worked on an agri world, they would never
have encountered one of those bloated and obese sacks of
stimm-injected muscle and sinew, too colossal to walk without breaking their spindly legs and force-fed high-nutrient
chem-soup to keep them growing in the pens. They would
never have come across a bovine, either, unless you counted
the thready strands of protein-extract pumped into their
ration-trays during sanctioned rest-breaks. Such things were
legends, in much the same category as relics of the Saints, the
Angels of Death or Manifest Acts of the Emperor – things that
definitely existed, but were unlikely ever to be encountered.

The bulk of vellum used throughout the Imperium was not,
of course, taken from such sources. Most of it was grown from
stock genetic material in bio-tanks, then cured in kilometre-
long reams before being sliced, rolled and pressed for deliv-
ery. Such stuff was hardy, inexpensive and plentiful – the
perfect qualities for a culture that prized quantity and uniformity above all things. For a few senior scribes, though,
that was not quite good enough. They wanted to run their
auto-quills across the hide of something once-living. They
wanted the iron tips to snag and catch on patches where
hair had grown, or where a blood-vessel had wriggled. They
wanted their documents to look like the ones in the mighty
tomes of the past, bound in real-leather and lined with gold
before being locked into vacuum-capsules and buried deep
in alarm-rigged vaults.

Whether bulk-produced or specialised, Terra alone sucked
in more imports of vellum than an entire subsector of less

exalted territory. Its scriptoria were the oldest and the most famed, steeped in traditions so ancient that their origins had taken on the lustre of true myth. In the greatest of such places, entire spire-pinnacles were given over to the business of inscribing, illuminating, copying, re-copying, redacting, interpreting and compiling. Rows of lamplit desks stretching far into the smoky darkness were fully occupied by cowled scribes, their scrawny grey hands clutching steel-tipped quills, their augmetic eyepieces zooming and panning before committing ink to parchment. Every tithe paid was recorded, every report from every battle was recorded, every court-hearing was recorded and every heretic's confession was recorded. It was all then stashed away in the mountainous repositories, tended by skulls and servitors, where it slowly mouldered, part of the landslide of unread testimony that would one day stifle its creators.

For the connoisseurs, the final processing of real vellum was done on Terra. Batches of unfinished stock were airlifted to the few remaining manufactoria, where they were unloaded, scrutinised for quality, doused, scraped, then hung on iron hooks until the characteristic stretched surface was obtained. Entire families were devoted to such work, and in some places production could be reliably dated back thousands of years at the same site, with the same bloodline and the same equipment.

Mordant was one such place. It was housed in a run-down industrial zone overlooked on all sides by the soaring flanks of promethium refineries, making the air more smuts than oxygen. Its antiquarian buildings were ramshackle and overlapping, a confusing jumble of steep-pitched, iron-tiled roofs and piped extractor housings. Gouts of steam from the settlement tanks rose up above them all, before pooling in a fug of milky condensation, swirling about the sensor-vanes like the mists of some primordial forest.

Revus took his Shade in close, setting it down amid a berth already occupied by several big orbital landers. Each of those was marked with the gothic 'M' of the Mordant brand, and were as well-appointed and maintained as any such vessels ever were. A few service menials and servitors were working in the semi-darkness as he got out, hammering at open engine-hatches or guiding in heaps of unfinished material on grav-loaders. None of them paid him much attention, and he walked into the facility without challenge.

Inside, the air was humid and stinking. Orderlies bustled along high gantries wearing stiff aprons, their faces hidden behind environment masks. Enormous vats bubbled, over which hung chains and hook-lines in a seething atmosphere of chemical vapours. Servitors with engorged upper bodies lumbered past him, hauling drums of solvents and metal pallets for onward distribution, their faces riveted with blinkers and their mouths clamped closed with permanent tox-filters. The far end of the chamber was entirely lost in hissing palls of steam, but Revus guessed this was just the start of the production line. From somewhere, he could hear what sounded like animal screams, which indicated, however improbably, that some living creatures had been brought here for slaughter and processing.

He made his way up pressed-metal stairways, higher and higher until he was far above the vat-level. Long rows of administratum chambers ran under the eaves of the facility's steep roofline, angled between the tangle of bracings and loader-crane supports. One of them, slightly larger than the others, was marked with a sodium-lumen panel indicating the site foreman. Revus headed for that one, and pushed the door open.

The room beyond was occupied by a single figure – a fat man with a bald pate and bottle-lenses suckered over his eyes. He was surrounded by tottering heaps of rotting vellum, most of which had been shoved around and atop a single creaking cogitator unit housed in a chipped pea-green metal casing. Old protein-ration casings littered the floor, and the place smelled strongly of meat. An electro-date reckoner hung on the far wall, showing the Standard Terran Measure from forty years ago. There was a plastek figurine of Saint Alicia Dominicia on a side table amid a few burned-out tallow candles, and a greasy pict-screen showing cycle-images of sun-drenched paradise worlds.

As Revus entered, the fat man looked up, and went white and sweatier.

'Look, I spoke to the adept from the sector-tithe office last week,' he said. 'We explained everything then.'

'I am looking for Elija Roodeker,' said Revus. 'One of your technicians.'

The fat man blanched even more. His chubby fingers, stained with ink, pressed together into a cat's-cradle. 'Roodeker?' he repeated. 'Who are you, then? I'll need to see an ident.'

Revus let his gaze run idly over the clutter. 'No, you won't,' he said, and waited.

It didn't take the man long, even in the murk, to spot the storm trooper insignia on his breast, and that made things quicker. 'Ah, I, then she must be in her hab still,' he offered, uncertainly. 'She's not reported in for several days. I meant to arrange a discipline schedule, but we've been overwhelmed with this tithe misunderstanding, and so–'

'You did not enquire after her welfare?'

The man squirmed. 'I meant to, but–'

'Where is her hab?'

'Next level along, unit forty-five, thirty-four, though–'

'I was not here. We did not have this conversation.'

'But I–'

'You have a successful operation here. You do not want to waste it.'

'No, it–'

'Clean this place, and yourself, up. Both are a disgrace.'

Revus turned on his heel and walked out of the chamber, closing the door behind him firmly. From there, he walked along the gantry corridor, glancing down at the churning vats below. Further down the production lines, sheets of bleached and hairless hides were being hauled out of the chemical baths by creaking knuckleboom cranes, then swung around to be pinned to ranks of drying racks, each one mounted on mobile gurneys and propelled by more bulked-up servitors. High-ranking workers with shiny black protective suits and whirring oculi patrolled the long rows with flensing knives, scouring the pinned parchment sheets. Further on still, members of another labour-caste prepared dyes and branding irons for the finished pieces. None of them looked up. For all they were concerned, this crucible of curing and stretching and pinning might have been the entire world.

Revus' route took him away from it all soon enough, following a bridge over the industrial chasm below, a hundred metres down a connective gangway and back into the more utilitarian surroundings of a standard hab-block. After passing through a stuffy transition hall and taking a elevator six levels up, he found himself in one of those corridors that could have been anywhere on Terra – lightless, airless, stained with the smells of refuse and pockmarked with individual hab-unit doorways. He walked along until he found the one he wanted. As he went, the lone flyblown lumen popped on and off, as if marking time. A door slid open further down, and a straggle-bearded, emaciated face emerged. Its owner looked at him for a moment with startled, red-rimmed eyes, before blurting 'And shall He be ever-watchful in these times!' and retreating rapidly.

Alone again, Revus faced the doorway to unit 45-34. He ran a quick scan for heat signatures on the far side, and got nothing. He stood to one side and pressed the entry chime. Still nothing. He drew his laspistol in his right hand and took out a lock-tumbler with his left. The device clamped on to the cheap fittings of the doorway, whirred for a second or two, then clicked it open.

He went in. The layout was standard for a worker of Roodeker's station – living chamber, bed-chamber, hygiene chamber. The lumens were out, so he activated his night-sights and closed the door behind him. The first room – the living chamber – was intact and tidy. A single table stood against the far wall with the remains of a meal on it. A single plasfibre couch, threadbare from use, faced a picter-unit that had been powered down. Hired vid-capsules were arranged on top of it – nothing unusual, just the standard motivational fare.

He could hear thudding footsteps from the unit above, only barely muffled by the poor soundproofing. From somewhere below came the tinny hiss of a music-player running through military-band standards. It smelled, badly – a smell Revus was all too familiar with.

Keeping his laspistol tracking ahead, he gently eased the door to the bed-chamber open. A double-width cot stood in the far corner, its sheets tangled. Elija Roodeker lay half propped up against a broken headboard, her grey face slumped onto her chest. Her tunic was soaked with blood from a single torso shot. She had a gun of her own in her right hand – a Callax R4 single-action revolver. Revus looked around, seeing a messy burst of blood on the opposite wall, and a spotty trail of it on the floor leading to the hygiene chamber.

He went over to the corpse and blink-clinked for a helm-scan of her exposed right arm. The flesh was grey, cold and still stiff, indicating death within the last few standard days. He twisted the revolver out of her grip, and checked the chamber. A single bullet was missing.

He took picts of the scene, then moved towards the hygiene-chamber. The door mechanism was faulty, and he had to manually haul it open. The space on the far side was tiny – a washstand, pulse-shower unit and lavatory. Roodeker had draped her lumen housing – also blown – with a collection of prayer-beads. Grainy printed picts of what Revus took to be her legal parents and work acquaintances had been pinned around the cracked mirror. They looked vivacious and agreeable. The dead man lying in her pulse-shower cubi-cle, on the other hand, did not.

Revus stowed his weapon and squatted down to examine the corpse. This one, too, had a single gunshot wound just below his shoulder. He had dropped his own weapon – a more powerful Hammerglaive VX projectile-pistol – into the shower pan, where it lay atop a dry pool of his own blood. He was wearing basic mesh protective gear, but noth-ing extravagant, and evidently insufficient to stop a Callax fired at close range. His head had rolled back, exposing the snow-grey flesh of his neck under a close-fitting helm. No sigils adorned his armour. The pattern was not distinctive – any hired operative would have access to similar. Revus lifted the man's jacket, searched the pockets of his fatigues.

Nothing. He pulled a glove off and took a fingerprint scan, then removed the helm and did the same with the eyeball.

It was unlikely anything here would find a match with Huk's records. This had very evidently not been a sophisticated hit, and the man almost certainly was not known to Courvain's systems. He was, in all probability, some under-hive trash gifted a gun and a mission, as anonymous in death as he had been in life. The chances of getting something substantive out of it all were slight, and there were other avenues still to check.

And yet, Roodeker had been an informant for both Crowl and Gloch, and Roodeker was now dead.

Revus activated the secure link to Courvain.

'Yes, captain,' came Aneela's crisp voice.

'Clean-up team to my coordinates,' said Revus, standing up and activating his loc-beacon. 'Two bodies to bring in. Prime Erunion for study when we get back – we'll need to take a closer look at this.'

CHAPTER SEVEN

You did not see the Hall of Judgement until you were close to it. That was one of the surprising things about the ultimate home of the Adeptus Arbites, whose palaces throughout the Imperium were often the largest and most imposing constructions on any world. On Terra, however, the haunt of the most senior Judges of all did not tower over its surroundings like the Imperial Palace or the Nexus Axiomatic, for it was sited in a region of already gargantuan Administratum spires and was far older than any of them. As if preferring to slump in their shadows, the Hall's onyx-black walls crept up almost unawares, before suddenly looming over you in a glittering facade of semi-mirrored darkness. Its sheer, steep sides were carved with the likeness of hook-beaked eagles, staring with obsidian-hard gazes through the drifting smog. The symbol of the Arbites – a clenched gauntlet holding a pair of scales – was engraved in lozenges twenty metres high on every facing panel. Pale blue lumens underlit the overhanging eaves of the great halls, interconnected by tightly crenelated walkways. A few scrawny pinnacles rose up into the higher airs, studded with advanced comms-nodes and sensor-spikes, but the greater mass of the place was set heavy, tomb-like in aspect, a warren of dense, lightless coffins spreading like an infection through the surrounding urban zones.

They said that the Hall had been delved far deeper than it had been raised high, and that its true size was carefully hidden to avoid giving away the scale of the Arbites' grip on temporal power. They said that its gaols still housed prisoners from the oldest ages of humanity, kept alive through their madness and decay to rave secrets into the ears of patient examiners. They said that there were secret courts buried at the very base of its internal labyrinth in which the face of the Emperor Himself would appear, reflected dimly in tarnished mirrors, to pass judgement over the living just as He did for the dead.

They said so many things about the Hall of Judgement that some of them, surely, must have been true.

Search-lumens swept across its many facets endlessly, tracing pools of hard white light over glossy, razor wire-topped battlements. Hunter-killers swarmed in packs, hovering low over guarded landing stages. Its cavernous hangar-maws were clogged with incoming and departing craft of all shapes and sizes – windowless felon carriers, talon-like Scrutiny gunships, gaudy formal transports bedecked with images of blindfolded angels. Every ship was tracked coming in, and every ship was tracked going out. Servo-skulls flocked like wingless sparrows around each ingress point and lumen bank, trailing their spinal segment-chains behind them as they darted and wheeled.

At ground level, the many gates were all of the same design – high gothic arches raised atop long, wide stairways. Crowds were forever braving the gunsights of the enforcers to climb those stairs, whether to report wrong-doing, to plead innocence before the austere pulpit of the magistrates within, or perhaps to inquire after the fate of a relative or friend hauled into the cells. Such was the scale of the place that even finding the right gate could be the work of months. Once inside, navigating through the coal-black warrens was a task of similarly daunting magnitude. Hundreds of thousands of scholar-adepts shuffled through the innards of the Hall, its subordinate chambers and its auxiliary precincts, ferrying documents between courtrooms and investigation-silos, shadowed at all times by the ever-present enforcers.

The reputation of the Hall was so fearful that the mere mention of it was often enough to cow the renegade and reform the sinful. Its inhabitants were the ultimate guardians of the Lex, that impenetrable thicket of laws and precedents that bound every living human so tightly that even a scream was impossible. As a keen student of the law herself, Spinoza had always admired its agents – they had a purity of purpose about them that made them worthy of respect. Less numerous than the Astra Militarum, less powerful than the Adeptus Astartes, less specialised than the Inquisition; nonetheless, for the average citizen the Arbites were perhaps the most enduring and potent symbol of the Emperor's power, the one they were most likely to come into contact with or know just a little about.

Now dressed in the black armour-plate of a proctor, with Hegain kitted out as her attendant enforcer, she had a flavour of what it meant to wear the uniform in public. As the two of them strode up the high stairs towards the gate plaza, the many citizens clustered around her scampered to get out of the way. Unlike her Inquisition rosette, which only generated terror when glimpsed up-close, this night-dark kit – all heavy angles and exaggerated, ostentatious weaponry – was a clenched fist-crunch to the face, unsubtle and remorseless. The thick plates were unpowered, making her movements ponderous in comparison with her usual physical fluency. Even Hegain, whose standard storm trooper carapace plate was of much higher quality, looked like he was wading through mud.

'I do not, as it is, much like the looks of all this here,' he voxed to her on their closed comm system.

'I know what you mean,' Spinoza said, forging a laborious path up to the gate level before striding out across the plaza. 'Has there been some triggering event? Something to provoke them?'

'Nothing at all, not a thing that I have been aware of,' said Hegain grimly, keeping close, his hand resting on the handle of his shock baton.

The mob was restive and numerous, pushing up towards the arch like a surge-tide, before breaking and ebbing under the attentions of the enforcers lined up ahead. Some of them seemed to be shouting, though the words were lost in the general roar of noise and movement. Several gunships dropped low, blasting their turbines straight into the thickest knots of bodies, but even that aggressive move failed to drive them back by much. As Spinoza and Hegain neared the gates, where the enforcers waited with weapons drawn, the air of ugliness got more intense.

'It is like an illness,' Spinoza mused, studying them all from behind the anonymity of her full-face helm. 'They should be driven from the gates.'

But that might not have been easy, not without considerable violence, and even then it was a large crowd to cow. For now, the assembled security forces seemed content to hold the Hall's perimeter, merely preventing things from becoming worse. In all likelihood, watch officers were using servo-skulls to pinpoint the ringleaders, ready for surgical strikes from the gunships if needed. The Arbites would not want to provoke an all-out riot on their doorstep if they could help it – better to let the cattle burn off their energy now and enact considered retribution later.

'Almost there,' said Hegain, shoving aside a robed, face-swaddled woman who hadn't seen him until too late. She whirled to face him, her eyes flashing angrily, before realising who had pushed her. Even then she held her ground, staring at the two of them as if they were the worst devils of the outer dark, her fists balled. 'And glad of it, I will say,' he muttered, pressing on. 'This is madness.'

Spinoza barged more citizens aside to reach the open ground before the lines of enforcers. 'Now we see how good the information from Revre was,' she murmured. Maintaining her stride, she approached the regulator in charge of the defence lines and snappily displayed her credentials. 'What is this all about?' she demanded.

The officer made the aquila. Despite his bulk and armour, he gave off a faint air of indecision. 'Unknown, proctor,' he replied, his voice muffled behind the wadding of his helm. 'Awaiting orders to disperse.'

Spinoza glanced back over her shoulder. It looked like even more were coming to join the mobs, streaming out from the ranked hab-towers beyond. 'Do not wait too long, regulator,' she said, taking her ident-wafer back.

'No, proctor,' he replied, distracted by the gathering unrest, his trigger-finger looking itchy. 'In His service.'

She passed through the line of troopers, Hegain close at

her heels. Once across the gate threshold, under the shadow of the yawning arch, it became easier to move. The giant Adeptus Arbites sigil hanging over them seemed to stare defiantly outward, as if daring the mob to follow them in. They would not have got far, had they tried to, but the fact that they were there at all was concerning.

Spinoza and Hegain moved within the precincts of the Hall proper, and presented credentials at three further security cordons before a pair of heavy iron doors swung open. After that, their surroundings sunk into that ambience so familiar in all courtrooms of the Imperium – the musty, mouldering air; the oppressive lighting; the muffled squeaks of boots on high-polished floors. Several squads of enforcers jogged past them, heading up to the gates to reinforce the perimeter. All saluted as they went by. Two servo-skulls with high-range oculi hummed overhead soon afterwards, heading the same way. One of them scanned Spinoza, presumably an automatic process, and picked up the subtle response systems embedded in her armour. Unperturbed, the skull bobbed onwards, its grav-unit whining.

'This equipment is adequate, at least,' Spinoza remarked as they kept walking.

'Erunion works hard,' Hegain agreed. 'He will be pleased to hear of it, when we return.'

Without advance planning and access to restricted schematics, finding a path through the warrens beyond would have been nigh-impossible. The corridors soon branched, then branched again, splitting up into dozens of different subterranean avenues. Every surface was highly polished and smelled of chemical cleaners. Every door was iron-barred and unmarked, save for small, cryptic iron glyphs set into the lintels. Adepts scurried all over the place, hauling materials from the repositories to the court-chambers and back again, their gaunt faces hidden under the ubiquitous scholars' cowls. It quickly became clammy, and the grind of atmospheric processors made the floors thrum. Once within the steel trap of outer security, few dared challenge a proctor and her escort, and the numerous armed guards made the aquila respectfully whenever they were encountered. Only the automatic scanning systems continued to challenge them, which happened at regular intervals as they progressed further inside.

They ignored the corridors leading to the courtrooms and gaols, as well as those descending to the interrogation suites and holding cells, but followed Revre's directions towards the third great portion of the Hall's interior – the investigation archives. Over the millennia of the Hall's ceaseless activity, these repositories had become truly immense, filling chamber after chamber with tight-packed files and vellum-bundles. Some sections were devoted to the accounts of notable judgements, others to academic tomes of esoteric jurisprudence, yet more to the mundane business of recording the minute-by-minute conduct of active enforcement work. As ever, the volume of material soon outpaced the ability of any single administration to process, and so a secondary industry of intensive tome-mining had sprung up within the Hall's cavernous vaults. Whole branches of its standing army of scholiasts were devoted to mounting extensive expeditions into the furthest and oldest reaches of the lower levels, set on uncovering lost jewels of wisdom or relocating the corpuses of the revered foundational Judges. Every senior official of the Adeptus Arbites, wherever they were stationed in the Imperium, had the ambition to make the pilgrimage to this place, just once, in order to assist this effort, perhaps to rediscover something truly significant in the deeps, maybe to learn some hidden truth of the Lex, or possibly just to breathe in the leathery air of the sealed chambers and gaze in rapture along the cases of ancient, flaking spines. It was even rumoured that, from time to time, some of the most fanatical of them took up permanent habitation in the furthest reaches of the archive-pits, eking out a famished existence in the dust and darkness before they finally expired among their beloved parchment-scraps, surrounded by burned-out candles and the scrawl of hasty, obsessive notes.

Of course, most of the archives were neither as important nor as well-hidden as those legendary screeds – records stretching back over the past few centuries were still reasonably accessible and frequently made use of. Hall XXVI of Level 458 was virtually at the repository's surface-stratum, though even using Revre's data it still required a long hike to find it. The bustle of the upper corridors slowly receded and the lumens dipped even lower, until the two of them were trudging through a twilight underworld of stacked vellum walls, each volume crammed on to iron shelves that seemed to stretch on forever.

'Folio thirty-three...' Hegain mumbled, scanning with a handheld augur to gain a fix on the correct location. 'Folio fifty-nine... Hells below, are these not in *any* kind of order?'

Spinoza took in the surroundings carefully. Grav-loaders had been stationed at the intersection of every major tome-casing. Boxy cogitator stations dotted the floor level. On the edge of hearing, she could detect other scholars at work in the far distance, their taps and scrapes echoing along the long avenues. Her helm's tactical display picked up the intermittent flicker of servo-skull movement. Even here, even in these barren reaches, there were still eyes to see and ears to hear.

'This is what we want,' she said, using Revre's information to home in on a sealed set of records.

They came to a halt in front of a barred metal section, behind which steel crates had been stacked. Spinoza scanned the catalogue panels with her own augur unit. After confirming the codes against Revre's figures, she applied a lock-cycler to the bars. With a rusty clunk they slid open, revealing the crates within. Hegain pulled one out, then tried Revre's seal-codes, one by one, until he found a match. The lid of the crate eased open, revealing an empty interior.

'Anything at all?' asked Spinoza, peering inside.

Hegain rummaged for a moment, using his helm-visor to scan for trace elements. 'There was material placed in this, yes,' he said, running his fingers along the bottom. 'Standard archive-vellum. Very much gone now.'

They pulled out another crate, and then another. All were empty. They worked their way down, looking for records filed in the adjacent cases, and found nothing.

'These were communications made at the highest level,' Spinoza said, reaching for another crate. 'Few would dare to destroy them, I think, without similarly high-level authorisation.'

'The physical copies, yes,' said Hegain, leaning against the casing. 'But Revre, if I recall it, gave us scan-codes, did he not?'

'The same, in all likelihood,' said Spinoza. 'But we have come this far – we must be thorough.'

They replaced the crates and re-sealed the casings. Then they trudged down the long avenue towards the nearest cogitator station. It was a huge, old contraption, with corrosion-spotted heat-sinks and a smeared, angle-poise viewer-lens. Heavy cabling snaked from its rear down into the floor, where it joined clustered wiring from the other linked units within the hall.

Spinoza took a seat before the terminal and activated the interrogation-unit. The machine-spirit coughed, spat, then blurted into life. She pulled out a typeslate, then adjusted the lens so the glyph-projector lined up with her eyes.

'Record access,' she said, speaking into the vox-grille, and holding her badge of status up against a sight-verifier.

The cogitator thought about that for a while, clattering internally, before a glowing line of runes chuntered across the lens.

Welcome, proctor. Security code, please.

Spinoza entered the first of Revre's figures, causing the cogitator to clatter some more.

No records held under that file-heading. Do you have another request?

Spinoza halted the recall and entered a realtext-query.

Have prior records on this topic been removed?

The cogitator ran the logic, and the transistors along its back flashed as power was drawn to the calculus-engine.

Yes, proctor.

By whom?

Undetermined, proctor. Do you have another request?

Spinoza entered more of Revre's codes, using each one to interrogate a different archive-silo. The answer was always the same.

No records held under that file-heading. Do you have another request?

In every case, the cogitator was prepared to divulge that the cases had once been populated, but had no data on the reason for them being emptied. It was a clean removal with no omissions. This was a dead end. If any link had once existed between the Provost Marshal and the Speaker's office, it had been terminated some time ago, and all traces of it expunged.

Hegain began to grow restive. He had been pacing up around, keeping an eye on the avenues ahead and behind. They were all deserted, but that could change at any time.

'Details of any further catalogue items in this silo referring to representatives of the Speaker of the Chartist Captains,' Spinoza finally voxed at the grille, for completeness.

Another round of clicking and whirring. *None held, proctor. Do you have another request?*

'If I may, lord,' Hegain ventured, peering out into the darkness, 'I believe we have all we are going to get.'

Spinoza ignored him. She had one access code left, the last one Revre had given her before his mind had begun to fade. It had not been a pleasant task, nor an honourable one, leveraging that wretch. It would be better to get something out of it, making the deed a little less sordid than the pointless murder of a weak man.

'Almost there,' she said, inputting the final sequence.

The cogitator rattled. It clunked. Then it stopped. For a moment, there was nothing – just the creak of the shelves around them.

Then, without warning, it shut down entirely. The meagre lumens hung far above went out, turning the gloom into perfect darkness.

From somewhere far away, right on the edge of detection, an alarm clanged into life.

Spinoza smiled dryly. 'I did not think he had it in him,' she said to herself.

Then she got up, pulling her hand-cannon from its holster. Hegain was already moving, stowing his shock baton and pulling out an autopistol. Both activated their night-sights.

'Forgive me, sergeant,' said Spinoza, breaking into a stride and heading swiftly back the way they had come. 'I fear that was one code too many.'

'Nothing to forgive, lord,' replied Hegain, chortling. 'I don't like to hide if I can help it. Best to fight harder on two feet, you think, yes?'

Spinoza remembered Crowl's orders.

We have no defence, once we are exposed.

'Just maintain your cover,' said Spinoza, picking up the pace as the alarms grew louder. 'We get out alive, then we worry about what comes next.'

From the terminus berths, Crowl and Bajan took a mag-train further inside the Nexus. Gorgias hung low over Crowl's shoulder, silent and subservient. As they went, the opulence of the interior gradually unfurled around them. The elevated track wound through a series of halls, each one larger than the one before, all well-lit and shining from expensive equipment and glassy fittings. The floors were white marble, the staff dressed in crisp blue tabards. The mounted Imperial aquila was present, blindly overseeing the activity on the floors below, but not as often as the symbol of the Chartists, which adorned almost every surface.

There should have been little surprise about this. All knew that the Chartists were phenomenally wealthy. Unlike the military orders of the Imperium, which were forever run ragged trying to police its long frontiers, the merchants had it good, here at its centre where all coin eventually found its home. Crowl found himself wondering what the average Militarum trooper, stranded out in the freezing, mud-clogged trenches of the main combat zones, would have felt if they knew what their sacrifice was buying. Not that any of them would ever get this far to see it – there was a reason why the Nexus guarded its perimeter so tightly.

'What is that?' Crowl asked, as the mag-train glided through another large hall.

The track was over ten metres up, sending them far over the heads of the adepts labouring below. In this chamber, enormous crystalflex screens had been erected, on which cartographic symbols glowed softly. A complex web of trade-routes overlaid one another, marked by status runes and trigonometric equations. Every so often, the lattice would update, ticking over to register the arrival of another big convoy or the completion of a major contract. Most of the datascreens depicted local systems, just a few warp-stages across, and here the level of information was impressive – a gently scrolling list of manifolds and fulfilments, placed orders and newly launched hulls. On the largest, though, the one that dominated the centre of the hall, things were more schematic. It was impossible not to recognise the straggling swirl of the western galactic arm, marked with Terra at its centre. That map was familiar to any child of a good schola, as were the many system names that were learned by rote.

It was a figurative diagram, of course – there was no way, in a universe dominated by astropathic communication and the vagaries of warp-travel, to generate real-time snapshots of every fleet movement and every landing. The schematic of the Imperium was by necessity half-allegorical, with the usual astrological symbols mixed in with the astronomical ones, tied together with benedictions to the Emperor-as-Navigator and old injunctions against the caprice of the void's tides. And yet, there was a broad picture to be read there, something that could be interpreted meaningfully, something that was clearly evolving. A long swath of that map was marked in red, tearing across the northern galactic sectors like a cut made by a jagged blade. Within that zone, whole systems throbbed with alert runes, their trade-routes and warp-conduits darkened, faded or erased.

Bajan followed Crowl's gaze. 'The anomalous regions?' he asked coolly. 'There is some uncertainty. As with all such things, the schema is only a rough indication. We compile distress signals, regular fleet bulletins, the usual sources.'

'Those systems are marked as lost.'

'Not lost, inspector. Uncertain. There is some doubt as to their current status and reporting reliability.'

The mag-train brushed along, heading steadily towards the exit portal at the far end of the hall. Below, activity continued much as it must always have done – a steady, professional bustle of scholiasts and analysers bent low over tabulators and scrivenodes. Chronometers ticked away on the walls, each fashioned to look like the centrepiece of a ship's command bridge, marking the estimated local time-date benchmark at major muster-centres. No one seemed concerned.

'But the pattern is immense,' said Crowl, unable to take his eyes from the map. 'And it begins in the Ocularis Terribus. Has this information been passed on to the Council?'

'Of course,' said Bajan. 'Everything is communicated in the usual way – I can show you the records, if you are interested.'

Crowl looked hard at the signals adept. There was a faint tightness around his mouth, a slight tension around his eyes. Nothing unusual, when faced with a member of the Inspectorate of Shipping. Was he really that relaxed about it? Had he been ordered to be? 'What response did you get?'

'I would not know, inspector,' Bajan said. The mag-train passed into another tunnel, and the brightness of the hall faded into the flashing lumen-pattern of the Nexus' interior.

'That is something the Speaker's office may be able to determine, were you able to ask them. But you will understand from your time in the scheduling stations that anomalies come and go. Sometimes they are very large, sometimes less so. We plan for them, we accommodate them, just as always.'

Crowl settled back into his clamshell seat. There was something surreal about the complacency. Still, these people knew their business. He himself had not been on a truly long void-passage for a very long time, and could hardly be held up as an expert on such things.

'The galaxy must be compassed,' he said, echoing the Chartists' motto.

'Quite.'

They moved on, travelling through more cartographic halls, then narrower chambers that appeared entirely devoted to enormous ledgers of goods and tithes. The scale of operations became somewhat numbing, a constant buzz of computation and calculation, never-ending in scope, remorseless in intensity. Most of it was utterly impenetrable to outsiders, an arcane business of profit-prediction and goods-distribution conducted over truly awe-inspiring distances and timeframes.

These were powerful people. In some respects, these were the most powerful people in the Imperium.

'Here we are,' Bajan said, getting up.

The mag-train glided to a halt. They disembarked and entered a glass-roofed atrium. Water – uncontaminated, by the look of it – ran from fountains into long ornamental pools. The adepts shuffling across the slate floors here were senior, clad in fine multihued robes and wearing elaborate headdresses. Bajan took Crowl into a palatial office, one that overlooked the cityscape beyond. That meant they were very high up, in the cluster of towers at the Nexus' summit, and the hab-spires stretched off in a cool haze of grey, bleached by the diffuse light of the cloud-barred sun. Black specks of air-traffic flitted past in silent mobs, like billows of dust in the wind.

'Drink, inspector?' Bajan asked, heading to a heavy-set ahl-wood desk with mournful caryatids for legs.

Crowl could have killed for one, but Calavine, unfortunately, was teetotal. Or rather had been teetotal, prior to his accident on the landing stages coming in from the Eleucine orbital transfer platform. Such a tragedy, that.

'No,' he said, taking the seat set opposite the desk. 'We'll get started.'

'Very well,' said Bajan. 'I have prepared a selection of recent–'

'I did not come all this way to scrutinise material you have already sanitised.' Calavine had been an irritable man. Mimicking him proved rather enjoyable. 'I have questions of my own.'

Bajan smiled tartly. 'I see.'

'You keep accurate records.'

'We pride ourselves on that.'

'And your responsibilities include the Laurentis subsector.'

'They do. Among many others.'

'Are you familiar with the name Naaman Vinal?'

Bajan frowned. 'I do not believe so.'

'He was a rogue trader.'

'Then, as you know, he would not fall under our auspices.'

'Interesting. He thought differently.' Crowl leaned forward, resting his elbows on his knees. The movement made his joints ache, but it was an affectation of Calavine's. 'He was in communication with your department regularly. Why was that, do you think?'

Bajan's right eyelid flickered, just by a fraction. 'You have the records of this?'

'Answer the question.'

'I do not understand, inspector. How does this relate to our scheduled business?'

'It does not.'

Bajan looked properly confused now. 'I had anticipated–'

Crowl curled his fingers. 'Tell me, then, about deposit account three-eight-seven-six-five, registered at Borlatte Vois accumulators.'

Now Bajan looked scared. 'None of this relates to our work here.'

'I know, adept. That is the point. It is a very well-stocked account, for all that – far in excess of what might be expected for a private citizen in the service of the Throne. Its owner is Gerhardus Aolph. Of course, and as you know, no such person exists.'

Bajan's mouth tightened. 'I have prepared reports. On shipping patterns.'

Crowl ignored him. 'You hid your tracks fairly well. The path back to you is convoluted – nine registered holding vehicles, of which the last – Aletto Urban – is entirely legal. If I did not have good forensic scholars in my departmento, you might have got away with it entirely.'

Bajan leaned forward a fraction, his hand creeping towards a drawer. Gorgias noticed, and rose up threateningly, needle-gun extending.

'I wouldn't,' Crowl recommended, staying perfectly immobile. 'My skull has an erratic temperament but a good aim.'

Bajan's hand froze. His expression remained blank enough, but Crowl was experienced enough to perceive the frantic calculations going on behind his eyes. 'Really, I do not–'

'This should be the end for you, Harker Bajan,' Crowl said. 'Filtering that much coin from your oversight contracts is just greedy, and I doubt even the most jaded overseer would be able to ignore it, once my report hit their desk. But you are in luck. Let us start again, shall we? With the things I am truly interested in. Why was Naaman Vinal in communication with your office?'

Bajan's eyes flickered, as he tried to keep up with what was going on. After a moment of thought, he seemed to understand, and slumped back in his chair. 'Is this testimony protected under Inspectorate confidentiality?'

'Yes. Not that you're in a position to demand much protection.'

'And my name will be kept out of it?'

'Start talking – I do not have infinite patience.'

'I do not know,' Bajan said. 'Honestly, I do not. The canisters were prepared from astropathic accounts and kept sealed. They were sent higher up – I only supervised the transmission.'

'On whose orders?'

'It had Ultra-Six classification. That is not questioned. I assume all the way to the top.'

'I was given the name Cassandara Glucher,' Crowl said.

'She used to work here. I don't know if she's even still alive. The incoming register-address might have been hers, but that means little. We oversaw onward movement, kept the canisters safe and off-book, then cleaned up the acceptance records.'

'It this normal procedure?'

'It's not as uncommon as you might think.'

'Then I'll need access to those files.'

Bajan laughed, more nervously than with any kind of humour. 'You are operating well above your clearance now, inspector.'

'That is hardly your judgement to make. Where can I find them?'

'For all the good it will do you, they were signed off by the Ninth Magister Calculo Horarium.'

'You had project codes when processing this work,' said Crowl, reaching for a data-slug and handing it to Bajan. 'I'll need those too.'

Bajan took up the slug, looked at it for a moment, then grudgingly entered a series of digits. 'I don't want my name associated with this,' he said again.

Crowl smiled. 'You're consistent, I'll give you that.' He took the slug back. 'Under the regulations of your office, as you well know, your position is now forfeit. The regulators at Borlatte are not sympathetic people. If I were you, I'd find some reason to get off-world. Then I'd stay there. You might even be able to access some of your funds if you move quickly enough, as I'll be busy with this Magister – assuming, that is, you've given me the right names. If not, then we'll be talking again soon.'

'No, no, it's all correct.' Bajan looked miserable. 'But my family–'

'Take them too. Consider this a lesson in morality. Learn from it, cleave to a better understanding of His example, and you may yet make something of your avaricious life.'

Bajan made to rise, then hesitated, eyeing Gorgias warily. 'So what are you going to do now, inspector? You can't possibly make use of this information. Just one for the files, is it?'

Crowl rose, ignoring the spasm up his spine. He had a long journey ahead of him now, and his mind was already turning to what must come next. 'That's right, adept,' he said. 'Just one for the files.'

CHAPTER EIGHT

The two corpses lay under Erunion's harsh lumens, every blemish and wound unforgivingly exposed. Both were naked, one man and one woman, side by side on polished metal slabs. Medicae drones the size of clenched fists mobbed them, taking measurements, recording picts.

Revus watched it all dispassionately. Erunion had been busy for a while, his gloves damp with blood, the instruments in their steel bowls spotted with it.

Eventually, the chirurgeon unfurled, stretching his shoulders back. He unclipped his visor from its shackles, leaving a pink ring around each eye.

'Simple enough,' he said, scratching his nose. 'The Callax revolver fired once. The Hammerglaive twice. Your killer entered the hab unit, perhaps expecting to find her asleep. She wasn't. He fired first, but either she was able to evade it or his aim was bad. She had her own weapon somewhere close to hand – sensible girl – and returned fire. She hit him, but did not kill him outright. He fired again, this time more effectively. After completing his assignment, he managed to make it to the hygiene chamber, but succumbed there to his injury. If you had sent someone to do such work, captain, you would not have been happy.'

Revus snorted. 'I'd have done it myself.' He leaned over the woman's face. There was nothing remarkable there – her ash-blonde hair was thinning, her cheeks were a little sunken, but otherwise she looked in reasonable health. Operating as an informer for one of the various security agencies was a decent way of supplementing food rations and getting hold of medical credits. That alone made it worth the considerable risks, at least most of the time.

'Was she a good contact?' Erunion asked idly, stooping to clean a long scalpel.

'I don't know,' said Revus. 'She fed her material to a priest in Salvator. I doubt he gave her the credit for his information, but I asked Huk to check. Small stuff, I suspect. How much are you really going to get in a parchment-works?'

Erunion chuckled. 'Keep your ear to the ground, anywhere much. You'll hear a thing, sooner or later.'

Revus remembered the picts in the woman's hygiene station. Since returning to Courvain he'd tracked the parents down. They, and her employers, had been told that Elija Roodeker had succumbed to a sudden outbreak of bile-clot, something that had to be cleaned up immediately, the body incinerated. The apartment had already been scoured by a biotoxin team and would soon be assigned to another occupant. Revus had made sure that the legal expenses of recording the death and registering it with the local scriveners were covered and a no-further-investigation note placed on the file. The family had already been the victim of one crime; they didn't need to be preyed on further.

'So what do you make of him?' Revus asked.

'Matches no one on our files,' said Erunion, bleakly. 'Huk's running further searches, but I doubt she'll turn anything up. Underhive trash, just as you suspected – virtually impossible to trace. I doubt he'd even fired a proper gun before they got him to do this.'

Revus looked at him. He was scrawny, his skin drawn tight across prominent bones. He had the sallow, bruised look of a man who'd lived his short life in the absence of natural light. Many of his teeth were missing from a rattish mouth, and his eyeballs protruded bulbously. Erunion's scans had already shown up a cocktail of diseases bubbling through his system. No wonder that single shot had been enough to kill him – a stiff breeze might have done the same, on another day.

'Sloppy work,' he murmured disapprovingly.

'So, what's your supposition?' Erunion asked.

'I don't know,' Revus admitted, unable to take his eyes off the wretch before him. 'There's little enough reason for Gloch to knock out one of his own informants, unless he's erasing his tracks down there for some reason. Maybe someone else was looking for him.'

'Not much sign of a conversation taking place.'

'We don't know that.' Revus resisted the urge to massage his temples. It had been a long time since he'd taken a rest period. 'Seems we don't know anything much. Before I file this, do you have anything else?'

Erunion wiped his gloves on his apron, and turned to an electro-scanner station. He activated the power-lever and routed the current to a polished picter-lens. Humming absently, he cycled through feeds garnered by the drone-augurs. Blotchy images flickered in sequence across the plexiglass – bones, muscle bundles, the twisting terrain of half-clogged arteries.

'Now, then,' he murmured, halting the procession. Revus moved closer to the lens. Erunion scanned in tighter, turning a brass dial up several notches. 'What is this?'

The subdermal scan was of the lower neck, close to where it joined the shoulder. There was a lump there, harder and more defined that the various clots and lesions that polluted the viewfield. It gave off no electromagnetic signature and had evidently been small enough and sufficiently benign to escape detection by the routine sensor-sweep.

'What's this trash doing with an augmetic bead?' Erunion mused, panning and swivelling some more. 'Close to the spine. A neural-clamp?'

'Too small,' said Revus, peering closely. 'A pain-spike, possibly. To keep him in line.'

'Hardly necessary. This rat would have worked for food.'

'An ident-emitter, then. Something to give him access to where he needed to be.'

Erunion nodded. 'Maybe so. Want me to extract it?'

Revus hesitated. He had already spent a great deal of time on this subject, and there were other things he ought to be attending to. He was half-minded to let it go, to order both corpses to the incinerators and mark the trail as ended, but then Crowl had always been one for the details. It might be something.

'Let's take a look,' he said.

Erunion smiled, and reached for the scalpel again. 'No stone left unturned,' he said.

The blade went in, propelled by expert fingers. Soon the flesh was peeled back, revealing a tiny black knot, lodged in the neck-muscle. A tiny thread led from it, looking as if it wormed its way all the way in towards the spinal cord. 'Hm,' Erunion murmured. 'I'll have to make an incision to get it out. Happy for me to cut?'

Revus nodded.

The blade nicked in further. Just as it did so, a burst of white noise, high-pitched and ear-splitting, rang out from the bead.

Erunion recoiled, clamping his hand over the wound even as Revus reached for his hellpistol. Almost as soon as it had broken out, the noise ended, leaving the picters scrambled with static and lumens flickering wildly.

'What was that?' Erunion asked, confounded.

Revus pushed him aside and grabbed the bead, yanking it from its bloody cradle and holding it up to the lumen. 'Is this place comm-shielded?' he demanded.

'Of course.'

Revus squinted for a closer look. It was so innocuous, lying there in his palm. Amid the spots of red, though, were tight curls of microelectronics, wound together in ways that gave away its extremely sophisticated manufacture.

'Damn,' Revus said, closing his fist over the device. A little gentle pressure, and it was crushed. 'Not an ident-bead.'

Erunion looked up at him, confused. 'What, then?'

By then, Revus was already moving. 'A tripwire,' he snarled, feeling the hot flush of failure wash through his system. 'One we just crashed straight through.'

Erunion swallowed, all his assurance gone. 'What now?'

Revus halted at the doorway, fixing him with a bleak stare. 'Burn them both,' he said. 'Lock everything down, get the Lord Crowl back here.' He flung the remnants of the bead into the trash-unit. 'If that thing was powerful enough to push through our shields, then whoever planted it now knows just where to find it again.'

'*Who*, though?' Erunion asked, querulously.

'No idea,' growled Revus, turning back to the course that would take him straight to the armoury. 'Get it done.'

Spinoza ran hard. She and Hegain scaled the first set of stairs without incident, but the alarms got louder with every stride, as did the clang and echo of boots hitting the floors above.

It was too damned dark, and her proctor's helm, despite Erunion's modifications, did not compensate for it as well as her own. She heard her breathing in her earpiece, close and rapid. The route out spun in front of her, a false-colour web of retina-projected overlay, but it was difficult to decipher at speed and with so few reference points.

Ahead of her, twenty metres off, a door slid open, exposing a rectangle of blinding yellow light and the silhouette of an armoured guard. Hegain got his shot off first – beautifully aimed, a shoulder-impact that sent the silhouetted figure spinning backwards. Another guard leapt through the gap, and this time it was her shot that felled him – low, smashing his shins.

It would be non-lethal, if possible. These were loyal servants of the Throne, doing their duty.

She reached the foot of a second stairway. More alarms were going off now, overlapping and filling the air with competing brays. The schematic whirled around across her viewfield, shaking with lines of white noise.

'This way, if you please it,' Hegain offered, scanning down the corridor ahead with his gunsight.

Spinoza paused. The sergeant was right – that was the quickest route out.

'Not yet,' she said, gesturing up the stairwell. 'Up here.'

She ran up the metal steps ponderously, clunking as her armour weighed her down. As she reached the summit, an enforcer in full suppression-garb skidded through the doorway. She punched him, jabbing at the neck with gauntlet-fingers locked and extended, and he crunched into the wall, clutching at his dented gorget-seal. She dropped him with the heel of her hand cannon, then stamped hard through his armour's knee-joint.

Hegain caught up, dropping to one knee to sweep the corridor ahead. A combat lumen was flashing up above, sending blood-red light blinking from the polished walls.

'This is very strange,' he observed, drawing no targets.

'So it is,' Spinoza agreed, running again.

They made faster progress after that, shooting down a lone scanner-skull that swerved into their path, and knocking out another two enforcers. Only one of those managed to get a vox-challenge out before Hegain, who might have been the best shot in Revus' entire detachment, sent him cartwheeling from an impeccable helm-strike.

'If I have the right of things–' Hegain muttered, panting as he clattered along in his heavy blast-plate.

'–there should be more of them,' Spinoza said, reaching the corridor's end and skidding a fraction on the reflective floors. 'Many more. So I do not believe that all those alarms can be for us.'

They rounded a corner, jogged across an intersection and headed upwards, ascending rapidly now. There was a knack to gaining speed in Arbites armour, Spinoza found. It was all about momentum – once you had enough of it, the weight became easier to handle. No wonder the enforcers had a reputation for doggedness.

As they reached a circular chamber studded with numerous slide-doors, a six-strong detachment of black-clad troopers trundled in from the opposite direction. Hegain made to open fire, but Spinoza shut him down, instead gesturing sharply to their leader.

'You,' she barked. 'Your orders. Now.'

'Perimeter, proctor,' the woman replied, making the aquila hastily. 'Sector D-4, overlook bastion.'

'Then you are with me,' Spinoza ordered, moving off again, using her schematic to pinpoint D-4. 'Stay close. This is weak. Damned weak.'

Hegain, to his credit, didn't miss a beat. Whatever alerts had gone out concerning a data-breach in the archives, clearly something else had taken priority now.

The eight of them travelled as a unit, heading ever higher, out from the inner courts and up towards the Hall's perimeter. Once back in the upper chambers, the corridors filled with slamming bootfalls – adepts hurrying away from the exposed regions, enforcers and troopers racing in the opposite direction. The few senior officers were clearly occupied with their own missions, and were doing much as they were – getting to a position where they could be useful. The closer they all got to the outer walls, the more they all heard it – a roar, vast and sullen, like a sea coming in.

The final doorway slid open, ushering in the smog and hot-air tang of the Terran night. Spinoza was first out, breaking through a blast-portal and onto a wide landing stage. The platform was over thirty metres across, perched atop an octagonal bastion tower. Two gunships were being prepped for take-off, ready to join the dozens that were already airborne. Additional troopers were stationed around its rim, a low rampart protected by a flak-screen, and all were busy. Smoke, much more than was usual, rolled up from the plazas below, acrid and eye-watering. The landing stage was perhaps twenty metres up from the nominal ground level, but the wall of sound was still impressive, blotting out the ever-present traffic grind with a rolling surge of human anger.

'The *sky*, lord,' Hegain observed, sounding shocked.

It was impossible not to notice it. Slivers of lightning danced far above them. The clouds that spilled and split through the hive pinnacles were blotched too, like ink spilled into water. Sparks flew and drifted across the moving belts of brown-black, spiralling like loosed fireworks. A pungent aroma rolled with them – hard to place, powerful as cathedral incense-clusters.

Spinoza headed straight to the wall's edge and peered through a gap in the flak-screen. On their initial approach to the Hall of Judgement, those spaces had been crowded. Now they were rammed tight, filled to bursting with a carpet of bodies. The owners of those bodies were not merely surly and restive, as they had been before. Now they were furious, and they were charging the Hall's defences.

For a moment, despite all her training, she looked on in shock. The attackers were dying rapidly, for the Arbites had been forced to respond, and that response was suitably and professionally brutal. Ranks of enforcers all across the walls were opening up with autoguns and bolt-pistols, carving great swaths through the mobs rushing the defences.

It wasn't deterring them. For every desperate citizen felled at the front lines, it seemed that more were prepared to surge forward, welling up out of the urban sumps to run, witless and furious, straight into the fire-lanes.

It was madness. It was beyond madness.

'Take your positions,' Spinoza ordered the troopers who had come with them, gesturing towards vacant slots in the ramparts. Those already stationed there kept on doing what they had been doing – picking leaders and knocking them out, adding the fizz and flash of ranged las-fire to the crack and smack of solid-round ordnance.

She turned to one of the gunships. Its crew were pulling

on their helms and preparing to board. Two ugly rotary cannons under its slab-wings had been loaded with feeder-boxes of ammunition, and it looked like spasm-gas canisters had been clamped along its flanks.

'I'll take this one,' she said, pushing the pilot aside and holstering her sidearm.

The pilot looked up at her, startled, but withdrew quickly enough once he saw her badge of office.

Spinoza clambered inside, with Hegain taking the other cockpit seat. The gunship's two auxiliary gunners were already in place behind them, clamped into the vehicle's augur systems and linked up to their cannons' machine-spirits.

'Er, do you know, lord, in truth, how to fly this?' Hegain asked, over the private channel.

There was very little in the colossal Imperial arsenal that Spinoza didn't know how to control, or couldn't work out with a little time in the pilot's seat. This was a Brawler T8 – a typically blunt but otherwise capable ground-attack unit, one that major Adeptus Arbites stations used through the sector and beyond. It was not entirely dissimilar, though far smaller and less powerful, to a Navy Vulture, a machine Spinoza had flown very many times.

'That was an uncharacteristically stupid question, sergeant,' Spinoza said, activating the power unit. 'Buckle up, now.'

The turbines blasted into life, throwing waves of grit across the platform. The gunship belched, gave a squeal of poorly aligned gears, then roared into motion, swinging upwards in a semi-drunken lurch. Hegain held on to the chassis, saying nothing. Spinoza worked the controls, compensating for the hard slew to starboard and pushing more power to the main engines. The Brawler found its equilibrium, dipped its nose and swooped low over the bastion perimeter.

Once past the Hall's outer walls, the full scale of the assault became apparent – the crowds stretched back for kilometres, filling every causeway and approach gradient. Most of them looked to be ordinary workers, still clad in their production-line drab, somehow roused to take on a fortress designed to resist the assault of entire armies. Hundreds of them had been cut down by repeated volleys from the enforcers at ground level and up on the ramparts. Even as Spinoza pushed the gunship out further, a column of Repressor troop-carriers bludgeoned its way down a long access ramp and into the centre of the throngs, gradually slowing up as the press of bodies around them got thicker.

'I can't see a command group,' Spinoza voxed, the thunder of the engines making the cockpit shake violently. 'But this can't be spontaneous.'

Hegain peered out of the narrow armourglass viewport, scanning the boiling masses below. 'The arch, lord,' he offered, doubtfully. 'Concentration's greater there.'

Spinoza nodded, and pulled the gunship around. The two Arbites seated gunners behind them were by now firing in controlled bursts, targetting any figures in the crowd that they deemed to be leading the mania. Towards the rear of the plaza, where the knots of bodies were thicker than ever, a triumphal arch had been erected celebrating the heroic sacrifice of the Adeptus Arbites throughout the galaxy. A stylised enforcer carrying a power maul had been rendered in granite, thirty metres high, notched and soiled by the punishing Terran atmosphere.

Spinoza powered the gunship closer, staying as low as she could. Grey faces gazed up at them, blasted by the downdraught. Rocks and masonry thunked and clattered against the vessel's underside armour. The gunners stayed busy, thinning out the numbers but doing little to stem the fury.

'Target acquired,' said Spinoza calmly, picking out a woman standing under the arch's apex. She was swinging what looked like a long metal flail over her head, wheeling it around and around. Those about her were screaming, goading the others, and the crowds surged past them like a river in storm-flood.

'Confirmed,' reported Hegain, taking control of the Brawler's nose-mounted bolter and lining up the reticules.

The woman must have seen them coming. Even amid that noise and clamour, she must have seen the heavy gunship swagger its way out of the night, its lights glaring, its flank-weapons discharging. She never made a move to evade the danger. By the time her face swam into visual range, Spinoza could see that she was laughing hard, her eyes alight with fervour. She was shaking, winding the flail harder, shouting out words that could not be made out over the gunship's roar but which were clearly driving those around her to an ever-greater pitch of frenzy.

Hegain fired just once, sending a tight burst of bolt-shells right at her. They exploded on impact, ripping her apart and sending the flail-segments spinning into the night. As the gunship banked, the rear gunners kept up a steady rate of fire, crippling and maiming.

Spinoza watched it all from the pilot's seat. Nothing changed. A man leapt up to take the woman's place, clambering over her shredded body. Others took up pieces of the flail and began to lash it against themselves and those about them. The drum of rocks against the gunship's armour picked up. The lightning raked against the spires. The screams, the roars, they never let up.

'We could empty the magazines,' Spinoza murmured, pulling the Brawler higher. 'It wouldn't make a dent.'

Hegain nodded grimly. 'Never seen the like of it, lord,' he said.

Spinoza found herself caught between instincts. In truth, there was little to be done here now, save to add to the futile rain of shells punching through this insensate crowd. The Hall itself was probably impregnable, but whether even the assembled enforcers there had the ammunition to break the will of such numbers was doubtful. This would be a slaughter before the end, and not a glorious one. Even so, her sense of duty pulled her towards staying in position and rendering what assistance she could.

In the end, she didn't have to make the choice. She hauled the gunship away from the arch, heading back to the Hall perimeter, when Revus' call-sign flashed up on her visor.

'Priority recall: the Lord Crowl, Interrogator Spinoza, all personnel in the field. Courvain security compromised. Repeat: Courvain security compromised, priority recall, all personnel.'

Hegain looked up at her sharply. She pulled the control-column, swinging the gunship back towards the citadel. Once on the correct trajectory, she opened up the power, sending the Brawler burning hard across the crowded plaza. After a few moments, they were out of the exposed spaces and back within the narrow twilit canyons between hive-spires.

Once beyond las-fire range, Spinoza set the gunship down briefly atop a hab-tower's landing stage, keeping the engines thundering. Hegain leaned over into the rear cabin.

'Out. Now,' he ordered the gunners, gesturing to the rear access hatch.

They didn't comply immediately. One even protested. Hegain had to draw his sidearm, then flash the sigil of his storm trooper detachment, before they saw sense, detaching their augur-cables and dropping cumbersomely from the hatches.

'Not the brightest stars in the night sky, if I may say it,' Hegain muttered, holstering his weapon as the gunship gained loft again.

Then they were back to full power, charging along the slender gulfs between the towering spires. Once given its head, the Brawler could pick up tremendous speed, and the turbines were soon screaming.

'So then, what do you think it can be?' Hegain asked, shuffling down into his seat and re-clipping his restraint harness.

'I have no idea,' said Spinoza, watching the sky get steadily blacker. 'But I fear, from the evidence before us, it cannot be anything good.'

CHAPTER NINE

He was Calavine now, to all intents and purposes. It wasn't just the uniform and the prosthetics, or the security passes, or knowledge of the man's history, duties and mannerisms. There were subtler changes, too – he could pass a retinal scan, or feed a blood-tester the required type. After a while, consumed by the mission, you could begin to forget yourself entirely, and let the mimicry take over.

Apart from the pain, of course. And apart from the visions of that other inimitable face, buried at the heart of the world, grinning, grinning. No amount of masks and guise-methods could make that go away.

Still, externally he went confidently, mimicking the inspector's strident gait. Gorgias, stripped down to resemble a typical Mercatura servo-unit, bobbed along with a degree less surety than usual – Gorgias hated deception, and would have happily taken a more basic approach to this mission.

'You are doing very well, my friend,' Crowl murmured, keen to maintain the skull's uncharacteristic restraint.

'Unworthy,' Gorgias hissed back. *'Indignus in maxima.'*

'For the cause, Gorgias. For the cause.'

Bajan had given them what they needed. That, and the research compiled from Huk's files, meant that they could travel with certainty. The layout of the Nexus was not as steeply classified as some of the more famous fortresses in the Imperial capital, and it was pleasing to discover a close correspondence between what they had predicted and what was presented to them in reality.

For all that, there were regular checkpoints. At each one, he presented credentials, or gave an account of his business, or issued one of Bajan's passcodes, and then went deeper into the labyrinth.

The Nexus' gleaming upper levels concealed an older kernel. The walls became a little less polished, the floors a little more pocked and cracked. Machinery, welded and bolted into the structure of the building, gained the patina and aspect of age. Signs of repair were everywhere – panels riveted over earlier work, pipes soldered with webs of metal.

It became hotter, as the air filtration struggled to compensate. The officials he passed in the corridors went more furtively, and their numbers thinned. It was a world away from the bright-lit halls with those galactic maps, the calm and efficient processing of signals from all corners of the sprawling empire of mankind. This was the true centre. This was where the core work of the Speaker's court was done, the real decisions made and the real concessions adopted.

This was the world of the Magisters Calculo Horarium, those select souls chosen to guide and interpret the passage of trade across mankind's far-flung dominions. Few living souls had ever encountered such creatures, and the stories, as ever in the Imperium, ran wild. Some said they were immortal, born in the earliest years of humankind's evolution and kept alive through the regular transfusion of blood from younger bodies. Others maintained they were mutants of such vileness that the Nexus' defences had been constructed entirely to keep them from being discovered by the Inquisition. Most believed that they were ciphers, their role long since taken over by magna-cogitators, but of all the rumours, Crowl knew that one was certainly false. The Imperium trusted cogitators as little as possible, hemmed in by ancient fears and more recent Mechanicus doctrines. Machines were employed when they had to be, but where it was possible to use a human mind, a human mind was used.

Crowl had often reflected on this, when inclined to consider the limitations of the institution he served. In some ways, only the blindest of fools could fail to see that much that had once been pristine and powerful had degraded over time, falling in disuse and disrepair. In other respects, the Imperium's power had never been greater, not even during the fabled ages long past. Where its mechanical inventiveness had long since faded, its biological prowess had remained dazzlingly proficient. A man with sufficient coin could extend his life beyond the dreams of ancient humankind. A woman with enough power could maintain her health even within the thickest of toxic smogs. Humanity might have forgotten much, but it could still manipulate cells and tweak synapses, tug at chromosomes and splice limbic systems.

The reliance on the mortal, on flesh over silicon, was not, like so much else, simply a product of desperation. It was more of an aesthetic choice, born out of long and deep-held antipathies. The human mind, whether psychic or no, had capabilities that no cogitator had ever truly matched, and if that power were combined with the dark arts of the neuropath and the chirurgeon-philosophical, then the potentialities were virtually limitless. The Navigator, the savant, the Space Marine, the sanctioned psyker – all of these opened doors and performed functions well in excess of any unaugmented mortal mind. In a galaxy of extraordinary fecundity, where a billion billion lives began every moment, stringent utilisation of the biological made a perfect, if typically ruthless, sense. Effective cogitator STCs were rare; brain-tissue ripe for surgical extension was as common as dirt.

For all that, a Nexus Magister remained a mystery. Crowl began to allow his imagination to play a little. Would it be a monster? Or a mortal? Or one of the many stages in between?

Soon, a high portal rose above him, verdigris-speckled and dripping with a faint sheen of glistening fluids. The floor below was hidden in a low fog of condensation, and the air smelled strongly caustic. All pretence at glassy refinement had long gone – this was a place of old and esoteric construction, studded with brass rivets and engraved with a riot of astrological symbols. Prominent among the images was the star-and-quill sigil, though of an older, more elaborate design than that reproduced in the upper reaches. The hands that had carved these shapes had been consigned to the grave a very long time ago.

Beyond the portal lay a long corridor, tall and vaulted, glowing from floor level with a soft, green light. The chemical smell was stronger down there, wafting up from a metal grid under which gurgled dark fluids. Crowl paused on the threshold. The last few checkpoints had been catered for by Bajan's passcodes, but gaining access to the chambers after this point would be less simple.

'Prepared?' he murmured to Gorgias.

'*In perpetuo,*' the skull affirmed, and dropped away into the plentiful shadows, bobbing carefully.

Crowl's boots sunk into the layer of mist. He walked past bas-relief panels depicting various stellar milestones. There was a geometrical representation of the first warp engine, with a robed figure resting one hand on its casing while raising the other to the starlit skies above. Next came what appeared to be a schematic of a prototype Geller generator, with flows of rune-marked energy around a symbolic unpacking of the core shield harmonics. The same figure was depicted there too, an austere character with sombre eyes, gesturing across the circuit diagrams as if pointing out some potent theological truth. After that came further images, some hard to make any sense of at all. There was a throne, seemingly placed in the heart of the void and connected to a figurative galactic map of swirls and tunnels, then a foetus curled up in a cartouche-shaped vial with a flame burning in the midst of its forehead. It was all rather more reminiscent of a Ministorum chapel than a temple of commerce.

At the end of the vault, the corridor took a sharp turn to the right. Heavy cables hung from the ceiling, wrapped about one another like iron snakes, all of them glittering with the same strands of moisture.

'No further,' came a vox-filtered voice from the far end.

Crowl halted. Just ahead, dimly visible through a green haze, stood a heavy brass door. On either side of the door stood two brass pillars etched with hieroglyphs, and over its lintel were carved the words *Per Sacrificium Ad Astra* and the single figure IX. In front of the door stood two figures, robed in deep green and masked with blank, bronze face-plates. Both carried staffs studded with electro-vanes, and the faint stink of ozone hung around them.

'State your business,' one of the guardians said, in a soft, almost whispering voice.

'Inspector Ferlad Calavine, Sol Sector Command,' Crowl said, bowing and making the aquila. 'Pursuant to inquiries concerning major irregularities in scheduling, as directed by the Speaker's representatives.'

'The Inspectorate has no jurisdiction here,' the guardian said. 'Go back to where you came from.'

'With respect, I cannot. The Magister must be informed of these things in person. I have the passcodes relevant to my investigations, should you wish to see them.'

The guardian remained unmoved. 'Those are of no use here. Return to your work.'

'I have come a long way for this. It is of the highest importance.'

'Return to your work.' The staff angled forward a fraction, and the vanes sparked into life. 'Or I shall send you there myself.'

Crowl's next movement was far faster than the real Calavine would have been able to achieve. It was prompted by a glanded spurt of motovine and came with a cost – a sharp bite of spinal agony – but was nonetheless sufficient to send three tranq-bolts into the second guardian's stomach before he could react, hurling him back against the bronze pillar and spidering his robes with three pinpoint bursts of blood.

The first guardian lunged at him, then froze almost as quickly, his staff crackling with undischarged energy.

'Wise,' said Crowl, dropping the pretence at Calavine's voice and holstering his laspistol. Just visible behind the guardian's helm was Gorgias, who had crept up silently and extended a needle into the back of the man's neck. 'Now say nothing,' said Crowl. 'Listen with utmost care. My skull here is delivering a substance into your bloodstream that will shortly render you both immobile and insensible. Prior to that, you will find yourself becoming amenable to suggestion. I suggest you do not fight it.'

The guardian snarled, and tried to raise the staff. Gorgias pumped a little extra in, and the gesture petered out. Slowly, the man's body relaxed. The sparks on the electro-vanes gusted out, his arms went limp.

'I require entry, nothing more,' Crowl told him calmly. 'No blame can be attached to you for that, and no harm need come to your master, should he cooperate.'

'No... blame,' repeated the guardian, slurrily.

'Open the door, let us pass,' said Crowl, taking the staff from slack fingers as Gorgias extracted the needle. 'Then seal us in, and allow no communication to disturb us. This is the work of the Throne, and by aiding me you are aiding His will.'

'His... will,' echoed the guardian, turning shakily to a panel set into the wall behind him. He extended a gauntlet into a recess, and something heavy clunked within the mechanism. The door hissed, snapped, then began to grind open, send-ing fresh squalls of green haze spilling across the milky floor. The aroma of chemicals became almost overwhelming, a tart cocktail that made the nostrils sting. A wave of wet heat came in its wake, humid and strangely alien.

'Good,' said Crowl, watching him carefully the whole time. It was important to be sure – the drugs in his bloodstream were potent but not infallible. If all worked as it should, both guardians should soon be safely unconscious for sev-eral hours. 'Now remember – no communication while we are inside. Once we are gone, all shall be as it was, and none shall know we were ever here.'

'Ever... here,' slurred the guardian, activating more dials and levers, before standing aside to allow them entry.

Crowl allowed himself to take a deep breath. It was dark under the lintel, almost pitch-black, and strange noises were coming from the aperture.

Gorgias floated up beside him, spinning anxiously. 'Incoming *transmissio*,' he hissed. 'Signal *tenuis* – just a little longer – *iterum…*'

Crowl shook his head. 'It can wait,' he said, stepping over the threshold. 'This cannot.'

Khazad woke again, this time into a state of full alertness.

She blinked. She tensed her muscles. She pushed her blanket down and swung her legs over the edge of the cot.

She was not in the chirurgeon's care. She was in a chamber on her own, one that had presumably been assigned to her a while ago. She stretched her arms out in front of her, flexing the fingers. Aside from a little muscle tenderness, everything seemed to be as it should be.

A single lumen fixed to the ceiling above her gave out a hard, unforgiving light. Her skin looked paler than it had done, making the tattoos on her forearms stand out vividly. A canister of water stood on a table next to her cot's headboard – she took it and drank it down.

Then she got up and cocked her head to one side, listening. From outside, she could hear the sound of boots thudding against the floor. There were noises both above and below her, more than she remembered from the last time.

In the corner of the chamber was a washstand, and next to that were her clothes laid out neatly – boots, a bodyglove, mesh under-armour, and the suit she had worn in Phaelias' service. It all looked to have been reconditioned and repaired, although the cameleo plates were still inoperative. Next to it hung her power sword. She took it up, depressed the activation rune and watched with approval as the energy field snarled into life along the blade's edge.

The noises outside the chamber grew louder. She dressed quickly, snapping her armour-pieces into place and fixing the interlock hooks. It felt better. Someone had clearly done a lot of work on it. A part of her was irritated at that – all this had been done without her consent, while she was still in recovery. Still, once completed, the intact shell made her feel much like her old self again. A little rustiness, a slight headache – that could all be fixed.

She took up the blade – a Shoba gladius-length sword with the tribal death-name *Okira*. They had been together for a very long time, the two of them – it would have felt wrong had she not been there, by her side.

Now the noises were very close – shouted orders, the jangle of armed personnel running. She went to the door and activated the lock-panel. It slid open, revealing a small antechamber. More food had been left there in a cold-cabinet, a few pieces of legal-looking parchment and two inactive data-slates. She walked through the antechamber and opened the outer door.

A group ran past the entrance – three adepts in dark robes, two soldiers. She let them go, and they ignored her. Overhead, a lumen was blinking red. The sound of engines revving rose up from underfoot.

She slipped out, not knowing exactly where to go, but sure that she couldn't stay where she was. She made her way past more jogging personnel until she reached a muster-chamber at the intersection of six corridors. A sergeant from Revus' detachment was giving orders to a group of storm troopers. They were all checking their hellguns over and making final adjustments to their armour and combat webbing.

'I seek Captain Revus,' she said, walking up to him.

He seemed to recognise her. That was something of a surprise – she didn't know who he was.

'Planning on throwing me to the floor again?' he asked. It took her a moment to realise he was joking.

'No,' she said, truthfully.

He grinned, and gestured upward with his thumb. 'Command unit, three levels up,' he said. 'I'll vox him that you're coming – he'll be pleased.'

She followed the direction. Three wrong turns later, and she had to ask again before landing on the right stairwell. The building seemed to have been designed to madden – half the corridors ended abruptly in dead ends, the rest snaked back and forth without signage or reason. As she moved, she realised just how out of condition she had become – it would take much training to get back to even a semblance of battle-readiness.

Eventually she made her way to what the sergeant had referred to as the command unit – a chamber much like the rest of them, all dark metal and gloomy recesses. A circular table dominated the centre of the space, around which a number of officials were gathered. A hololith of a tower – the place she found herself in – rose up from its surface, flashing with translucent runes. Revus was there at the heart of it, gesturing at the schematic and consulting with those about him, most of whom were in storm trooper uniforms too.

'Captain,' she announced.

He looked up. 'Carry on, sergeant,' he said to the woman next to him, then came up to Khazad. 'Glad to see you're back to yourself, assassin. How do you feel?'

'I am fine.'

'Planning on another wrist-lock?'

'No. Why I am being asked these things?'

'Forget it. Come with me.'

They passed through the command chamber, entering another room beyond. This one had maps on the walls, etched in steel and marked with various Gothic labels, all looking like sides of meat cut open and marked for butchery. For the first time, she glimpsed something of Courvain's full internal complexity.

'Combat-ready yet?' Revus asked her.

'No,' she said. Then, as he raised an eyebrow, 'By my standards.'

'I'd like to have you on station.'

'Something is occurred?'

'Our location has been given away. As you said yourself, assassin – they will come for us.'

'Gloch,' she said, making the word sound like an expletive.

'Possibly. There are webs of loyalty out there.'

Khazad stared at the diagrams carefully. 'Hard to seal off, this place.'

Revus nodded. 'The lower levels, yes. But there are failsafes, and we have had time to prepare.' He moved over to the nearest schematic. 'The upper reaches are virtually impregnable from the outside. Any intruders would have to break in lower down, and move up. That is not straightforward, but we must guard carefully against infiltration.'

'I can hunt.'

Revus smiled. She had not seen him smile before, and had never gained the impression it was a common event. 'I know,' he said. 'For now, these are just precautions. The Lord Crowl will be returning shortly, as will Interrogator Spinoza.'

As he spoke, though, there was a sudden crash, one so violent that the floor shook underfoot. All across the schematic, red lights blinked on.

'This is Crowl?' Khazad asked, doubtfully.

Another boom, and the lumens flickered above them. Then more – heavy impacts, all coming from outside. Revus' gorget lit up with incoming comm-signals.

He grabbed his helm and twisted it on, hastening back the way he had come.

'No, it is not,' he said, his voice made cold and distorted by his helm's vox-filter. 'It seems you woke up at just the right time, assassin. Someone has come knocking.'

CHAPTER TEN

It was everywhere. It was growing, burgeoning, swelling, spilling from the high portals of the spires and out into the already congested courtyards and transitways. The air was crackling with it, the towers were sparking with it.

Fervour. Fear. Fury.

Spinoza drove the gunship as hard as she could, sweeping along the narrow urban chasms and skirting the very edges of the overhanging terraces. The sky ahead was a bruised mix of grey and black, scored by ranks of lightning that played across a tormented horizon. It had become hot, far more so than usual, even with the gunship's rudimentary atmospheric compensators working at full tilt.

Ahead of them, a big Ministorum gun-float was languishing, listing badly, its turbines whining. Bodies were dropping from its sides as it foundered, and if it could not right itself soon, it would collide with the hab-units drawing steadily closer. Across the other side of the canyon, a commercial vox-emitter bank had gone haywire and had started blaring nonsense from its groundcar-sized speakers. There was no sign of an Arbites presence amid all the disturbance, which was unusual – perhaps suppression units had been recalled to the Hall of Judgement.

'Do you have a loc-reading for the Lord Crowl yet?' Spinoza asked.

'I do not,' Hegain replied. 'But I also do not have a loc-reading for anyone else. I am struggling, in the truth of it, with all comms.'

Spinoza swore under her breath. Maintaining reliable feeds on a teeming, crumbling world like Terra was always a challenge, and now the skies themselves seemed to be intervening unhelpfully. 'Courvain?' she asked.

'Intermittent,' he said. 'But they know we are coming.'

She glanced at the flight console, and noted the citadel's marker-rune drifting into the forward scanner. 'Throne, this is congested,' she muttered.

There was never a time when Terra's skies were not scarred and piled with fleets of intermingling vehicles, all flocking and darting and lumbering among themselves and between their thousands of receiving hangars, but something did seem to be shifting in greater numbers now, like some great blind and panicked migration, converging from a number of separate compass-points and piling into the choked airspace.

'Almost there now,' Hegain offered.

'Ever seen a storm like this, sergeant?' Spinoza asked, maintaining her high speed despite the narrowing volume of space.

'I have not, lord,' he said.

'Any idea what could have caused it?'

'None at all, lord.'

Spinoza grunted, pulling hard to starboard to avoid colliding with a big personnel carrier decked out in the livery of an urban-sector contagion controller. The sodium-glare of hab-lumens smeared past them, long streaks in a mess of angry crimson. She found herself recognising some of the spire profiles as those of central Salvator, and realised just how habituated she had become to her new home.

'Damn it all,' she swore, ducking under the heavy linked containers of a cargo-lifter. A bulky adamantium ore-casket swept overhead, nearly snagging on the gunship's rear tail-fin, then she had to pull hard to swing them round before tumbling into the oncoming air-intake of a worker transport.

Hegain made no comment, but quietly gripped the cockpit's moulded doorframe.

'More up ahead,' Spinoza grunted, tilting the Brawler to angle it between a phalanx of private grav-cars.

Hegain leaned forward, studying the scanners. 'They look...' he started, then ran his fingers over the augur controls.

Courvain finally appeared up ahead, its wizened, crow-dark flanks overlooked by the titanic spires clustered around it. For a moment, framed by the mountainous architecture and illuminated by the bloody electrical storm, it all looked horribly vulnerable, lit up by lightning flashes, bright-white against the dark stone.

'But that is not lightning,' said Hegain, taking up the bolter controls again.

It was las-fire, a whole storm of it, flickering and smacking from the muzzles of dozens of aircraft, all spiralling and ducking around Courvain's spiked summit like flies drawn to a sucrose-stick.

'Damn,' Spinoza swore again, dragging the Brawler out wide to avoid colliding with a drifting procession of commodity-transports. 'Any insignia on those ships?'

'None that I can see,' Hegain reported, training his sights on the closest of them. They were still too far out for a shot, too blocked by the flabby shoals of lesser craft. 'I do not, I surmise, even recognise the profiles.'

Spinoza squinted, dropping the gunship lower then shooting clear around a static-crackling comm-relay tower. 'Neither do I. Some of ours are up there, though.'

The augurs picked up friendlies, and overlaid them on the tactical screen. A few Shades were fighting hard, outnumbered and burning, and some Nighthawks were also still airborne, firing back in a tiered series of corkscrewing dogfights. These were horribly outnumbered, and as the Brawler closed in, Spinoza saw one blown apart by a volley of hard-round hits, its rear engines detonating in a shower of sparks.

'I shall attempt to break through,' Spinoza said, swerving clear of the final dregs of traffic and boosting straight at Courvain's embattled turrets. 'Though I do not like these numbers.'

Even in the confusion of the darkness, the ceaseless movement, the backdrop of crowded skies, it was clear the enemy vessels far outnumbered those scrambled by Courvain's hangars. These aircraft were mainline battle fighters – bigger than the citadel's gunships, sleeker, liveried in a nondescript dark grey. Their short, swung-forward wings were designed for aerial manoeuvrability, and they appeared to be decked out with high-power las weaponry. At least one of Courvain's hangar entrances was burning and semi-blocked with wreckage, and more shots were landing. At ground level, where dozens of transitways intersected with entrance gates across many vertical levels, palls of smoke rose, bitter with the stench of spilled promethium.

Hegain pinned one of the enemy craft with the Brawler's attack augur, marking it on the scanners with a crimson skull-rune. Spinoza adjusted her angle to give him as clear a shot as possible, and they hurtled into range. Hegain opened fire, raking it with bolts that pinged and exploded across heavy armour plate.

The vessel immediately ducked out of contact, tilting heavily and dropping like a stone. Spinoza went after it, throwing the Brawler into a dive. Hegain fired again, smacking three shots into the rear of the fighter, impacting on the afterburning thruster and triggering the first explosion. It tumbled over and over, igniting more blasts, before careening straight into a transitway. The wreckage blew apart, throwing ground vehicles off the main reservation and cracking the asphalt open.

Three more fighters immediately swerved from the main attack, breaking away from their assault on the citadel to intercept.

'That got their attention,' Spinoza said, yanking the Brawler round hard. Hegain switched to control of the starboard cannon and sent a volley of projectiles spraying at the incoming fighters, none of which appeared to trouble their armour much. ·

Lasfire soon streaked in, spiking in disciplined bursts. Spinoza banked, waggling the Brawler's stocky wings to generate unpredictable flight, but several bolts hit home, slicing cleanly through the gunship's ventral plating.

Hegain switched back to the main bolter, punching a burst of shots across the diving noses of the incoming fighters. One was struck directly, its cockpit exploding in a rain of armourglass, but the other two angled away expertly, maintaining their own counter-barrage of las-fire.

Spinoza cut power to the main turbines, forcing the Brawler into a dizzying plummet, before sweeping back up barely twenty metres away from Courvain's steep-angled sides. Hegain worked the bolter again, striking another fighter but this time failing to pierce its armour.

By now, Courvain's few remaining Nighthawks were being picked off, and more of the grey fighters were turning inward to mop up the remains. Even as the Brawler thrust hard to gain loft, a Shade cartwheeled away down into the canyon depths, its back aflame and leaking ink-thick smoke. The fires below raged more intensely, slapping the knees of the citadel, fanned and fuelled by the dropping carcasses of downed aircraft.

They were hit again, a salvo from the left-hand side that nearly slammed them straight into the citadel's outer skin. Spinoza grabbed the control column two-handed and wrenched them back on course, pushing over the raking attack from one fighter before wheeling away from a pincer movement from another.

'If I may say it, lord…' Hegain began calmly, now firing steadily at anything in range.

'I *know*, sergeant,' Spinoza spat, riding the judder and spinning them away from a combined las-spear. 'Almost there.'

Now they were getting hit hard. The gunship's left wing perforated, the engines shrieked. Even as they shot up towards the citadel's summit, a scatter of las-bolts peppered their undercarriage, cracking the outer hull open and spearing up into the rear compartments. The cockpit filled with whistling air as the pressure-seals failed.

Hegain took a final shot, emptying the main bolter's ammo feed and managing to smash the wings from a banking fighter, but by now the consoles were smoking and the armourglass was spidered with cracks. More fighters tilted, coming around for the final attack, far too many to stop.

Spinoza cut the engines' power completely. The gunship, which had been streaking near-vertically, slammed to a near-halt. A whole swarm of las-bolts punched into the citadel's armour above them, lancing through the volume of airspace they would have occupied a split-second later.

The drop in momentum was impeccably timed – they drew up alongside the last of the unencumbered hangar entrances, and Spinoza kicked the power back in. The gunship swivelled, toppling back to horizontal. The hangar bay opened up before them – a metal-strewn mass of burning chassis – before they were hit again, knocking them inside and sending the Brawler tilting crazily over on its side.

'Brace!' Spinoza shouted, grabbing the cockpit's inner frame.

They hit the apron, dragging along and tumbling over, smashing a wing and sending the cannon-barrels flying. They smashed into the remains of a downed Shade, which brought their skid to a shuddering halt. The engines blew in a welter of superheated propeller blades, and the last panes of armourglass exploded into shards.

'Still with me, sergeant?' shouted Spinoza, feeling the hot trickle of blood down the inside of her helm.

'Absolutely, lord, yes, I very much am,' said Hegain groggily, pushing the remains of his control column from him and trying to clamber out of the mishmash of metal.

'Good,' said Spinoza, reaching for her weapon and pushing the cockpit door-release. 'We are alive, we are inside – this isn't over yet.'

The chamber hummed with the muffled throb of many machines. Every surface vibrated. The air felt soup-thick and resonant. Cables lay everywhere, coiled together, tangled up, lashed into bundles and piled high across the mist-wreathed floor. Some were the thickness of a child's waist, ribbed with iron bands and studded with glowing status monitors. Others hung from the distant roof in loops, or slithered down the bare metal walls amid rows of hooks, glistening in the darkness with coiled ophidian reflectiveness.

The only light was a faint green tinge, welling up from hidden floor-level sources and barely scraping across the mass of iron and plastek. The entire place was choked and claustrophobic, like the space-spare interior of some starship engine, wrapped up with conduits, valves and feeder lines. Every tread risked stepping on another slippery length of cabling or sinking into an oily pool of coolant. From up ahead, hidden by the steam and the darkness, came the echoing sound of breathing, slow and halting.

Gorgias bobbed gingerly, his lumens casting white pools across the jumbled ephemera, illuminating very little.

'*Obscura*,' he murmured, keeping his needle-gun extended.

Crowl activated night-augmentation across both his implant lenses, sharpening things up a little, but still the gloom was suffocating. Breathing was hard. The place seemed as much like a natural cavern as a manmade space, a relic of some old water-gouged sinkhole that had somehow erupted up into the guts of the Nexus' rockcrete foundations.

'Ahead,' he said, ignoring a number of orifices that led both left and right through the jungle of pipework. 'Follow the breathing.'

Progress was slow and treacherous. One enormous fibre-bundle had to be clambered over with effort, and Crowl's gloves slipped from its greasy surface. By the time he slid down the far side, his uniform was smeared with gelatinous stains.

The breaths became louder, welling up through the narrow passages ahead, neither speeding up nor slowing down. After a while, something else underpinned it – the *thud-thud, thud-thud* of a deeper heartbeat, slightly staggered, as if heard through a faulty stethoscope. The chamber's loops and coils shivered in time with it, such that the entire labyrinth began to feel like some vast internal organ, lubricated with bodily fluids, all as hot as blood.

Eventually they crept through a final aperture and emerged into what felt like a much larger space, though its true extent could only be guessed at due to the immense volume of cabling that now clogged and criss-crossed its entire volume. Every one of the hundreds of strands and fibres met here, wrapped around one another and plaited up and hung and plugged into a gaggle of reason-defying complexity. Every surface was draped in the arachnid twists, an orgy of coupling and decoupling, its moist uniformity broken only by the faint pulses of green light that darted down the carriage of the greater trunks.

All inputs terminated ahead, drawn together and gathered up into an organ-like screen of hammered iron. Mechanical devices ticked and chuntered in front of it, interposed with ancient-looking chronometers and timepieces. A hundred picter lenses flickered and scrolled, each one displaying screeds of minuscule runes, though there were no servitors or adepts to tend them.

Beyond the clots of webbing, a high arch rose up more than ten metres. Under the arch was a thick screen of what looked to be plexiglass, and behind the screen was a boiling, green-hued miasma. The cables entered the tank through a series of heavy iron plugs, disappearing into the liquid murk beyond and thereafter drawn, blurrily, towards a hidden central point behind the glass.

Crowl looked up at the screen, studied it for a moment, then bowed respectfully.

'Magister,' he said, crossing his arms. Then he waited.

Within the tank, the blurred cables twitched. A line of bubbles rose up from the depths, rising slowly through thick liquid. The heartbeat, which still sounded oddly layered, picked up, just a little, as did the echoing breaths that went with it.

Gorgias hung back warily. '*Monstroso.*'

The liquid stirred, and sediment filtered up from the tank's depths. A shadow swam lazily out of the haze, first indistinct, then thickening and broadening, dragging cables with it. More bubbles churned, spiralling in clusters against the inner surface of the glass. The shadow darkened further, became more defined, drifting forward and upward, until an outline became properly discernible.

It had been a man, once, perhaps. Or more than a man, possibly – it was hard to tell in the brackish murk. Surely more than one set of atrophied limbs hung there, swaying gently in the tank's currents. Everything was swathed by the thick sediment, but it seemed as if more than one body hung in suspension, tightly bound up and wrapped in its amalgamated filaments. The input fronds spread out from the tangle of flesh like the spokes of a great wheel, at once holding it up and tying it down, shackling it deep within its translucent nutrient broth.

A withered, puffy mass of flesh loomed up towards the glass barrier. Its skin was folded and crumpled, like a drowned corpse, so much so that the individual features were difficult to pick out. There was an impossibly high forehead, bulging and swollen to more than five times the size of a mortal cranium. The bone mass looked to have grown exponentially, erupting in a grotesque series of bulbous ridges. Under knots of gristle, a pair of deep-sunk eyes blinked slowly. Further down the sliding crevices of pale skin, another pair of lids remained closed, lodged within a gnarled, tumescent tangle. Atrophied arms hung like tentacles in the mire, their elongated fingers slack and half-webbed. A bony, twisted torso was punctured with dozens of input jacks, each one strobing gently with tiny motes of electric discharge. The entire spectacle resembled nothing so much as a carrion-flesh jellyfish dragged up from one of Terra's mythical, pollution-acrid oceans.

It did not speak. It wasn't obvious where its mouthparts were. Its active pair of eyes blinked slowly. A rattle-ribbed chest shuddered, drawing in oxygen through ironwork gill-filters carved into what might once have been a throat. The heartbeats, now clearly distinct and overlapping, maintained an echoing rhythm. Other life-support machinery could be dimly made out within the tank's depths, wheezing, bubbling, filtering.

One of the picter lenses cleared, becoming briefly black and empty. Then a new line of text scrolled across it.

Who are you?

Crowl glanced up at the screen, before returning his gaze to the monster hanging over him. 'Inspector Ferlad Cala–'

Who are you?

'It's as good a name as any other.'

A pause. *My input streams have been terminated.*

'Yes. My doing.'

Such a thing has not happened in a hundred years.

'Many strange things have happened recently.'

The spectral outline within the tank twitched, making its trailing limbs wobble. There were definitely more than two legs there.

This is death for you.

'Perhaps.'

What do you want?

Crowl let his eyes run over some of the half-hidden equipment in the chamber as he spoke. Everything smelled foul, like chlorine mixed with excrement. The heat, the dark, the stink. It was hard to see how the thing before him, if had ever been a baseline human, could have maintained its sanity in such a place. Perhaps it hadn't.

'I toured your realm a little,' Crowl said. 'I saw things that greatly interested me. A galactic chart, showing a wound drawn across the stars. Do you know of this?'

I know of everything. That is my function.

'What is it?'

An anomaly.

'Can it be corrected?'

The eyes blinked. Fresh pulses scampered down the web of cables, making the nutrient-soup shimmer briefly.

I hear the voices of a thousand worlds in every breath I take. I feel the passage of fleets through the abyss with every heartbeat. I dream of emptiness, and I then I dream of the lines we draw across it. I calculate what must be calculated. I compass the void.

Crowl's eyes narrowed. 'Not quite the answer I was hoping for.'

You should not be here.

'But I am. That is a fact. You deal in those, I take it? And this is important, so please summon up what remains of yourself, and listen.'

The spectre hung there, unsteady on its web.

'There was a ship,' said Crowl. 'A rogue trader's galleon, plying the Laurentis subsector. It was lost, but when salvaged, records of communication were found, directed to an adept named Cassandara Glucher, who was linked to this departmento. No such woman existed at the time the messages were sent. I believe, as a result of inquiry, that those messages came to you.'

I hear the voices of a thousand worlds.

'Did you hear the voice of Naaman Vinal?'

The void shall be compassed.

'*Insanus,*' muttered Gorgias, getting agitated.

'You know why the messages were sent,' Crowl pressed. 'A xenos was to be brought to Terra. It was collected in the Torquatus Nebula, before being taken onto Vinal's ship. Then your forces ensured he and his crew were erased, and another conveyer was pressed into service. One under the Speaker's direct control, a bulker named *Rhadamanthys* with a more pliant captain.'

Do you know how many signals I process every hour? Can you even conceive of it? It is breathing to me. It is the blood in my veins.

'That ship was intended to carry the creature all the way here, but word got out. A loyal subject within this Nexus, perhaps? Or maybe just carelessness. The authorities were alerted. A search was begun. It might have succeeded, had it not been for the intervention of the Mechanicus vessel *Ohtar*, which carried the subject out of harm's way. Two great offices of state, both implicated. But I know there was another involved. You know this too. Tell me the name. Tell me the purpose of it all, and I will leave you to your schedules.'

A billion ships. All moving. All in peril. Who should mark it, if they fail? Who should mark it, if they arrive? The cargo must be landed. The blood must flow. The void must be compassed.

Crowl drew his weapon. Not the borrowed pistol with its tranq-setting, as used on the guardians, but Sanguine, his favoured revolver, taken out from its hiding place under his inspector's coat. He aimed it at the glass before him.

'Cease this babbling,' he said. 'I came here for answers.'

We hear all. We process all. As we are ended, all is ended. The head cannot endure, if the heart be stopped.

Gorgias began to rove around the edge of the tank, getting impatient, looking for something more promising to interrogate.

'I will not leave before I have a name,' Crowl said, patiently.

I hear the voices of a thousand worlds.

Crowl cocked the pistol, choosing a spot at the base of the armourglass. The volume of liquid within the tank was hard to gauge, but the chamber was substantial. On the balance of probabilities, the creature would suffer more from its destruction than he would.

'Tell me the name,' he said again.

You are wasting your time.

Gorgias spun around, startled. Crowl kept his revolver trained on the glass. Another terminal had activated. Within the nutrient broth, the second pair of eyes flickered, twitched, then opened.

Luna-made. It should have a twin, too. A fine piece, inquisitor.

Crowl lowered his revolver. 'To whom am I speaking now?'

The same. We have been together a long time. His mind is devoted to the great lattice, mine to the minor lattice. I sleep, when I can. He never does.

Gorgias swept in close again, scanning harder. '*Fratres*,' he murmured, intrigued. '*Conjuncta.*'

How could it be otherwise?

'But you are lucid,' Crowl said. 'And you know your weapon-marques.'

I understand a great deal. Such as your name and rank, Lord Phaelias of the Ordo Xenos.

'Ah. Well, there you have me.'

I am impressed you are still alive.

'My questions remain the same.'

The Magister twitched in the tank. Its greater half, with the swollen cerebrum, appeared uncomfortable, and a withered limb slapped against the glass, leaving a long smear.

As I told you, this is a waste of your time. If my mistress ever had much of an interest in this scheme, it is over. The instigators have moved on, the moment has passed. Records of her involvement will be impossible to retrieve now, here or elsewhere.

'I find it hard to believe this was just a passing fancy.'

She has more pressing matters to attend to.

'Such as the missing signals from the north galactic arm.'

So you may suppose.

'What *is* that?'

Something that does not concern you.

Gorgias hissed in frustration. Crowl walked up to one of the major cable-clusters, and ran Sanguine's muzzle idly down its spine. 'It must be a living nightmare,' he said, lifting the barrel and watching the watery slime trickle down it. 'Force-fed all this data, hour after hour.'

You cannot comprehend it.

'Try me.'

The eyelids blinked in the broth, sending tiny bubbles rising up again. *Every major convoy reports every hour. Determinations are sent to astropathic choirs. They are relayed to sector commands. Collations are transmitted here, interpreted and ordered. He sees it all. He sees it as a mortal man sees a painting – all in one glance.*

We process all.

And when you understand the Imperium in this way, when you see it as a single organism, unified within time and space, you understand where its deficiencies lie, where its needs are greatest, where scarce coin maybe be best employed.

'And you would see it preserved.'

For eternity.

'Then *help* me,' Crowl urged, spinning back to face the glass. 'I need a name, the purpose behind it, then I will leave you in peace.'

Why do you care so much? It was a failure. If a High Lord can walk away from it, why can't you?

In a flash, he saw the dream-face superimposed there, projected on to those warped and melded features, licking its lips, goading him, never letting him sleep.

'You have your duty,' he said stiffly. 'I have mine.'

The creature rose up, its web pulling taut. *No more of this. Go now. I already told you – there is nothing for you here.*

A billion ships. All moving.

Crowl withdrew a few paces, taking cover behind a heap of cabling, and aimed Sanguine again, picking a spot near the base of the armourglass.

'A name,' he said.

The Magister withdrew into its nutrients, trailing black lines behind it.

Go now.

Gorgias took cover. 'Do it now!' the skull shrieked. '*Rapido*, quick-quick!'

Crowl tensed. This would likely be unpleasant.

'You had your chance,' he muttered grimly, and fired.

CHAPTER ELEVEN

Revus hit cover, crouched down, took aim, and fired his hellpistol.

One of the grey-clad attackers took the shot in the chest and flew backwards, crashing into a cargo-crate and cracking its plasteel bracing. The warriors running with him scrambled for protection, skidding behind more piles of crates and chain-shackled metal tubes. Revus' own squad – five strong – took up position around him and picked their targets.

The chamber was a big one – a receiving depot for sundry goods ordered by the quartermaster's department. At one end stood tall slide doors capable of receiving a beta-grade land-transport, all but one of which were closed and locked, the final one blown open and dangling on a single hinge. At the other end, where Revus had entered, was a row of smaller openings leading back into the citadel's innards. In between was a heaped maze of containers, many piled up close to the roof. Between those containers and the various piles of items waiting for onward transmission were a series of narrow trackways for slaved servitors. A couple of mech-lifters, powered-down and dormant, stood up ahead, already blackened from las-burns.

As he hunkered down, the las-fire scything overhead, Revus' helm-feed swam with updates from elsewhere in the citadel. It was already looking bad. They had not been hit by a lone infiltrator, nor even a small group of them, but an entire army. It beggared belief that a force so capable and so large had been mustered and deployed so quickly – unless, of course, they had been held prepped and ready for this very eventuality.

'Hold the refectory level,' Revus voxed to the command-group stationed there. 'Vaf's heavy weapons will be there in moments.' He switched scope to the main elevator-spine, where the fighting was already fierce. 'Pull back to intersection five,' he ordered. 'You're taking too many casualties.'

He was firing the whole time, emerging from cover for split-seconds before pulling back again.

The invaders filtered forward using the plentiful cover. Whatever else they might have been, they were well-trained. Having blasted their way in, they were now overlapping one another and advancing up the narrow passages. They seemed to be universally kitted out with lasrifles, perhaps not the equal of the storm trooper's enhanced hellguns, but certainly on a par with Militarum-issue weapons. Their armour was light but effective. They wore closed-face helms with narrow eye-slits, all in dark grey with no livery visible. None of them had spoken or issued demands – they had just smashed through the air-cordon, landed troop-carriers and burst out across a whole gamut of the lower levels.

Revus scampered down the length of the container, reached the far end, swung round, fired blind, then snapped back into cover. A pain-filled grunt from the end of the chamber told him he'd hit something, but the storm of las-bolts coming back at him, frying and chipping the container's edge, also told him there were plenty more.

He slid down to the ground, knocked the spent powerpack out of the holder and slammed a fresh one in. The air was beginning to smell of burning, and the chamber echoed to the strangely muted sounds of lasgun combat.

Over to the right, two of his troops, a man named Jusdin and a woman named Ilu, were creeping forward under the protection of long, chained-up metal tubes. Behind him, the three others – Hafal, Pieter and Slovia – were attempting to edge left. Revus stayed where he was, hugging the container's charred metal edging, trying to get an augur scan of numbers. The container must have held food supplies, for the stink of protein-sticks filled his nostrils.

He heard a thud, a smack, and the clatter of boots – they were attempting to rush him.

He spun back the way he'd come, dropping low and rolling face-down into the trackway. He got three shots off, hitting two invaders, before return fire forced him to wriggle back out of view. Jusdin managed to clamber higher and unleashed a volley down at the onrushers, dropping one of them. Slovia pulled the pin on a frag grenade and sent it spinning into the channel. It detonated in a cloud of metal shards, shredding through a three-metre tower of packing units and making the whole space echo from the explosion.

Hafal and Revus took advantage of the blast to move forward again, holding their bodies low and firing through the debris. More cries from the tottering crates told of shots finding their mark, and the two of them reached the shadow of a mech-lifter stuck in the midst of a tarp-wrapped heap of sacking.

The enemy troops fell back. Revus' helm display lit up with detected heat signatures – more than two-dozen now, creeping closer. Out of the corner of his eye, he glimpsed more shadows against the distant left-hand wall. He saw Pieter and Slovia sidling up to his position, and waved them back.

Too many, he indicated in battle-sign.

Then there was another explosion, and a column of cargo-crates blasted apart. Grey-armoured shapes charged through the wreckage.

Revus ducked out of cover, still holding himself low. He heard Hafal cry out but had to keep moving, sprinting back towards the containers as more grenades detonated. One impact-wave caught him, nearly throwing him from his feet, but he crashed into the edge of the container and used it to keep him upright. He saw a flash of grey amid the tumbling fragments and took a snapshot, hitting an oncoming warrior in the visor.

Then there were more of them, charging up through the splinters, firing as they came. Revus dived for cover again, feeling the hot ping of las-fire at his feet. He could hear Slovia shouting something, but couldn't see where she was.

He whirled around, glimpsing an enemy bursting out just ahead of him, no more than five metres away. He fired, striking him in the torso, but another leapt up behind the first and fired back. Revus was struck in the shoulder, knocked from his feet and sent skidding. He tried to brace, to get another shot out, but something else – something blurred with speed and movement and velocity – got in the way.

Momentarily disorientated, it took him a moment to recognise Khazad, springing from the shadows, flinging herself out into the open without heed for cover or protection. She seemed to spin straight through the las-beams, arcing around and across them, before crunching in close to the grey-armoured soldier. Her blade flashed gold, and he toppled, his breastplate torn open. She pounced back, hitting another, slicing across his throat, before checking against the edge of the lifter and springing into contact with a third.

Revus clambered back to his feet, his ears ringing. Hafal's life-reading was gone, and he saw Pieter hobbling backwards, trying to reload even as fresh las-bolts whizzed past. Out on the far side of the chamber, where the broken slide-door remained open, he saw a personnel carrier rumble into the depot. It looked to have flamers mounted on its armoured back, already swinging round and looking for targets.

He reached for his own frag grenade, primed it and threw it down the central trackway.

Pull back, he signed, voxing the same command over the squad-comm.

They responded instantly – he saw Slovia darting down the flank, weaving between crates. Jusdin fired a blistering las-volley down from his vantage before leaping away as the crates were blown apart, crunching to the floor then running.

Revus was the last, retreating ahead of the advancing carrier and dropping any infantry that got too eager for the chase. Khazad loped past him, freed up by the covering fire laid down by Ilu and Pieter. They reached the first of the open portals, released a final mass of las-bolts, then piled through and slammed the blast-doors closed as the storm of return fire scorched the frame. Hafal wasn't with them.

Slovia ran down the corridor, locking the rest of the portals. Jusdin reloaded while Pieter pulled a reel of plastape from his medipac and wrapped it around a thigh-wound. Khazad leaned over, her armour splattered with crimson, panting hard.

'Doors will not hold them long,' she said.

Already there were thuds from within the depot, the scrape of heavier weapons being drawn up. The carrier itself might not be able to come further in, but its contents were clearly being unloaded.

Revus consulted his tactical scope. 'We'll rendezvous with Milo's squads here,' he said, transmitting the coordinates of the next choke-point up, the conjunction of three major passages into the main spine columns. 'Keep moving.'

Ilu laced each doorway with wire-spring charges, and then they were running again, back up, away from the ingress points. This was their third fighting retreat, and the same thing was happening all across the lower levels.

'Too many,' voxed Khazad, sounding disgusted. 'Where are from?'

'I do not know,' replied Revus, his mind already turning to the next set of encounters. He didn't have the numbers. It didn't matter how many invaders they dropped, for they seemingly had the resources to spare, and his defenders were running out of room. A few more levels up, and they'd be into Courvain's command structure, and after that the Lord Crowl's own chambers. They were being forced upwards, squeezed like blood in a vein.

'We hold them at the next one,' Khazad urged, her activated powerblade swinging as she ran. 'Bleed them good.'

He wanted to agree. All across his feed, he could see the signals of his units being forced back, forced up, crammed into the dead-end that would see them all crushed up together.

'Keep moving,' he said again, grimly, feeling the wound in his shoulder start to burn. 'We'll do what we can.'

Huk heard them coming before she saw them. That was often the way with her – tied-down into the structure of the citadel by her synapse cabling, she had come to think herself as a part of it, a spur jutting from its bones, a cell within its bloodstream. She might not be explicitly told much, nor get out to see for herself what was taking place, but she felt the tremors and listened to the echoes.

So now she waited patiently as the vibrations grew. She felt the walls shudder, and knew that they must have broken through the airborne defences and through the outer walls. That was something that had never happened before, not in her experience at least. As far as she knew, there were no records of the citadel ever being successfully invaded, though even her tomes didn't stretch all the way back to the place's foundation, so you never knew.

'Crowl will be angry,' she said, tutting. She hoisted her ragged skirts and shuffled over to her ring of cogitator columns. 'I wonder if he can be back yet.'

The shelves above her, rising up to the summit of the archive's vaulted ceiling, were empty of servitors. Some of the books had already been carted away, but most remained. There was no room elsewhere for the tonnes and tonnes of material that needed to be stored – the depositories here occupied a considerable portion of Courvain's bulk, stretching deep into the dark recesses of its creaking structure.

She reached the cogitators, and adjusted the chain across her shoulders. Her oculus whirred, giving her a scan-view of the chamber-floor. It smelled very musty. It smelled of decay. She hadn't noticed that before, and wondered why she did so now. Perhaps it was the girl, Spinoza. Huk liked Spinoza, for all that she was a starched, stiff product of her education and breeding. Her instincts were in the right place.

There was another crash, then a squeal of metal against metal. The floor juddered, throwing up little wavelets of dust.

Huk frowned. It should never have got that dusty, not without her being aware of it. Had she slipped that far? Had she forgotten about the small things, amid all the constant demands?

It had been different, in the beginning. Her robes had been finer, her sense of confinement less onerous. It was still a prestigious job, and Crowl had always made sure her contribution was recognised. Somewhere, though, somehow, things had become stale. She had retreated into herself, letting the high walls of the archive hem her in. For a long time, all there had been for her were the old parchments, the ragged leather spines, staring at her from their high eyries. Perhaps she had let that happen. Perhaps there should have been more.

'The girl was right,' Huk murmured. 'This is disordered.'

There was a boom, one that rang up along the high space and shook more dust down from the shelves. The great metal doors, the ones she had locked closed herself just a few moments ago, flexed inward.

Huk turned to face them, a wry smile cracking her desiccated features. She placed her hands, with their long iron fingers, across her lap.

A second boom, and the doors blew open. Smoke tumbled across the stone floor, and warriors entered through it. They were grim-looking, bearing no icon or sigil that she recognised. Their armour was dark-grey, their helms blank. They carried lasguns two-handed, treading warily into the open and scanning for threats.

One of them, their captain presumably, approached her. She watched him come. His troops fanned out, pointing their gun-muzzles up into the high vault. She counted thirty, with more no doubt outside. She could hear the sounds of fighting from the corridors – the snap of las-fire, the thud of bodies hitting the deck, the cries of the wounded.

He came to a halt, regarding her. It seemed he was trying to work out what kind of thing she was. That was understandable. For a long time, Yulia Huk had been engaged in much the same activity.

'This is the main archive, boy,' she said, smiling sweetly. 'There's nothing for you here. If you have a quarrel with the master of this place, I suggest you keep heading upwards. Though I can't imagine why you'd have a quarrel with him, or any of us.'

The captain looked up, peering into the distance. Then he swung his gaze around, scanning across the metres and metres of shelving. Although it was impossible to get a sense of his expression under all that grey plate, everything in his stance and manner indicated disdain.

He looked back at her.

'Of course,' Huk said, tweaking the cables around her a little, 'if you had a request for something specific, I'm sure I could find it for you.'

He lifted his lasgun, pointing it right at her.

'No?' asked Huk, resignedly. 'Very well. I was nothing if not polite.'

She let the electro-pulse run down her cables and into the archive's central retrieval lattice. The response was instantaneous, like a nervous system twinging. Plates blew open, chains rattled down, grapple-hooks flew. From every cubbyhole, every alcove, every storage hopper, the servitors burst out, capering on their over-muscled arms. Their eyes blank, their mouths gaping, they hurled themselves at the invaders, smashing into armour and tearing at it with their knife-sharp fingers. They scrabbled and scattered like grey-fleshed, metal-pinned primates, flailing and capering before ripping into those who had crossed the threshold into their hidden realm.

Courvain's archives were large and well-tended. Over a hundred retrieval drones worked here, built for access-speed and agility across the high places. Their cortexes were simple, but their bodies were unusually honed for a servitor-cadre, with digital augmetics that could serve just as well as combat-blades if the need arose. Huk controlled them all with absolute precision – one of the very few advantages of her unfortunate, locked-down status.

The captain whirled away from her, switching his aim towards the bestial figures suddenly leaping at his men.

Deftly, smoothly, Huk withdrew the old gun she'd used once as Crowl's savant, the one that she'd had to relearn how to use with her new iron fingers. She aimed it at the man's back, and fired. The las-beam burned a tight hole in his armour, felling him instantly.

'Still got it,' she murmured, with a definite air of self-congratulation, then picked her next target.

CHAPTER TWELVE

The glass, taut under pressure from the liquid behind it, exploded into thick, spinning pieces.

Crowl dropped to his knees as the heavy fragments smashed into him, crashing across his hunched body and nearly sending him careening into the walls behind. Amid the roar and foaming, he was dimly aware of Gorgias riding high above it all, shrieking something, as always, about traitors and vengeance.

For a moment it felt like he'd be borne clear from his feet and dashed like a piece of flotsam on the tide's fury. Everything smashed and whirled. He staggered, slipped back, fighting back against the swell, but then, mercifully, the worst passed.

He steadied himself, drenched by the fast-draining torrent, only to see the Magister coming right at him amid the last dregs of its tank's contents.

Crowl fired again, winging the creature, but it was surprisingly fast, shrugging off its mooring strands and swinging down to attack him. It was still semi-tethered, borne up by its main electro-pulse cables, but out of its suspension fluid it was even fouler than it had been before – a half-rotted, blanched twist of puffy flesh and cartilage. Its huge cranial mass unbalanced it, toppling crazily like an infant's head atop a withered scrap of sinew, but, for all that, its thick web of rope-ties kept it upright and directed. The core cables were steel-wound lengths with a prehensile strength of their own, making the Magister the central node of a whole network of lashing strands.

Crowl fired a third time, retreating steadily. The stench of it was intense. It screamed – somehow, for no mouth-parts were visible – in a painful, gurgling wail, spilling fluids from its every gushing orifice.

Gorgias flew in close, peppering it with shots before being swatted away by one of the flail-like cables. The skull smacked hard into a glistening bulkhead, its spinal trail sparking.

Then the monster was on Crowl, sweeping down from its wrecked tank, reaching out to claw at him with its atrophied limbs. For an instant, just as he looked up into its combined, overlapping mess of once-human features, he saw the familiar, hateful dream-image imposed there, just as grey, just as foul, laughing.

'No!' he roared out loud, firing again, right into the monster's cortex-folds. Blood spurted from the wound, black as oil, adding to the slicks of fluids spurting and caking everything.

It slapped down on him heavily, its sagging flesh smothering, its drapery of strands winding rapidly around his limbs. Something burst along its haunches, flooding more thick liquid across the already swimming floor.

Crowl struggled to breathe. Its weight was alarming, and only out of the tank did its true size become apparent – despite the withering of its birth-limbs, its residual body must have been pumped with stimms while hanging in that broth, its brain and facial tissue swelling beyond all reason.

He pushed back, his arm-muscles shrieking with pain, and managed to shove it to one side. He gulped a breath, scrambling to get out from under it. As he did so, its secondary pair of eyes glared at him from within the folds and humps of mottled skin, bloodshot and furious. Crowl somehow kept hold of Sanguine, and tried to haul it out of the gaggle of dripping limbs and cables. One of the strands whipped around his throat, tightening up with appalling speed.

Crowl grabbed at the garrotte with his free hand, yanking it clear from his neck, then tried to get another shot away. The smell was overpowering, a wet stink of putrified muscle and chemicals. The Magister was abhorrently strong, but also palpably weakening. The gill-flaps along its chest were trembling, trying to drag in the liquid that was no longer there.

More cables snapped at him, whistling around his neck, his chest, his arms, locking him down. The bulbous head loomed higher, a twisted, intermingled mess of twin faces, one massive, one dwarfed. The primary twin's expression was contorted, its eyes glazed and unfocused. The secondary twin's mangled features were still more coherent, albeit sharpened into fury.

The throat-cables tightened. Crowl began to feel his vision blackening, and ripped harder at the coils. He managed to wrest Sanguine out of the creature's grasp, and fired again at point-blank range. The bullet punched wetly into the Magister's hide, folded up into the sucking mass of fat and muscle, and that slowed the creature down. Several of the strands went limp, including the one around his neck.

Gasping in deeper breaths, Crowl fought back, kicking out against the whirling mass of cables. He could feel his strength waning, just as the creature's was – this had to be decided quickly.

Finally, Gorgias returned to the fray, his oculus fizzing with static but his needle-gun evidently intact. The skull flew at the Magister's primary face, spraying him with darts. The tumescent structure shrunk back, its tethered limbs spasming, and Crowl seized his chance. He thrust Sanguine into what passed for the lesser twin's throat – a wattle of slack skin and nodules – and held it there.

'That's *enough*,' he snarled, twisting the muzzle into the press of loose flesh.

The secondary eyes narrowed. The creature shivered, its gill-flaps sucking emptily, its twisted chest cavity heaving.

Crowl hauled cables from his shoulders and pulled himself free of the creature's embrace, all the while keeping the revolver pressed against the throat. Gorgias spun around, jerking and bumping, sending a final volley of needles into the thing's twisted spine-ridge.

The Magister shuddered. Its feeble lungs spasmed, once, twice. Its limbs flapped wetly on the draining floor.

'What purpose can you have now… for keeping this secret?' Crowl panted, throwing the last of the cables off, pushing himself free of the clutching flesh. 'Even now, it is not too late. You could be restored. Tell me what I need to know. A medicae team can be here within moments.'

The Magister twitched, coughing out bloody-flecked liquid. After a moment, Crowl realised that was as close as it could get to a laugh. He glanced up at the picter lens above him, wondering if the link was still intact.

Why do you think

The runes ran across the lens slowly now, tracking under the cracked glass as if being typed by a child.

having seen this, having seen all this,

Suddenly Crowl knew what it was going to say. He knew why the creature had goaded him, denying him information, making him angry.

that we would wish to live?

Then it shuddered, its foul body going limp, its eyes staring, its tentacles falling slack.

'*Miserabilis*,' spat Gorgias contemptuously, drifting lower to hover over its ruined features.

Crowl slumped a little. All this effort, all this risk, for nothing. Slowly, he pushed the last of the slackened cabling from his limbs, untangling himself from the matrix of overlapping tresses.

He stood, shakily, feeling the effects of the fight bear down on him. He needed to get back, now. He needed help from Erunion.

'*Iterum*,' Gorgias said, bobbing up higher again.

'I think not,' said Crowl, wearily holstering Sanguine. 'It is ended.'

'*Stupidus!*' the skull blurted, agitated again. 'Other one! Hurry, *momento – alterum geminae*.'

Of course. The conjoined twin, the one that had been turned into a biological data processor, its waking mind long gone. Crowl scrabbled to reach it, stretching out across the corpse and hauling it over, turning it so that the swollen cranium rolled clumsily into view.

The primary set of eyes was still open, blinking in confusion. Its gill-flaps were still wobbling, trying futilely to suck.

Crowl knelt over it.

'You had the harder path,' he said softly. 'If there is anything left within you, any residual memory of duty, you can still redeem it all.'

The eyes looked up at him in bewilderment, almost lost under the knots and crags of its grotesque skull. How long had it taken to turn a mortal man, albeit of a unique kind, into this tortured landslip of agony?

'The transmissions came here,' Crowl said, patiently. 'You processed them. You know who conceived this plan, and who will try it again. Tell me. Tell me now, and I can end your pain forever.'

Another blink. Now there was fluid pooling under the lids. The gills stopped trembling.

Crowl dared to look up at the first set of lenses, the ones it had used to speak through. Nothing new appeared.

'Anything that you can,' he said, watching in hope. 'Any data, of whatever kind, before the end.'

It quivered, then thrashed out, as if suddenly consumed by fear. Then it fell still.

Slowly, Crowl bowed his head, balling his fists in frustration. He remained like that for a few moments. Then he straightened, reached out, and closed the creature's grey lids. He stood up, sluicing down the worst of the sticky fluids from his uniform.

'So, that's that,' he said, grimly.

But then, overhead, the picter lens flickered again. Perhaps caught by some delay-loop, or maybe the last glimmer of dying neural ganglia, words appeared.

There was a sea of glass.

Crowl looked up at it. Gorgias swooped down to get a view. The same text repeated.

There was a sea of glass.

Crowl frowned. Gorgias spun around, irritated.

'Nonsense,' the skull opined. '*Ineptias.*'

'Its life, I suppose, as it saw it,' Crowl said, eyes narrowing.

He looked back at the shattered screen, the only thing it had known for such a very long time. 'Its whole world.'

A final line, terminated abruptly.

There was a sea o

The picter's cursor blinked, on, off, though no further characters emerged.

Gorgias lost interest.

'Have to get out,' the skull said, swinging back to face the way they had come. 'Now now, *celero, celero.*'

Crowl knew the truth of it. Somewhere, in one of the Nexus' many hundred cells, someone would surely have noticed by now that the Magister Calculo Horarium IX's output had terminated, and be requesting a service team to investigate.

His uniform coat was filthy. The guardians at the gates would be reviving at some point. The journey back to the transport would be as long as the inward passage, but with less effective cover and more reason to be stopped.

He began to reload Sanguine, though even that familiar gesture made his fingers ache. As the last of the nutrient-fluid drained into the culverts, he turned away from the stinking scene of carnage.

'Home again,' he said to Gorgias, working to summon the energy that would be needed. 'With nothing much to show save destruction. We must hope that Spinoza has done better.'

Spinoza pivoted around, dropping to her knee and aiming her hand cannon. The pursuing troops rounded the corner, and she shot into them, blasting two against the far wall before the rest scrambled to retreat.

Hegain, crouching at her shoulder, reloaded his autopistol. 'Recognise them?' he asked, slamming the magazine home.

By then Spinoza was retreating again, running back down into Courvain's heart. 'No,' she said. 'Was hoping you might.'

Hegain kept up with her, breathing heavily. Since breaking into the hangar, it had been non-stop fire-fights against the gangs of invaders, who seemed to have penetrated multiple levels of the citadel and were converging with speed on the main access routes. They were like an army of blanks – voiceless, demand-less, without identity or badge. They fought professionally but recklessly, throwing bodies at problems. That approach might have been wasteful, but it was effective – the corridors rang with alarms and there were the sounds of distant explosions everywhere, but Revus' long-prepared defences seemed to have been brutally smashed aside, at least in the sectors they were running through.

They reached a wider, better-lit passage. Armoury-lockers ran along one wall, though all were empty now – the contents taken, Throne willing, by defenders who were now using them elsewhere. A long series of black burn-marks ran along the opposite wall, and the remnants of broken carapace armour littered the floor. The lumens at the far end had begun to flicker, and sparking cables hung like vines from shattered panels in the ceiling.

'Strongpoint up ahead,' said Hegain, clumping along in his cumbersome enforcer gear.

'If it's still manned,' Spinoza muttered.

They sped through the locker-corridor and across an empty arming chamber. Bodies littered the floor here, both grey-armoured and those in Courvain's night-dark livery. The doors at the far end had been smashed open, and there were more corpses slumped over broken blast-panels.

Spinoza kicked through them, and saw a narrow, high-ceilinged transit artery running straight ahead. Its lumens were blown completely, and the floor-sunk servitor-rail deck was humped with more bodies, most of which had puncture wounds and las-scorches on their armour. At the far end of the corridor – a space perhaps four metres across – was a makeshift barricade, over which a bristling hedge of lasgun-muzzles protruded.

'Stay!' Spinoza shouted, holding her weapon aloft and breaking her rosette out.

Hegain advanced warily alongside her, looking over his shoulder – the sounds of pursuit had started up again, and it felt like there were more bootfalls than before.

Spinoza reached the barricade, rosette still held high. It was a staggered wall of dropped-in rockcrete sections, manned along its width by storm troopers. Their commander – a sergeant Tallis, by his unit badge – made the aquila.

'Lord Interrogator,' he said, looking somewhat doubtfully at her Arbites armour. 'Good to have you back.'

'Where is the Lord Crowl?' Spinoza demanded, taking her place behind the barricade. A trooper handed her a fully-charged hellgun, which she took up. Hegain also replaced his weapon, hunkering down next to his comrades and nestling the muzzle on the chipped surface.

'Unknown, lord.'

'Status, then.'

'Multiple hostile units attacked at chronomark zero-four-fifty, coordinated and moving fast. They have taken the lower levels, all air-access hangars and groundcar depots. We are cut off from the exits, and have lost the primary elevator columns at base station.'

'Captain Revus?'

'Holding the central convening chambers at level twenty-eight.'

The barricade was manned by fewer than thirty storm troopers, plus a scattering of Courvain's adept personnel in ill-fitting flak-armour. From the echoing clangs behind her, it sounded like a great deal more than that were coming down the corridor after them.

'Your orders, sergeant?' Spinoza asked.

'Delay them here until full personnel withdrawal to Corvus Ring complete.'

The Corvus Ring was the final layer of defence near Courvain's summit – a failsafe of military-grade blast-doors and bulwarks, capable of being defended by less than a third of Revus' full complement of troopers. The citadel was not operable for any length of time beyond that zone – its main power generators, core supply reserves and operational chambers were all located below that level – but it had been put in place as a strictly temporary measure, a response to catastrophic levels of infiltration that could only last until fresh reinforcements were called in from other ordo fortresses. The fact it was even being considered in an environment in which any reinforcement from outside was unlikely to be available showed how desperate things had already become.

'Signals incoming,' reported a trooper, crouched down behind the barricade, his helm-visor glowing from the battlefield augur-units clustered in front of him.

'Inform the captain of my location,' Spinoza ordered. 'Tell him I will rendezvous with him when I can.'

Then they arrived.

The advance was heralded by a brace of smoke-canisters thrown down the artery, tumbling and exploding in a wave of blue-tinged smog. The storm troopers opened fire immediately, piercing the wall of smoke with dozens of las-lines. Blurry shapes emerged from the far end, moving at speed.

'Frags,' ordered Spinoza, and storm troopers heaved two grenades into the murk. They exploded about fifteen metres along, shredding the clouds with their shrapnel, throwing at least one dark silhouette hard against the right-hand wall.

Lasfire burst back, punching out of the smoke and fizzing into the rockcrete wall. Storm troopers on the barricade ducked down, pausing for the barrage to subside before bobbing up again and returning fire. The ground between the forces erupted into a cat's-cradle of burning and sizzling.

The first of the enemy emerged into clarity, carrying heavy flak-shields and running straight at the barrier. Spinoza snapped a blast at the lead warrior, catching his shield and yanking it backwards. Another trooper got the next shot in, upending the shieldbearer in a splatter of blood.

Behind that one, though, came three more, all running hard and firing one-handed past their shields. The storm troopers opened up at them, blasting two to the rail-deck, but the third ducked around and gained the barricade. He was cut down there, his helm fried by a close-range las-blast even as a bayonet-thrust jabbed into his torso, but all that did was clear the way for more warriors to leap up out of the smoke.

Hegain fired incessantly, picking targets at speed. An enemy's las-bolt hit the storm trooper hunched at his side, burning between carapace plates and driving deep into the mesh-layer beneath. Spinoza shot back, but a second shieldbearer reached the barricades, crunching a defender aside and pulling a grenade out.

Spinoza saw the danger and pounced, smashing him into the rockcrete and crunching his arm under her boot. She stamped down, once, twice, as Hegain shuffled forward to cover her. She kicked the unprimed grenade away, then jammed her hellgun into his neck and fired once, searing a tunnel through the armour-seal and stilling his thrashing.

The intensity of las-fire picked up, snapping in at close quarters and making the air simmer. The enemy troops were rushing in numbers now, ignoring their dead and leaping for the barricades. The first rank of storm troopers reached for combat blades.

Hegain pushed forward, slashing his knife into the throat of a vaulting warrior. Another one breached the defences, and Spinoza shot him in the chest. He shrugged off the wound, kicking aside a storm trooper and going straight for her. Spinoza swivelled on her heel, striking out with her clenched gauntlet, catching him full in the face even as he went for a shot. Then she hit him again, and again, cracking his helm open and sending him reeling. She went after the toppling body, grabbing it by the neck-joint and hurling it around, throwing him back into the oncoming figure of yet another invader.

'Get *back!*' she roared, opening fire again as both bodies crashed to the ground, striding right into the breach, uncaring of the las-beams crackling past her. 'This is *our home!*'

She might have been back on Forfoda, charging into close-contact alongside the Imperial Fists, except that then she had been the weak link amid a strike force of demigods and now she was the linchpin of this defence. It would have been good to have Argent in her clenched fist then, to sweep it round in a welter of disruptor energies and cut through this chaff, but she only had her cumbersome armour, her heavy gauntlets and her standard issue firearm.

Hegain came with her, roaring defiance, somehow both firing accurately and slashing out with his combat knife. Tallis, on the far side of the barricade, led a more measured assault, retaking the barricade where it had been swarmed across.

The enemy fell back, with more bodies dropping as the storm

troopers' disciplined volleys caught them. For a moment, Spinoza was tempted to go after them, to hound them back to the hangars and retake the initiative. The interlopers did not know the way of the corridors like they did, the nooks and zigzags that could be used to pin an enemy down.

She resisted the temptation. She emptied the dregs of her hellgun's powerpack, then dropped back into the barricade's cover. The invaders stumbled away through the drifting snags of smoke, ducking and scampering to evade the last of the las-beams.

The bootfalls died out, the last of the smog sunk into smuts. The corridor ahead of them was heaped with bodies, most still and blotched with blood, some still moving.

Hegain drew alongside her. There was blood on his forearm, and he was panting hard.

'Our home,' he said, approvingly. 'Those were good words, lord.'

She had, indeed, spoken them. Not that she knew where they had come from.

Medics rushed to tend to the wounded. Tallis' signals operative ducked down to consult the augurs.

'Multiple signals again.' He looked up at Tallis. 'We have more incoming.'

Spinoza went over and took a look at the schematics. They were already quite high up Courvain's main structure, though still several levels below the Corvus Ring approaches. They could be cut off easily, if the enemy penetrated the service tunnels above them.

She reached for another powerpack.

'You've done all you can here, sergeant,' she said to Tallis. 'We fall back to Captain Revus' position now – get your troops together.'

Tallis nodded smartly and turned to the others, calling out orders.

Hegain looked up at her. He'd seen the signals too. 'Too many, I do believe,' he said, grimly. 'Even at the Corvus.'

'For shame, sergeant,' said Spinoza, reloading. 'Trust in Him – there will be a way.'

CHAPTER THIRTEEN

Crowl walked as an inspector would walk – not too fast, not too slow, head held high, daring anyone else to look at him.

It had not been possible to do more than a cursory clean of his uniform. He was painfully aware of what a shabby spectacle he must have looked then, with the last strands of the Magister's nutrient slime still glistening on his epaulettes. He could see the shocked stares from the bustling adepts, hastily averted. One of them, sooner or later, would start making enquiries.

He did not take the same route back as he had done coming in. Those paths were too exposed, too open to the many scrutiny lenses that floated like hummingbirds up in the globe-lit vaults. The research he had commissioned from Huk paid off now, and he was able to take a circuitous path up to different landing stages, passing through less exalted chambers – refectories, boiler-rooms, communal recreation spaces where section superintendents read out Ministorum-approved moral texts from high pulpits.

Gorgias seemed more or less recovered, though the

crustaceous mass of sensors across his cranium had been disarranged, and some fault in them now made him more repetitious than ever.

'*Rapido rapido rapido,*' he hissed, at least having the sense to keep his chirping to a barely audible level. 'Must get out must get out must get out.'

Crowl barely looked around him as they travelled, projecting the air of an official calmly going about his business. Out of the corner of his eye, though, it was evident that something had unsettled the adepts, and it wasn't just him. Several chambers were stuffed with technicians, all poring over their bulky cogitator terminals. He heard expressions of disbelief, followed by the patter of feet as menials ran to report whatever disturbing findings were coming in.

'You said you had an incoming transmission,' Crowl said under his breath as they passed along a semi-deserted corridor with only a few cowled adepts clustered at the far end.

'Lost lost lost,' Gorgias blurted. Clearly something had gone wrong with his processing units. Crowl's own comm-bead had picked up damage during the struggle with the Magister, and now coursed with white noise when accessed. The lack of contact with the outside world made him uneasy. The Nexus was vast and heavily protected – it would be all too easy to be buried here.

They reached a elevator station and took an unoccupied cage up as far as it would go. As the levels slatted by, flickering and jerking, the background hubbub of disquiet only grew. He caught a fleeting glimpse of Mercatura troops running, and half-reached for Sanguine, only to see them tearing down a long slope heading elsewhere.

He began to dare to hope. They were making good progress, and the entire citadel was strangely distracted, suddenly focused on some other infiltration or system fault. A series of more populated chambers followed, each clustered with cranial-plugged servitors and sensorium adepts with high-crested helms. Astropathic relay crystals hung from the ceiling, swimming with pulsing light. The interpreter lenses were crammed with text, as if suddenly half the worlds of the Imperium were all sending in transmissions at the same time. Here, too, the milling staff were far too busy to pay attention to him, no matter how outlandish his appearance, and he made it up to the departure level for the main transport berths.

'Almost there,' he murmured.

Perhaps that over-confidence did it. Perhaps that sentiment offended whichever machine-spirits governed the operation of this place. He and Gorgias slipped into a narrow walkway running up from the main concourse and into the feeder lines for the shuttles. The place initially appeared deserted, and the same blue light filtered out from wall-set lumens. As they reached the end of the tunnel, though, five figures stepped out of the circular access portal to greet them. Four were Mercatura troopers carrying laspistols. The fifth was Bajan, looking bilious in the unnatural lighting.

'That's far enough, I think,' the adept said, barring passage through the portal.

'What is the meaning of this?' Crowl demanded, adopting Calavine's demeanour once again.

'Just what it looks like, inspector.' Bajan smiled. 'Did you get anything out of the Magister? I'd be impressed if you did. No one else can. I wonder if the two things might be connected.'

As Bajan spoke, Crowl assessed the preparedness of the guards around him. They looked competent and alert, which was an irritant. He was still in considerable pain from the earlier encounter – taking four of them on, plus anything Bajan could muster, might well be asking too much. He had no idea what Gorgias was capable of adding the situation.

'That doesn't concern you,' Crowl said, staying just on the right side of surliness. 'You'd have been better to have taken my advice, and got off-world. When this comes out, it–'

'It won't be coming out anywhere, though, will it?' Bajan said. 'I've done some digging of my own, and I don't quite believe you are who you say you are. I also don't quite believe your business here is as sanctioned as it should be, and that worries me a very great deal.'

'This is a foolish game, Bajan. Stand aside.'

'Something's going on,' Bajan said. 'The whole Nexus is unsettled, and I can't but think that it has something to do with you. Surrender your weapon and call off your skull – I think it's time we spoke again.'

Crowl began to isolate the options. He could potentially take out the two troopers closest to him, but Gorgias in his current state might struggle to tie up the other two. It would have to be done soon, though the prospect of it, and the likely outcome, made his heart sink. He let a little dose slip into his bloodstream, giving him the boost he needed.

Just as he tensed to move, though, another figure ducked clumsily through the portal – a scatty-looking woman with green-tinged hair dressed in an off-white secretarial tabard. She was bearing a pile of data-slates.

'My lord,' she said, bowing clumsily at Bajan. 'Brought straight to you, as you requested.'

The adept shot a glance at her, scowling in irritation. 'Not *now*,' he hissed. 'I'll look at them back in the–'

Then his eyes went wide, his hand flew to his throat, and he choked up a glut of blood.

The data-slates fell from the woman's fingers, clattering on the floor to reveal the tiny spike-pistol nestled in her palm.

Crowl moved instantly, barging one trooper into the wall with an elbow-thrust to his throat. He snapped Sanguine out with the next breath, hitting the second in the stomach. The woman fired again to knock out the third, and Gorgias, demonstrating he still had command of at least some of his senses, accounted for the fourth with a flurry of needles that smashed through his helm visor.

It was all over in a second. Crowl made sure the first one wouldn't be getting up again with a sharp stamp to the throat, then glanced over at Bajan's immobile body. 'Impeccable timing as ever, Aneela,' he said.

'A pleasure, lord,' Aneela replied, pulling the wig from her scalp and shaking her head to clear the flecks of green. 'The transport has been cleared to depart and is ready to detach, though we may need to use our initiative a little – this place is in some disarray.'

'I'd noticed,' said Crowl, stepping through the portal doors and hurrying up the ramp. 'What's going on?'

'Unsure, lord,' said Aneela, following him. 'But it seems widespread – we've had transmissions from Courvain too. Did you receive them?'

Something about the way she said that made his stomach turn.

'No, I was sealed away,' he said, reaching for the airlock release valve. 'Tell me swiftly – I fear we may have been away too long.'

Revus marched down the long central hall, flanked by the remains of his command group. They would be the last ones up before the Corvus Ring was sealed. The very fact he had been forced to enact the order so soon troubled him intently.

The invasion had been so sudden, then prosecuted so rapidly, that there had been little time to do anything other than fight, but that didn't erase the nagging voice in his head, reminding him in every snatch of rare down-time, that he had brought this on the citadel. He, who had been charged with defending it, in the full knowledge that any slip would attract the attention of those with the power to snuff them out, had smuggled in the tripwire corpse, rigged to betray involvement and send out a signal to those listening.

The device must have been extremely sophisticated, both to have evaded detection by the routine quarantine scans and to have pushed its comm-burst past Courvain's scaffold of transmission protectors. It may be that no one could have reasonably foreseen the eventuality, given that bodies were routinely brought in and out of the citadel in pursuit of various investigations. It may be that it was not, in any sense, his fault.

That did not make him feel better. Every soldier who had died under his command during the grubby engagement stabbed at his conscience. He had fought harder than any of them, staying longer at the barricades and taking his fury out on those who had violated the portals, but that did not assuage his guilt for long, for they were still losing so very badly.

Khazad was at his side now, just as she had been since the start. His opinion of her martial prowess had, if anything, grown. He had watched her single-handedly plough into an enemy squad, at close-range as always, cleaving them apart with her gold-flecked blade. If he had somehow been able to call on fifty such fighters, this thing might still be salvageable. As it was, the outcome was remorselessly zeroing down to the one scenario he had been dreading from the start.

Up ahead, at the top of a steep flight of coal-black stairs, stood the last of the unsealed Corvus Ring portals. It was blunt and solid – a monolith of moulded adamantium, surmounted by the Inquisitorial skull and banded with force-repelling struts. On either side of the great doors were anti-personnel bolter turrets, each one linked to great magazines of ammunition. Once shut, those doors were formidable obstacles.

The final members of his command trudged wearily up the steps, backing up with their faces turned towards the hall, weapons still trained just in case the enemy made it here too soon.

Khazad looked over at him, her helm banded with blood. 'We go in now?' she asked.

No doubt she'd prefer to stay outside, where she could engage the enemy face-to-face, but even she'd stopped protesting the strategy a while back, aware of the risk of losing everything.

Revus waited. 'Almost,' he said.

Even as he spoke the words, Spinoza emerged from the gloom of the hall's entrance lobby, striding at the head of Tallis' detachment, still dressed in her Arbites garb and looking as ravaged as all the rest of them.

To her credit, the interrogator didn't ask him what had happened. She didn't fulminate or demand answers then and there, but merely acknowledged him with a weary nod.

'Any more to come?' she asked.

'No, lord. You're the last.'

'Then we go in.'

'By your command.'

They trooped up the stairs. As they went, the first sounds of pursuit welled up from the chambers below – booby-traps going off, blowing the tight net of corridors into rubble, hopefully keeping the pursuers bogged down for a while yet.

Revus ushered Spinoza over the threshold before stepping after her and issuing the command to seal. Huge blast-doors rolled closed, grinding inward from their sockets to slam closed across the breach. Long adamantium bolts hissed tight, and the edges crackled with the telltale gauze of molecular shielding.

The chamber beyond was considerably smaller than the one they'd just passed through, and already congested with bodies and equipment. Wounded storm troopers and security personnel limped off to be tended to, while those still combat-capable took up positions well back from the doors.

Spinoza removed her helm, revealing the depth of her shock at what had taken place.

'So what now, captain?' she demanded.

Revus said nothing, but led her, Hegain, Tallis and Khazad into an anteroom, itself guarded by heavy doors. The walls were reinforced metal, lined with banks of pict-screens and cogitator consoles. A single control column fashioned from glossy alabaster rose up from the centre of the floor. More Inquisition skulls surmounted it, ringing a single steel plunger.

'The Lord Crowl made no signal,' Revus reported. 'I do not know if he ever received my transmission. Soon after the assault all our comms were jammed, so there is no way of knowing if he will return.'

Khazad sunk down to her haunches. She looked spent.

'Then we must hold out here long enough for him to organise a relief force,' said Spinoza.

Revus didn't quite know what to say to that. Crowl was a powerful man in some ways, but that did not extend to being able to summon armies on demand. In any case, one glimpse outside the walls showed that the entire urban sector seemed to be suffering from riots and looting – this was just a small part of some greater upheaval, and the authorities, if indeed they had any significant presence in the locale, were likely already busy with more pressing concerns.

Before he could formulate a reply, though, the doors behind him opened again, and two of his troops entered, dragging the body of an enemy warrior between them. Erunion shuffled along in their wake, looking paler than ever. The chirurgeon normally cast a fussy, confident profile in his own domains. Now, for reasons that no doubt echoed Revus' own, he appeared very much diminished.

The captured soldier was helmless, and a long, livid weal ran down the right-hand side of his face. His eyes were vague, and his head lolled heavily on his shoulders. He had a black web of augmetics along one temple, and his skin was an almost pigmentless white.

The storm troopers dumped him in a metal chair, then lashed his wrists and ankles to the frame.

'Who are you?' Spinoza demanded.

The man looked up at her. He was scared. His gauntlets gripped the edge of the chair.

'Operative four-five-seven,' he replied. 'Squad thirty-four.'

Spinoza drew closer to him. 'No – who *sent* you?'

The man looked briefly confused. 'I don't know,' he said.

Spinoza struck him on the cheek, and his head snapped painfully to one side. 'Who sent you?' she asked again.

The man winced, and struggled to answer. For a second, his lips formed up, but then his gaze went blank. He looked up at her again, now properly scared. 'I… don't know,' he said.

Spinoza clenched her fist, ready to strike again, but Erunion laid a restraining hand on her forearm.

'Selective mind-wipe,' he said. 'Good work, too. You could beat him to a pulp and he couldn't tell you anything.'

Spinoza glared at the man in fury, looking as if she would like to test the hypothesis.

Revus walked up to the captive and began to study his armour. It was high-quality carapace plate, well-fitted, though of no design he had ever encountered.

'What is your mission?' he asked.

The man swallowed. 'Take the citadel. Recover its master alive, if possible. If not, destroy it.'

'Where are you planning on taking him?' Revus pressed.

The man looked panicked again.

'He doesn't know that either,' said Erunion. 'All he's able to do is repeat the mission parameters. I doubt his commanders are even present in the battlefield. Yet.'

Spinoza turned on the chirurgeon. 'There must be something you can do. A mind-wipe can be unpicked.'

Erunion shrugged. 'Some can. We have other subjects in the lab right now, being worked on. But it takes time.'

Revus shook his head. 'We don't have that time.'

'Then we must *make* time,' said Spinoza, impatiently. 'We are behind the bastion, we still have a fighting force to hold them. This is not over yet.'

Hegain looked at Revus. Tallis looked at the floor.

Revus drew in a long breath. 'We have a breathing space,' he said. 'The citadel's heaviest defences were on the outer walls and the main gates – if they breached those so rapidly, we must assume they can breach these too. And in any case, they have control of much of the citadel already. If they decide that their true quarry is not to be found here, or it becomes too much trouble to break us open, there will be ways for them to destroy the entire place.'

Khazad looked up, a fierce light in her eyes. 'Then we rest, just a moment, and get back into fight,' she hissed. 'Better to die on feet than like cats in trap.'

Throne, she was admirable. 'That is one option,' Revus admitted.

Spinoza clenched her fists, in what seemed like a reflexive movement. 'In that case, captain, just what is the point of this exercise?' she asked testily. 'We fall back, only to have them come after us. We hole up in here, to find that they can chisel us out. Are you merely finding us slower ways to die, or is there some purpose to this constant withdrawal you have yet to share?'

Revus looked over at the control column. 'Of course there is a purpose,' he said quietly.

Several of the pict-screens flickered into life. A vid-capture showed the chamber at the base of the stairs outside suddenly filling with ricochets – the automatic gun-turrets had opened fire. From below them, the steady crack of ammo-drums emptying made the floors vibrate. Amid the thundering cycles of ordnance, something bulky and armoured was advancing, sparking with impacts, but coming on all the same.

'Then I think,' Spinoza said coolly, her eyes turning from the monitors to hold his own, 'as we are clearly running out of time, that you had better tell me what it is.'

They did not take the same craft for the outward journey. Aneela had arrived at the Nexus in a Mercatura transit flyer, and it had always been the intention to withdraw in that one if possible. The flyer had been berthed in one of the less prestigious spots within the fortress' colossal docking innards, all the better for slipping away undetected.

They were not the only ones, though. Whole ranks of

ship-tethers were active, flickering with marker lights and running with electro-pulses. The internal comms were clogged, filled with requests for disembarkation and increasingly strident demands for the lock-claws to be released.

Aneela took up position in the pilot's seat, pulling the head-set on and powering up the main console. Crowl settled in beside her, his bones aching. Gorgias spun around somewhere behind them, mumbling repetitive dirges.

'I must apologise for my appearance,' Crowl said, pulling the restraint straps on. 'That was an unpleasant place.'

'Noted, lord,' Aneela said, her fingers dancing across the console. 'I didn't like it in there much myself.'

There was a heavy clank, and the shuttle's chassis thunked downward. A hiss followed, and then the tinny slide of comms-lines withdrawing.

Crowl leaned back against the headrest. 'Everyone's keen to leave, it seems.'

'There has been considerable turbulence within the last few hours,' Aneela said, opening up power to the thrusters. 'A lot of the adepts have opted to get out, if they can.'

'What caused that? The riots?'

'I do not know, lord.'

The shuttle's structure trembled as its motive force came up against the hold-claws. Ahead of them, dozens of craft were filtering out of the narrow canyon and towards the narrow sliver of the night sky beyond. One ship – a merchant's urban skimmer, by its profile – seemed to have got stuck, either because its pilot had powered up too quickly or because the administrators had refused it permission to leave. Its engines had flared up, flooding the metal cliffs behind it with plasma. If that didn't get resolved quickly, there would be an almighty explosion soon.

'Is that likely to happen to us?' Crowl asked, watching it calmly.

The shuttle's holding claw cracked open, and they floated free of the berth.

'I made sure it wouldn't,' Aneela said, concentrating on the press of traffic ahead.

'You really are very good, Aneela,' said Crowl.

They fell in amongst the other vessels, slowly drifting along the canyon and further out from under the Nexus' shadow. The patch of sky ahead steadily grew, although it was darker than before and seething with stormclouds.

'You said there had been transmissions from Courvain,' Crowl said.

'One, lord.' Aneela played Revus' message over the cockpit's audex.

Crowl frowned. 'I don't like the sound of that. You received nothing more?'

'That was the last I heard. I could not establish a link back, and I could not reach you, either.'

'When we are clear of the perimeter checks, drive this craft as hard as you dare.'

'There was another transmission,' she said, ducking a little lower to edge past a lumbering atmospheric transporter. The sky ahead was now plainly visible – a mottled patch of ripped clouds, shifting closely like stirred coal-dust. 'I was unable to open it directly as it came in from the Representative's office. Do you wish me to shunt it to you now?'

Crowl frowned. 'Do it.'

A lens rose up from a device on the console in front of him, unfolding a bundled ident-reader as it did so. A sigil flickered into ghostly life across it – the skull-inset 'I' of the ordos. A scatter of verification runes followed, indicating that the transmission came from the chambers of the Inquisitorial Representative, Kleopatra Arx. Such direct communication was extremely rare – the various fortresses and conclaves operating on Terra were generally expected to go about their business unimpeded.

Crowl reached forward, taking his rosette out from its cache at his breast and pressing it to the ident-reader. He then leaned forward for a retinal scan. 'Crowl, Erasmus, Ordo Hereticus,' he said, letting the logic-engine process his voice-pattern.

Only then did the screen clear of the sigil, and fill with tracking runes.

Priority message to all members of the Holy Ordos of the Emperor's Inquisition operating on Terra or within standard void passage range of Terra, issued by the Office of the Representative to the High Council.

Following irrefutable evidence obtained from scryers and portenders stationed within the inner observatories of the Ordo Malleus, this world is currently subject to a theta-grade anomaly warning, according to the Karcher scale. All operatives and agents, staff and retainers of the Holy Orders present on the Throneworld are advised to travel immediately to locations within or adjacent to the Outer Palace precincts, where secure communications will be established for subsequent bulletins.

No guarantees can be given that the anomaly level will not rise in subsequent announcements. This message supersedes all previous instructions. Temporal authorities advise that unrest across all districts is significant and rising, with no assurance that protection will continue to be extended beyond the highest-tier assets identified in the standard operational manual's crisis lists. Warning is duly given; no further broadcast messages on this subject will be given outside of the designated muster precincts.

The Emperor Protects.

Crowl's brow furrowed, and he clasped his hands together. In his long years of service on Terra, no such transmission had ever been made. Unbidden, his mind immediately flashed back to the horror of the tunnels under the Palace itself, the warrens of darkness where that creature had slithered, the pleading face of Rassilo as she tried to persuade him not to intervene.

They cannot repair the Throne. You understand that? You see what that means?

Aneela increased the power to the engines slightly, pulling up towards the Nexus' outer rim. The tormented sky opened up above them. 'Do you wish to give me fresh orders, lord?' she asked carefully.

Crowl didn't reply immediately. Everything about this was troubling in the extreme. The air of unrest and anger had been growing for weeks. Perhaps it had already been there during Sanguinala itself – you could never have told then, for that was always an occasion of religious frenzy. He had been so caught up in his own hunt since then, unable to sleep, unable to rest, that he had barely given it consideration. Perhaps that was as it should be – his holy calling was not, and never had been, to investigate the structural misalignments of the ether. That was for his esteemed colleagues of the Ordo Malleus.

But the signs had been there. He had his responsibilities.

'No,' he said, shutting down the terminal. 'Maintain course for Courvain. Captain Revus would not have made contact without good reason – I wish to learn what that was.'

CHAPTER FOURTEEN

Yessika huddled in the corner, wrapping her arms around her knees and trying to shrink into the shadows.

She had always been good at that. There were many shadows in Courvain, and it paid to know how to shrink into them, to merge with them, to avoid being seen, to avoid being heard.

Yessika was hardly alone in this. A signal attribute of all the citadel's menial class was its capacity to dissolve into nothing, to be unnoticeable, to blend into the background like one of the timeworn mottos carved into the lines of steel panels. They went with their heads lowered, with their hands clasped, with their feet pressed softly against the stone. Yessika, however, was particularly good at it. She was tiny, a waif of a girl, with limbs that looked so thin they might snap under a finger's pressure. She was like a breath of wind, her mother had told her. Like a gust of hot, silt-pocked air from the outside, caught for a moment under the yellow glare of a lumen, before sliding out again towards Throne only knew where.

It was not that the regime in Courvain was particularly

onerous – there was no outright cruelty from the superiors, at least not the abuse that tales said was rife across many other closed Imperial institutions – but all of them knew, to some degree or other, the clandestine nature of what went on in the cells and hidden chambers. It did not pay to hear too much, just in case a stray secret might creep out from under a locked door and attach itself to you. There was always work to do – supplies to carry, surfaces to wash with the caustic blocks of antisep, errands to run for the lords of the Upper Tower – and that made it easier to clear one's mind of uncomfortable thoughts. At the close of each dark, cloistered day, there was gruel and synth-lactose, and tubs of water to wash in, and hard cots free of lice, and that was a good and fortuitous thing, so best not to ruin it by paying too much attention or being noticed.

Of course, Yessika had been noticed now, by the new interrogator. She remained in awe of her, in truth. Her armour, her bearing, her speech. She must be infinitely wise, must Spinoza, and infinitely powerful, perhaps only a little less so than the Lord Crowl himself. They had not spoken together for a long time, but Yessika still remembered the single piece of fruit she had been given, and the way it had burst across her chapped lips, and the juice that had trickled into her mouth, and the secret pact that had been sealed. In return, she had only been able to give her tiny snippets, things that most people in the citadel already knew, but she had done as she had been bid, and kept her eyes open. One day, she knew, she would see something truly important, and then she would creep up the levels to the cell where she had been given the fruit, knowing that she had a gift for her mistress now, one that would repay that past kindness.

'Thank you, Yessika,' Spinoza would say then, smiling at

her, lifting up her chin with a finger. 'You have done me a great service. And, through me, you have done the Throne a great service. Well done.'

Perhaps this was the time, Yessika thought. Things had been strange for a while. There had been the running, and the shouting, and the orders coming down from Gerog's people all the time, making them scurry. It had felt as if everything was being made and then re-made, and towards the end of it, the storm troopers had rifled through the menials' living quarters, looking for anything out of place. They hadn't found anything, of course, for all were loyal in Courvain.

But then there had been the bigger noises, the louder shouts, the booms that had made the walls echo and the floors shake. She had kept her head down then even more than usual, hoping it would all pass over.

It hadn't. More storm troopers came, only these wore grey, not black. They burst into the dormitories, bringing with them the stink of smoke. They had blank helms and empty eye-slits, and pulled the menials from their cots before throwing them onto the floor. Then they rummaged through the sheets, and tore out the food processors, and kicked in the lockers where they all stored their few private belongings.

They didn't ask any questions. They didn't speak at all. They were rough, and clubbed a few of the older menials with the ends of their lasguns to make them move, but that was the limit of their brutality. They seemed to be a great hurry, wanting to sweep through the lower chambers before heading on up to do whatever they had come to the citadel to do.

Yessika watched them all the while. She did what they wanted, and stayed small and on the edge, watching. She tried to remember the little things – how they moved, what they smelled like, who was in command and if they could be identified by a particular mark or manner. It was hard to keep everything in her head as they were jostled and herded out of the dormitories and down into the big refectory, so she mouthed the facts to herself silently, over and over.

Once the grey storm troopers had gathered them all up in the main hall, most left, leaving just a few to watch over them all. Yessika saw adepts in that place as well, clad in their finer cowled robes. Some of these, after a little while, jumped up and rushed against the grey guards and tried to disarm them. The fighting was brutal and swift, with predictable results. Once it was over, the leader of the storm troopers killed the instigators and left their bodies lying on the tiled floor. The rest of them, menial and adept alike, hunkered down. Some of them looked scared. A few looked resigned. Yessika merely observed, knowing that Lord Spinoza, by the time she arrived to sort all this out, would want to know the details.

For a long time, it seemed, the noises of fighting felt very close by, as if there were entire riots going on in the corridors outside. Those gradually moved away, heading upwards, until the refectory was left in an awkward state of near silence. Menials coughed quietly. Adepts sat back against the walls, their eyes closed. Those who had been taken from sickbeds moaned from time to time.

After a while, it became hard to keep her eyes open. Some of the older ones lay down on the floor, trying to grab some rest. Yessika looked up, straight into the overhead lumens, determined to stay alert.

As a result, it was possible that, of all of them there, she was the first to notice the narrow vents around the edge of the high ceiling – the ones that she had noticed from time to time in the past but never paid much heed to – activate.

She narrowed her eyes. This was interesting. They were only

little things – circular nozzles, with lenses that were spiralling open – but they were silent, and no one else had seen them.

She smiled to herself. She was the only one. Perhaps this was part of Spinoza's plan. Or perhaps she would want to know when it happened, in which case Yessika would be the one to tell her.

She began to feel strange. Light-headed. The lumens overhead seemed brighter, and hurt her eyes. It also seemed that, for as long as she stared at them, the nozzles were becoming hazier.

She rubbed her eyes, and looked away from them. Now, it appeared, others were doing similar things. In the far corner of the chamber, a woman suddenly bent over and retched. One of the adepts got to his feet shakily, before tottering and falling over again. The guards became instantly jittery – one trained his weapon at the ceiling, while another started to clutch at his throat.

Yessika smiled again. She was feeling terribly sick – something to do with the gruel ration she'd had earlier that day, no doubt – and was having great trouble focusing, but something was clearly happening.

She clasped her hands together, and concentrated on staying alert.

'She will want the details,' she said to herself, willing the sickness to fade away by remembering how that fruit had tasted. 'All the details. To do great service to her. To do great service to the Throne.'

They were still fighting. They were too stupid to stop; too brain-clamped and nerve-numb to anything but their neural-jack-sparked orders.

Huk found herself inordinately proud of them all. She had

lived down here with them for a long time now, and they had been her companions for the entirety of that time. It had become hard to think of them as they were – sacks of vat-grown meat hardwired to slaved cortex implants, destined for a five-year life of perpetually stacking, sorting and retrieving books they would never read for clients they would never see. In principle, they had been delivered for use as identical models, given one of the lowest Mechanicus service-ratings and deployed for a strict subset of monotonous tasks. In practice, Huk had found ways to make things more interesting. Some years ago she had gained access to some of their basic machine-spirit glyph-patterns through the cogitator-hub at the heart of her domain. Through a long process of tinkering and experimentation – there was little else to do when the lords of the citadel did not demand her expert services – she had found ways to make them a little more variegated. One of them had even been taught to smile at her when it was dragged out of its rest-pit. That smile had been a toothless, black-gummed horror show, but at least it had been a vestige of something like humanity.

And now they were fighting for her. They didn't know what they were doing or why they were doing it, but it was possible to imagine that they cared, and imagination was all that she really needed then.

Of course, they were getting cut apart. Once the shock of their first assault had died away, the grey-armoured interlopers had fought back well enough. They were initially heavily outnumbered, and had to fall back to the archive's gilt-lined entrance to avoid being torn to pieces, but Huk's little army had no genuine weapons, and no tactics other than the blanket order she had given them on auto-repeat in their tiny pseudo-minds.

A few stray las-bolts must have flown into the sea of shelves at some point, setting alight the tinder-dry leaves, so now the fighting took place under the wavering flicker of flames. If she'd had time, she would have shuffled over to the precious cases and activated the dry-chemical dousers, but that was already impossible. Her flesh-puppet army was being driven back towards the central cogitator hub, sliced and burned now by disciplined strikes of las-weaponry.

Huk had lost contact with Courvain's main augur-feed, and so had heard nothing over the mainline comms since this thing started. Lasbeams had scythed through one of her main synapse-cables, making it hard to order the few servitors she could still direct. Her own sidearm was nearly out of power, and the flames were only getting stronger.

She started to laugh. She clambered over one of her cogitator-banks, hoisting her ragged skirts to clear a bulbous screed-entry maw. She had a few shots left, and it would be good to end a few more of them before they got close enough to defile the data-coils.

It was as she did so that she heard it. A normal mortal might not have done, for the noise of combat in that echoing vault was significant, but then Huk had always been gifted in many perceptive and hard-to-quantify ways.

A hiss, like a long outlet of breath. Then another, overlapping and growing in strength, until it was a solid gush.

'No,' she murmured, staring up at the distant ceiling, now part-obscured by snags of smoke. 'No, not that.'

More las-beams criss-crossed the space overhead, sizzling into the ranks of leather-spined books and kindling more bonfires.

She got angry. She had not been angry, properly angry, since she had woken up and found herself here, tied down and locked away, her mind half-functional and her limbs bound up with iron.

'Who ordered this?' she shouted, flinging her arms around, whirling amid the crossfire as if she could pinpoint where and how and why. '*Who ordered this?*'

The servitors were toppling now, and not from incoming shots. She saw one of the grey-armoured invaders stumble, gagging, vomit bursting from the narrow slit at his neck. Her vision began to blur, like grease spread over a lens.

She fell to her knees, buoyed only by her remaining synapse cables.

'I wanted to talk to him again,' she mumbled, thrashing amid the wreck of her kingdom, trying to stay upright. Now all she could hear was the whooshing of the vents. 'He said he'd be back, and we'd talk again.'

She wanted to shout that out, but wasn't going to be able to do that now. She knew a terrifying amount about what would happen to her next, and how agonising it would be.

She toppled over. As she did so, she watched one of her servitors expire, its face as blank and expressionless as ever.

Her iron fingers clawed at the floor. The flames fanned higher, making the parchment scraps crackle and fly.

'Who ordered this?' she croaked, before her tongue stopped moving.

Spinoza kept her hand on the plunger the whole time, as if by maintaining a physical link with it, she could somehow appreciate what was happening down below.

She had kept her eyes open, staring at the cylinder of steel as it had slid smoothly into its sheath. The skulls arranged around the summit were a theatrical touch, and she hadn't been able to decide whether they were entirely crass or eminently suitable. An Inquisitorial fortress was stuffed with skulls. They were the badge of the organisation. They were virtually the badge of the Imperium. So strange, to twist a symbol of abject mortality into one, supposedly, of institutional strength. What did that say about them, as a species? When had they stopped noticing the irony of it?

But now she sounded like Crowl, whose lack of fortitude was so troubling. That would not do at all – one of them at least had to remain resolute, focused on the larger picture and not obsessed with the minutiae of this singular quest for answers of doubtful value.

The conversation she had undertaken with Revus before taking action remained stained on her mind, playing through it as if on auto-loop. They were all still clustered around her – Revus, Khazad, the storm trooper officers, Erunion. The arguments had been run through now, exhausted, and she had made her decision, just as she had been trained to do.

'The Corvus Ring is not primarily a physical barrier,' Revus had told her. 'It can hold an assault for a matter of hours, but its principal purpose is to maintain a molecular seal across the citadel at the point where its diameter and functional arrangement makes such an arrangement practical.'

She had instantly understood the implications of that. There would be no point in creating such a seal unless the counterpart facility were also in place – the means to flood the levels below with chemical agents. She had not fully grasped the purpose of Revus' preparations before that – they had seemed strangely ordered and unnecessary. Now she realised what he had been doing, among all his other duties – ensuring that the vents were in good working order, just in case.

'The invaders have decent armour protection,' Revus had

gone on, his voice almost a monotone. 'But it is not fully chem-sealed. Counter-measures will be effective.'

As they had spoken, the grinding thrum of assault from below had grown. The enemy had brought up metal-boring machines, and the chamber's remote oculus-feeds had filled with the blaze of turbo-drills.

Spinoza had looked away from those pictures. 'How many of our people are still below the limiter?'

Revus had looked her directly in the eye. 'We pulled as many back as we could,' he had said. 'That was the purpose of my strategy, once it became clear what we were up against.'

'I did not ask you that. I asked you how many are still below the limiter.'

'A third of the citadel's complement. Mostly lower-grade menial staff, but significant numbers of mid-grade adepts. Some of my detachment. Prisoners, cell guards. The archivists.'

The thrum had grown louder. She had heard shouted orders from the chamber next door, as the stationed troops had prepared to defend it from attack.

'There would also be significant collateral damage,' Revus had intoned, sounding more and more like he was delivering a funeral oration. 'Delivering the volume of nerve agent necessary to cleanse the citadel will result in leakage to the surrounding areas. Casualties there will be significant.'

She had nodded. He had been commendably thorough. Perhaps unworthily, she had reflected then on what would have happened if she and Hegain had not rendezvoused with him when they had done. Would he have contemplated this still, knowing that she was on the wrong side of the barrier?

Khazad had interjected then, her eyes live with indignation. 'You cannot be making this!' she had blurted, looking to her for support. 'We can fight, here.'

Revus hadn't looked at her. He had looked at Spinoza the whole time, as if trying to assuage some sense of guilt that the order would now be given by her, rather than him.

At that point, the noise of the drills below had picked up. She remembered wondering if they were already too late, and whether the bulkheads had been pierced. Still, she had not been able to press the plunger. She had resisted even putting her hand on it, knowing that once she did that, there would be no way back.

A final question.

'Any word from the Lord Crowl?' she had asked.

Revus had shaken his head.

Now she stood, her hand still pressed on the metal. It had taken far less time than she might have imagined. The tubes must have threaded down through the inhabited levels like veins, chamber after chamber, protruding just a little from the crannies and the corners, almost unnoticeable. Such a system would have been hard to retrofit, surely. Courvain must always have had it, she guessed, baked into its atrophying structure by its long-dead designers, a product of an age of paranoia and insecurity. Perhaps it had been used many times over the centuries. Perhaps this was the first time. Perhaps there had been souls who had deployed it and felt nothing. Perhaps others had been haunted by their decision forever.

She remembered her last conversation with Huk.

This place is disordered. You were a savant. You should fix it.

Slowly, she withdrew her gauntlet. Khazad was glaring at her. Hegain, seemingly, could not meet her gaze.

The chamber's picter lenses showed the devastation below. The assault on the bastion had halted. Two tracked drill-machines lay immobile, their crew slumped around them.

Other lenses were cycling through images from further down – silent halls, crammed with bodies; empty corridors strewn with wreckage; automatic machinery ticking over in the shadows as if nothing had ever happened to threaten it. The tactical displays, which had been filled with signals, were now black and empty.

'How long before we can get back down there?' she asked, her voice sounding hollow in her ears.

'Volumes are already dissipating,' Revus reported, going over to an augur terminal to monitor levels. 'A few hours, suitably protected.'

She felt cold, as if carved from the stone of the walls around her. 'Enemy aircraft still active?'

'Some. I have given orders for the turret gunners to target them.'

'Good.' She withdrew from the control column, once more feeling the weight of her unfamiliar armour on her shoulders. 'I will return to my chambers now. Do not disturb me unless necessary.' She paused at the doorway, resting her gauntlet against the fluted granite. She felt nauseous, and the feeling would only grow. 'But notify me as soon as the Lord Crowl returns. He will wish to be briefed on what has taken place, I am sure, in person.'

Revus watched her go.

He had not yet had a chance to tell her what had caused the security breach. That would have to be done some time soon – all would have to be disclosed. For now, though, he was still needed. He had orders to give, arrangements to make, timetables to establish. Every indication was that the chemicals had done their work, and that the citadel was now secured.

A third of the citadel's complement.

As he had spoken those words, he had felt the guilt stab at him like knives. He had served Crowl for a long time, and knew many of those stranded, by sight at least. Some of his own troops hadn't made it, and their deaths were added to the tally of those his mistake had condemned.

He pushed such thoughts out of his mind, striding out of the command chamber and back into the hall where most of those remaining under his command had been gathered. The portal leading to the levels below was still tightly shut, its shimmer of shielding still in place. A team of adepts in biohazard suits was making its way down the central aisle towards the control mechanism, poised to be the first through the gap once the all-clear was given. For now, though, the warning panels were still pulsing red, forbidding passage beyond the Corvus Ring.

He went through his remaining tasks methodically, placing them in order of priority, not moving on until each was completed. He travelled to the control chambers for the exterior gun emplacements, and watched as the last of the enemy's lingering attack craft were either brought down or driven off. He briefed the reclamation teams on their priorities, once transit beyond the Ring could be established – flush all confined spaces, install test devices at all intersections, set up anti-tox stations wherever readings remained high and summon the biohazard teams. Once access had been restored, it would be essential to clear the corpses quickly and get them incinerated, lest infection spread through the air filtration network. Counterseptic programmes would have to be rigorous and rapid. The adepts, even those used to working in the scriptoria and the signals units, would have to get involved. The hangars and main ground-level portals would have to be reclaimed and sealed, to prevent ingress while they were so weak. Some kind of guard would have to be set up. The list of tasks was almost endless.

A third of the citadel's complement.

He didn't so much as catch an idle breath for the next few hours. The painful process of establishing control absorbed him completely. When fatigue crept up – a reminder that he had been on his feet and fighting for a very long time – he treated it as just admonishment for his failings, and redoubled his efforts.

His duties only took him to the medicae bay once. Erunion had already made his way up there, and was busy preparing his own teams for reinsertion below. His slabs were fully occupied – enemy corpses, most betraying catastrophic battle wounds, a couple showing evidence of selective excruciation. Clearly, some effort to counter the mind-wipe had been undertaken. The few survivors were corralled in a secure unit. They were looking shell-shocked, sitting under the glare of white lumens, saying nothing.

'You have what you need?' Revus asked him.

Erunion nodded. 'Captain, I–' he started, looking thoroughly miserable.

'It was my order, chirurgeon,' Revus said, heavily. 'My order. I'll tell Crowl.' He rolled his shoulders, trying to fend the exhaustion off a little longer. 'Keep a few alive for interrogation. And accelerate the clean up – I want teams back across the boundary within the hour.'

Erunion hesitated, looking as if he wanted to say something more. Perhaps it was guilt with him, too. Or maybe just fear. 'By your will,' was all he offered, eventually, before shambling back to his bloody slabs.

After that Revus found himself alone again, heading back towards his private cell. His comm-feed was still jammed with incoming messages. Nothing had come in yet from Crowl. As soon as they were back on their feet, something would have to be done about that. A squad sent out, perhaps. Then again, the entire world seemed to be in almost open revolt – it might not be possible to arrange anything before the hangars were cleared.

He reached the corridor leading to his cell. The lights were out, making the already dark stone look like the void itself.

A figure was waiting for him. As soon as he recognised Khazad, he felt just a fraction better.

'Assassin,' he said, walking up to her. 'You should be resting.'

She darted a quick look at him, though it was hard to make out her expression in the dark. 'Cannot rest.'

'You should try, though. We have only won a temporary reprieve.'

She smiled. 'Will be back. I told you this.'

'I know.' He was close to her now. 'I should say... You fought well.'

Her face clarified a little in the glow of his armour lumens. He saw then that her smile was not mirthful, but bitter. 'Fight well,' she said sourly. 'I ask it – how can you live with yourself?'

That took him aback. 'What do you–'

'Too quick, captain. Too quick to retreat.'

He stiffened. 'It was an army. We would have lost the citadel.'

'Not honourable.'

'It was war.'

'War? Who against, really? See who has died now.'

And then she turned away, limping back down the narrow corridor. Revus watched her go, half wanting to follow, half too surprised to move.

Then he turned, slowly, and took the access wafer from

his belt. He slotted it into the door mechanism, and it slid open to reveal his bare chamber beyond.

Treading heavily, he made it to his hard cot and collapsed on to it. He looked up at the whitewashed ceiling, where mould speckles clustered around the ventilation housing.

His comm-bead pulsed. It pulsed again.

A third of the citadel's complement.

Silently, wearily, he closed his eyes.

CHAPTER FIFTEEN

They came in through tortured skies.

Close to Salvator's edge, an entire hab-tower was on fire. It glowed internally, red as fresh-cut entrails, bleeding into the night. The flames lapped up, higher and higher, sheets of energy that made the air shake. The smoke from its burning rose up in a massive pillar, black against black, overarching and stolid.

Crowl watched it in silence. It took them a while to pass it, such was its bulk and heat-wash. A big tower like that would house thousands. Maybe tens of thousands. Take in its catacombs, no doubt now cooking or collapsing, and the numbers would only rise. Dimly, half-perceptible in the thick smog, he saw figures streaming away from the furnace across every intact span and transitway. Most were fleeing in panic. A few were rushing the other way, tearing headlong into the inferno.

'*Insanus insanus insanus*,' Gorgias mumbled, too shocked to be truly outraged.

Lightning shot down between the remaining towers. It did

not leap like natural lightning, but plummeted like falling lead ingots, punching into the suffering world below. The clouds above raced and churned, stirred into turmoil by superheated winds.

For the first time he could remember, the airspace was freeing up. Those shuttles still aloft were beating for home now, hammering their path through the tumbling ash like gulls before a squall. They were being replaced, in part, by far bigger military craft. He saw a convoy of Imperial Navy transports grinding north, towards the Palace regions, surrounded by escorts of atmospheric fighters. Then, further away, he saw a big orbital lander coming down, wallowing in re-entry flame and tilting badly. Throne only knew where it was hoping to come down – there were no suitable landing stages for kilometres around.

'Anything from the citadel yet?' he asked, for the third time since leaving the Nexus.

'Just static,' said Aneela. Then, as an afterthought, 'It may be the storm. I'm getting nothing from anywhere else, either.'

They flew on. Aneela was as good a pilot as Crowl had ever known, but she struggled to keep them on an even keel. Violent updraughts buffeted them, nearly tipping them over more than once. The lightning strikes grew ever more frequent, lancing down and cracking into the febrile hypercity below.

'I saw some troubling things in the Nexus,' Crowl said eventually, needing to break the silence. 'While you were there, with Bajan, did anything notable cross his desk?'

'Not much,' Aneela said, never taking her eyes off the path ahead. 'But they were all getting worried. An anomaly, they said, affecting the galactic north.'

'Yes, that was what they were tracking. A long way away, you'd think.'

'Yes.'

'Too far away, to be responsible for this.'

'Surely.'

He sunk into silence again. It felt too convenient, as if the entire thing had been arranged to divert the world's attention from the true threat at its base, the hidden one, worming its way under the towers and the battlements. Perhaps that was what had kept Navradaran quiet for so long. The ways of the Custodians were strange. From his brief encounter with them, he had seen a court dyed in aspic, frozen amid rites ten thousand years old. It was hard to imagine them taking the initiative on anything much – the dust had been gathering on their fine armour for too long, steadily thickening with each long generation. Perhaps Spinoza was right about them. Perhaps they could not see the world as it was anymore, only how it had been.

The Magister had known about the xenos, and did not care. If he was to be believed, his mistress no longer cared either. Spinoza, he appreciated, did not truly believe in the hunt either. Perhaps they were all right. Perhaps the xenos had got under his skin, preventing him from seeing things clearly. Perhaps this was something that should be put aside now, filed in a drawer for possible future reference, or turned over to the expert hunters of the Ordo Xenos for their consideration. Rassilo might have been overstating the importance of the Project she had so assiduously worked for, after all. Pride was a common affliction among their kind.

'Coming into visual range now, lord,' Aneela reported, as they pulled past the lumen-flickering bole of another mighty spire-trunk.

Crowl looked up. The familiar hooked and serrated profile of Salvator's many hab-blocks jutted up around them.

More fires had been kindled in the teeming bowels, sending palls rolling into the sparsely-occupied heavens. As the flyer burned towards its destination, it looked for a moment as if something had gone wrong with the instruments, for Courvain did not exist at all. And then, as they got closer, he saw that its lights were out, save for a dim scatter at the summit of the citadel. Fires were burning at its base, too – a whole gamut of them, strewn across the network of bridges and thoroughfares that bound the place into the grasping roots of the surrounding conurbations.

'Are those… fighters?' Crowl asked, reaching for the shuttle's viewport augmentation controls.

None of them were in the air. The wreckage of what seemed like dozens of atmospheric attack craft littered Courvain's flanks and the shoulders of the hab-units around. Most were still smouldering, kicking more acrid smoke into an already gauzy fug. The hangar entrances, ground-level portals and upper take-off stages were all mangled and glowing red-hot.

'I am not sure how we're going to land there, lord,' Aneela said, running her own scan of the damage.

'Get us in, somehow,' Crowl said grimly. The more he looked, the less he liked what he saw. 'There are lights on further up. We're closer now – can you get anything over the comm yet?'

She tried again. After a few seconds of the now-familiar static-snarls, the link finally clarified.

'–owl. Throne be praised. Please do not approach the main hanger maws. Repeat – do not approach the main hangar maws. Contamination has yet to be cleared there. If it please you, follow coordinates to be transmitted, and I shall do my greatest to guide you into the service bay on level twenty-three.'

Crowl recognised the voice – it was Hegain. Why was he directing this?

'What has happened, sergeant?' Crowl demanded.

The link went dead for a moment.

'If it please you,' Hegain voxed again, 'that is a most difficult matter. Please follow directions – it is not safe in the air. I shall inform the Lord Spinoza you are returned. She can brief you fully.'

The link cut.

Crowl looked at Aneela. 'A most difficult matter,' he said, dryly. 'What do you make of that?'

'I do not know, lord,' she replied, picking up Hegain's marker trail and guiding the flyer down towards his suggested ingress point. 'I shall leave that to you to determine, if I may – this approach may be challenging.'

But by then he wasn't listening. He was looking at the damage.

'Just what, by the nine devils of all hell, can have happened here?' he muttered.

Prayer had filled the hours since her decision. Spinoza had knelt before her altar, her fingers clutching the chain of devotion, her head bowed.

It had felt good to get out of that foreign plate and don her true robes of office again, but that only fixed the external, not the internal. As her lips moved, at times she felt as if she could almost taste the nerve gas, filtering up from the chambers she had poisoned, wafted by some divine buoyancy by those who had suffered.

The devotions did little to ease her spirit. After a while, she got back to her feet. She put her armour back on, not because she felt it necessary, but because it made her feel like herself again. Whatever came next, she would face it in her full regalia, her weapon ready, her allegiance displayed.

She checked her backed-up comm feeds. The Courvain

traffic was predictable enough, albeit with the addendum, sourced from multiple emitters, that the Lord Crowl had returned.

That ought to have made her glad. He was her sanctioned master, and his absence had no doubt contributed to the debacle here. Instead, though, all she felt was dread. Perhaps he would be angry. It might even be good to provoke anger from him, rather than the world-weary lethargy that marked his usual speech and manner. Or perhaps he would be crushed, witnessing for himself the vengeance of those whom he had chosen to cross.

In addition to all that, there was now another element from outside, one that had seemingly been delayed by the jamming devices used by the enemy during the assault.

Priority message to all members of the Holy Ordos of the Emperor's Inquisition operating on Terra or within standard void passage range of Terra, issued by the Office of the Representative to the High Council.

She read on, and took in the full statement. So that was that. Crowl's ambition would have to be curtailed now. Clearly the contagion she had witnessed at the Hall of Judgement had spread rapidly. It was impossible not to wonder what must have transpired to have forced the Representative's hand. Disorder on a planetary scale was hardly unknown in the Imperium – she had witnessed it herself under Tur's tutelage, together with the suitable responses and their continent-scouring consequences – but this was no ordinary planet. Any systematic unrest on Terra would have to be dealt with on its own terms, spire by spire.

Her summon-chime went off. She was being asked to attend the council chamber again. Crowl had wasted no time.

She drew in a deep breath, adjusted her cloak, and left the

chamber. As she walked through the narrow ways, the candles fluttered in their pools of wax, untended for too long. The air tasted even more metallic than usual, no doubt due to the curtailing of the citadel's circulatory pathways. The surroundings were so similar to the way they always had been, and yet, there could be no doubt, everything had changed.

The passageways were crowded. Revus had managed to pull as many souls as possible above the Corvus Ring before the situation became critical, and now there were adepts clustered in every chamber and intersection, some sitting disconsolately, others attempting to go about their business as if nothing much had changed. When they made the aquila to her as she passed, it was impossible not to imagine their eyes following her afterwards, perhaps pitying, perhaps judging.

She reached Crowl's rooms. Here, too, the council chamber looked much as it had done before, with the high-polished table, the patterned rugs lost in semi-darkness, the crystal decanters and the recessed lighting. Revus had arrived ahead of her, and was already seated on the far side of the table. He looked exhausted. Crowl was in his usual place, also back in his familiar robes. He had a half-empty goblet in one hand. As she entered, he beckoned for her to take a seat.

Awkwardly, he shuffled forwards on to his elbows, moving with some stiffness. There was a strange aroma coming from him, something toxic. He didn't look noticeably worse, physically speaking, than when they had last spoken. Something, though, had changed – like a strut, hidden but structural, snapping. He had been sick before. Now, he looked wounded.

'Spinoza,' he said, as she took her seat. 'I thank the Throne you are preserved.'

'And that you are too, lord,' she said, trying not to make that into a lie. It wasn't, not truly, although it was so hard to summon the right level of feeling. Why was that? Why, even now, was she still struggling with these same things?

She caught Revus' eye, and saw how his habitual front had been restored. Aside from the fatigue, he looked much as he always did – like a granite outcrop, weather-worn, immutable.

Crowl turned to him first.

'So, tell me from the start,' he said. As he reached for another sip, Spinoza could see the faint tremble in his fingers.

'It was my error, lord,' Revus said, baldly. 'I pursued a lead, hoping for evidence of Gloch's presence within Salvator. I found what looked like a killing – a contact of a contact. I brought the bodies back here, wishing to draw something from the killer's corpse, something to work on. But there was no killer, merely bait. While we were examining the cadaver, a locator-beacon emitted, giving away our involvement.'

'It broke through the sensor-wards?' Crowl asked.

'Evidently. And also got through our routine scans on the way in. I do not say this to excuse the error.'

'What happened next?'

Revus was sitting perfectly upright, his spine ramrod straight. 'We enacted lockdown,' he said. 'I attempted to recall all off-site personnel, and put a check on movement at the gates.'

'But that was not enough.'

'They reacted too quickly. They were too numerous. I do not believe, given what was sent here, that anything could have prevented them gaining access. Once inside, they took control rapidly, and we lost a great many of our people. I pulled back to the upper levels once it was clear that we could not expel them by force.'

Crowl took another draught. 'Who are they?'

'Unknown. We captured several, but their minds have been

altered. Subjects, both living and dead, are still held here. Erunion is working on them.'

'And they wanted to destroy the citadel?'

Revus hesitated. 'Only if they failed to capture its master.'

Crowl smiled sourly. 'I see. Did they mention what they wanted with me?'

'They do not know.'

Crowl nodded. He reached the end of the goblet, and got up to pour more. 'And that led you to enact the Corvus protocol.'

Spinoza leaned forward a little. 'I gave the order,' she said.

'Yes, Spinoza,' said Crowl, taking his seat again. 'Do carry on the tale now.'

'I returned to the citadel after the fighting had already started. I concur with Captain Revus' assessment of the situation – we were being overrun. I was presented with the simple choice – enact the protocol, or attempt to hold the bastion. I judged that we could not do the latter.'

'You tried, though.'

'We held out for as long as we could.'

'You agree with that, Revus?'

'I do,' Revus said.

'Damn you both,' Crowl muttered, drinking again. There could be no mistaking it now – his hands were shaking. He swallowed, then looked up at the ceiling, stretching his arms out across the tabletop. 'The one requirement. The *one requirement*. Keep it secret.' He drew in a long, bitter breath, then shot a look of uncharacteristic venom at Revus. 'You did not think, at any point, that this corpse could have been planted?'

Revus shook his head, just a fractional movement. Spinoza might have answered in his place then, pointing out that bodies were brought in and out of Courvain all the time. This whole thing had started with one such cadaver, hauled out of Gulagh's flesh-strippers and given over to Erunion for study.

'You surprise me,' Crowl said, bitterly. 'And you disappoint me.'

Silence fell. For a long time, none of them spoke. The ticking of a clock could be heard in the recesses of the chamber.

Eventually, Crowl sighed wearily. 'I have been the custodian of this place for many years. Too many, perhaps. In all that time, we never dared to use it. I had half-forgotten it was even there, before this all started.' He stared sullenly into the veneer. 'I could not allow Gorgias to be present for this. It would have broken him. He is undergoing work, and will awaken soon, and then I will have to try to explain. I do not relish that prospect.'

'If you wish it, lord–' Revus started.

'Do not dare,' Crowl shot back, instantly. 'Say nothing about penance, or resignation, or punishment. We have so little strength left, and so little time. It is done. It was always going to be hard to keep our names out of this.' He turned to Spinoza. 'What did you discover, before you returned?'

'Nothing, lord,' she said. 'No investigations are active. The records of the orbital cordon have been erased. It was a dead end.'

Crowl nodded again, slowly. 'Just as it was at the Nexus,' he said, allowing, so it seemed, a fractional resentment to enter his voice. 'Closing ranks, covering over, forgetting orders were ever given.' He smiled wryly. 'I met the creature responsible for Vinal's ship being scuttled. The Speaker has, it seems, repented of her involvement, and it was unwilling to divulge any useful information. So there is nothing for us there. The identity of the third conspirator is still hidden. It may be that he or she is the only active partner now, though they are clearly aware of us now. We must assume these killers will return, and in greater numbers.'

Spinoza found herself looking at her hands, and lifted her head. 'The wider city is in some disarray, lord,' she ventured. 'Travel is becoming perilous. It may be that the danger has abated, for now at least.'

'Maybe so,' said Crowl. He took another swig, and this time tiny beads of wine remained on his lower lip, glistening in the candlelight. 'But, for ourselves, we cannot rest. We must keep moving. We must keep enquiring. This must not be allowed to run away from us.'

Revus was like a tombstone now, mute and deferential.

'They have struck us,' Crowl went on, clenching one fist into a tight claw. 'They have wounded us, and that shall be the weakness. There will be something. Something they have neglected to hide. And when we find it...'

He seemed to run out of words.

'With respect, lord,' Spinoza offered, gently, firmly, knowing it was likely futile but still choosing to try, 'you will have seen the unrest in the city outside. If the Project even still exists–'

'It exists.'

'–if the Project still exists, there will be other burdens on the High Lords now. Their attention will be turned towards the Palace.'

Crowl shook his head, a jerky movement that made the sinews of his neck stand out. 'No, no,' he muttered, opening his fist, then closing it up again. 'That is what they wish you to think. That is the great trap.' He looked up at her, and she was shocked to see the fervour in his old eyes. 'Everything is linked. The Throne. The xenos. The anomaly. I do not see how, yet. I do not see how it can be. But it is. I looked into its eyes. You understand that? I saw what it intended. This is not a single thread, but a whole braid, twisting, twisting.'

Now Spinoza noticed a flicker of alarm in Revus' otherwise blank expression.

'They struck us first. That betrays fear. They had to destroy us, in this one hit, and they have failed. Now we must strike back, strike while the iron is bloody.' He grinned, a flicker of a smile that extinguished again almost instantly. 'The error is theirs. I have yet to see how we can turn it yet, but I will do. This cannot be the end. It is just another step on the same path.'

She was tempted to say a number of things in reply to that. She was tempted to say that they still had no idea who had attacked them, and that was of critical importance. She was tempted to say that if the Speaker's office and the Adeptus Arbites had decided to lay their involvement to one side, then perhaps that meant the whole affair was dead now and they were merely opening themselves up for destruction by pursuing it. She was tempted to say that a xenos infiltrating the Palace, as serious as that was, paled into insignificance besides the prospect of losing the Throneworld to anarchy.

But one look at her master, just then, told her that this was not the time nor the place. She shared a significant look with Revus, before bowing her head.

'By your will, lord,' she said, quietly.

CHAPTER SIXTEEN

After that, Spinoza waited some time before going to see him. The captain was as occupied as ever. He threw himself into his work, seemingly as some kind of penance. Or perhaps it was just easier to keep busy.

Eventually, however, even he had to rest. She observed him heading down towards the senior officers' refectory, and followed him. If he'd noticed her, he gave no sign, but headed to an auto-dispenser and poured himself a cup of caffeine. He pulled a protein-stick from the counter next to it, then went to sit, alone, at the far end of one of the long tables.

She retrieved a drink of her own – heated water, flavoured with a little sucrose-essence – and went to sit opposite him. For a while, he sipped his caffeine, chewed his protein-stick, and did not acknowledge her at all.

Spinoza looked around her. The refectory was virtually empty. A couple of adepts were hunched at the far end of the chamber. A menial worker looked to have fallen asleep from exhaustion in the opposite corner. Normally, she would have reported that one for discipline, but things were hardly normal.

'You do not like me much, do you, captain?' she said, taking a sip.

Revus looked up. His eyes were ringed with grey, his cheeks were sunken, his chin bristling with wire-brush stubble. 'Why would you think that, lord?' he asked, not sounding terribly concerned either way.

'Ever since I arrived,' Spinoza said, 'that is the impression I have gained.'

Revus shrugged. 'It is not my job to like or dislike. If I have not given adequate service, then–'

'It has always been exemplary,' she said.

He said nothing in reply. He drank again, cradling the metal cup in both hands as if needing its warmth to keep himself alive.

'You saw the way he was,' Spinoza said carefully.

No response.

'You have known him longer than I. Has he ever been like this before?'

Still no response.

'I got close to the creature myself,' she said. 'I still see its face whenever I blink. He, though – he spoke to it. It breathed on him. I do not think he has been the same since.' She toyed with her cup, tilting it idly. 'I am not saying the hunt is not worthy. I am not saying we should do anything other than our duty. I am merely voicing concern for his welfare, and for the wider situation.'

Revus did not look up. 'I saw it, too,' he said, eventually. 'I tried to bring it down, and failed. I was not as close as you were. Not as close as him. But… Yes, it stays with me. The smell of it.'

Spinoza regarded him carefully. 'Then you know of what I speak.'

'Maybe. Right now, I do not place much faith in my judgement.'

She tried a different tack. 'You were out in Salvator, before this all took place. What was it like?'

'Restive.'

'Worse than you've known it?'

'Yes. And now, after this, much worse.'

Spinoza leaned forward, lowering her voice further. 'There is concern at the highest level. I have seen transmissions that indicate this is a planetary phenomenon. *Planetary*. I do not get any sense that the worst of it is over. In such circumstances, I am unsure that pursuing this business, as we are being asked to do, can be the right course of action.'

She had overstepped with that, and knew it instantly. Revus' grey eyes flickered up towards her, hard as ice. 'He is the inquisitor.'

'Yes,' she admitted, rowing back. 'I know.'

'That is a judgement for him.'

'You are correct.'

An awkward silence fell. Revus drank again. Spinoza left hers untouched.

'I do not know if he will find anything,' she said eventually. 'My enquiries were useless. It seems he discovered little, too. But I am under no illusions – he has a formidable mind. If he should find a way to take this forward, and we are still confronted with the worsening situation in the city, and it comes down to a choice of duties...'

There were no easy ways to finish that sentence.

'Tell me what you came to tell me,' Revus said, still not making eye contact.

She drew in a breath. 'I came to Terra, of all worlds, for a reason. Well, more than one, but one in particular that meant something, given my past, given what I still believe is important.' She kept her voice low, her head close to Revus'.

'If a moment comes, only if, but if a moment comes, a crisis, a significant crisis... then I can call on help.'

'What kind of help?'

'Help.'

Revus smiled dryly. 'Ah.'

Now she was on dangerous ground. 'I only mention it–'

'No, I understand.' He finally looked up at her. 'But I believe you came to speak to me about what comes next.'

He was no one's fool. 'Just so. We have been damaged. We have made choices. We must move beyond them.'

'I agree.'

'I made the call on the Corvus protocol,' she said, pushing her cup away. 'Guilt is an unworthy emotion, captain. Get over yourself.'

The ghost of the same smile flickered across his lips. 'By your will, lord,' he said.

'The portals in the lower citadel are safe to enter now. I will survey them, and send my findings to you. Any deficiencies, I shall expect you to remedy them.'

'By your will.'

'Very good, captain.' She rose, shoving the metal bench back and making to leave.

He looked up at her. 'For what it is worth, I do not remember ever disliking you, interrogator,' he said. 'I do not dislike many people. Even those I have to kill. They are just faces, just names. You have to understand – there have been very many of them.'

Spinoza did understand. 'This is Terra, after all.'

'It will consume you. If you let it.'

She nodded. 'Then we will speak again.'

'Aye,' Revus said, returning to his drink. 'We will.'

* * *

The biohazard teams worked quickly, once the first set of all-clears were given. They went methodically, level by level, clearing up the bodies, hosing down the blood, raking the debris away and re-opening the portals. Slowly, steadily, contact was re-established with all the major external doorways. They were re-sealed, then re-guarded.

Many things became apparent during the process. The enemy had not had things entirely their own way – a few knots of resistance were discovered. A couple of storm troopers, cut off from the main squads, had led counter-attacks in one isolated corner. Some of the prisoners' cells had been broken open, letting out some extremely dangerous people, who had gone on to cause their own kind of havoc. In truth, though, Revus' tactical decisions were largely vindicated by the sheer numbers of enemy bodies the hazard teams came across. There were heaps of them, piled up at every choke-point and intersection, their limbs stretched out and their mouths open and gasping. Tracked vehicles had been brought in to the larger chambers, most armoured, all with heavy weapons mounted on their backs, the engines still growling and kicking out smoke.

None of those encountered, defender or invader, had survived the chemical attack. They lay where they had fallen, twisted and choking, their armour-plate or robes flecked with blood.

Crowl walked alone through the debris. He had been present on many battlefields of various kinds during his long life, but this was by far the most painful. The stains and chips on the walls gave away the ferocity of the initial firefights, but all was now frozen in a kind of stasis – a freeze-frame image of momentary, fleeting torture.

He should have sought sleep. His mind was getting even

murkier. He could feel his thoughts slowing down, just as he could feel his limbs begin to seize up. He would have to retire soon, or his body would shut down entirely.

Sleep, though, brought dreams. And, besides that, there was so much to do.

He found the entrance to the archives in disarray. The reclamation teams had not been there long, and lifting work was still under way. A masked storm trooper on duty saluted as he approached. Servitors lumbered past him, dragging bodies behind them.

He passed within, treading carefully. The place was charred black and stank of smoke. Fire suppression squads had got in late, just in time to save a portion of the archive shelving at the rear of the chamber. Much of it, though, was gone – a mess of melted steel braces and blackened parchment.

He walked up to Huk's cogitator station. It, too, was half-destroyed, burned away by a mess of las-shots and grenade detonations. Huk herself lay in the middle of it all, her crippled body folded up, her arms bent backwards around the cables that had both imprisoned and liberated her.

Crowl knelt down. No one had dared go near her yet – she was just as she had been when the nerve agents had started flowing. He smoothed a tangle of matted hair away from her grey cheek. Her facial muscles were more relaxed now than they had been for a very long time. It made her look younger.

'I am so sorry, Yulia,' he said, with feeling. 'So sorry.'

He allowed himself, briefly, to remember how she had been. Vital, enthusiastic. Always eccentric, even before the accident, before the misjudgement, but that was to be expected. She had hated it down here, despite knowing the reasons.

As he knelt there, his ceramite-clad finger running down her skin, he heard the voice again in his mind – that mocking voice, dredged up from its alien sump of corruption, steeped in aeons of existential cruelty; needling and vicious.

You should have been here, Crowl, it said. *You should have taken the transmission.*

He stood up. He called over the officer in charge. 'Prepare this body for cremation,' he said. 'Let me know when all is ready. Take extreme care of it. I shall preside.'

The man made the aquila and withdrew, hurrying to pass the order on. By then, Crowl had moved on himself, driven by his latest compulsion, entering the vaults where the books had been. He had to tread carefully. The lower deck was littered with still-hot debris. Some servitor carcasses slumped in the corners, their overdeveloped upper bodies lacerated by las-fire. The chains that had once borne them up into the heights swung loosely, clinking.

Further back, beyond the inner layers of the great well of shelves, more archive silos stretched away into darkness. Many of these radial shafts were more or less intact, protected from the fires just long enough for counter-measures to halt the damage. He walked along one of them, letting his fingers run over rough, metal-studded spines.

Right at the end of the shaft, deep into the citadel's structure, the last of the light gave out. The tomes here were heavily proscribed, and all were bound in thick chains. Crowl knelt down in the black dust, searching near the base of the shelves. Here were forbidden books, books so dangerous that even an inquisitor might balk at admitting ownership. Some were written in ancient forms of Gothic that had long since passed out of use. Some were transcriptions, imperfect no doubt, from pre-Imperial languages – Francish, Inglish, Mandrin. Making sense of any of those was difficult for all but the most gifted lexicographers and archaeoscribes, though it could not be doubted that the contents were, to the right reader, precious beyond price.

Crowl paused at a volume marked *Ethica, Ordine Geometrico Demonstrata*, and smiled to himself. Then he was hunting deeper, pulling aside heavy slabs of bound vellum. After some rummaging, he found what he was after, and withdrew a cracked and iron-bound volume. This one was heavily chained, with two separate locking devices. It took him a while to unclasp the second, for it relied on a very old pass-phrase that he had to delve deep to recall. As he touched it, he felt a stasis-field over its front panel prick at his fingers. Only the rarest, the most obtuse and the most perverse books had such precautions attached.

He looked down at the spine title. This was a copy of a copy of a copy, made in a scriptorium that had been razed to the ground six thousand years ago. In the eyes of a man like Tur, its presence here alone might have constituted just cause for extermination.

Crowl parsed the text with difficulty, for the characters were not Gothic. *Offer-bearing*, was the best he could manage in the absence of a translexer.

Then he tucked the book under his arm, and walked back the way he had come.

When he emerged back into the light, he saw that Huk had been taken away, but Khazad was there instead, rooting around amid the destruction. He limped up to her.

'I am sorry for this,' he said, offering a grim smile of apology. 'You come here to work for us, and now... this.'

Khazad shrugged. She seemed to be back to herself. Her skin had regained its healthy glow – the longer she stayed on Terra, the more that would fade – and she carried herself with her old poise. 'Means nothing to me,' she said. 'I wished to fight longer.'

'Spinoza made the right judgement,' Crowl said. 'Painful as it is. There will be other days.'

She looked hard at him, her gaze as uncompromising as ever. 'You will not stop now, will you?' she asked. There was an element of desperation in the question.

He shook his head. 'No. We will find them.'

'Good.' She grinned, a flash of a savage smile, relieved. 'Good.'

Crowl found himself smiling too. It was the first time he had done so, without irony, for quite some time. 'You are a refreshing presence here, assassin.'

She shrugged again. 'I have vengeance-debt for my old master. And now, loyalty-debt to my new one. *Kataj* once, and now, *Saijan*.'

'Those are Shoba terms, are they not?'

'I leave the planet. The planet does not leave me.'

Crowl chuckled. 'Do not stay here for long, then. This world suffers no rivals for affection.' He hoisted the book under his armpit. It was heavy, and his limbs were aching. 'I won't insult you by warning you of the danger. They have missed the heart with their first strike. They will have to try again.'

Khazad appeared supremely contemptuous of that idea. She gazed around her, at the devastation and the signs of burning. 'They made mistake,' she said. 'Should have brought twice as many. So they are not without fault.' She sniffed. 'On Shoba, there is old war-manual. It is called *Elements*, by Ataya. We study it, all children. There is famous line. *In war, more is unknown than known. Assume your enemy understand more than you, and you will be slow to move against him.*' She raised an eyebrow – an odd gesture, which might have signified something different to her than it did to him. 'They are in dark, too, I think.'

Crowl thought on that. 'You may be right,' he said.

'So what is next?'

He hefted the book under his arm. 'Study,' he said. 'Sleep. Then we move again.'

'To where?'

He started to walk. That was the question.

'The answers will come,' he said, more confidently than he felt, retreating into the old ordo maxims. 'Apply, interrogate, and the answers will come.'

CHAPTER SEVENTEEN

Spinoza had been unconscious for less than an hour when the chime sounded at her bedside.

The wrench from sleep was painful, and it took her a few seconds to realise what was happening, her head still filled with semi-nightmarish dreams of lips and teeth and kohl-black eyes.

She raised herself onto her elbows, floundering to silence the chime's bleating. The lumen flickered on, and she gradually blinked her way into focus.

It was Crowl.

'I wish to see you in the observatory,' he said. 'Ensure you are in your full armour.'

The link cut before she could reply. She sat there for a moment, feeling drunk with fatigue. Her whole body protested, demanding that she return to sleep.

Sighing, she pulled herself from her cot. She stumbled from the bedchamber into the arming room, where her armour hung on its rack, ready for donning. As she laboriously applied the pieces, feeling the weight of them snap into place, something like alertness returned. She took a swig of water, rinsing it around her mouth and spitting it into the sink. Then she ran her fingers through her short hair.

The corridors outside were quiet. It was the deep of the night, and only the watch-shifts were in operation. With the re-occupation of the main citadel, the command sections felt empty and echoing, starved of occupants by the death-toll during the raid. There were barely enough bodies left to man the sentinel stations, let alone keep the myriad functions of a fully operational citadel ticking over as they should. Courvain felt sicker and more threadbare than ever – an ague-weakened body on faltering life-support.

The observatory was, as one might have expected, placed right at the summit of the main pinnacle, only overshadowed by the long comms towers with which it was linked. It jutted from the flank of the upper horn-tip of the fortress, a hemispherical protuberance with ornately inlaid windows that gave the distant impression of compound eyes. The most sensitive of the citadel's listening equipment was housed there, together with the mid- and long-range augur arrays. The space was cluttered with linked machines, tended carefully by trained menials, continually clicking and cycling and churning out ribbons of etched parchment.

When she arrived, the place was flooded with red light. It wavered across the floors, making the tall banks of cogitators appear to sway and tremble. Erunion and Crowl were waiting for her, alongside the duty menials in their robes.

The light came from outside. It looked as if half the horizon were aflame now, and the silhouettes of the greater spires stood against a backdrop of angry, lava-like turmoil. A low rumble could be heard through the armourglass – louder than the usual grind of vehicles, a kind of glowering reverberation that got under the skin.

'Good,' Crowl said as she entered. 'Now we can begin.'

Erunion looked as shattered as she felt. He shot her a weary half-smile, before turning to one of the great creations of valves and transistor-crystals and fiddling with the wires.

Of all of them, Crowl was the most animated. His eyes were glistening, his movements were agile. Perhaps, Spinoza thought, a little too agile. There was an element of brittleness to his demeanour, as if he had taken something potent to keep him going.

He came up to her, smiling that reptilian smile of his. 'It was Khazad, really,' he said. 'I like her. I like her attitude. That is what we need right now.'

Spinoza steeled herself. She had a feeling that she would not like what came next. Crowl looked restive, agitated, and couldn't stay still. He walked around the machines, back towards her, then over to Erunion again. 'I had forgotten the first insight we had,' he said as he moved. 'The very first one. We know that Rassilo is dead. We know those with her were taken by the Custodians. We forgot that they do not. They do not know what happened to her. They will be anxious about that. They will be worried that she is currently in some dungeon somewhere, apt to be interrogated. That must be their great fear now, for she knew all there was to know.'

His hands were kneading one another. He kept pacing.

'And now we know that Gloch is still missing, too,' he went on, speaking rapidly. 'They do not know where he is, either. So they found his contacts and implanted the tripwire devices, trusting that those holding him, or perhaps looking for him too, would wish to tidy away the loose threads. This is about their weakness, and our strength. They are scared of us, what we might know.' He laughed. The sound was a little forced, a little febrile. 'They were trying to *protect* themselves.'

Spinoza tried to follow the reasoning, which seemed convoluted to her still. 'Then we would have been better,' she ventured carefully, 'not to have gone after Gloch at all.'

'No, no, not at all. We had to be sure. We had to know he was out of the picture, and now we do.' Crowl went over to Erunion, checking over the work he was doing and nodding with approval. 'They did not set out to destroy this place from the outset, though they plausibly had the power to do so. They wanted information. They wanted to know whether we had him in our cells. Or Rassilo, even. They wanted to talk to me, to find out what we had uncovered, and if we had discovered the links that led back to them.'

Spinoza drew in a deep breath. That was, in all likelihood, true. It didn't alter the facts, as far as she could see. 'Then, are we–'

'Consider it, Spinoza!' Crowl blurted, clapping his hands together. 'They were monitoring Gloch's contact web. They were monitoring all the links he had established, in Salvator and elsewhere. As we must assume, they still are. Not just his. Rassilo's, too.'

Suddenly, she realised why he had asked her to wear her armour. 'I... see,' she said, warily.

'Instruments prepared, lord,' Erunion reported, stepping back from the batteries of machines. From up above them, a gantry shifted, aligning a series of receiver dishes on the outside of the observatory. A flash of neon strobed up the length of the comms towers, and static jumped between the brass spheres perched at their limit.

'Even now, they cannot be sure,' Crowl said. 'They did not get what they wanted here, so their surveillance must still be in place.' He limped back up to her. Now there could be no doubt – the animation in his eyes was of chemical origin. Had he slept at any time over the past few days? Before that, even? 'They will be monitoring every link, every scrap of communication that Rassilo ever had. Everything will be tripwired, of course, but that hardly matters, since we have already sprung the trap. So you see why I needed you here?'

'I do, lord.'

'So you can still make contact? You still have the means?'

'I do not know.'

'But you can try.'

She glanced at Erunion, who avoided her gaze, keeping himself busy with the monitoring equipment. 'If I may ask,' Spinoza said, 'what good will opening the link do us? Even if someone is monitoring her old network, how does that help?'

'Because it was a two-way link, was it not?' Crowl asked, wringing his hands again and pacing some more. 'You had a reply to your communication? If we know of that in advance, if we have access at this end, there are things we can do. Provoke a reply, any kind of reply, and we may learn where it came from.'

Hence the observatory. Hence the sensor arrays all being activated, the cogitators already running algorithms, the menials getting into position to process encoded data-gluts.

He had worked quickly. He might even be right.

'What do you want me to do, then?' she asked.

'Just as you did before,' Crowl said. 'Open the link. Give whatever code-phrase you were asked to before. Let the vox verification do its work. The operator at the other end will be different, but they'll know the protocols. And that's it. All we need is a reply.'

'It might be dormant now.'

'It might.'

'They might not respond.'

There was a faint sheen of desperation in his eyes. 'If they're there, they'll respond. They have to. Why are you resisting this?'

Why was she? Was it the injunction from Arx, the command that she wanted to obey in favour of this increasingly obsessive quest? Or was it just the prospect of Crowl being right, and using what had been her original weakness to gain a weapon against an enemy whose face they had yet to see?

She unclipped the seal around her gorget, exposing the secure comm-bead used before. Erunion came up to her, bearing a long snaking input spike, which he slid into a receiver nodule just above it. The cogitator lenses filled with status runes, dotting the transmission protocols one by one.

Crowl fidgeted the whole time, hanging back, then half-stepping forward, his lips twitching.

'Ready?' Erunion asked, when all had been connected up.

Spinoza nodded.

'Keep it open as long as you can,' Crowl said. 'Any feedback will be routed to the main console.'

Spinoza looked up at a large semi-circular lens with its overhanging lumen pod. Its glassy surface was empty as yet, but a lime-green cursor blinked, ready to scroll with data.

She reached up and depressed the bead.

The first time she had opened this link, a duty officer under Rassilo's command had answered. Now, all she got was white noise. The lenses filled with routing data, all encoded, but no substantive content.

'Spinoza, Luce,' she said, just as before. 'Code sequence beta-beta-chimeric.'

Still nothing. The quality of audex received fluctuated, as if something was getting in the way.

Erunion frowned, reaching out for his equipment controls. 'We have a thread into something,' he mumbled, pulling at a jewel-tipped lever. 'Nothing solid yet.'

Spinoza looked at Crowl.

'Again,' he urged, pressing his fingers together too hard.

'Spinoza, Luce,' she repeated. 'Beta-beta-chimeric.'

The white noise grew in volume, fluctuating, then rippling as if it were liable to shear away entirely. They listened for a few moments more. Erunion made more adjustments. The lenses remained empty.

Spinoza raised her hand, poised to cut the link. Just as she did so, the main lens suddenly scrawled with runes. They were gibberish – routing information and frequency parameters. Crowl, who had started to become distracted, suddenly snapped his chin up.

'This is–' he started.

Then the screams began. They crowded into the feed, overlapping and incoherent and incredibly loud. Erunion scrambled for the volume controls, but they just kept coming.

Spinoza recoiled, her finger hovering over the bead, but Crowl gestured frantically for her to keep it open.

'Mercy of the Throne! Mercy of the Thr–'

It was a woman's voice, perhaps, or some distorted version of one, or maybe a man's that had been ramped up the registers by fear. Other voices crowded in, guttural, bestial. There were words in a language Spinoza didn't understand, ones that made her ears ring.

The lens filled with random data, picking up speed. The chronometers started to clatter round. Crowl stared up at them in alarm, and menials scrambled to isolate the main input jacks.

Spinoza found herself recoiling. There were other noises

on the feed – fleshy, squelchy noises. High-pitched, por-cine shrieks in the background went on and on, crowded out only by the foreground cries. She heard what sounded like gun shots, and heavy crashes.

A new voice broke through the cacophony, a man's this time, shouting over the tumult in another unfamiliar lan-guage. Solid-round gunfire broke out, hammering into a crescendo and drowning out most of the agonised screams.

Someone got close to the transmitter and spilled out more desperate injunctions. *'Help us! Help us! Help–'*

Then there was a scrape, a snarl, an animalistic snap of aggression. More gunfire hammered out, growing in volume.

The link cut out.

She found that her heart was beating faster. Gingerly, she reached up to her comm-bead to ensure the audex could not re-establish. The lenses around her flickered with whole screeds of rune-data.

Erunion looked shocked. He drew in an unsteady breath and looked over at Crowl.

The inquisitor was lost in thought.

'Did you get anything… useful?' Spinoza asked Erunion.

The chirurgeon stared up at the lenses. 'Ah, well…' he started, before steadying himself. 'These are all vox-containing elements. Nothing I can use yet. No location markers. Not yet.'

'You must have something.'

Erunion shot her an irritated glance. 'What did you make of the screams, interrogator? Your department, I would think.'

The insolence stung her. 'I would advise you to watch your tongue, chirurgeon,' she snapped, clenching her gauntleted fist and taking a step towards him.

'Enough,' came Crowl's distracted voice. His brow was still

knotted. 'An unpleasant surprise. We must reflect on it, not fight over it.'

'What is there to reflect on?' Spinoza asked, feeling her patience fraying. 'Whoever was at the other end of this long-dead link has been caught up in the madness overtaking this whole world. The madness we should be doing something about. You heard it! Those were proscribed words, or they were gibberish.'

'Some of it was.' Crowl looked up at her. 'Some was anguish. Some was indeed proscribed. But some was battle-language. Of a secret kind, of course, but it has always been my business to uncover secrets.'

Erunion stared at him. Spinoza realised the truth then, and her heart sank.

'I know precisely where it came from,' Crowl said, looking almost dazed. 'And so I know, now, at last, where we have to go.'

The two Spiderwidow gunships were the only aircraft in the citadel's armoury still fit to fly. Being orbit-capable vehicles with limited atmospheric manoeuvrability, they had not been scrambled during the assault, and so were now hastily prepped and loaded by teams of menials.

The lead vessel now stood on the apron, gouting with steam, its access hatches open and every intake valve trailing fuel lines. All non-essential items were being carried away by servitors, lightening it and creating room for the storm troopers that would soon be encased within.

'We can barely guard the citadel as it is,' Revus said as they entered the hangars, not as a complaint, but as a bald statement of fact.

'I know,' Crowl told him. 'If times were otherwise, we might be able to make arrangements, but they are not, and so we can't.' He halted, placing a hand on the captain's arm. 'But it has all come down to this, Revus. One gamble, made possible by fate. We would never be forgiven if we did not take it.'

It was impossible to miss the signs now. Crowl's eyes were too bright, his movements too jerky. Even Gorgias seemed uncertain, keeping his distance and saying nothing.

'I've done what I can,' Revus said. 'The gates must be guarded – there will be underhive trash to ward off, if nothing else.'

Crowl started walking again, his steps halting in his armour. 'They don't matter,' he said, waving one hand breezily in the air. 'There have been riots before. There will be again. *This* is the true danger.'

The hangar's far end was mangled and open to the elements, flying with filth and dust blown in from outside. The launch ramps had been cleared, but rubble and smashed metal still littered the spaces on either side of the gunships' launch trajectories.

Spiderwidows, despite their bulk, did not have large crew compartments. Ten storm troopers would go in one; five, plus Revus, Khazad, Spinoza, Hegain and Crowl, would go in the other. The fact that such a paltry complement was enough to strip Courvain's defences to the marrow was a crushing indictment of the damage that had already been caused.

All remaining space was taken up with ammo-loops for the prow-mounted bolters, auxiliary generators for the lascannons and stowed replacement weapons for the infantry on board. In addition to the usual hellguns, the squads also packed plasma guns and bolt pistols.

Spinoza and Khazad were waiting for them on the apron, both fully armoured. The assassin looked lithe and lethal, Spinoza stolid and immovable. They were both helmed, as were the storm troopers clambering up into the gunships. Spinoza carried her crozius arcanum with her now, which Revus thought, not for the first time, made her complete.

'The time for secrecy has passed,' Crowl announced, greeting them both. 'We succeed in this, or perish in the attempt. The Emperor knows the righteousness of our cause, and will judge us if we fail.'

'By your will,' Spinoza replied curtly. Khazad bowed floridly. Revus had not spoken to her since their last encounter, and she did not make eye contact with him at all. She looked ready, though – bristling with energy and spoiling to make up for the perceived failures of the last engagement.

Then Crowl was climbing to take his place in the cockpit, next to Aneela. Revus hauled himself into the crew bay behind, followed by the interrogator and the assassin. As the hatches slammed closed, sealing them in, the fuel-lines slithered loose and the giant engines snarled into shaking, roaring life.

He reached for the restraint harness, snapping the locks home. Hegain was sitting opposite him in the dark, and nodded in greeting.

'Back into action, captain,' the sergeant said, cheerily enough. 'Something to welcome, in the truth of it.'

Revus said nothing. He had fuelled up on protein-sticks and carb-bars in the short time he had been given, and had a stock of stimms to keep him alert when they arrived, but he still felt drained, hollowed out. Perhaps he was getting too old for this. Perhaps the fires were on their way to dying now, and this was how military careers – and lives – came to an end.

The gunship's structure shook, and the engine-whines rose in pitch and volume. From outside the gunship's armoured exterior, shouted voices could be heard completing the pre-flight checks, and heavy chocks slid across the rockcrete.

Then, with an accelerated growl of turbines booming into full power, the last of the shackles slammed clear, and the alert klaxons broke into throaty life. Menials scampered out of danger, servitors trundled out of the blast-zone. The hangar's shutters came down, and the Spiderwidows lifted off the ground on cushions of driving thrust. Through the narrow viewport, Revus watched the hangar walls drop lower, then slide by, faster and faster, before they were out, thundering into the night.

The aircraft swung wide immediately, tilting over hard and boosting for a slender gap between hive spires. It was hours yet before dawn, and the skies were still as dark as pitch. In normal times those skies would have been punctuated with a billion lumen points, gaudy against the deep velvet of the overcast heavens. Now, though, everything was stained red from the many fires. They were burning along whole avenues now, upwelling in the sheer chasms between towers, flooding a crimson glow up the long ranks of deep-set windows. The airspace above them was thick with smoke, a choking pall that masked out the lightning-danced nimbus of the ever-present cloud cover.

It looked hellish. It looked ripe to boil over, to spill up and out and cover the world in an angry tide of blood and darkness. The storm winds made the Spiderwidows shake, throwing them both around in a mess of turbulence and unnatural thermals. One moment they would be screaming along at full tilt, the next dropping like a stone. The panels within the crew bay shook hard, rattling as if they would pull the rivets with them.

The volume of noise made talking next to impossible.

Revus thought he caught Khazad and Spinoza shouting at one another over the din.

'He is sure?' the assassin was asking.

'He is sure,' Spinoza replied, her helm making it impossible to know what she thought of that.

The spires swept past them, one after the other, streaks of lumen-dappled black against the flames. He saw mighty warehouses, each one the size of a Mechanicus coffin ship, slumping into ruin as the fires tore through them, leaving skeletal lattices of iron across the booming heart of the inferno. He saw whole urban sectors seemingly without power, their towers and their transitways like the twisted forests of some forgotten nightmare-world. The only other aircraft abroad now were military or Arbites, struggling against the ash-laden winds just as they were. A big Militarum gun transport roared its way north, its grav-plates glowing white and its leviathan engines labouring. The sound of gunfire ebbed and waxed within the symphony of other sounds, giving evidence of the running battles taking place across half the sector's streets.

After a while, they flew over more sparsely inhabited areas. Great refinery complexes reared up on either side of them, flanked by cooling towers that belched steam into the cauldrons of dirty smoke. A subsector power reactor was still evidently in operation, its vast rockcrete walls studded with a maddening complexity of pipes and feeder-lines, its bulbous roof floodlit and pinned by a hundred sensor vanes. Tox-stained wastes emerged, studded with empty carcasses of old manufactoria, their empty windows lashed by the storm's wrath.

They were headed north-east, climbing steadily as the land rose. It was almost impossible to tell by eye, since Terra's horizons were never clear of competing turrets and towers, but Salvator had been built in something of a depression. The great structures of the central core were raised atop ancient mountains. The centuries of delving, elevating, re-delving and scouring had erased their primordial magnificence and interred it all under ranked layers of rockcrete, but the altimeters still betrayed evidence of the first contours of the Imperial capital.

Away north, beyond sight and across a flaming horizon, loomed the mighty Palace itself – its temples, its bastion walls, its sarcophagi of administration. The lightning storms seemed strongest there, as if forces within the heavens above had launched themselves at one another and now crunched into ruinous contact, each unable to drive the other into submission.

Their course took them east of that, out past the industrial wastes and further into clearly impoverished districts, with half-ruined walls standing like tombstones amid cheap-looking conurbs and hab-ziggurats. The reason for the destitution became clear soon enough – a mighty ravine had been gouged straight through it all, a kilometre wide and two hundred metres deep. The canyon was lined with iron-black metalwork, banded and ridged like a mortal spine. A cluster of massive cables, each the diameter of a Warlord Titan and surrounded in layers of protective scaffolding, ran along its base, snaking like some gargantuan powerline amid the semi-derelict structures on either side. Mournful watchtowers rose up at regular intervals, each one a fortress in its own right and surmounted by rotating lascannon emplacements. The telltale flicker of void shielding shimmered over the canyon's roof, sealing in the semi-buried conduits below. Every so often, enormous tangles of machinery erupted out from the sloping walls of the trench, bearing the unmistakeable mark of the Mechanicus – power transformers, plasma-sinks, electro-magnetic flux absorbers, psy-coils.

The ravine went on for kilometre after kilometre, carving through whatever it encountered. Static fizzed and crackled along it, sparking where the shield-gauze hit the hard edges. Red lumens glowed at intervals down in the depths between the colossal tubes, indicating pits below that churned with great pumping houses or climatic stabilisers. No rioters came near that place, perhaps deterred by the many watchtowers, but more likely by the aura of profound dread that emanated from every part of it.

Revus felt it himself, even high above its snaking path. His heart was beating just a little too fast, his palms were just a fraction too sweaty. The structure below was far from inert. The power thundering through it could be sensed, like a sub-audible vibration that jarred, that needled, making teeth grind and fingers press tightly into one another.

All knew where that great trench originated. Far to the west, it gouged and blasted its way through steadily grander constructions, plunging deep underground and boring through cathedral-sized vaults before linking up with the immense psionic receptors lodged deep in the planet's crust.

They were not travelling to its origin, though. They were headed east, along its coursing route towards its terminus. And now, steadily, kilometre by kilometre, that terminus was gradually appearing on the forward scopes.

Revus looked away from the viewports and switched on a grainy augur-feed from the gunship's racing prow. It slewed, cycled, and then settled down to show the landscape ahead.

More towers were rising, though these were darker, more esoteric and more aesthetically challenging that those behind them. A great press of spiked spire-clusters soared up in front of the storm-torn horizon, twisting in elaborate ways and interconnected by dizzying lattices of conjoining bridges. At the heart of the mass rose eight massive spikes of dark metal, thrusting higher even than the spires around them, jutting as a single coronet into the skies. And within the heart of that iron crown, more massive than anything else, jet-black, frosted like glass, a hemisphere of such aching perfection that it made the urban sprawl lapping up to its perimeter look like a tide of thrown rubble.

The lightning was drawn to the dome, licking and slithering around it in an unending cascade of attraction. Its smooth face swam with eldritch light, reflecting the lacerating discharge of the firmament.

All on Terra knew what that place was. Most of those in the Imperium with any education knew what that place was. Even more so than the Imperial Palace itself, they knew that they would never go there. No pilgrims made their way to its sanctuaries. No ambassadors attended its dark courts, and no politicians gravitated towards its vaulted assembly chambers. The only qualification for entering that obsidian dome was to be damned already, condemned to burn your soul out in furtherance of humanity's greatest and most irreplaceable psychic accomplishment.

Revus found he was gripping his own thigh too hard. He could not take his eyes away from the images. No one in the crew bay attempted to speak. They were all doing the same thing, watching it grow.

In the end, when Crowl broke the silence over the internal comm, his words crackling with interference, it felt like some kind of trespass into their private, sanctified thoughts.

'Behold,' the inquisitor announced, his transmitted voice

a strange mix of both heady anticipation and profound disquiet. 'The Hollow Mountain.'

CHAPTER EIGHTEEN

It had been made, like so much else on Terra, so far in the past that its origins were now little more than myth. Some held that the Emperor Himself had laid the first stone. It was almost universally believed that He had designed it, drawing up the plans that would one day connect its central chamber to the mechanisms of the Golden Throne itself.

For many diligent adherents to the Imperial Truth, this posed something of a theological conundrum. All were taught that the Emperor powered and controlled the great Beacon that enabled His warships to ply the void. All were also taught that He did this from His Throne, from where He also governed the lives of His people and engaged in eternal spiritual warfare against the Ruinous Powers of the Outer Dark. However, it was also taught in the orthodox Ministorum schools that the Emperor had only retired to the Throne after defeating the Devil Horus, from where He could be sustained for all time in the service of His people. Did that mean that, at one time, the Beacon had powered itself? Or that the Emperor had been able to direct it while being free of the Throne's confines? Or did it meant that the Beacon had only come into existence once He had taken His eternal place on the Throne? In which case, how had warp travel been maintained during the legendary days of the Great Crusade, when the Master of Mankind and His Nine Primarchs had walked among mortals?

Entire learned theses had been written on the topic, attempting to prise open the relationship between the Throne and the Mountain, speculating endlessly over which had been raised first, and how they had been linked, and why both were now necessary in order to guide humanity's vessels through the living hell of the ether. Many of those scholars striking near the truth of its functioning had eventually gone missing, been censured, or even burned as witches. It was most comforting to accept things in their broadest elements – the Astronomican originated with the Emperor and was directed by Him; by such means did He shine a light into the eternal darkness; it would go on forever, just as His reign would go on forever.

The majority of those left engaging in such work therefore knew nothing of the Black Ships that ran their long circuits through the lonely paths of the void. They knew nothing of the ancient harvest of the gifted, who had once been destined to form the vanguard of a new humanity, but were now fated to become something just a little more exalted than psychic firewood. They knew nothing of the months-long voyages in those creaking, heavily warded behemoths. They knew nothing of the null-soulled guardians plucking the strange and the changed from their childhood homes. They knew nothing of the long journeys back home, assailed on all sides by madness within and without, until they came back to the Sol System at last, unmarked and unmonitored, to dock with the stygian orbital facilities rotating silently over Terra's skies. They knew nothing of the choices made by age-ravaged ancients, selecting those who might survive to prosper under the guidance of the Adeptus Astra Telepathica to become the soul-seers and seekers of dreams that the Imperium relied upon in order to communicate with itself. They did not know that a few select individuals among that harvest might be elevated to the highest echelons of all – the mysterious Librarians of the Space Marines, or the sanctioned psykers of the Astra Militarum and the Inquisition itself – and that of those, many in turn would be selected for service within the Forbidden Fortress.

So it was that the black-liveried landers would descend on prescribed nights, slipping out of orbit and down into the Throneworld's crowded skies. Once disembarked, the chosen would file through the great arched gates, their heads shaved, their bodies stripped naked and their names taken from them. They would be given new raiment – nightshade robes, controller collars, spinal implants and steel-ringed input nodes at the bases of their skulls. They would be instructed in the lore and the mysteries of their craft, and learn to control the beasts that coiled within their minds.

Many would die during that training. Others would succumb to insanity and be turned over to the tech-priests for servitor-meat. For those who survived, a mind-altering journey of discovery awaited them, one denied to almost all other members of their species. They would learn the true nature of the ether. They would learn of the beings that dwelt within it. They would learn of the few ways that a mortal could employ its powers safely, and the many ways that a mortal could wreak destruction through hubris, malevolence or error. They would write treatises on the philosophy of the empyrean, and compose music reflecting its shifting harmonics. They would be tested, over and over again, for signs of taint, sickness or open-mindedness. They would be drilled in the worship of the Emperor, through whom all their gifts were made perfect. They would come to believe, in time, that annihilation in His service was the highest calling any mortal human could ever hope for. They would dream of it. They would long for it. And, when the call finally came, they already knew the words they would sing, endlessly, rapturously, as their eyelids burned away and their skin began to crisp.

Such was the purpose of the Mountain. No one now living, save He who sat on the Throne, remembered how it had been conceived. The great sphere at its heart had surely been there from the very earliest phase of its life, carved out of the heart of its enclosing peak to house the Chamber of the Astronomican. Perhaps, once, that had been enough. Perhaps the simple geometry of that construction had been all that was needed to angle and reflect the great Beacon into the stars, maintaining the light the Navigators cleaved to amid the worst of warp storms.

It was not enough now. Over the long, dissolute millennia, the first psionic amplifiers had been constructed under Martian direction, initially as a simple means of purifying and augmenting the signal, and then, later, as essential tools for arresting its degradation. More machinery had been bolted on, retrofitted and infiltrated into the earlier, more elegant, designs. Additional psy-conduits were laid down, each one larger than the last, to boost the signal from the distant Imperial Palace. The immense spikes around the original sphere that looked so much like mighty hab-towers were in fact psionic machinery, added to every year by armies of enginseers and psyker-artisans. Their roots extended far below the Fortress' foundations, and their pinnacles now ascended higher still, until they were colossal fingers of resonant iron, reaching up, claw-like, to scrape the skies.

As the new age of strife had arrived and mankind's grip on its domains had faltered, this complex too had become bloated, run to fat, half-derelict at its base and semi-understood even by its most senior occupants. The power drain it required passed beyond all reason, such that a minor fluctuation in demand could wipe out the charge-supply for a whole urban subsector. The build-up of psychic power in its major reso-nators was so enormous that the air hummed and crackled for a hundred miles in every direction, causing sickness and tumours and sending minds into torpor. Whoever its origi-nal designers had been, they could surely never have foreseen the throughput of human souls now required to stoke that great psychic furnace. The years of discharge had worn away at the tottering foundations, clogging the Fortress' creaking arteries, for now more than a hundred souls were burned up every day, only to be replaced within the sphere by the steady shuffle of new blood brought in by the overworked and overextended Black Ships.

So the choir continued. The hymns continued. In defiance of the heavy grind of entropy and the weakness of mortal strength, the Beacon still burned, threading together human-ity's rotting empire of a million worlds.

And now Crowl watched it approach, filling the forward viewers with its obsidian majesty.

He had never travelled even close to it before, but it was not hard to guess that something in the air was different to how it should have been. Something in the harmonic resonance, the subtle thrum of molecules and particles, was wrong. Light-ning lanced down across the great dome, jerky static charge snapped between the pinnacles of the iron crown. This was Holy Terra, where all wards were strongest and the walls were manned by demigods clad in the gold of ages, but still the cracks had begun to snake out. Nowhere was immune. Nowhere was insulated.

He remembered how it had been at the other end of the great conduit, where the psychic concentration had been so overpowering that he had wanted to fall on his knees before it. Here, it was different. He could sense the same gathering of unearthly energies, but they were wilder, unrestrained, flapping like a loose sail in the wind. It was as if the moorings had slipped now, the vessel drifting free even as the swell gained in strength under the keel.

'Any challenge-hails?' he asked Aneela.

She shook her head, keeping them on a steady course towards the heart of it. The Fortress grew larger and larger, swelling up until it obscured and blanked the skies ahead. It had once been a mountain of rock and snow, rearing up in unparalleled natural majesty. Now it was dark and mangled, just as gigantic, still rooted in its aeons-old tectonic foundations.

'Nothing at all?'

'I will notify, if any come in,' Aneela said.

Her voice was tense. Crowl was tense. It felt as if any movement, any breath, might release some snap of static, break some pact, provoke some catastrophic and malevolent presence to devour them all.

They had already passed many watchtowers, shooting low over the landscape of pipes and flare-plumes. They should have been halted there, asked for credentials, even shot at. Instead, there was nothing – an empty hiss on the comm-lines, the curl and whip of lightning arcs across pitch-black adamantium.

'I'd have preferred some interference,' Crowl muttered. 'Something to tell me there are still souls alive in there.'

The gunships angled upward, reaching the metal-clad foothills of the immense construction, moving like tiny specks against the ebon cliff-face. More watchtowers swept by, each larger than the last, each crowned with lascannons and psy-lances and marked with the sombre sigils of the Adeptus Astronomica. Some were dark and silent, their gaunt profiles not even broken by functional marker-lumens. Others crackled with electric discharge, sparking like decorative candles in the surge of the storm's anger. A few were on fire, though the flames were blue-tinged and wavered strangely.

Below the flyers, close to the line of the enormous trench, the skeleton of a big lander languished amid shattered spurs, its spine smouldering. Enough remained of its corpse to determine that it had been travelling from a Black Ship. Those things were some of the most tightly protected vessels in the entire Imperium, equipped with every failsafe imaginable, and now one lay in pieces, dashed against the cyclopean flanks of its final destination with nothing but silence from the sentinel stations around it.

'I have coordinates for an intake hangar, close to the main control spires,' Aneela announced, guiding them further up and further in. Two of the great iron spike-vanes, hazy in the murk, were now on either side of them, and the curve of the inner sphere rose up beyond, glistening as if wet. The surface looked like glass, almost, as if you could somehow see within it if you got close enough.

'Take it,' said Crowl. 'Something is very wrong here.'

They flew tightly, keeping close to the steadily rising artificial terrain. They passed within two enormous piers of black stone, each one surmounted by an outward-facing nova cannon barrel, though neither had any signs of activation. At the terminus of the chasm between the piers was a steep iron-faced surface, gouged and pitted with age. A bank of lumens running along its top was blank and dormant, and none of the many fibre bundles criss-crossing its outer face flickered with light. A carved icon of the Adeptus Astronomica was only barely visible in the low light, glinting weakly from the reflected glare of the distant lightning strikes. At the centre of it all was a horizontal cleft in the metal, over a hundred metres across and more than twenty in height. The entrance was barred, its outer doors down and clamped together like jaws. No guide-lights were operative either above or below it.

Aneela brought the gunship up in front of the barrier. The second one rose up alongside, both facing the closed portal. They hovered there, engines labouring in the buffeting winds.

'Run standard docking requests,' Crowl ordered.

Aneela did so. 'Nothing, lord.'

'You used the Inquisitiorial seal?'

'Of course.'

'Repeat it.'

As she complied, Crowl gazed out at the fortress wall before him. It looked entirely dead, like the façade of some nightmarish sarcophagus. The hard-to-shake sense of dread intensified. If the Beacon had suffered some catastrophic malfunction, surely forces would be on their way to remedy it. Surely someone in the Palace would have reacted by now – the Fortress couldn't be this inert in normal times, surely.

And yet, as he remembered the fires in the endless city beyond, the collapse in order, the running battles and the clearing of the skies, it was not impossible to entertain an even more troubling thought.

They know something is wrong, but they cannot do anything about it.

'No response to interrogation on any channel,' Aneela finally reported.

'We don't have time for this,' Crowl muttered, opening a link to the other gunship. 'Break us in.'

Both Spiderwidows withdrew to a safe distance, then opened up with bolter and lascannon. A torrent of hard-rounds crashed into the barrier, hammering into the thick metal. Lasbeams interleaved with the bolt-shell impacts, sizzling into the unyielding adamantium.

For a while, little impression was made. The surface chipped and sparked, but remained intact. Slowly, though, under the relentless barrage, the outer layers began to heat up. A red glow spread, turning steadily to white. The bolt explosions rattled across the external face, blasting divots and eating into the melting layers of protection.

Finally, with an echoing boom, one panel imploded and collapsed in on itself, flying back into the hangar as the bolt-rounds smacked against it.

A gaping chasm opened up on the far side, blacker than any natural night. The shadow seemed to leak out of the wound, dribbling through the jagged hangar-doors like oil.

Both Spiderwidows switched to forward lumens, and pools of hard white streamed into the gap. Despite the power of the floodlights, they made little headway into that murk.

Crowl found that he was sweating.

'Take us in,' he ordered.

The first thing Spinoza noticed was the stink of blood – thick and pungent, inescapable, almost unbearable.

She jumped down from the gunship and landed heavily on

the deck. The hangar itself was huge, stretching back into the interior of the Fortress further than she could see. Ranks of large vessels stood in the darkness, all deactivated, all silent.

There was no interior illumination at all – everything they could see was picked out by the gunships' lumens or those mounted on their helms. The darkness felt like it had a life and presence of its own. Whenever she moved her head, shadows moved to eat up the sparse light, slithering up over it, drowning it.

The movements of the storm troopers disembarking echoed eerily. She saw Khazad treading carefully, venturing further in. She went after her. They had barely exchanged words since it had all begun again, caught up in their various assignments.

'I see you are restored,' Spinoza voxed.

The assassin nodded. 'Almost so.'

'I am glad to have you back with us.'

'And am glad to be back.' Khazad was almost invisible in the gloom, her matt-black armour sinking into it. She looked wary, as if not sure what to say to her. 'You understand this, though – I am here for Phaelias.'

'It seems we are all caught up in that man's business, one way or the other.'

It had been intended as a part-jest, something she rarely attempted. Khazad's lack of response told her the general strategy was a sound one.

'Listen,' Spinoza started, hesitantly. 'What happened, in Courvain–'

'No, not that,' Khazad said, abruptly, moving off into the dark. 'Not here.'

Spinoza almost followed her, but then Crowl was signalling to them. The storm troopers formed up in two squads, one headed by Hegain at the rear, the other by Revus. Crowl paced ahead, his black-and-silver armour picked out by Gorgias' erratic lumen-beams.

'Now stay close,' Crowl ordered. 'Follow me, and keep moving.'

They moved further up into the hangar's interior. The storm troopers trained their weapons into the grasping dark, sweeping their viewfinders warily. Crowl had unholstered Sanguine, which glinted silver. Khazad's blade was out too, though unactivated.

Spinoza kept Argent at her belt. It was too heavy to bear unless needed for combat, but already she felt her fingers itch for it.

Their footfalls echoed up into the high vaults above, though no other sounds penetrated the thick atmosphere. The stench of blood grew more pronounced the further they went. Soon there was something else alongside it, something Spinoza could not place. It was a little like... rot.

They reached a heavy door set into the hangar's rear wall. It was closed and locked. One of Revus' troops went up to the lock-panel and attempted to open it. After a few failed attempts, he placed a microcharge over the unit. The charge fizzed, ticked, then blew, shattering the lock panel. The trooper went back to it, and applied a breaker to the exposed electronics.

The doors coughed, jerked, then slid open.

The storm trooper immediately gagged.

Blood trickled across the threshold. In the corridor beyond, the floor was caked with it, glistening blackly under the sweep of the lumens.

Two storm troopers crept forward, angling their hellguns around the corner before disappearing into the enveloping gloom. Spinoza followed close behind Crowl and Khazad.

Once inside the corridor, they caught sight of the first bodies.

'Keep moving,' Crowl said again.

Spinoza glanced at the corpses as she went past. They had been adepts of some kind, clad in dark robes that sucked to the flesh like liquid. Their skin was ivory-white in the glare of the helm-beams. They looked thin, almost skeletal, and their arms were outstretched. Their shaven heads were marked with iron implants, including input-rings at the base of the scalp. Their blood lay on the floor, old and stale and viscous. It appeared as if they had been running, possibly, though their bodies were mangled badly and it was hard to tell.

They advanced down the length of the corridor, reached an airlock seal, forced it open, and went through it. Everywhere they looked, everywhere they went, it was the same – suffocating dark, utter silence, corpses lying pale and still. Spatters of blood ran across the walls, thrown like paint-streaks.

'All the same, so it seems,' Hegain mused, softly. 'Adepts, menials. No one from the outside.'

'Yet,' said Spinoza.

The further they went in, the worse it got. The bodies were mutilated, contorted, pressed into tiny spaces. They entered a narrow through-passage and saw corpses hanging from the ceiling, twisting slowly in the shadows. Some of them had been despoiled – teeth-marks, claw-rents, angry holes caused by gnawing. A few adepts looked like they had been trying to get out of the chambers and had been dragged down by pursuers. Others looked like they had killed themselves using whatever means they had to hand. In one chamber – once some kind of communal instructional archive – all the pict-screens had been smashed. The operators had used the long shards on themselves.

It became hard to process it all. Spinoza heard her own breathing resonate in her ears, close and moist. Her pulse picked up, beating like a soft drum. Every movement, every glance, brought a flash or blur of something horrific, caught in the sporadic pools of lumen-glare.

Suddenly, from up ahead, a hellgun went off. She dropped to her knees, grabbing Argent's hilt and kicking the disruptor into shimmering light. More shots zipped out, flashing painfully, making the black walls briefly dazzle.

Revus hurried past her, clamping it all down. She heard mutters of, 'Nothing, nothing,' over the comm.

She relaxed her grip on Argent, and stood again.

As she did so, she caught sight of *it* – the xenos – reaching out of the shadows to her right. In a cold panic, she swung instinctively, smashing it back against the wall, tensing to go after it, before realising she had smashed a carved gargoyle from its mount. The broken stone rocked on the floor, sticky amid the blood. She exhaled, furious with herself.

'Fortitude,' Crowl warned over the comm, speaking to them all. 'We can assume it will get worse. Remember – His truth wards against the lies of the senses.'

Then they were edging through the dark again, treading carefully among the corpses. Khazad drew silently alongside her then, placing a hand gently on hers.

'I see them too,' she hissed quietly. 'Ghosts. This place is more than tomb.'

Spinoza said nothing, torn between anger at her lapse and the gathering sense of nausea that threatened to overwhelm her. Even in normal times, this place would have been hateful – its walls swirled with baroque ironwork, sweeping in unnatural eddies and enclosing strange, semi-figurative sculptures. Everything was black, semi-reflective and oppressive.

The Fortress had been dwelt in by psyker-breeds for too long, and it reflected their uncanny, tortured perceptions.

They crossed a high chamber bisected with long lines of slender pillars. Their lumen-beams rippled across great bas-relief images cut into the metal. Mournful theological images of the Holy Primarchs were set against stranger things – serpents, beasts with many heads, whirlpools in which limbs and torsos melded and diverged. More bodies were encountered, each with fresh evidence of horrific ends – spines curving clean away from red-raw flesh, skin stripped from muscle, organs yanked wetly from spreadeagled torsos.

And then, up ahead, something moved. The storm troopers froze. Spinoza shuffled to the fore, where Crowl had also hunched down, breathing hard through his helm's respirator.

In the distance, indistinct amid the angled interplay of lumen-beams, a diminutive figure was limping towards them. It was human in outline, albeit too small to be an adult. Spinoza adjusted the gain on her helm's night-vision augmenter, and saw the grainy profile of a male youth, bare-headed, implants nestling against his pale skin, limping.

Every hellgun was trained on him. He seemed not to have noticed them at all, and his head hung down against his chest.

'Survivor?' Revus voxed.

'Stay back,' warned Crowl. 'Maybe.'

The youth stopped moving. He seemed to be dragging something behind him. He stayed perfectly still for a moment, his lips moving soundlessly.

Then the face snapped up, catching the lumens. It was white, just as all the others had been, but the forehead bulged horribly, threaded with black veins. The boy's eyes were gone too, and streaks of black blood ran down his chin. He was dragging the top half of what had once been another body.

'*The Wound!*' he cried wildly, in a voice that sounded like an animal with its throat crammed full of swarf.

'End it,' Crowl ordered, opening fire.

The hellguns snapped in unison, flooding the chamber with light. For a second, Spinoza thought they had dropped it, only to witness the thing leap through the las-beams with horrific agility, pouncing and loping towards them in a judder of extreme speed. It squatted briefly, insect-like, against the bole of a pillar.

A storm trooper darted forward, firing continuously. The boy-horror flicked a wrist, and the storm trooper was propelled across the chamber as if kicked by some massive boot, cracking into the far wall with a wet thud. It scampered towards the rest of them, weaving between bolt-shells and las-blasts, going straight for Crowl.

Spinoza charged, swinging Argent up to velocity, its energy field now flaring, but she was a fraction too slow – Khazad was on it, slashing down with her blade, cutting cleanly between shoulder-blade and neck. The edge ran through the boy-horror's torso diagonally, emerging under its right arm.

It slapped to the ground, wriggling, and Spinoza saw its empty eye sockets stare blindly at her. It should have been dead – Khazad's blow had gone straight through it. She strode forward, swinging Argent heavily, bringing it down on the creature's head.

The thrown storm trooper had not got up. Hegain hurried over to him, bent over to investigate, then stood up slowly, looked at Revus and shook his head.

Crowl joined Spinoza, staring at the bone-flecked remains of the psyker-youth. He dropped down to his haunches, extending a probing finger into the mess of skin and brain matter. 'Extensive physical corruption,' he said. 'Enlarged cranium, major internal changes. How can this have happened, here of all places?'

'Augurs detecting movement ahead,' Revus reported, edging protectively in front of Crowl. 'Many, many signals.'

Crowl got up and calmly reloaded. 'There will be a command chamber somewhere up ahead. We must find answers.'

Then he was off again, limping into the darkness. The storm troopers went with him, fanning out on either side, covering one another watchfully.

Spinoza shared a long look with Revus. Then he too was moving, staying close to the inquisitor, not giving her a backward glance. Khazad prowled ahead with a hunter's enthusiasm, her deathmask helm underlit with her blade's energy field.

She shook her head resignedly, and followed them into the dark.

CHAPTER NINETEEN

Revus felt like throwing up. His throat was full of phlegm, his eyes were stinging.

He knew what it was. They all knew what it was. Every soul still alive within this place had some kind of psychic gift. It was like a stench, albeit one that competed with the very real aromas of vivisection. The fug made it hard to concentrate, hard to focus on what was real and what was not.

He had seen things in the shadows. The scrawny killer he had brought to Courvain had appeared more than once, hanging back under the shadow of leering gargoyles and carved dragons. Roodeker, too. Every time he moved his head, apparitions flickered briefly at the edge of the lumen-flare.

Concentrate, he told himself.

The only one of them who went onward with unfettered enthusiasm was Crowl. The inquisitor was pushing the pace now, pressing ahead, driving them hard. They had quickly moved out of comms range of the gunships, perhaps due to this place's internal density, but more likely due to the psychic effervescence that played havoc with every piece of equipment in their armoury. Now they were isolated within the gigantic fortress, and already one man down.

Revus didn't even know precisely what they were doing there. Spinoza had been the one to tell him before they had mounted up for the crossing, and her face had betrayed her long-seated doubts.

'We activated a link from Rassilo's network,' she had told him. 'In what came back, the Lord Crowl recognised snatches of battle language from the Forbidden Fortress. We therefore believe the third member of the conspiracy is the Master of the Astronomican.'

We believe.

Still, having arrived here now, it was impossible not to see that something terrible had taken place. Had it been his decision, he would have withdrawn immediately and called for back-up, broadcasting to all and any receptors in range.

Crowl had just pressed on, reiterating the need to detain the Master before the chance went, thrusting deeper into the pitch darkness of the interior.

Now they were far from help. No comm signal would escape this colossal edifice. Either Crowl understood more than he was letting on, or they were taking a reckless chance. The inquisitor had taken gambles before, and every time Revus had gone along with them. The fact that both of them were still alive after so many years working together demonstrated the soundness of the general doctrine, and he had learned to trust the old man's instincts.

Until now. Now, the sickness could no longer be ignored.

They climbed a long, broad stair, stepping over the long slicks of blood. One skeletal adept had been jammed between the spindles of the stone banister, her skull cracked, her ribs protruding like bone fingers. Another had, so it seemed, torn his own innards out.

They reached the landing above, where a dark crystal chandelier had once hung but was now dashed into pieces across the black floor. He checked his malfunctioning proximity meter, and caught a few jerky signals, flickering uncertainly. Out of the corner of his eye, he saw the shadows writhe again, playing tricks on his mind.

Except they were not tricks. A robed horror sprang from the dark, swinging down the hem of a long, velvet curtain. A second creature darted out from under a heap of twisted corpses, its face punctured with hooks.

Revus opened fire, missing with his first shots. His troops reacted too slowly, dulled by the weight of mental confusion, and the las-bolts skittered ill-directedly. The corrupted adepts moved as if they were half out of time and space – lurching and shifting, sliding eerily through the swivelling shadows. The lumen beams spun as the storm troopers scattered, trying to gain a hit. Revus thought he saw the first psyker – a horribly emaciated wretch with tattered robes flapping around a cane-thin torso – rise up into the air, before its mind-blast hit him, hurling him from his feet.

The touch was freezing, an agony of frost, slicing through his armour as if it weren't there and bending him double. He cried out, just one of many shouts and bolt-blasts, making his ears ring and his vision shake.

He unfolded with effort and tried to find a target – any target – in the swing and flash of half-perceived impressions. He saw another one of his own troops sail past him, arms cartwheeling, cracking into the chandelier's remnants with a sickening crunch.

'*Enough,*' he spat, furious with himself.

He opened fire, clamping his finger to the trigger and punching las-beams right into the onrushing hook-face.

'The Wound!' it cried, writhing in obscene ecstasy as the bolts sliced into it. It stumbled, carried through the las-fire by its momentum, and lurched out to claw at him.

He couldn't move. He just fired and fired, tearing the flesh from its bones, but still it came on, dragging itself into him. A half-skinned face reared up, pulled into a raw grin by the hooks, its black-in-black eyes wide with hunger.

The charge-pack clicked empty, and Revus swung the hell-gun round to smash the stock into its face. By then Hegain was piling in too, hammering at it with his own weapon. A third storm trooper joined in, and they beat it down into the ground, smashing its bones, grinding it into the floor, their movements frantic. Revus heard someone shouting, roaring, *screaming* – and only slowly realised it was him. Horrified, he jerked away, dragging himself from the wreck of what had once been a human, swivelling around to try to locate the other one.

Hegain and the other soldier withdrew as well, all breathing heavily. The corrupted psyker lay on the stone between them, its tortured body broken. It was still breathing – gargling on its own blood, but somehow dragging breaths in. With a liquid gurgle, it started to slither after him.

Spinoza emerged from the shadows, easing Hegain aside to get into contact. Her crozius was flaming. With brutal efficiency, she swung the maul down over the prone psyker, finally snuffing out those terrible, snuffling gasps.

'Move,' she commanded, breaking back the way she had come and beckoning him to follow. 'Faster, now.'

They did as she said, breaking into a jog. As he went, Revus forced himself to remember the basics – snap a new charge in, keep moving, keep looking out and up. He blinked through the flicker-dazzle of jumping lumens, trying to catch sight of the other creature amid the flash of light-dark. He caught glimpses of more bodies on the floor – his own troops, this time, broken against the walls, bent backwards, thrown aside like puppets.

Hegain limped along with him, aiming his hellgun jerkily as he went, his breathing a little too rapid. Up ahead, a heavy set of doors loomed. Their edges were blurred, sliding around as they sprinted towards them. Revus began to feel like he might pass out, and willed himself to keep going. From somewhere behind he heard a high-pitched scream, then the smack of bolt-rounds striking something hard and unyielding.

They piled through the doors. Once across the threshold, Revus dropped down and swung around, attempting again to find something to aim at in the murk. He felt other bodies blunder past him, Crowl among them, then the assassin, then, last of all, Spinoza, striding tall in her blood-red armour.

Someone hit a control, and the shutters clattered down. Blast-panels slid together behind them, sealing them in with a tight, final snap.

The noises of combat echoed away. Revus stayed hunched down. His blood thundered in his temples. His hands were shaking, his legs were like liquid.

Get a grip, he told himself. *It's just witchery.*

They were in a circular chamber. Sensorium equipment lined the walls. A hololith column dominated the central space, marred by three corpses draped across it like macabre decorations. Crowl had sunk to his knees too, one curled fist resting on the floor, recovering himself. Revus could see ten of his storm troopers there, plus the assassin and the interrogator. Gorgias darted around, back and forth, his lumen beam winking and flaring in the dark.

'Did we get the second one?' Khazad asked, her voice uncharacteristically uncertain.

'I shot it,' Hegain offered weakly, sounding like he only half knew where he was. 'Do not know, in truth, if that was the end of it.'

'The place is infested,' Spinoza muttered, checking the door-seal.

Crowl got awkwardly to his feet. 'So it seems.' He limped over to the hololith column. 'And we are in the dark, most literally. Sergeant, if you please?'

Hegain roused himself and hurried to assist. Revus joined them.

This chamber was much like all the others they had passed through already – depowered, completely dark. They dragged the bodies away from the main column and examined the power inputs. Everything was cold and dead. Hegain pulled a portable cell from his webbing and adjusted the interface. He set the cell for maximum drain and slotted it into the column's auxiliary power feed.

The mechanism reacted instantly. Lights strobed up its baroque base-station before spinning out across the flat iron surface. A series of rune-controls glowed into life, all sickly green against the deep dark.

Crowl leaned forward, his breathing shallow, condensation steaming from his helm. 'Good,' he said, studying the interface. 'This is a start.'

He depressed one of the runes, and a hololith of the Fortress spiralled into instantiation over the column's octagonal top.

Revus forced himself to focus, to absorb himself in the

schematic. It took a moment for his eyes to even focus properly, but he narrowed them and blinked hard until they did.

The Astronomican's central sphere was clearly visible at the heart of the complex. A bewildering array of internal chambers and corridors were picked out in translucent lines around that core, all slowly rotating. Status indicators and personnel locators blinked all across the network, clustered in various locations like corpuscles in a bloodstream.

'Life-signs,' Spinoza said, indicating a series of markers making their way steadily inwards. 'Withdrawing to the central region.'

Crowl nodded. 'An inner defence layer. Some survived, at least.'

Hegain moved over to a pict-screen, and connected it to the newly powered cell-grid. More runes blinked into life across the crystal surface. 'Not many,' he said. 'Reports here from all over the Fortress. Sudden breakdown in controls. Sector after sector... they did not have any time.'

'What caused it?' Crowl asked.

'Unknown.'

Spinoza peered intently at the schema. 'Why no distress calls?'

Hegain worked the dials, prompting more runes to skid across the display. He shook his head. 'Unsure, lord. There are confused reports... Comms towers overrun, that is plain.' He looked up. 'If they lost the transmitters–'

'Someone would still notice,' Spinoza said. 'This is the Fortress.'

'A thousand fires are burning,' Revus said. 'Unless a persistent distress call made it out...'

Crowl laughed. The sound was so strange, so jarring, that for a moment Revus didn't know where it had come from.

'That is it, captain,' he said. 'Pride. They left it too late, tried to keep a lid on it, and now their mouthpiece has been taken away from them.' He leaned in closer, gripping the edge of the column. '*He* is still in there, though. The one we came for. He cannot run now.'

'That may be true, lord,' said Spinoza. 'But you can see what has happened. We must find a way to raise the alarm.'

'Not what we came for,' said Crowl, staring intently into the heart of the hololith.

Revus looked over at Spinoza. Hegain too broke off from his work and looked up at Crowl. Even Gorgias stopped spinning.

'This is the Astronomican, lord,' Spinoza said, quietly. 'This is the Emperor's Light.'

'Yes, Spinoza. That it is.'

'You have seen the… corrupted. We must summon aid. We cannot halt it by ourselves.'

'We did not come to halt it.' Crowl straightened, seemingly having seen enough. 'We came for the Master. I have memorised the path – come, we must be swift, lest they complete their inner defence and lock us out.'

He moved away from the hololith, clearly expecting the rest of them to come with him.

Spinoza, though, stayed where she was. 'You cannot be in earnest, lord,' she said.

Crowl halted. 'I am always in earnest, interrogator. Some catastrophe has befallen this place – that may hamper our task, but it cannot prevent it.'

'The Fortress is overrun.'

'That is not our concern.'

In eight years of service, Revus had never spoken against his master. There had never been the cause for it. For a moment, even then, he struggled. He knew his mind was under unnatural psychic stress. He knew that his fear and his fatigue made him susceptible to error. He had already committed one great mistake, one that another master might have had him sanctioned, or even executed, for.

But this was now madness.

'The interrogator is correct, lord,' he interjected, feeling as if he had to drag the words out with pincers.

Crowl snapped around to face him. 'Revus,' he breathed, disbelievingly. 'What is this, now?'

'As I said, lord. The interrogator is correct.'

Another laugh blurted from Crowl's vox-grille, just as harsh, just as laced with the evidence of stimms. 'I think you are forgetting your duty, captain,' he said, an edge of menace in his normally equable voice.

'It is duty that compels me,' Revus replied, trying to keep his voice calm. He hated this. He hated this with every fibre of his being. 'You have seen the horrors here. They cannot be allowed to endanger–'

'So it has infected you.' Crowl spoke as if a great insight had just come to him. He looked over at Spinoza. 'You were there, too. It has infected both of you.' He backed away from them, keeping Sanguine in his hand. The storm troopers in the chamber did not intervene. Some looked to Revus, some to Crowl. 'Jarrod told me it could affect minds. It could whisper, long after the event. You told me so yourself, did you not, Spinoza? Now we are close, its poison will not let you strike. It speaks to you still, and you are too weak to see it.'

In a flicker of battle-sign, Spinoza gestured for the storm troopers to keep their weapons lowered and make no move. 'I have attempted to counsel you, lord,' she said. 'Such was my duty. When that counsel was discarded, I attempted to serve. Such was my duty. But now, in all conscience, I can no longer obey. We must make haste to draw reinforcements here, or we will lose the Beacon.'

'You wish to delay me,' Crowl accused, moving towards a second door on the far side of the chamber. 'You wish to keep the traitor from justice at my hand.'

Gorgias became seriously agitated then. '*Insanus!*' he croaked, unsure which way to float. 'Listen to her!'

'We can secure the Fortress,' Revus offered, trying again. 'Restore comms, summon assistance. Then, when the danger is past, we can pursue the one you desire to speak to. He can hardly escape.'

Crowl laughed a third time. 'You fool. That is what he wishes for. Fate has trapped him here, caught in some mire of his own making, and you wish to break him out of it.' He began to fumble with the door release. 'So be it. Your treachery damns you. All of you. If you do not have the stomach for the hunt, you may go your own way.'

Spinoza risked a step towards him, reaching out with her gauntlet. 'My lord,' she said. 'Do not leave. You have seen what waits in the dark.'

'Afraid of it?' Crowl asked, mockingly. 'No matter. You shall not have to face it. I always preferred hunting alone.'

'Not alone.' The voice was Khazad's. Unseen, unnoticed, she had edged closer to Crowl. Now she moved to stand beside him, blade in hand. 'If he is in there, I come with you too.'

'Good!' Crowl said, delighted. '*Kataj*. I knew I was right to take you in.'

Revus watched Khazad in disbelief. The whole place screamed with madness. All judgement was affected – hers too, seemingly.

'No one else moves,' Spinoza ordered, addressing the storm troopers. 'Stay where you are – your duty is plain.'

Crowl finally activated the locks, and doors slid open. The darkness beyond was almost painful in its completeness.

'I pity you, Spinoza,' he said, and the edge of mania made his words sound almost jaunty. 'The chance to achieve greatness comes but once in a lifetime.'

For a moment, he and Khazad stood before the chasm into darkness, as solid as ever.

'I pray you will see your folly in time,' Spinoza said. 'I pray that He preserves you.'

Then the two of them melted into the blackness. The doorway gaped emptily, ushering in the fresh stink of blood.

Revus looked at Spinoza, feeling more wretched than he had ever done. 'What now?'

Spinoza stood for a moment, seemingly unable to move. Then she gripped Argent. The crozius was still activated, and a flicker of stray power ran down its shaft.

'Close the doors, captain,' she said, her voice cold and firm. 'We have work to do.'

CHAPTER TWENTY

This was vindication. This was confirmation of everything he had been working for since the Palace, drawing the threads together, tying them into the cord that had led him here, at last, to the source, to the architect.

His mind was working well, very well, much faster now. The Fortress, strangely enough, was helping with that. He could see things in the dark, flashes of memories and ideas, and they were the things that had brought him here, his angels of perception, the fragments of the whole. The xenos was there too, of course, goading him, driving him onward. He had long since stopped being surprised or shocked by its regular appearances – reflected in the black crystal surfaces, caught at the edge of sight when he turned his head, growling something unintelligible behind the speech of others.

Running helped, too. His body felt looser now. He could feel blood in his armour and guessed that something had broken, somewhere, but he couldn't attend to that now. He was awake again. It was still hard to breathe, but if he just kept going, just kept moving, it would all be fine.

He couldn't stop. If he stopped, he might hear Spinoza's doubts again. He might see *her face*, rather than *its face*, with that pious, insufferable concern written all over it.

She was a good acolyte, Spinoza. He was fond of her, despite her stiffness, her obsession with the regulations of their ordo. She would regret not coming with him, when all was finally revealed. She would regret missing her chance to *understand*.

Khazad loped alongside him, running freely, almost invisible in the gloom. That was a reassurance, if he was honest. Now that he was back in the tunnels, heading through the blood-soaked chambers with their markers of madness and excruciation, it was good to have a blade at his side, one who had already proved her worth.

Perhaps Khazad would have made a better acolyte. Perhaps, as fate willed it, that had been Spinoza's function all along – to bring the assassin into the fold. Perhaps, after this, another adjustment would have to be made.

'The wound,' he muttered, as he hobbled along. 'The wound.'

'Why do they say it?' Khazad asked, lighting the way ahead with the gold-silver illumination from her blade.

Crowl thought quickly. His mind was racing now, burning ahead. It was so much easier to think in here. 'They are soulbound,' he whispered. 'They see things. They know things and they feel things. They see things even the Magister did not.' He chuckled. 'A wound in the galaxy. There is some doubt as to their current status and reporting reliability. Bajan was a greater fool than his master. I hear the voices of a thousand worlds. There is a link. The anomaly. The xenos. The dead of the Astronomican.'

Khazad did not reply. She seemed to have sunk into a kind of battle-trance, and uttered few words now. She, too, appeared to have been enhanced by the psychic pressure in the air, stripped down to her essentials, shorn of all things but her remaining death-oath.

The chambers were getting bigger, becoming finer. Dark crystal surfaces were everywhere, reflecting the images of horror and pain like augmenting reflectors. Senior adepts slumped among the dead now, their fur-lined robes sticky with blood, their teeth pulled and their eyes gouged. In one hall – something ceremonial he guessed, going by the proscenium arch and ranked stages – dozens were strung up, flayed, changed, damaged, stretched. Someone had scrawled *The Wound* across a wall made of mirrors, tracing the words out in bloody handprints.

One of the killers was still there, gorging on raw flesh, her own nightshade robes disarranged and her hair stiff with blood over an enlarged skull. Her eyes, like all of their eyes, were black-in-black, empty, pupil-less, but still somehow capable of something like sight. She screamed at them, whirling a blackwood staff until it whipped the bloody flecks into a storm around her.

Khazad did what Khazad did best, darting and dancing in close, cutting the staff up with two rapid flickers of her blade, but the woman blasted her away with a fist-clench, then rose up unsteadily into the air, her robes fluttering.

Crowl shot her. He shot her again. He shot her a third time. His aim was impeccable. His reactions were superlative. His fingers appeared to be bleeding, and there was something sharp and urgent taking place in his chest cavity, but he could not pay any attention to that. The creature bent over itself as the bullets hit, jerking back and forth before being driven back against an old hexagrammatic ward graven into the crystal walls. When she hit it, she screamed and thrashed, her robes bursting into blue-edged flame. She couldn't get away from it. She stuck fast, like an insect on a pin, shrieking and writhing. Crowl watched it unfold, enthralled.

Khazad got back to her feet, and hobbled to his side.

'Must keep moving,' she muttered.

So they did, leaving the witch to burn. They raced away from the hall, entered the next, crept unseen through the procession of chambers, each one of them as black in their armour as the Fortress around them. As they hurried, Crowl found that he couldn't stop talking, even if it was only to himself now.

'Battle-language,' he murmured, remembering how he had worked it out. 'One of many hundreds in use. An esoteric dialect, based on pre-Vandire lexical forms. Suits this place. I told Palv it would be worth making a study of them, all of them, their origins, their types, but he never agreed, and now look where it has led us.'

He halted suddenly, drawing up before a baroque altarpiece encrusted with blinded angels and hawk-faced, lion-bodied sentinels. 'Where is Gorgias?' he asked, aware for the first time that the skull was not there.

'The skull does not come,' Khazad said, prowling ahead, her boots sucking on the wet floor.

Crowl shook his head. 'Even him,' he said mournfully.

Then they were moving again, limping, scampering, hugging the dark, squelching through the dampness where the violence had been. The vibrations in the air became even more intense. A pressure built up, making his sinuses ache. The silence was broken now, underpinned by a low, grinding thrum, one that ran through every structure and shivered every column.

They passed through a long, narrow capillary passageway

before breaking out into the biggest hall they had yet encountered. The change in air pressure was palpable. They crept across the floor. Giant supporting columns glinted at them in the gloom, each one engraved with defaced warding runes and astrological devices. Crowl caught sight of the xenos again, peering out from behind one of the pillars, smiling at him, before darting back into hiding, and he almost smiled back at it.

'Fighters,' Khazad warned, suddenly racing over to the chamber's central aisle.

Crowl went after her, tripping over an extended arm on the floor, then slipping on the still-warm matter underfoot.

A tangle of bodies lay in the open centre of the hall. Most were just as the others had been – acolytes and menials of the Fortress, clad in nightshade, their sunlight-starved flesh as white as alabaster. But among them were others – soldiers, clad in well-made carapace armour. Khazad dropped down beside the nearest of them, bringing her snarling blade up close to illuminate it. The battle-plate was dark grey, unmarked, with a narrow-slit helm.

She looked up at Crowl. 'Same ones as before,' she said.

'Good,' Crowl said, looking up and out into the shadows. From up ahead, more sounds could be made out, only faintly, but there nevertheless. 'They're still fighting. Retreating, but still fighting.'

He could smell it now. He could feel it too, rising up from the floors, permeating the crystal around them, curling up like smoke. It made him feel as he had done at the Eternity Gate, only this time the blood-rush made him exhilarated rather than terrified. Something immense lay up ahead. Something burning and burning and thundering like an unending watercourse. He pictured it in his mind's eye, recalling the detail of the hololith perfectly. He knew where they had to go, but time was running out. They would be lowering the internal doors soon, shutting out the madness, believing that by locking themselves down they could ride out the storm.

'Hurry, assassin,' Crowl said, getting up and limping down the long aisle. 'Hurry, hurry. Must not be late.'

Khazad looked down at the corpse again. She kicked it once, watching the head rock. She looked around her, at the mass of limbs and skin. Then she came after him, her blade crackling in the dark.

Revus slumped into a corner. Ten of his storm troopers had made it in, but two of those were badly wounded. One of them couldn't speak, it seemed. Gorgias was darting back and forth, caught between his usual fury and a more unusual sense of remorse. The skull didn't know what to do now. Revus could sympathise.

Hegain busied himself with the control column, trying to find out more about the situation. The rest recharged their weapons, wrapped bandages around wounds, recited battle litanies.

If Spinoza had been shocked by what had just happened, she didn't initially show it. She worked with Hegain for a while, trying to figure out how far they had come and what to do next. Revus attended to his weapon, ensuring it could be used again. His sense of panic was fading now, leaving a hollow feeling in its wake.

He remembered the Custodians. He remembered the endless hours of training, the desire to learn. He remembered the snarl of their golden halberds.

Spinoza came over then, squatting down in front of him. 'Thank you, captain,' she said, quietly.

Somehow, that made it much worse. 'You were right,' he said, for the want of anything better to say.

'We were right,' she corrected.

'Crowl is not himself,' he said. 'But the assassin?'

'Be thankful they are together, even in misjudgement.' She made to get up. 'Come, we cannot linger here.'

They rose and went over to the central column. Hegain looked up at them from his glowing lens port.

'Hard to get much more out, in truth,' he said. 'All instruments are playing badly. But the Lord Crowl was right – I think they left things too long, trying to fix them. They have not issued distress calls. Or, if they did, they were not answered.'

Spinoza rested a weary hand on the column's edge. 'Then we need to do so for them. I take it we do not have the numbers to do much here on our own?'

Hegain shook his head. 'There were thousands stationed in these sections. If even a fraction of them survived, we will not last long.'

'Can we get back to the gunships?' Revus asked, trying to make sense of the schematic.

'Possibly,' said Hegain, indicating the respective positions. 'But they have limited range transmitters, and would not carry verification markers for this location.'

Spinoza leaned further over. 'That is a communications tower, is it not?' she asked, pointing out a spire jutting from the Fortress' edge, close to their current position. 'Is it active?'

'Everything is inactive, lord,' Hegain said. 'But, if we could get there, it might be salvageable.'

Revus calculated the distances. 'Not far,' he said. 'If we moved now, before more of them got our scent, we could make it.'

'And we could broadcast a signal from there to the Palace?' Spinoza asked.

'If the equipment could be made functional,' said Hegain, 'to wherever you like.'

Spinoza looked over at Revus, who nodded his agreement.

The interrogator stood tall then, turning to address the remaining members of the detachment. 'You came here under the command of the Lord Crowl,' she told them. 'In his absence, you are now under mine. This Fortress is at risk of destruction, and that cannot be countenanced. We must strike out to secure the tower and broadcast a priority distress signal. Then, and only then, if we can, we shall attempt to go after the inquisitor. You have served with him for a long time. You have been loyal to him. I understand that. But I need to know, now, that you will do this for me.'

Revus stood at her side, making his feelings plain. Hegain did the same.

Gorgias swung low. '*Affirmativo*,' he rasped, though with less of his usual ebullience. 'Now, quick-quick.'

None of the others demurred. Spinoza turned back to Revus.

'Very well, then,' she said. 'Prepare yourselves – we move out.'

CHAPTER TWENTY-ONE

They kept their bodies low, embracing the deep shadow.

Every so often, they would hear evidence of the debased adepts, usually from far off. Occasionally they would see them at a distance, limping in gangs through the passageways with stringy hunks of meat clutched in their pale fingers. The dead outnumbered the corrupted, but the corrupted were still numerous, their foreheads swollen and their eyes blackened.

At times, they had to fight to make progress. Khazad led the way, using her blade in order to reduce the sounds of combat, supported by Crowl's marksmanship when necessary. They had to surprise the enemy, if possible – some of the psykers still had command of uncanny abilities, and telekinetic assaults had almost overwhelmed them more than once.

'Getting dangerous now,' Khazad told him, her voice low, as she nursed a gash along her right thigh. She strapped it up, her hands moving quickly in the gloom. 'Too many.'

Crowl nodded, reloading Sanguine. Despite his restraint,

he was running low on ammunition. 'Not far now,' he said, hoping he had calculated the route correctly.

'And what then, when we get there?' Khazad asked, sealing her makeshift wrapping and cutting the bandage off. 'We fight them all, too?'

'No, no,' said Crowl, sounding more confident than he felt. 'We won't have to.'

They set off again, padding through the murk. They entered a maze of some kind, perhaps designed according to ritual purposes. Crowl ran his fingers along the walls, feeling the engraved surfaces click against his gauntlet-tips, and wondered what was depicted on them. Something likely unsettling and esoteric. This mountain-city, even in normal times, was an arcane place, a home for the soul-cursed. Everything was symbolic, arranged to channel and conduct the psychic power that curled up tight at its heart. The corridors, the halls, the great vaults and the baroque chambers – all of them were part of a complex web, growing like a cancer around and beneath the central orb.

'Yes, yes,' he murmured, recognising the ways the paths took them. 'This is right.'

They passed through tighter confines, squeezing through a series of narrow service corridors. The bloodstains were fewer here, though even the servitors had not been spared – several lay at the gaping portal of some dormant refuse furnace, ripped apart, their blank eyes reflecting dully in Crowl's helm-lumens.

Soon, lights flickered up ahead. The sound of bootfalls, then low voices, welled up from below. They edged out, emerging from the service tunnels. They were high up, it seemed, having crawled into an empty gallery above a larger space below. Both Crowl and Khazad stayed on all fours, worming through the gaps between the empty seats and pressing themselves up against a spiked metal railing.

Below them, five metres down, was a grand chamber, lit up by the movements of dozens of armour-mounted lumens. Its floor was a chequerboard of blue-black marble, its walls the same dark crystal that lined every surface in the Fortress. Statues stood at regular intervals, some of vaguely human form, others of more indeterminate – and troubling, to the non-psyker – shapes. A few wall-inset lumens still burned, though most were smashed. Armourglass fragments littered the floor, alongside the familiar detritus of bloodletting.

Over to their right-hand side, where the chamber terminated, rose a sheer wall. It was black, and inscribed with occult symbols linked by geometric swirls of inlaid silver. It reminded Crowl a little of the maps in the Nexus Axiomatic. The skull-and-eye of the Adeptus Astronomica gazed out from a giant obsidian lozenge. At the base of the wall were a pair of reinforced siege doors, each one still raised, but clearly poised to drop soon. Steam pooled from the heavy lift-columns, spreading like condensation across the debris-strewn floor. Several squads of grey-armoured guards lingered, looking anxious to get inside. Perhaps more importantly, fine-grained hexagrammatic wards were engraved on almost every surface, overlapping one another, intersecting with one another, creating a perceptible, tangible barrier against the psychic.

'Here they come,' Crowl whispered.

Over to their left, another set of doors slid open. More figures emerged into the uncertain light, all hurrying, some limping, others dragging wounded with them. Most were in the dark grey armour of the Fortress guardians, but some were decked in nightshade robes, their pale skin standing out amid the wash of gloom.

Crowl narrowed his eyes, studying carefully. These adepts looked older than most of those they had encountered already. One, the most senior by her look, wore an elaborate lace ruff at her neck and walked with an ebony cane. She was bald, like they all were, with that mix of pale skin and black augmetic enhancement so reminiscent of the cadaverous.

They were agitated. Even as they made their way towards the waiting siege doors, fresh noises of scampering pursuit could be heard.

'You can make this?' Khazad asked him doubtfully, gesturing towards the long drop.

Crowl smiled grimly. 'No real alternative, is there?' he said. 'My armour will take the brunt.'

Now that he was stationary again, the pain in every joint had come back with a vengeance. It was harder to maintain the belief that this place was making things better. That now seemed, like a number of other things, to have been something of a misjudgement. He was getting tired. Very tired.

Khazad peered over the edge. Her blade was inert, held ready. The cavalcade approached the siege doors, and some of the adepts were ushered inside. The woman paused, conferring with one of the guards. They were almost directly beneath the gallery's edge.

Crowl looked at Khazad.

'Now?' she asked.

'Now,' he confirmed.

They both got up, grabbed the railing, and vaulted over, dropping to the marble floor. Khazad landed in a fluid crouch before springing up and setting her blade alight. She sprang towards the woman, going for her throat.

Crowl crashed to earth alongside her, overbalancing a fraction before correcting, whipping Sanguine out and aiming it at the woman, aware that a dozen lasguns were now also aimed at him.

Khazad had frozen. She was in mid-stride, one leg off the ground, her blade held high, entirely static.

The woman looked at both of them coolly. Up close, it was apparent she was very old. Her skin was crinkled like fine lace, her augmetics wire-thin and delicately made. Her nightshade robes were of rich velvet and mottled with subtle damask, though there were dark stains splattered at the hem.

Some movement was still possible, at least for him. Crowl slowly reached for his rosette, keeping Sanguine trained on her the whole time.

'An inquisitor,' the woman said. Her voice was dry, arch and penetrating. What was most disconcerting, though, was the fact her mouth never moved. 'What a night of surprises.'

'Greetings, mamzel,' Crowl said. 'You will want to take us in there with you.'

'I do not think so.'

'I must speak to your master.'

'He has other things on his mind.'

'He will make the time for me,' Crowl said.

The noises from the far end of the chamber began to grow in volume. Something was coming their way, heading rapidly up out of the darkness. Some of the guards began to look a little jumpy.

The woman signalled to those stationed at the doors, and the steam gouted out more powerfully. Slowly, grindingly, the siege doors began to drop. One by one, the grey-armoured troops filtered inside, along with the last of the more junior adepts, ducking as they entered. Soon only the three of them remained outside.

Crowl could see Khazad struggling against the psychic lock.

He began to wonder if he'd even be able to pull the trigger, if it came to it. The woman did not seem overly concerned at the threat.

'I suggest you go back the way you came,' she said, gathering up her robes and walking towards the portal. 'I wish you luck.'

'Four beasts,' said Crowl. 'Four beasts, full of eyes, before and behind.'

She halted.

'Three beasts have been uncovered,' Crowl went on. 'Who is the fourth? I will discover it. Perhaps it is me. Ask him about that, when you see him.'

She turned back. Her face remained a mask, taut as a screen of ivory. She looked at him, long and hard. She glanced at his rosette again, then over at the still-struggling Khazad. An unearthly scream rang out, echoing up from the chambers at the other end of the hall. More followed, louder and closer.

For a moment, he thought she would remain firm. She closed her eyes briefly, as if communing with someone or something. The doors kept coming down. Soon they would be below shoulder-height.

Then her eyes opened again. Khazad was released, though her blade spun from her fingers and embedded, shivering, in the stone floor.

'A night of surprises,' the woman said again, her mouth as rigid as a stone. 'Stow your weapon. Remove your helm. You have bought yourself a little more time. Let us see what you can do with it.'

Spinoza stood before the closed doors, her crozius snarling. She took a final moment to memorise the route ahead, calibrating that with the numbers left to them and their capabilities.

Losing Khazad was a blow – she was invaluable in a close-range fight, and now she was gone, haring after Crowl on a mission that would surely see them both dead soon.

The prospect of that, of both of them being lost in this horrific place, racked her. Everything about the Fortress did. She knew why, of course, but that didn't make it much easier to deal with. Maybe she should have spoken out earlier, at the final meeting in Courvain, but it was hard, almost impossibly so, to break the lifetime habit of fealty under all circumstances.

Doubts crowded at her mind, even as she tried to think past them. She saw Crowl's disbelieving face staring at her, over and over. She had never disobeyed a direct order from a superior before. Tur would likely have shot her on the spot, rather than let her get away with it.

That was not Crowl's style, of course. And it had to be remembered that, as Revus had said, the man was not himself. If things had been less critical, if the situation had been otherwise, she would never have done it. Now, though, as Hegain had demonstrated, the decision was surely the right one. Losing tracts of hab-units to anarchy was regrettable; losing the Astronomican was unthinkable.

'Ready, captain?' she asked Revus, who stood on the opposite side.

Revus nodded. The others were all in place, lined up facing the doors in two ranks, the first kneeling, the second standing. Gorgias had unsheathed his needle-gun, his eye glowing a determined dark crimson. Once out, they would have to move fast and keep moving. They could already hear the scrape of fingernails down the outside of the portal, and more were arriving all the time.

'May He guide you all,' she said, crouching down, and released the lock.

The corrupted cascaded inside immediately, clawing and drooling. The storm troopers opened fire – a mixed barrage of las-beams, plasma bolts and hard rounds, shredding and cutting and sending the corrupted adepts scattering backwards.

Spinoza and Revus swivelled around the door's edges and launched into the flanks, cutting and blasting. A flesh-stretched face leered up at her out of the gloom, and she smashed it aside with her crackling maul. A scrawny claw grabbed at her ankles, and she kicked it away.

The first rank of storm troopers, having loosed their concentrated wave of las-fire, leapt up and charged. Two grenades spiralled overhead, bursting right at the heart of the press of horror-creatures and throwing their broken bodies against the corridor walls. The foremost storm troopers reached for combat blades even as the second rank raced to cover them with pinpoint las-blasts. In such tight confines, the tactic was effective, and the corridor ahead was blasted clear, its floor half-buried in a glut of twitching, claw-flexing bodies.

'Now *run*,' Spinoza ordered, leading by example.

They charged out of the chamber, barging the remaining corpses aside and sprinting down the long capillary.

From up above, where the vaults ran away into darkness, a chorus of hissing drifted down. The distant roofs ran with the sound of scuttling, as if an army of rats had been stirred into motion.

Spinoza ignored the sounds, keeping the mental map of the way ahead fixed in her mind. They had to reach one of the steep stairwells running close to the inside skin of the outer walls, get up it and fight their way into one of the major communications towers perched on the western-facing battlements. The distance was not great, but the passages were confined and tortuous.

Just like Courvain's, she thought to herself, with a pang of memory.

They reached a rectangular hallway, smeared with the evidence of extravagant tortures, at the end of which rose the first of the stairs. She had nearly made it when something leapt at her from under the heaps of flesh.

A dozen las-beams scythed into the creature, sending it slamming back into a twisted glut of cold bodies. Then, from the other side of the pitch-dark hallway, two more adepts burst from cover. Each was a vision of derangement – foreheads bulging as if fit to burst, striated with pulsing veins, the eyes compressed into black slits. They extended their arms, and a wall of pressure burst out from their blood-stained fingers.

Spinoza saw a storm trooper stumble, dropping to his knees, before blood burst from his helm-seals and armour-joints. Another one bent double, caught in the pressure-wave, crushed to the ground and burst apart like ripe fruit.

She hurled herself into the nearest psyker, heaving Argent into its stomach where the disruptor blazed and boiled. Revus got a shot away at the second, pinging its shoulder and sending it spinning. Gorgias flew in hard overhead, spraying needles and shrieking *'Diabolis extremis!'* at the top of his vox-emitter.

Another storm trooper, possibly Hegain, leapt atop the first corrupted adept, stabbing up and down in a frenzy. The second creature recovered itself in the swinging dark, baring a black-toothed mouth and hissing. It threw its arms out again, and the metal walls around them flexed. A pressure-wave hurtled down the hallway, catching two more storm troopers and kicking them over in sprays of blood.

Spinoza lurched with effort towards it, fighting the skirts of the effect, punching Argent two-handed into a spike-crusted chin. Its neck snapped cleanly, and she whirled back around, trying to see if any more had emerged.

None had. One of the downed troopers got back up, clutching his side, still bent double. The others did not.

'Keep moving,' she ordered again.

She broke back into a run, reaching the stairs and vaulting up them two at a time. Revus came close behind, followed by the rest. They clattered up the stairway, and unearthly screams followed them.

An adept was waiting for them at the top of the stairs. Spinoza didn't even break stride, lashing out with the full force of the disruptor charge, breaking its limbs and sending the bloody pieces careening into the shadows.

Across another vaulted hall, then up more spiral stairs, through an antechamber, and there it was – the slide doors to the communication tower. The panels were wedged open by a corpse that had got caught in the mechanism.

Spinoza dropped to her knees.

'Blind them,' she ordered. Hegain pulled a flare-grenade from his belt and threw it through the gap. They both averted their eyes as the flash went off, a microsecond of retina-burning illumination. 'Now, inside.'

They raced to make the gap, just as the first of the pursuing adepts crested the summit of the stairs behind them. Revus and another storm trooper stooped to drag the body from the gap and piled inside. Others shot the momentarily blinded adepts blundering about within, and once the last of the storm troopers had staggered over the threshold, Spinoza kicked the close mechanism. The doors slid jerkily together, just as the chasing creatures scampered across the antechamber towards them. The two panels fused with a hiss and a clunk, followed by multiple thuds as frustrated fists hammered on the other side.

Spinoza turned around, panting hard. Seven of them had made it in, including Revus and Hegain. They were hauling in breaths now, reloading, edging ahead warily.

The chamber was a large one, maybe fifteen metres across. On the far side were high armourglass windows, each more than ten metres high, lined with gothic arches in lead tracery. Banks of communication equipment covered every surface, extending up into the vaults above them, where large copper vanes hung amid entrail-like coils and signal-enhancers. Just as elsewhere, the excruciated bodies of those unfortunate enough to have been caught up in the bloodletting were everywhere, and the console tops were scratched with desperate fingernail trails.

The view outside was almost as troubling as the one within – the skies were black-red now, underlit by the raging infernos. The lightning was frenzied, snapping against the external walls as if trying to prise its way in. After so long in the oppressive darkness, to see the surfaces lit up by the flash and flicker of the storm made her eyes sting.

Revus stalked ahead with two others, prodding every static body with the muzzle of his hellgun. Spinoza signalled for two more to stand guard at the doorway, which was already being thumped hard from the outside. It might have been her imagination, but the metal looked to be flexing, as if some enormous force were being applied. She motioned to Hegain, and together they went up to the main comms station. She deactivated Argent's energy field, and adjusted a set of runes on its haft.

Hegain fiddled with the station controls before bringing out another portable power cell, connecting it and coaxing the transmitters into life. Far above them, out of sight but within hearing, the immense external emitters slowly turned westward.

'Full spectrum broadcast,' Hegain announced. 'All channels, maximum power. I can set it to auto-cycle, if you will it.'

Spinoza knelt down in front of the control console. 'Very good, sergeant. I shall require a closed input link.'

Hegain rummaged around in the hopper at his feet, before unravelling a wrist-thick cord. One plug went into the comms console, and he proffered the other to Spinoza.

She inserted it into Argent's shaft, just below the maul-head, then adjusted a control dial. Lights flickered into life along the crozius' length, and corresponding strobes lit up on the console.

Now there could be no mistaking it – the doors had began to bulge. A sound like the scrape of metal on metal rang out, as if knives had been brought to bear, or maybe claws.

Spinoza glanced up at Revus, who gave her the signal for all-clear.

His troops slowly took up positions behind cover, their guns facing the swelling door panels.

'Now then,' said Spinoza to herself, turning the other way, looking out across the burning city beyond the tower's edge, 'we shall see what an oath is truly worth.'

Once inside the inner defence circuit, things got better. The power was functional here, feeding lines of blue-tinged lumens. The air smelled less of blood and more of incense. The oppressiveness did not go away though. The pressure at the temples did not lessen. With every step, it grew a little stronger, pressing down, exerting its uneasy and unquantifiable sense of dread.

'Can you tell me your name?' Crowl asked the woman as they walked down a long, bare passageway.

'I am one of his Resonances,' she said.

'Are there many of you?'

She turned to him. 'Just what is it that ails you, inquisitor? You took your helm off, and I thought I was looking at a corpse.'

Crowl smiled grimly. 'It's been a long journey.'

Khazad was sullen and withdrawn. Losing her blade was, Crowl guessed, a major blow to her sense of self. Perhaps she was regretting her decision to accompany him.

He was in a somewhat similar position. His earlier euphoria was wearing off. Erunion's last doses were losing their potency. Or, maybe, as they moved out of the worst of the psychic maelstrom, things were settling down a little. He wondered how Spinoza was faring, back in those horror-drenched chambers, and the thought of her, back there, pained him.

They passed through more sets of doors. As they went, somewhat against expectation, the decoration became less ornate. The first portals were silver-inlaid riots of dream-images and astrological allegories, as if the architects had tried to conjure up the inner life of their charges in stone and steel. The ornamentation gradually fell away until they were back in an industrial milieu. The muffled grind of great machines rose up through the grilles of floor-decking. Surfaces became bare metal again, stamped with Astronomica sigils, but chipped, worn, and edged with corrosion.

The temperature began to drop. Surfaces were first clouded with condensation, then frosted with brittle spikes. The edges of things – doorways, lintels, lumen-casings – seemed somehow sharper, as if the air had become thinner, or perhaps electrically charged.

They reached the most mundane set of doors yet, a pair of beaten-iron slabs on rail-runners. Heavy levers controlled the cog-mechanisms to open it. The sharp stink of engine-oils now rivalled that of the incense.

As if sensing his thoughts, the Resonance turned towards him. 'This is a machine,' she said, her lips still perfectly static. 'Never forget that.'

The doors ground their way open, squealing on their rails. On the other side was an immense gulf, across which the way ahead shot straight as a spear, suspended high above a steam-choked void.

Crowl looked all around him, up and down, left and right, marvelling at the complexity of the devices cloistered below and hanging above. Everything had the stamp of Mars on it – the bronzed casings, the heavy frames, the old rust, the raw and brutal functionality. Great engines hammered, connected to drivetrains and gearing arrays, in turn connected to generators, power converters and energy-fins. Sparks of static flew across the chasms between the elements, half-lost in the fogs of vapour. Some areas flickered with greenish energy, snaking and writhing around conductor-spikes. Others were entirely lost amid noxious fumes, spilling from exhaust vents the size of orbital lifters. Some constructions, the largest of them all, defied interpretation entirely. There were ranks and ranks of wafer-like gold mesh, all crackling with wriggles of raw force and ringed with iron torcs. There were black spheres, suspended by electromagnetic force above receiving dishes, studded with snaking cables and input-whirls. There were crystals, each tens of metres high, glowing with eerie inner light, held in place by webs of sensor-whips. Nestled amid all those gigantic elements was an astonishingly complex system of gantries, scaffolds and ladder-cages. Some movement

was detectable in the very deepest reaches – servitors, perhaps, or maybe tech-priests, shuffling about agitatedly in the
smoke-choked gloom.

It took a long time to cross that gulf. By the time they
reached the far side, it was almost possible to forget about
the horrors in the outer chambers. It felt as if they had passed
into another world again.

A final doorway loomed. This had almost no adornment
at all – it was a circular hatch, four metres in diameter, studded with rivets and cross-barred with adamantium braces.
The impression of extreme age leaking from it was striking. A faded, worn-away sigil could just be made out on the
curved surface – a raptor's head, maybe, over a jagged lightning strike. Somehow, perhaps due to the unnatural energies
lashing and flaring all around them, Crowl could almost taste
its antiquity – this thing had been there, in that position, for
longer than a Palace had stood on Terra.

The roar, the thrum, the constant ramp-up of pressure, it all
came from the other side of that door. Even if he had known
nothing of the Astronomican at all, not even the rudimentary fragments that any schola child was taught, he would
have known then that something colossal was on the other
side, something perilous, something lethal and elemental,
something so grotesquely powerful that a single soul, set
against it, counted for less than a speck of dust against the
arc of eternity.

The Resonance glanced at him as the bolts were drawn
back. For the first time, her lips twitched.

'I would tell you to prepare yourself,' she said. 'But there
really isn't much you can do.'

Then the door swung open, and they went inside. A long
tunnel followed. Crowl ran his finger along the wall as he

walked – it was naked rock now, worn smooth and polished to a high sheen. A rectangle of light waited for them at the far end, glowing so brightly that his eyes watered. Every step brought them closer to that light, and with the light came a melange of noises – the roar he had been hearing since they first set foot in this place, mixed with a whole array of other, harder-to-place sounds. Crackling, maybe, like flames? Murmuring, as if a crowd of thousands was talking to itself? Singing, even?

They reached the end, and stepped out into the light. A long spur ran straight ahead, composed of the same rock as the tunnel walls, extending far into the gulf beyond. In all other directions, the ground fell away to nothingness. They stood against the inner curve of a gigantic sphere. Its lower half was hewn from the stone of the mountain; the upper half looked like glass.

The scale of it was hard to process – the zenith and nadir stretched so far overhead and underfoot that both were lost in the haze of distance. All across the sphere's inner surface were points of light, thousands of them, some blazing brightly, others dim. Murmuring, shouting, chanting filled the entire space, reflecting and echoing back and forth until it seemed that there must be millions of sources there, fissured, overlapping, interplaying.

At the very centre, far out beyond the end of the spur, was a huge orb of light, dancing, spinning, whirling like a neutron star. It was not static, but it vibrated to an uncertain rhythm, contracting and expanding like a lung taking in air. Tendrils of ephemeral force ran into the orb, connecting it to the thousands of lights at the sphere's edge. Pulses travelled down the tendrils, all moving in the same direction – towards the centre.

It should have been beautiful. The light was blue-white, dazzling in its purity, making the glass dome ripple like sunlight on water. The singing was harmonious, the proportions of the sphere were perfect.

Instead, it was hateful. It was abominable. Crowl looked up at it, and felt his soul tugged away. He could barely maintain his focus. The light played around him, dancing in concentric circles, winking and sliding from the rock facets and the frost-mottled crystal, and it made him want to scream out loud. Every one of those brilliant points contained, at its heart, an iron throne. On every throne writhed a mortal man or woman, locked down by iron collars, their skin punctured by control jacks, their temples weighed down by psy-resonant tiaras, burning themselves to death.

This was a furnace. A cold, hard furnace. Each point of light was slowly being drained to nothing, sucked into the orb in order to generate the signal that burned through the warp itself.

'This is a place of pain,' he said out loud, his lips moving unbidden.

The Resonance inclined her head, walking beside him out on to the spur. 'A fraction of the pain He endures,' she said. 'Consider that.'

He had to keep moving. Now that he was here, he had to keep placing one step in front of the other. A part of him wanted nothing more than to crawl away, to turn his face from the pristine light and return to the world of shadows and deterioration. Nothing should have been that... stringent.

A single figure was waiting for them at the far end of the spur. Initially it was almost invisible, lost in the nimbus of the orb above. As they got closer, a black silhouette formed against the amorphous light, firming up, solidifying into the profile of a mortal man.

Certain features emerged. He was tall, very tall, thin as a javelin, and dressed in a dark, thigh-length, tailored coat. Like all the denizens of this place, his skin was pearl-white. As the man turned to face them, he revealed a plain black rebreather covering the lower portion of his face. Tiny black tubes snaked from his earlobes, from plugs at his cranium, from behind his eyes. He looked neat, precise, composed. His hands were clasped in front of him, clad in a pair of sleek silk gloves.

Crowl came to a halt. Everything hurt. Everything ached. Khazad stood silently at his side, staring with raw distrust at the dancing lights. The Resonance hung back, as did her guards.

'Inquisitor Crowl,' the man said, inclining his long face a little.

Slowly, haltingly, Crowl reached for his rosette. He brought it up into the light, his hand shaking as he did so.

'Say nothing,' he said, his voice hoarse and cracked against the terrible beauty of the celestial choir. 'Listen with utmost care. High Lord Leops Franck, Master of the Astronomican, I charge you in the name of the Emperor of Mankind with treachery against the Throne, consorting with aliens, and conspiracy to pervert the course of Imperial justice. You shall be taken from this place and subjected to just interrogation in order to establish the degree of your undoubted guilt. How do you plead?'

CHAPTER TWENTY-TWO

They were going to get in.

Spinoza backed away from the doors, Argent crackling, watching the metal dent and flex.

'On my command,' she said, tensing.

It sounded like there were dozens now on the far side, scraping and thudding. They might have had a battering ram, for all that the steel was being tortured, but she had seen enough of their psychic prowess to guess what was really hurting the structure.

If the messages had ever got through, there was no guarantee that the recipients would be in a position to respond. Spinoza found it hard to believe that no prior messages at all had made it out, given the vastness of the Fortress and its importance. If its Master had truly kept his failure quiet out of some misplaced sense of pride, then that was as damnable an offence as any. The entire world was burning. Its guardians, those who still answered the call of duty, were being run ragged. She had warned Crowl about the growing anarchy often and early, but he had been blind, so it seemed, to the signs. Perhaps he had been on Terra too long, learning to hate the world that kept him prisoner within it. Perhaps, when it had all started to come apart around him, he had no longer cared enough.

The door rattled on its pistons.

The surviving storm troopers had done what they could to find cover, and now crouched behind instrument banks and cogitator chassis. Revus, as ever, had taken the position of most danger, kneeling less than four metres from the doorway behind an overturned metal bench. Hegain was similarly positioned forward, with the rest of the survivors scattered across a loose arc facing the doors.

There was no way out now. The communications spire was hundreds of metres up the sheer western face of the Fortress, and flames and ash billowed up outside. The windows themselves were darkening, filling with the spread of sooty filth, cutting off even a visual link to the rest of the planet.

Spinoza began to wonder, dryly, whether her chosen way to die was any worse than her master's. At least he had acted consistently throughout, running down the scent they had uncovered together, never deviating from it even when it seemed the entire world was succumbing to insanity. Perhaps that was what an inquisitor needed to be. Perhaps that was what separated them from the rest of the Adeptus Terra, with its messy compromises and necessary imperfections. Perhaps that was not madness, but something to be admired.

The door shook again, and a crack rippled across the chamber. She could hear panting from the other side now, urgent and wet, like animals' voices.

Gorgias hovered at her shoulder, his needle gun swivelling towards every scrape and scratch.

'Maximum spread, please,' Spinoza asked, as politely as

she could. She had never really addressed the skull much before – he was Crowl's creature, sharing some link that obviously went back a long way. It felt inappropriate to be giving him orders, somehow.

Gorgias ducked down a fraction, his spinal trail flexing. *'Fortias, Interrogatrix,'* he said, in as companionable a tone as his primitive vox-emitter ever really managed. 'Kill-kill, *instantus*, very soon.'

The door panels shivered. Another great bulge, like the clenched fingers of a fist, swelled out, pushing the mangled steel close to the shatter-point. The hissing got louder.

The windows behind her rattled, whipped against by the driving wind. The entire structure seemed to be shaking, as if the furious elements outside were capable of rocking it down to its ancient foundations.

Another crack opened, and the metal shrieked. More hammer-blows came in now, faster and faster.

'In His name,' she said through gritted teeth, bending her knees and preparing to meet the first wave, 'bring *them down*.'

The broken doors burst apart. What seemed like a single massive creature swarmed through the breach, splitting rapidly into a close-pressed scrum of nightshade-clad adepts, their black eyes wide and staring, their bloody mouths open to gnaw.

Every lasgun opened fire, filling the chamber with neon spears. Some of the corrupted were caught, spilling over themselves, though others quickly pounced through the gaps, shoving their own kind aside to get at the raw flesh ahead.

Spinoza rose up, spinning to gather momentum and smashing Argent into a flying, black-eyed adept. The maul-head smacked into it, driving fragile ribs in. A second horror lurched up, and the maul slammed back down, boiling with blood and plasma.

From the corner of her eye, half-lost in the whirl of movement, she saw a storm trooper borne down by several horrors at once, fingers scrabbling for her throat. She heard Revus roaring in fury and pain, and smelled the acrid tang of plasma weaponry burning through flesh. The room thundered with noise, a gathering crescendo that vied with the whines and bullet-impacts and shrieks. Even amid the confusion and adrenaline of the assault, she thought that was strange – where was it coming from?

She lashed out again, cutting down another corrupted adept, only to see one of the brain-swollen psykers coming right at her. She felt a tightness around her neck, and immediately black stars crowded her vision. She tried to shake it off, to break free and bring her maul back to bear, but the constriction grew.

She let rip with a half-strangled cry, struggling to stay on her feet, attempting to drive the crozius with arms that now felt like they were sunk into a swamp. Other adepts capered towards her, taking advantage of her sudden lethargy, their pupil-less eyes blazing.

Then the windows blew in. Every pane shattered at once, throwing armourglass across the chamber in a racing horizontal rain. The roar became a scream – a crashing, driving growl that drowned out everything else.

The grip on her throat disappeared. Its architect collapsed in on itself amid a flurry of blown glass shards. Hot wind scoured through the chamber, bringing with it ash-flakes and flecks of still-burning metal. She whirled around, just in time to see the first of them crash through the open window frame.

She had forgotten just how big they were. She had forgotten just how heavy, how intimidating, how *magnificent*, they were.

The Imperial Fists Space Marine landed perfectly, denting

the floor with his weight but never losing poise. He was firing even before he landed, filling the space ahead of him with a blistering rain of mass reactive bolts. More Space Marines smashed through the window alongside him – first two, then three – just as huge, just as fast. Behind them, half-lost in the squalls, hovered the massive shadow of a Thunderhawk gunship.

Spinoza dropped face-down to the floor, crawling out of the path of the bolt-shells. She could see the others doing the same, slithering away from the hurricane that had been unleashed at her request.

The Imperial Fists strode through the wreckage of the chamber, the storm-surge flying about them in a welter of fire and filth. They were not so much fighting the enemy as grinding it away, bludgeoning the corruption aside and crushing it back to the metal. Psychic blasts or pressure-waves were shrugged off, then punished with eye-burning volumes of retributory bolt shells. The brutality of it, the unremitting violence of it, was breathtaking.

The first Space Marine reached her position. Already his bolter-barrage was slowing, shorn now of targets to hit. The entire far end of the chamber smouldered, a crater-pitted wreck of bent and blasted ironwork, laced with scraps of cooking mortal matter.

A huge, pitted, snarled-faced helm angled down at her, its lenses glowing faintly. He smelled like something industrial – a smelting furnace, a turbo-hammer.

'You were the one?' he asked, his voice a low-timbre growl through his helm's systems.

She got to her knees, shakily. 'Interrogator Luce Spinoza,' she said, showing him the crozius. 'Gifted by Chaplain Erastus on Forfoda.'

The Space Marine regarded it carefully. 'Argent,' he said. 'That was how your signal reached the Keep.'

'It came with an oath. A promise of aid.'

'For you?'

'For this place,' she said, a little stung. 'For the Beacon.'

The Space Marine took another look at the crozius, as if he couldn't quite believe it was there, in her hands, in this place. As he did so, more of his warriors broke through the gaping wall-breach. Soon there were ten of them there, a full tactical squad. That alone was astonishing. They were busy finishing off the last dregs of the enemy now, moving up towards the bolt-cracked doorway and preparing to lumber through it.

The Space Marine reached down to help her up. His gauntlet swallowed hers, enclosing her hand in a heavy sheath of ceramite.

'Brother-Sergeant Haessler,' he said. 'Reinforcements are incoming, interrogator, but will take time to get here. You can still fight?'

The words alone made her heart swell.

'By His will,' she said, activating Argent's disruptor again. 'Yes, I can.'

Khazad had been struggling the whole time. After the psychic clamp placed on her limbs outside the portal, the woman had allowed her to move again, but an invisible straitjacket still lingered over her movements. She could feel the weight of it, just beyond true sensation, a denseness poised and hanging out of the reach of her fingertips.

She had not spoken during the long walk through the heart of the machine. Every step she had taken had been a testing of boundaries – an uncoiling and alignment of certain muscles, an imposition of mental energy. Crowl had seemed fascinated the whole way in, caught up in the spectacle of it all, or perhaps with his own mortal obsessions. For her, it had meant very little – just a transition to where she needed to be.

Now, placed at the heart of it all, surrounded and enveloped by that numinous chorus of pain, she prepared herself. She observed how the bodies on the rock spur were arranged. Crowl had gone ahead of her, speaking to the man he called the Master, who she now knew was the murderer she had been seeking ever since her own inquisitor had been killed. The Resonance stood to one side, keeping Khazad tightly in check, holding her on her invisible leash. Four of the Fortress guards stood a little further back. Their presence seemed more for the sake of protocol than anything else.

Crowl's first words to the Master had felt hollow, rather than bold, as if the necessary formalities had to be observed but that all of them knew where the true power balance lay. Suitably enough, the man had smiled coolly, his eyes creasing above the line of his rebreather.

'How gallant,' he had said, glancing perfunctorily at Crowl's rosette. 'But you have come a long way. Come, let us talk.'

And then they had both moved further down the length of the spur, one walking easily, the other failing to conceal his limp.

Khazad watched them go, aware the whole time of the Resonance's eyes on her.

'Your hatred is impressively focused,' the woman said. Her lips still did not move – a cheap trick that Khazad found more irritating than daunting. 'He is here out of duty. With you, it is personal.'

Khazad ignored the observation – one hardly needed to be psychic to detect her degree of hatred – and paid greater attention to her surroundings. She tested the bounds of her psychic shackles again. She could move her head, her shoulders, even her limbs, just a little, but beyond that the heaviness was deadening. If she attempted sudden movement, she knew the clamp would return instantly, freezing her fists before they could fly into the woman's face.

She glanced upward, out across the gulf where the giant orb of light pulsed. It was truly immense, that thing – a sphere of pure energy suspended within the empty core of the greater physical sphere, radiating steadily like the heart of a cold sun.

'The physical emanation of the ecstatic souls,' the Resonance said, noticing her interest. 'It is majestic, is it not? And yet, it is but a shallow reflection of the true power of this place. That power is unseen, generated by those who serve, and guided by Him alone.'

The woman's seeming need to talk was also an irritant. It was almost as if, having spent her entire life here and been suffused into its mysteries, she was compelled to share something of it, to justify her existence to those who had now stumbled through its broken gates.

'Failing,' Khazad said.

The woman frowned. 'The empyrean is in great turmoil,' she said. 'These are, as you can see, dangerous times.'

Khazad's eyes scanned across the distant sphere's inner wall, and she witnessed more signs of damage. Flecks of darkness played over the orb's translucent surface, blotting its purity for a few seconds before being swallowed up again by the gelatinous churn. The thousands of iron thrones, all hanging in their long serried ranks, were marred with what looked like burn scars – some of them were missing entirely, their place taken by empty apertures that fizzed and crackled with wild force.

The people here were deluded. They were insane. They had spent so much time gazing into the maw of the deep that they were no longer capable of seeing the physical catastrophe unfolding around them. Their adepts were dead or dying, their great machine was clanking out of control, and still they nodded and smiled, maintaining the icy demeanour of men and women used to presiding over the elements of eternity, confident it would all be back as it should be soon.

This was Terra in microcosm. This was a world on the edge of annihilation, washed by the first shockwaves of a greater conflagration to come, and still its people busied themselves with their age-old rituals and functions. They lived, they fought, they laboured, and all the while their doom crept steadily closer, in full sight, undisguised yet ignored.

In that respect, Khazad was no better than any of them. She had come here, not for the sake of the Throneworld, but to get close to one man, a man who now stood less than a single leap away from her, unarmoured, his neck exposed.

It would be good to keep the woman talking.

'You will die here, I think,' she said.

The Resonance looked briefly startled. 'Do you think we have never seen turbulence before?' she asked. 'We regret the bloodshed, that is true. So much careful training, wasted. But the balance will be restored, the harmonics will align, and then the gates will open, the ships will return. The thrones must be filled. That has always been the way of it.'

As the Resonance reeled off her platitudes, Khazad entered the Shoba discipline of *kao-kokoro* – one face, two minds. She maintained a façade of careful attention, while inwardly she prepared to move. Every sinew tightened, her weight shifted by a fraction. Her blade was gone, but she still had her hands, which in their lightweight armour casing were as deadly as claw-hammers.

'This comes from far away,' the Resonance said, looking up at the dome. 'This is the result of distant wards breaking, ones that have been in place for millennia. It shall be endured, though. We have always endured.'

The ground beneath their feet began to tremble. The Resonance's attention was briefly diverted, and Khazad felt the pressure lift. She was on the edge now, her strength gathered up, her recovery complete. It felt as if everything that had happened since waking up in Crowl's apothecarion had led her here, step by step, for this. Something like joy flooded through her. Psychic clamp or no, the crisis was coming, and when it did, she would be ready.

'I would not expect you to understand,' the Resonance went on. 'Nor your master. These are learned matters, and your time here will be, I am afraid, brief.'

Steadily, Khazad turned her face back towards her.

'Tell me, though,' she said, selecting the place where the first bone-break would occur. 'I am very fast learner.'

CHAPTER TWENTY-THREE

Revus watched the new arrivals get to work. Once the chamber was secured, they brought over equipment from their hovering gunship – power-units, long-range comms-bundles, heavy coils of ammunition. They moved quickly, methodically, barely saying a word to one another.

Some of what they did was just insane. Their gunship remained at station a few metres out from the comms tower, its massive engines burning hard. In order to retrieve some of the heavier items, the Space Marines would casually leap across the gap, momentarily suspended hundreds of metres up, before coming back the same way, heavy equipment swinging in their fists that would have torn his muscles just to lift.

Soon the chamber was fully lit again, its equipment pulsing with power. One of the warriors consulted with Hegain, summoning up fresh hololithic schemas of the labyrinth within. The one who had called himself Haessler – a sergeant of the Third Company, by his markings – spoke with Spinoza.

Revus got up, feeling the stiffness in his limbs, and went over to them.

'The outer Fortress is completely overrun,' Spinoza was telling Haessler. 'The inner sanctuary seems to have been sealed off, but that may not help if the corrupted gain access to the main power generators.'

The Imperial Fist nodded, studying the hololiths. 'Those can be secured, here,' he said, pointing to a narrow choke-point many levels down, close to where the psionic conduits docked with the main citadel. 'But we'll need to get inside the centre, too.'

'My master, Inquisitor Crowl, aimed to reach the cordon before they shut the doors. He believed the Master of the Astronomican was in there.'

'Then we shall endeavour to reach both of them.'

Just listening to the Space Marine speak gave Revus a curious kind of reassurance. It was not a gentle voice – it was bone-hard, perfunctory, the kind of voice that had been giving orders for decades – but it was *solid*, where all else around them seemed to be collapsing into flux. If warriors such as these could be mobilised in numbers, if they still had their vigour and faith when all others lost theirs, then it became possible to believe the situation was still salvageable.

Revus had served for eight years in Salvator. In that time, he had proven equal to anything the Throneworld had hurled up at him. Now, in quick succession, fate had thrown him alongside different warrior-species of legend, each capable of performing feats that dwarfed anything he could hope to achieve. If this constituted some kind of providential injunction to remember his place in the scheme of things, the lesson was at risk of being quite heavily overstated.

Spinoza, in contrast, carried herself with a freedom that

he had seldom seen since her arrival at Courvain. In her full battle-plate, carrying her crozius, she did not look much out of place alongside the giants of the Adeptus Astartes. When they spoke to her, it was almost as if they spoke to one of their own.

'Ready, captain?' she asked him.

The storm troopers who had made it into the chamber were still capable of fighting. All of them were on their feet again now, recharging, reloading, flexing fatigue-tight limbs.

'On your command, lord,' Revus said.

'We shall need to move swiftly,' Haessler said, motioning for his squad to take up position before the shattered doors. He glanced at Revus. 'You must try to keep up.'

Revus smiled dryly under his helm. 'We'll do our best.'

Then the Imperial Fists moved off into the gap. Haessler led the assault, barging aside the tattered sheets of metal and plunging into the dark.

Once on the far side, everything changed. Their progress previously had been a matter of running for cover, seizing any islands of protection they could find before fleeing onward again. This was entirely different – the Space Marines made no attempt to hide, no attempt to trace hidden and tortuous routes, but burned the straightest path towards their goal, contemptuous of danger.

They split into two squads of five. The second squad headed down towards the Fortress' principal power convertor, buried deep where the psionic trench met the inner walls. Spinoza, Revus and the other survivors went with Haessler and four of his battle-brothers, and together they struck out towards the centre.

Their presence soon attracted attention. The dregs and scraps of the corrupted screamed up out of the pits and vaults towards them, throwing themselves at the armoured monsters who had violated their realm. The Space Marines took the brunt of every assault, never slowing, sheltering the storm troopers with their own bodies and loosing bolter-fire in vicious, unrestrained volleys.

Revus, as promised, did his best to keep up. He contributed when he could, adding his hellgun shots to the thundering chorus of boltguns. Amid all the broken shadows and fire-flecked explosions, even through his fatigue, he witnessed the way the Adeptus Astartes fought, and for the first time began to understand why Spinoza was so enamoured with them.

They were so different to the Custodians. Where those warriors had been artisans of combat, individually perfect, beautiful and dreadful, these were ostensibly cruder creations, blunter-edged, heavier. Soon, though, it became apparent that they were no less deadly. Their way of battle was to overwhelm, to shock, to render an opponent half-insensible before the first blows even landed. Within that rolling tide of sensory overload, fuelled by battle-roars and the incessant grind of servos and muzzle-flares, there was another kind of artistry present – a pinpoint precision, a flawless awareness of those around them. They were a seamless unit, the five of them, backing one another up, multiplying the others' firepower and killing potential.

As Revus ran, he felt the long tug of exhaustion snag at his muscles. The pace, as promised, was punishing. The Space Marines scorched their way back through blood-streaked halls, never pausing, tearing through hastily-thrown psychic bolts as if they were nothing.

Spinoza remained at the forefront, running alongside Haessler, guiding them in. They reached a long arched bridge that crossed a deep chasm, and sprinted across it. Screams swung at them eerily, some far below, some above. Revus gritted his teeth and kept going, feeling the sharp burn in his lungs. An Imperial Fist loped alongside him, his heavy boots cracking the stone with each footfall.

The corrupted adept came from nowhere. It must have been waiting for them on the underside of the bridge, hanging like a spider, poised to drag itself up over the edge. It slithered quickly into view, cloaked in snaggles of darkness, its toothless jaw locked into a snarl.

The Space Marine reacted instantly, bringing his bolter to bear, but reality suddenly popped around them, wobbling and distorting. He slipped, skidding close to the edge.

Revus, running just a little further back, opened up with his hellgun. Lasbeams sliced into the adept, every one hitting home, cutting straight through it and punching streamers of blood out the far side. He found himself shouting in rage, just as the Space Marines did, hurling invective at the creature even as its psychic distortion gusted out.

A second later, and the Imperial Fist had recovered himself. He lurched forward, grabbing the wretch by its neck and hurling it out into the void. Then he turned on Revus, his helm lenses glowing in the fractured dark.

For a moment, Revus thought the warrior would be angry, deprived of prey.

'How long have you been in here?' the Space Marine demanded.

Revus glanced at the mission chrono. 'Five-point-four hours, lord,' he replied.

The enormous helm nodded in salute. 'Impressive,' he said. 'You do honour to the Throne.'

He turned back, running again, racing to catch up with

the rest of the squad. Revus stood for a split second, startled, panting, aching.

You do honour to the Throne.

Then he too was running again, somehow feeling less pain than before, somehow dragging energy up from a place he had not yet tapped. His jaw set firm, his shoulders low, he kept his legs moving, rejoining the band as it tore deeper into the heart of the Fortress.

The Space Marines were still roaring battle-chants, creating that wall of sonic intimidation that travelled before them like a physical shockwave.

'For Him!' Revus cried out, joining in the charge, feeling the energy of it flood through his body, banishing both the dark and the agony. 'For the glory of Him on Earth!'

Crowl glanced back, just for a moment, at Khazad. She appeared to be listening to the Resonance while staring all the while intently at the Master. The expression of pure hatred in her eyes was impressive. If the Resonance had not been on hand to keep her in check, he had little doubt the man would already have been dead at her hands, powerblade or no.

He turned back to his host. The void below yawned away beneath him, and eddies of the sphere's internal winds pulled at his cloak.

'What happened here?' Crowl asked.

'It can be contained,' said Franck.

'Have you been outside?'

'It can be contained.' Franck gazed up at the pulsating orb. 'A new alignment is coming, inquisitor. A new age. We must expect birth pangs.'

Crowl followed the man's eyes. He had no means of judging, but the oscillations out in the centre of the sphere looked febrile to him, as if something was out of kilter. Even as he watched, black blotches appeared and disappeared in its heart, bursting and fading like blood clots.

'You have lost your acolytes to madness,' Crowl tried again. 'The few left alive are mindless wretches. This is more than an alignment.'

Franck sucked in a long breath through his device, making it wheeze. 'You and I are both old men. We have seen a great deal. But nothing compared to what must come now.' He turned, and fixed the inquisitor with two deep green eyes. 'I come here from the Senatorum. We nearly changed a law there that has stood for ten thousand years, one that has underpinned everything we have done since the days of glory. I argued against it, and for now it stands, but as for the future... who knows? There are agitated souls out there now. They have reason to be. We have lost Cadia.'

Crowl thought he must have misheard that. 'We have–'

'We have lost Cadia.' The Master smiled again, coldly. 'That will concentrate minds. Some of them should have been concentrated far earlier.'

'What is the Wound?'

'Ah, you heard them scream that, did you? That was the first inkling we had that something was wrong. They started writing it in their scriptorium classes, over and over. Then we couldn't stop them saying it. Then they started reaching for knives.'

'You should have reported it.'

'It can be contained.'

Crowl snorted. The orb above them flexed again, blotching black, before clearing. 'You know it can't.'

'There is a boundary between the ether and real space. It can be bent, it can be broken. In the usual run of things, breakages are localised, impermanent. But Cadia was important, and there were more than just physical walls on that world. The Wound is the mark of our failure. I do not know yet how large it will grow. It may never stop growing.'

'And it is sending your people mad.'

'They are attuned to the warp as few others are.'

Crowl remembered what Spinoza had said then. His words to her in that final chamber seemed like some strange dream, a fever-nightmare, and he could hardly believe he'd uttered them. 'You need assistance. You need help. The Beacon will be lost.'

'How did you get in here, Crowl? I thought our tracks had been covered adequately well, given the limitations of time and resources.'

Crowl stared at him for a moment, wondering how he could be quite so phlegmatic. His entire kingdom was on the verge of destruction. Even as he hesitated, a few more of the light-points on the sphere's edge went dark, provoking more spasms from the central orb.

'You took your inspiration from heresy,' Crowl said. 'Appropriately enough. I thought the Magister was merely mad, but its final words had a ring to them. I had heard something similar before, or maybe read it. It took me a while to remember, for my mind does not seem to be what it was, but it came to me in the end. I had a single copy of the forbidden manuscript, written before this world had a single language. Mine was in the Doitjer dialect, and transliterated, after a little work, to *Offenbarung*. Or, in the Gothic, *Revelation*. A suitably obscure passage to choose as your code-phrase. *And before the Throne there was a sea of glass, like unto crystal.*'

Franck nodded. '*And in the midst of the Throne, and round about the Throne, were four beasts, full of eyes, before and behind.* The text was not picked idly.'

'Rassilo told me the same thing. The Throne is failing.'

'And we were the beasts that stood about it, the only ones to see and understand the danger. Dhanda. Raskian. Myself.'

'And the fourth?'

'You have met it, I believe.'

'That creature is dead.'

Franck laughed. 'Come, now. You know that isn't true.'

The orb trembled, and black sparks shot from its heart. A tongue of flame kindled in the air above them, snapping briefly like a pennant before gusting out. A tremor ran across the earth far below them, core-deep and angry.

'Tell me what you have done,' Crowl said.

Franck clasped his hands together again, turning his face up to the light show above. 'It is already complete, inquisitor. Bringing the xenos here was our greatest mistake, but it had insisted on seeing the Throneworld in person. In truth, the main outline of the Project had already been agreed. When the creature went mad, that was regrettable, and momentarily dangerous, but it did not affect the matter of the scheme. Dhanda pulled out, which was a shame, but her role was always peripheral.'

Crowl listened, suppressing the hundred questions that simmered under the surface.

'They can help us. Without them, the Throne will not see out the next hundred years. It will go dark, poisoned both by age and the coming Wound in reality. You do not know what that means. You do not know what the Throne truly is, nor what it protects us from. You may believe, in your ignorance, that it is immune to harm, or that its failures can somehow be accommodated, but let me tell you, with the utmost surety born of perception of what lies beneath, that the horrors you have seen in here this night pale into nothing beside what would overtake us if it were allowed to fail.'

'They are liars,' Crowl said.

'The xenos? Most assuredly so.'

'They will betray us. They care nothing for us.'

The Master shrugged. 'The second point is certainly true. The first point may be true also. Risk exists in everything we do.'

Crowl had to restrain himself from leaping up then, clawing at the man's throat. He still had Sanguine at his belt. If he moved quickly enough, before the thought fully formed...

'What have you given them?'

'That is none of your concern.'

'You sold out your own species!' Crowl shouted. 'That makes it my concern.'

The flesh at the corner of Franck's eyes flickered a fraction. 'No price could be too high,' he said, defensive now, 'if it succeeded.'

Crowl edged closer to him, holding himself back with some difficulty. 'They are *abominations*,' he hissed. 'Nothing they have told you can be trusted. Whatever you have promised them will be lost forever. They live only for pain. *Our* pain.'

Franck rounded on him then, at last showing defiance. 'Yes, we are prey to them,' he said, his voice low and bitter. 'We always have been. And yet, if we are destroyed, then they understand that they must be next, for it is *we* – the weak, the deluded, the decaying children of Old Earth – who alone hold back the tide of unmaking. We are bound together in our mutual need.'

Crowl stared into the Master's eyes, and saw the utter certainty there. At the very least, the man believed what he said.

'Whatever you have done,' he said, his voice low, 'call it back.'

Franck smiled again, this time with a certain sadness in his eyes. 'I could not do so now, even if I wished it,' he said. 'You have been a most dogged pursuer, Crowl. I find myself pleased that you did not die in your lonely citadel, and that we have spoken these words. But the delegation has left. They are no longer on Terra. They take with them the final element of the Project, the very last thing they asked of us, and when they reach their destination, the contract will be sealed. It cannot be stopped now.'

Crowl tried to move then, to reach for his revolver, but found he couldn't. With a rising sense of panic, he found that his limbs were frozen, weighed down as if in liquid rockcrete.

He could still move his eyes. Above them, the orb was pluming more violently. It looked as if, far above them, a crack had formed in the glass. He tried to blurt out a warning, but his lips were clamped together.

'We must endure, now,' the Master said. 'We must wait, and ride out the coming storm.'

Crowl felt a twitch at his belt, and saw, with horror, that Sanguine was moving of its own accord from his holster. Out of the corner of his eye, he could see Khazad similarly locked in place, though struggling hard.

'I have sacrificed everything to see this come to pass,' Franck said. Above them, more flames licked into life, dancing like ghosts around the cold star at their heart. 'You understand me? *Everything.*'

Sanguine rose up smoothly before Crowl, swivelling on its axis until the barrel was lined up against his forehead. He struggled to move, and knew that the strength he had left in his withered limbs was laughably insufficient.

Sanguine floated closer, the muzzle's tip pressing lightly against his skin.

'The new age is upon us,' the Master said. 'I find myself sorry, truly sorry, that you will not live to see it.'

With nothing left to do, Crowl closed his eyes.

CHAPTER TWENTY-FOUR

Spinoza fought alongside Haessler, driving herself hard to keep somewhere close to his speed and power. She had forgotten just how arduous it was even to be in their presence, let alone attempt to accompany them into combat.

They were phenomenal, of course, barely giving her or the others a chance to shoot. Spinoza felt all the old adulation rush back at once – they were like furnaces, driving all before them, never relenting, never stopping. They must have been running well within themselves in order to allow her and the others to keep up, but the pace was still staggering, and soon they were closing on the inner Fortress.

'How long has it been like this?' Haessler asked as he loped along, sounding appalled.

'Unknown,' Spinoza replied, panting. 'Must have taken hold fast. They made no distress call.'

The sergeant grunted, clearly unimpressed. 'We nearly did not respond to you. A hundred other cries have been issued, many of them critical.'

'What is causing it?'

'Causes are your domain, interrogator,' Haessler said. 'We are here for what comes next.'

They made their way further in, following the course that Crowl must have taken. The cadavers never went away, still contorted into their various displays of agony, besmirched with signs and slogans daubed in their own blood. The same word was sprayed everywhere – *the Wound, the Wound, the Wound.*

'My sensors fail beyond this point,' Haessler reported calmly, as they sprinted down another long, echoing chamber. 'What can you tell me?'

Spinoza began to struggle to match pace. Only her pride, her determination not to lose face before such warriors, kept her ploughing on.

'My master came this way,' she said, sounding more certain than she felt.

Just as she spoke, the floor beneath her rocked, as if shaken by an earthquake. Debris streamed down from the roof, smashing apart as it hit the ground.

'Interrogator!' Haessler cried, grabbing her and pulling her clear just as a huge crack zig-zagged across the stone. The squad skidded to a halt, retreating from the widening chasm.

One of Haessler's battle-brothers grabbed a handheld sensor device. 'Major tectonic activity, imminent psionic rupture,' he reported. 'More shockwaves incoming. The epicentre is directly ahead.'

The sergeant put Spinoza down. 'It is unsafe to continue. We shall take it from here.'

Spinoza stood her ground. 'He may yet be alive.'

'I will not tell you again.'

'You will not have to. I am coming.'

The ground shook again, and a pillar cracked open, bisected from top to bottom. Further back, another shaft opened up and flames shot out from the gap, thundering like gas-plumes from a refinery chimney. The air around them suddenly shimmered, became denser, then shook back to normal, as if reality had briefly flexed.

Haessler laughed. 'Come, then.'

And then they were moving again, all of them, sprinting through the hall as it steadily disintegrated around them. Huge flashes of blue-white light flared up out of nowhere, spinning into the chasms before erupting into snaking maelstroms. More pillars toppled, rupturing as they smashed into the rockcrete floor.

The Space Marines formed up around Spinoza, Revus and the others, warding them from the worst of it. The confined space filled with dust, and the way ahead became even murkier than before. Explosions rang out both ahead and behind them, shivering the bones of the Fortress and sending blast-waves racing down the narrow tunnels.

The detonations were not just physical. Every impact brought a chorus of shrieks with it, coming from nowhere, sounding as if hundreds of voices, thousands of voices, were crying out in sudden and unbearable pain. The crystal walls blew apart, one by one, showering them all with spinning slivers.

Of all of the non-Space Marines, Revus seemed to be coping best. He was running harder now, looking as if he intended to break through the barriers ahead through force of will alone. Gorgias soared high above, driving his motive units hard, weaving between the falling wreckage. Spinoza felt as if her limbs would betray her at any moment, flooded with lactic acid and ready to give out. She barely noticed the destruction around her, only the way ahead, forged now by Haessler and kept clear by his squad.

Eventually, they broke into another long hall with galleries set high on either side. The chequerboard floor had erupted, and whole ranks of statues had collapsed into rocking chunks. Snaking lines of force lapped and whipped across the far wall, illuminating heaps of blood-drenched bodies amid the widening cracks. Some still lived, and shrieked when they saw the Space Marines break in. A few tried to summon up some kind of defensive power, but with the eldritch forces now running wild and unrestrained they were torn apart as soon as they raised their arms.

Haessler reached the siege doors. The brace-columns on either side of them were shaking, and spiderwebs of tiny cracks ran across the reinforced armour of the outer surface. The entire space vibrated, shaking like chaff in a thresher.

Spinoza hauled in painful breaths, dropping to one knee. Her vision was blurred, and when she blinked she saw, alternately, both Crowl and the xenos staring back at her from the bleary shadows.

'They are in there,' she panted, stating the obvious out of sheer desperation. There was no time. The outer Fortress was falling apart, and this door had been made to keep the world at bay.

Haessler studied it for a split second.

'Stand back,' he ordered, waving his own squad to withdraw. He took up a number of charges from his belt – melta-bombs, from their look – and mag-clamped them to the door-seal. Then he pulled back alongside the rest of them. All of them, storm troopers included, trained their weapons on the same point, readying themselves for the timed explosions.

Spinoza looked up above. More debris was now falling from the roof. The floor rippled like water, and the screaming was getting worse. Whatever was causing this was already well under way, building up to its inevitable crescendo.

'We are too late,' she murmured, watching the runes on the melta-bombs spin down to zero. 'For the love of the Throne, we are here too late.'

The air exploded. It kindled, flashed, sparked, then blew apart.

The Master reeled suddenly, and Sanguine, free of his control, clanked to the ground. He staggered, falling back towards the spur's edge, just as the psykers in the chamber, one by one, began to erupt.

Crowl was felled too, hurled back down onto his knees. The spur shook, feeling for a moment like it might snap off and tumble into the gulf below. He went after his revolver but missed it, his vision blurring.

The screams were everywhere now, inside his head, inside the sphere, swilling around, spilling over, deafening and unending. He saw lines of black force shoot across the sphere's heart, snapping into the orb and sending it dark. Flames rushed across the chamber's zenith, chewing through the thrones set into the curving walls, immolating them in bursts of shattered metal.

'Khazad!' he yelled, feeling as if the world were tilting away into the abyss. From the corner of his eye, he saw that the Resonance had been thrown aside too and now tottered on the edge of the spur. The assassin only needed a fraction of a second – freed of the psychic lock, she pounced, launching a flying kick at the woman and sending her sailing out into the seething ocean of burning souls. The surviving guards went after her, and Khazad swung around to take them on.

That left the Master.

Crowl grabbed Sanguine, clutched it in his shaky fist and

fired. The shot went wide, disappearing into the gathering inferno, and Franck regained his poise. One faltering step at a time, he advanced on Crowl.

'This delegation,' Crowl demanded, firing again. 'Where did you send them?'

Franck held up a palm, and the bullet exploded before reaching him, showering them both in fragments.

'Beyond help,' the Master said, pulling a powerblade from his belt. His outline shook with what looked like a heat-haze, and the blade's disruptor-flare pulled around him in wild tendrils. The air fizzed with psionic charge, kindling without warning, causing the air to sizzle and pop. Making aggressive use of the warp now was perilous – the combatants were reduced to the physical even as the very elements of reality turned into hellish plasma around them.

Crowl snarled, launching himself at Franck, his free gauntlet curling into a fist. He struck out, and the Master parried with the knife, catching Crowl's hand and snapping it back. Crowl punched out with Sanguine's heel, catching Franck in the ribs and knocking him, staggering, back towards the edge. The Master dropped down to his knees against the pull of the flying energies.

As he did so, the orb above them suddenly shrank radically, imploding into itself as if caught by some psychic black hole. The air in the chamber howled after it, sucking inward towards the rapidly blackening heart, and dark lightning blades leapt out from the sphere's edge. The screams became ear-burstingly unbearable.

Crowl shot a pained glance back towards Khazad, seeing that the assassin had dispatched the last of the guards. She swivelled on her heel, riding the surge of the unnatural winds, and galloped towards him.

Franck struggled back to his feet, facing them both. His coat rippled around him, pressed flat against his body.

'You can still redeem this!' Crowl shouted. 'Tell me where you sent them! Tell me what they took!'

The Master tensed, ready for the coming impacts. 'You are a persistent man!' he cried. 'Too persistent!'

Crowl fired a third time as the Master lunged again, hitting him in the chest and blowing a long line of blood out the other side. That barely slowed him, and Franck slashed the power-blade across Crowl's helm, driving the metal in. His vision dissolving into bloody blotches, Crowl reeled away, dropping Sanguine, only for Khazad to barrel into the Master, yelling Shoba curses so loudly that they were audible over the roaring tumult around them.

Half-stunned, Crowl scrambled after his weapon. He never got the chance to pick it up.

The black orb at the heart of the sphere suddenly pulsed, shuddered, then blew out.

A thunder-clap rang out across the gulf, shattering every remaining light-point across the crystal's edge. The screams extinguished. The fires guttered away. The psychic pressure accelerated into excruciating density, before it, too, blasted into nothingness. Blackness fell, as complete and choking as the void itself, broken only by the racing tongues of fire still guttering amid the preternatural hurricane.

Crowl cried aloud, his back arching, watching as iron fragments – thrones, tiaras, bolts – blasted across the void and rained down from the sphere's zenith. He crawled forward through the shadow, on his knees again, watching as the dark profiles of the Master and Khazad struggled desperately on the spur's edge, backlit by driving flame.

With the Beacon's destruction, the sense of loss was suddenly agonising, as if a chunk of his soul had been wrenched from his body, leaving only a shallow husk behind. They were still fighting, the two of them, their limbs blurred amid the driving rain of iron flecks. The Master had his blade, but Khazad had her armoured hands, and it wasn't clear which would prove decisive.

Snarling through the pain, Crowl pushed himself up onto all fours and scrabbled along the spur, closing in, going for Franck's trailing leg. As he did so, the final shockwave from the pulsar's demise hit the spur, rupturing the stone's surface and making it bounce like a storm-blown branch.

Both Khazad and the Master were thrown from their feet, their momentum carrying them out over the edge.

With a sudden burst of clarity, Crowl knew he could still reach them. His first thought was Franck – he could grab the Master, haul him back, get the answers he so desperately needed. His legs kicked straight, and he threw himself forward, his chest slamming into the stone floor. His left hand shot out, grasping an armoured wrist as it slithered down the steep rocky drop.

Shouting aloud from the pain, Crowl lodged his other hand into a crack in the rock, bracing against the stone, and pulled hard. For a moment, as the suspended body thudded against the overhang, he thought his spine would crack. His shoulder shrieked with pain, taking the full weight. If he had not been wearing his armour, no doubt the bone would have sprung from the socket.

He held on, breathing through gritted teeth. Wincing, he started to pull. Slowly, agonisingly, he dragged the deadweight back from the edge.

It worked. Khazad managed to get a foothold down below, somehow, and gradually reappeared over the rock's lip. Once she had hauled herself over the spur's edge, the two of them rolled onto their backs, panting hard.

Crowl stared up at the zenith of the sphere. Flecks of smouldering metal were still drifting. The screams had all gone now, snuffed out with the extinguishing of the Beacon's power.

Everything hurt. He could taste his own blood against his teeth. His lungs felt as if they had been scraped internally by a blunt razor.

Khazad was the first to recover the power of speech.

'Though you would… go for… him,' she gasped.

It took Crowl a while to be able to respond.

'Changed my mind,' he whispered. '*Kataj*, once. Now *Saijan*.'

She chuckled, painfully. After a while, she managed to get up. The rain of burning metal continued steadily, a scatter of dull red sparks against the darkening globe. Tremors still rumbled below them, and smoke was pouring out of the exit tunnel.

'Think you can go back in there?' she asked, concerned.

Crowl lifted his head painfully. He wasn't even sure he could get back to his feet. His shoulder was surely broken. His skull had been cut open where the Master had slashed against his helm. It was a struggle just to remain conscious.

What did it matter, anyway? The quest had been in vain. Franck had achieved what he had set out to do – his forces had left Terra, carrying with them all that was needed to make the contract irreversible. The Beacon was extinguished. Everything had failed. The Wound had come to the Throneworld, and the fury of the End Times rode on the hems of its ragged, death-stained cloak.

He was about to tell her that, and advise her to make her own way back alone, if she wished to, when he spied movement amid the smoke. At first he thought it must be one of the corrupted, staggering out of the hell they had created and ready to impose the final indignity, when he saw the first golden-yellow armour-profile break out from the swirls of roiling black.

He let his head crack weakly back against the stone.

'Spinoza,' he croaked, smiling bleakly under his ruined helm.

CHAPTER TWENTY-FIVE

Crowl didn't know very much about what came next. He only had fleeting impressions of armoured giants in the dark, lifting him, taking him back into tunnel, and then across the bridge where the buried machines now flailed and sparked. He never remembered how they got him back to the hangars and into the gunship. He didn't know whether they had pulled out again in one of Courvain's Spiderwidows, or one of the Space Marines' own massive transports. He had vague memories of many other troops arriving, pouring into the Fortress alongside red-robed priests. His unconsciousness ran very deep after that, and became completely dreamless. That, after all that had happened, was a relief.

When he awoke properly, two days later, he discovered that not very much had changed. The anarchy, which up until then had seemed unprecedented in its severity, had only got worse. The loss of the Beacon could be felt by everyone, as if a heat-source they had never known about was taken away, leaving them shivering and naked. The Space Marines hadn't lingered. There were too many fires to put out, even

337

for them. He asked Erunion where they had gone, and the chirurgeon couldn't tell him.

Later, they would call that time the Days of Blindness. Those days would not last forever, but then, just then, right in the heart of the storm, none of them knew that. Being awake was an ordeal. Trying to sleep was even worse. Entire sections of the planet became ungovernable. The comm-links hissed with nothingness. Starvation reared its head in the underhives, and there were tales of daemons rising from the despoiled earth to prey on the harried minds of mortal men.

Courvain, already damaged, became an island in a sea of danger. There was little rest for any of those who had survived. Revus took command of the defences, once he had recovered sufficiently, and was soon hard-pressed keeping the rabble from the gates, just as he had feared.

Crowl spent his own recovery in isolation, refusing all but the company of Gorgias and Erunion. The worst of his wounds started to heal, but the underlying damage was now profound. He lay in his bed, staring at the ceiling, feeling his bones ache.

On the third day, he managed to walk again, then dress himself. He felt strangely light, as if his innards had been stripped out, leaving him hollow and transparent. When he hobbled over to his hygiene-station, he looked into the mirror, and saw nothing but his own reflection.

That, too, was a relief.

On the fourth day, he summoned Spinoza to his chamber. She came promptly, just as always. She looked far better than he felt. Then again, she was younger, and stronger, and in every way a better representative of the ordo than he was.

She sat at the far end of the long table. Suspensors floated overhead, casting a weak light across the furniture. It was dusty, now. Not enough staff remained for the luxuries of cleanliness, only survival.

He sat at the other end. For a long time, neither of them said anything.

'So,' he said, eventually. 'What do we do now, Spinoza?'

She looked uncertain. 'I do not know, lord.'

'The last time we spoke, our exchange was not... friendly.'

'There was a madness, lord. It affected us all.'

'Some of us,' Crowl said. He found his fingers reaching for a goblet, even though he had ordered that none be put out. 'Tell me, how stands the Fortress?'

'I am told they have stabilised it. The chambers were purged. I believe that agents of Mars are in place now, attempting to repower the mechanisms.'

'Without a Master.'

'I assume so. Unless another has been appointed.'

'But there is a hope of saving it.'

'There is a hope.'

'As a result of your work, Spinoza. It might have passed beyond all recovery had you not acted as you did.'

'We do not know that.'

Crowl looked equivocal. 'A reasonable supposition.' His shoulder ached. 'And so, I have a dilemma. When we spoke here before, in this place, I told you my trust in you was absolute. I needed it to be. We were embarking on a dangerous mission. I needed to know that, if we were placed in peril, I could rely on you.'

Spinoza stiffened. It was always hard to read what she was thinking. Was she still resentful, now? Guilty, even? It was impossible to tell.

'I did not think,' she said carefully, 'that you were yourself.'

'Or perhaps,' he said, evenly, 'you thought that I was more myself than ever.'

'No, I would not put it like that.'

Crowl nodded. 'No, I would not put it like that either. Even so.'

Another silence fell.

'I will be honest,' Crowl said at last. 'I do not know what to do. My thoughts are still disarranged. I do not know what to do about what we discovered. I do not know what to do about Revus. I do not know what to do about you.' He paused, feeling the effects of his fatigue again. 'There may be nothing left to do. Perhaps this is the end, not only of what we started, but of all things.'

Spinoza said nothing. There might have been pain there, in her eyes. So hard to know.

'An inquisitor must be master of his domain, or he is nothing,' Crowl said, staring into the polished wood of the table. 'His trust must be unshakable. If he tolerates insurrection in his retinue, how can he root it out elsewhere? And yet...' He looked up at her again. 'You were right.'

There could be no doubt about it now. She was unable to hide her disquiet. 'What, then,' she asked, 'would you have me do?'

Crowl placed his hands together. 'Nothing, Spinoza. Nothing. I need to go away for a while. I need to reflect. I need to think.'

She looked concerned. 'Go away? Surely... It is dangerous.'

'So it is. Nonetheless, it must be done.'

It looked like she might protest, but evidently thought better of it. Then, and for the first time, she looked him directly in the eye.

'And after that,' she said, cautiously, 'after that is done, and when you know your own mind, what of us, lord? You and me?'

'I do not know,' he said, looking away again. 'That is the issue. I do not know.'

He left Courvain by himself, not asking Aneela to pilot him this time. Using a flyer, he followed the route they had taken together by groundcar, travelling far quicker. The evidence of disorder was everywhere, lit up by skies the colour of flame. The threads, which had been loose for so long, had now unravelled entirely, turning Terra's eternal city into one vast, untrammelled battlezone.

He found himself wondering what Navradaran must have made of it. The Custodians were surely aware, even from their lofty vantage, of what was taking place. Would they sit back and let it happen? Were they even still present, guarding the ancient walls, or had the passing of the Beacon seen them disappear too, like daemons banished with a word of power?

His speculations were becoming fanciful, uncontrolled. Such flights of imagination were not helpful.

He landed and passed inside the spire, carrying his weapon openly. The tunnels were empty, though strewn with the debris of running battles. Some of the habs were burned out. A few were still smouldering. He could hear armed clashes some way in the distance, and knew that they would spread this way soon enough.

Right up until he stood before Jarrod's old armoured portal, he had dared to hope that the security devices would be intact. Of course, they were not. The hidden guns had been smashed, the doors kicked in. Much of the old man's finery now lay, broken, in the street outside, its value unappreciated by those who had taken it.

Crowl went inside. The evidence of destruction was mixed. Some of it was looters, but they had not been the first ones to break in. Jarrod could have held out almost indefinitely against that trash. No, the ones who had destroyed the security cordon had been more professional, more disciplined, acting in greater numbers.

Crowl bent down, and picked up a sliver of dark grey armour. He looked at it for a moment, before letting it fall again.

'I told you not to investigate,' he murmured, rooting through the upturned artefacts, trying to ignore the stench. 'You could never resist a conundrum.'

Jarrod's tastes had been extravagant, and he had allowed his penchant for collection to overreach, but it was still heartbreaking to see it all in such a state, crushed and trodden into despoiled carpets. Hopefully, he had not lived long enough to witness the trampling of his precious accumulations.

Crowl entered the room where they had spoken before. He righted the chair he had sat in, and sat in it again. The windows were dark now, stained with soot, making the place murky.

He looked up at the mantelpiece. The gemstones were gone – looted either by Franck's troops or, more likely, the ones that had come after them. The long tusk remained in place, though, its bulletholes still present.

Something was different about it, though. Its tip was red. Crowl was sure it hadn't been before. He got up and reached for it, bringing it down from the mount.

It was heavy – heavier than it looked. He turned it over in his hands, and saw that one end had been hollowed out, and stoppered with fabric. He pulled it out, to find a roll of parchment inside.

He sat back in the chair and unrolled the vellum. At the top, written in a hasty hand, were the words *My Dear Erasmus.*

Crowl read on. As he did so, he felt his heart rate pick up.

When he had finished, he read it over again, just to make sure. Then he put the parchment down in his lap.

'You damned fool, Slek,' he muttered to himself.

He sat back in the chair, letting his head rest against its back. He looked up at the ceiling, flame-damaged, already beginning to sag.

He was weary. So much had already been sacrificed. His citadel was in ruins, his retinue in more or less open revolt, and the Imperium was disintegrating around them all.

He could leave, now. He could replace the parchment and forget he had ever found it.

But he couldn't forget it, of course. The knowledge would always be with him, whether he chose to make use of it or not. That was the trap. That was what had no doubt given Jarrod a smile – perhaps the last one he'd ever had.

He remembered Franck's last words then.

You are a persistent man. Too persistent.

He smiled to himself.

'I know where you sent them,' he said, already thinking what that might mean, what it might cost. 'And I know how to find them.'

Then he got up, taking the parchment with him. Limping still, but with a firmer tread than the one he had entered with, he walked the way he had come, out of the hab-unit, through to where the flyer waited, and back into the world.

ABOUT THE AUTHOR

Chris Wraight is the author of the Horus Heresy novels *Scars* and *The Path of Heaven*, the Primarchs novels *Leman Russ: The Great Wolf* and *Jaghatai Khan: Warhawk of Chogoris*, the novellas *Brotherhood of the Storm*, *Wolf King* and *Valdor: Birth of the Imperium*, and the audio drama *The Sigillite*. For Warhammer 40,000 he has written *The Lords of Silence*, *Vaults of Terra: The Carrion Throne*, *Vaults of Terra: The Hollow Mountain*, *Watchers of the Throne: The Emperor's Legion*, the Space Wolves novels *Blood of Asaheim* and *Stormcaller*, and many more. Additionally, he has many Warhammer novels to his name, including the Warhammer Chronicles novel *Master of Dragons*, which forms part of the War of Vengeance series. Chris lives and works in Bradford-on-Avon, in south-west England.

Consciousness, sudden and violent.

Her eyes snapped open and hellish light poured in. She sucked a breath down her red-raw throat, then coughed hard, doubled up, curling foetal on her side. Her eyelids flickered, and darkness threatened to swallow her again. Her mind kicked against it, fought back, surfaced. Another painful series of coughs wracked her, then subsided. She took a slow, shuddering breath, blinking quickly as her eyes adjusted to the glare.

Her surroundings resolved; her senses cleared, sight, sound, smell and touch coming slowly. She registered that she was lying on something hard and lumpy, an irregular surface that shifted beneath her as she moved. To her bleary gaze, it looked like a mound of pale stones and jagged debris, but no matter how much she blinked and frowned, she couldn't quite focus.

She could hear a low moan. The wind, she realised. It was warm, but not pleasantly so. Its touch was like the first bloom of fever-sweats that warned of illness to come. It bore a sharp tang. It took her long moments to place the stench. Sulphur, and something worse, some underlying stink of corruption that triggered primal revulsion within her. She pushed herself into a sitting position and redoubled her efforts to see straight.

What began as a fiery haze became a sky, though a more forbidding and ominous sight she could not have imagined. Blood-hued clouds roiled through a bruised void of purples and rotted greys. Vortices of black fumes whirled across the vista, ripping the bloody clouds to tatters and trailing crackling storms of lurid green lightning in their wake. Her gaze lowered, taking in the distant horizon with its jagged line of half-seen mountains. Fume-wreathed plains marched away from their feet.

She shifted again, fighting down feelings of dislocation. Her heart thumped as she realised that she had no idea where she was, or worse, even *who* she was. The questions almost escaped her lips aloud, before she realised there was no one there to answer. Something crunched beneath her palm, hard and splintering. She looked down with dawning horror.

Not stones.

Bone.

She snatched her hand back through the broken, brittle brow of an ancient skull. Bones ground beneath her as she moved, and this time she did let out an involuntary moan. She scrabbled backwards on hands and heels, as though to escape the carrion mound. Osseous matter cracked beneath her weight. Shards jabbed through the grey shift she wore, scraping her bare legs and arms. The macabre clatter of bone on bone grew, skulls and femurs and finger-bones grinding with her every movement.

She felt something cold and hard beneath her palms. She

dragged herself backwards with a gasp of gratitude, until she sat on a slab of black-painted metal several feet across. It was part of something larger, she realised, buried in layers of bone, rusting and studded with rivets and old bullet-holes. Dimly, she perceived the faded remnants of an insignia still clinging to the metal, but she had no more attention to spare. The slopes of bone stretched away on all sides, spilling down and down, broken by jutting metal wreckage, tatters of coloured cloth and other, more organic looking remnants that she didn't care to identify. She couldn't tear her eyes away.

'Not a mound...' she said, her voice a dry croak. 'This is a mountain.'

Questions chased one another through her mind. She shut them into cages forged from her iron will, there to languish until she could address them rationally. Panic spread like hoarfrost in her gut, surged up through her chest. It met the fire of her determination and melted back as quickly as it had come. She took a deep, slow breath and closed her eyes, centring herself.

'Emperor, protect me and light my way,' she said, the words coming unbidden to her lips. They felt right there, natural, reassuring. She could not say for sure who the Emperor was, but she drew strength from His name. Feeling calmer, she opened her eyes and took mental inventory.

She could see no signs of movement beyond the occasional stirring of wind-tugged cloth. Whatever macabre carrion peak she found herself atop, wherever this wasteland was, she was alone here. She realised she had clenched her fists in readiness to defend herself.

'A fighter, then, perhaps,' she murmured, finding comfort in the sound of her own voice. It was deep and strong, a voice made for firm statements, stern prayers and binding oaths. But prayers to whom? Oaths of what? Seeing no immediate danger, she resolved to begin by answering as many questions as she could about herself.

She would open her mental cages one at a time and interrogate the thoughts within.

She took personal inventory. Her grey shift was unadorned, its material coarse against her skin. The body it clad was a powerful one; she could feel graceful strength in her every movement, and see wiry, chorded muscle shift beneath the skin of her arms and legs.

Her hair was shoulder length, and she could see from holding it out before her eyes that it was raven-dark. Beyond that, without a reflective surface she could tell little more about her age or appearance. What she had gathered for now would have to be enough.

She let her fingertips explore her facial features, moving down over her chin to her throat. She gasped and pulled her hands away as she felt a ragged ring of scar tissue there, bespeaking a catastrophic wound. Feeling nauseated, but needing to know, she gingerly felt around the circumference of her neck. Sure enough, the scar ran all the way around, and for a moment she felt an echo of something within her mind.

Screaming.

Flames reflected in churning waters.

Something towering and monstrous.

A light.

The strange sense was gone as suddenly as it appeared, moonlight glimpsed through tattered cloud. She frowned in puzzlement as she realised that the scar was gone too. She felt at the flesh of her neck with increasing agitation as she tried to find the horrible mark.

'How is that possible?' she asked the empty mountaintop. 'How is *any* of this possible?'

She had no possessions, that much was clear. No weapons or armour with which to protect herself, no food, drink, any other items of clothing or gear. Nothing to suggest who she was, or to help her survive.

'And no idea how I came here,' she said. 'But I have myself. That is enough.'

She knew she could not simply sit atop a mountain of bones forever. There was no telling what kinds of ferocious storms the brooding sky might disgorge, and she felt no desire to be plucked from this peak by a screaming gale or caught amidst ferocious lightning blasts. Though she felt neither hunger nor thirst, she doubted that would remain the case forever. Starving to death and adding her bones to the mountain held even less appeal.

Yet the thing that drove her to her feet was the desire for answers. Who was she? What was she doing in such a ghastly place? How had she come to be here? Who was the Emperor? She needed to know, and she would find no insights here.

She stood atop the mountain, shift and hair blowing in the hot winds. She stared down the steep slopes. They vanished ever downward on all sides into a thick crimson mist.

'Nothing to suggest a route,' she said. 'No hint as to where I must go.' Strangely, the notion held no terror for her. Instinctive as breathing, she closed her eyes and offered up a wordless prayer to the Emperor for guidance. To her surprise, she felt a faint warmth upon her cheek, as though a candle flame had been brought close to it for the briefest of moments. The sensation was there and gone, yet it was enough, its touch somehow pure, distinct from the clammy caress of the winds.

'Are you a god, then? My protector, perhaps?' Her questions

fell dead and unanswered. Whatever the truth, she knew it would not be as easy as simply demanding answers.

She opened her eyes and turned in the direction from which she had felt the warmth. Steeling herself, she stepped carefully out, barefoot, onto the jagged carpet of bones. She began to make her slow and slithering way down the mountainside.